Particular
Intentions

L.L. Diamond

Particular Intentions

Particular Intentions
By L.L. Diamond

Published by L.L. Diamond and White Soup Press
Copyright ©2016 LL Diamond

Cover and internal design © 2016 L.L. Diamond
Cover design by L.L. Diamond/Diamondback Covers
Cover Art: *Pea Blossoms* - Edward Poynter (1890) and *Wivenhoe Park, Essex* - John Constable (1816)
Source: Wikimedia Commons.

ISBN-10: 099678912X
ISBN-13: 9780996789127

Facebook: https://www.facebook.com/LLDiamond
Twitter: @LLDiamond2
Blog: http://lldiamondwrites.com/
Austen Variations: http://austenvariations.com/

Other works by L.L. Diamond include:

Rain and Retribution	*A Matter of Chance*
An Unwavering Trust	*The Earl's Conquest*

Particular Intentions

To those who have helped me with my writing since I began, whether it was with one book or all of them—Lisa, Kristi, Debra Anne, Suzan, and Janet.
I can never thank you enough for your time, knowledge, opinions, and friendship! Thanks, ladies!

Particular Intentions

"Seldom, very seldom, does complete truth belong to any human disclosure; seldom can it happen that something is not a little disguised or a little mistaken." – Jane Austen (Emma)

Chapter 1

October 17th 1811

Another day of dreary clouds! Fitzwilliam Darcy stared at the overcast sky from the window of Netherfield's study and exhaled so the glass before him misted. The last few days of sport had been enjoyable. The weather had been cool yet pleasant, the sun peeking through the clouds overhead. What a blessed respite from London and his worries it had been!

A voice yelled, and he started at the sound breaking the quiet, drawing his attention to a carriage pulling before the house. Rather than disturb his friend Bingley, who was working at the ornate mahogany desk behind him, he paused. They expected the arrival of Bingley's sister Louisa and her husband, Reginald that afternoon; however, the Hursts numbered only two and a distinct third shadow could be discerned through the windows.

A knot formed in his gut. They would not have brought Miss Bingley, would they?

The step was placed before the door, which was swift to be opened, allowing the Hursts to exit. As they had never before laid eyes upon Netherfield, the couple looked the length of the building and around themselves at the grounds while Miss Bingley stepped from the equipage and halted to scan the façade of the large home. Her scorn for the property was evident as her expression appeared as though the house were made of the foulest dung imaginable.

He stiffened. Bingley would have to be informed at some point. Better to be done with it now than allow him to be surprised later. "Bingley? Did you perchance invite your youngest sister?"

His friend's head shot up from assessing the ledgers before him with his brow drawn low. "Caroline? I would never! I invited *you* to partake of some shooting and to be of aid to me as I attempt to learn the management of this estate. The last thing I would do is request my sister join us. Besides, Caroline is well aware she is unwelcome at Netherfield." He peered down to his book and then back. "Why do you ask?"

"I inquired because Mr. and Mrs. Hurst have just arrived with Miss Bingley in tow."

Bingley jumped to his feet, dashed to the window, and glared at the equipage. One would think the carriage had wronged him somehow by his fearsome countenance. "How dare she insinuate herself! And Louisa! I expressly told her Caroline was not to come!" His frown followed his sisters as they climbed the front steps. "I can guarantee Caroline has concocted some travesty in order to play on Louisa's sympathy, else she would not have journeyed in Hurst's carriage!"

Indeed, it was the scenario that made the most sense. Hurst did not relish Miss Bingley's company, which made his agreement to transport her all the more curious. No, something dire *must* have occurred which prevented Miss Bingley's remaining in London.

Charles Bingley strode with haste through the study door and to the front hall where his sisters and brother were removing their hats and gloves. "What is the meaning of this, Caroline? You were told not to come, and yet, here you stand! Did you not understand my explicit instructions?"

Miss Bingley's eyes widened, and she began to blink rapidly. "I did not believe you meant it. I never thought you could be so cruel!

How you could exclude me, your sister, from such a momentous time in your life? I..."

Bingley stepped forward with a furious scowl upon his usually cheerful visage. "Did I mean it when I informed you I would arrange your own establishment?"

His sister's face blanched. Bingley clenched his fists at his sides. "Did I mean it when I banished you from my home?"

"But, Charles—"

"Did I mean it when I set up a monthly allowance with specific instructions that you should never exceed those funds?" Her mouth began to open. "Did I?"

"Well, yes. But—"

"No! You brought this upon yourself, and I will give you no quarter!" Bingley turned to the butler, who stood nearby. "Mr. Reeves, we will require the carriage to be brought back around. Miss Bingley, her maid, her companion, and her trunk shall be returned to London with all due haste."

Mrs. Hurst motioned to the butler. "Mr. Reeves, wait a moment on that command." When she faced her brother, her hands were in front of her, her palms facing Bingley. "Caroline cannot return to town without a maid or a companion to accompany her."

"And where are her maid and her companion if they are not here?" He peered back and forth between his sisters. The elder, Mrs. Louisa Hurst shrank and took a step back, but the younger stared at her fingernails as though studying them, perhaps a bit pale, but not at all disturbed by her brother's ire.

"Oh, I do not remember the entirety of the discussion. Hazel found another position with the wife of a *tradesman*."

The last word was uttered with such dripping distaste that Bingley rolled his eyes. "*You* are the daughter of a tradesman."

Miss Bingley's lips twisted into a scornful expression. "As for Mrs. Rowley, her sister offered her a place to live so she would no longer be required to seek employment." Miss Bingley spoke in an off-hand fashion, as though the loss of a companion *and* a maid were commonplace.

Darcy bit the inside of his lip to keep himself from laughing. Bingley had been required to replace his sister's servants twice since he formed her establishment the year prior. He could not be surprised at the constancy of her bad behaviour, could he?

"Who else has left? Has the cook resigned her post? I warn you, sister, you will be preparing your own meals if I cannot find a replacement!"

"I have been nothing but kind and generous to that woman you hired—not that she would find employment in a home belonging to a member of the ton—"

"She was not hired to give dinner parties."

"Of course she was not! I have not the space to entertain! You ensured my spinsterhood when you chose such a small house!"

Mrs. Hurst placed a hand on her younger sister's arm. "Charles, we cannot send her back without a maid or a companion. We must first find someone suitable for the position, or at the very least, locate a female servant to accompany her on her return. Besides, it is late. The sun will set before she can reach London."

The butler still hovered nearby, having never departed due to Mrs. Hurst's earlier request.

"Mr. Reeves, we will not be requiring that carriage until we sort out the matter of a maid or a companion for Miss Bingley."

"Of course, sir."

Bingley pivoted so he faced the Hursts. "I should put you in the carriage with Caroline and return you all to London directly! You knew she was not invited, yet you brought her regardless of my wishes."

"We were supposed to leave her without a maid and a companion?" Mrs. Hurst's voice was appalled.

"She would have a housemaid and the cook. You should have conveyed the news of her companion and maid without bringing her with you. Her reputation would have survived the time required to find replacements."

His head whipped to Miss Bingley. "I shall not continue finding servants for you to abuse. If you persist, you shall be cooking your own food, fixing your own hair, and keeping yourself company!"

Miss Bingley gasped. "But Charles!"

"Do not test me on this, Caroline! Your character has become well-known, and it is becoming increasingly difficult to find servants willing to take a position in your home."

An uncharacteristic growl emanated from Bingley as he pinched the bridge of his nose. "Louisa, the unfortunate fact is I require a hostess, so you shall remain. Most of the men of the neighbourhood have called, and I informed Sir William Lucas I would have guests this evening. Caroline shall have to return to town as soon as arrangements can be made.

"Mrs. Nicholls, would you have the furthest room at the end of the west wing made up for Miss Bingley, and please place Mr. and Mrs. Hurst along that same corridor."

Darcy pressed his lips together. Thank goodness! Miss Bingley would be on the opposite end of the house from him!

The elderly housekeeper gave a swift nod. "Yes, sir."

He pointed towards the Hursts. "*You* will be responsible for Caroline. You brought her—against my wishes—and you will see to it she behaves herself."

"Now, Bingley—" began Hurst.

"Hurst, you were well aware she was not to come. You also knew the reason. I informed you a year ago when I formed her establishment that I would brook no dissension from either of you." He pointed an insistent finger in Miss Bingley's direction. "As you make your bed, so you must lie upon it." Bingley pivoted and took a step toward the study.

Miss Bingley made to follow. "But Charles! You have prevented me from obtaining invitations to the biggest events London has to offer. How am I to find a husband when you hinder me so?"

He swivelled back around to face her. "You would have secured a husband long ago, had you not decided to set your cap for my friend. I told you repeatedly that your machinations would not yield the desired result, but you heeded none of my warnings. You are well aware as to why I took the actions I did. If you have forgotten, I can always remind you should you require—"

Miss Bingley's eyes widened and darted between the servants and her brother. "No! That will not be necessary!"

"Good! I will be in my study." Bingley began to stride away, and with one last look at Miss Bingley and Mrs. Hurst, Darcy followed.

When the door was closed behind them, Bingley poured them both a glass of port. "I apologise, Darcy. If I had any idea that she would arrive unannounced as she has, I would have warned you."

Darcy cradled his glass in his hand as he met the apologetic gaze of his friend. "Over the past year, you have taken great pains to control her behaviour. I admire the fortitude you have displayed in the endeavour. We both know she can try the patience of Job."

"I had to do something. We were fortunate I noticed her missing that day."

Darcy took a large gulp of his drink. "I am thankful you noticed as well. I am still at a loss as to how your sister gained access to the mistress' suite. Mrs. Reynolds usually keeps those rooms locked up tighter than the Tower of London."

A chuckle escaped his friend's lips. "I believe she had her entire contingent of maids in the room after I removed Caroline, cleaning and scouring every nook and cranny. Did she burn the bed linens?"

"No." He shook his head and laughed. "She did have them laundered and the room aired for a few days. The room was pronounced clean when Mrs. Reynolds could no longer smell any traces of Miss Bingley's perfume."

"I would never force you to wed her. I hope you know."

Bingley's expression was earnest, and Darcy gave a nod. "I appreciate you saying as much, but I would never offer, even should she find her way into my rooms without a stitch of clothing upon her body." Lord, what a nightmare that would be! An involuntary shudder racked his body.

A small distinct gagging sound came from Bingley's throat, and he washed it down with a large swig of port. "What of this assembly tonight? You know how contemptuous Caroline is of country society. She will be insufferable. She and Louisa will overdress and pass judgement on every individual present without so much as a word of sensible conversation. I do not wish to offend the whole of Meryton with their company."

"Why not have Miss Bingley stay behind? She was not to come in the first place, so why allow her any amusement at all while she remains?"

"To be honest, I do not trust her here alone. She might see it as a perfect opportunity to rifle through your rooms. If she is at the assembly, we know where she is and what she is doing."

"I hate to admit it, but you have a valid point." He glanced through the windows for a moment. "You know, Miss Bingley's attendance might not be such a hardship." Bingley's jaw dropped. "There is always the possibility we might make the acquaintance of a potential suitor for her."

A loud, derisive laugh erupted from her beleaguered brother. "I should be so fortunate!" He set down his glass and exhaled a long breath. "I shall warn the footmen and servants. They can ensure she does not step foot in the east wing of the house, but have your valet search your chambers prior to entering—and lock your door. I would not be shocked to find that Caroline lied in regards to her maid and companion."

"Clarke will likely have a cot set up in the dressing room by the time I ready myself for the assembly. After Pemberley, he guards my chambers with a vigilance typically reserved for my wardrobe."

"Your staff does not want her as their mistress. I cannot say I blame them, either." Bingley walked around the desk and took a seat. "Before I go up to dress, I shall pen a letter to Caroline's cook. I require the precise situation. I must plan my sister's return to London as soon as may be."

With a crooked grin, Bingley glanced from his quill. "I assume you will be your usual charming self at the assembly?"

Darcy set his glass upon the tray. "I attend tonight for no other reason than to be of aid to you. I am ill qualified to recommend myself to strangers."

"They would not be strangers if you spoke to them."

"You are the one who will maintain this lease until you purchase your own estate, be it Netherfield or another estate in a different county, so it is you who must make the acquaintance of your neighbours—not I."

"I would not be so fastidious as you are for a kingdom, Darcy."

Bingley's long-time joke brought a small smile to his lips. "I should go dress. Will we depart on time if Miss Bingley is late?"

His friend grinned. "Of course, and while we enjoy ourselves, the carriage will return for her and the Hursts since I wager Louisa will be just as tardy."

Darcy rose and strode to the door.

"Darcy?"

With a start, he turned and raised his eyebrows.

"Though I am unaware the reason, I know you did not wish to leave Georgiana. I thank you for coming, for your assistance, *and* for not departing the moment Caroline strolled through the door."

His hand rested on the knob as he gave a grin. "Do not thank me just yet. If Miss Bingley is too insufferable, I might just leave at first light on the morrow."

As he exited the room, an amused bark came from the study. Departing for London was tempting, but he had made a promise to a friend, one he intended to fulfil whether he was required to dance with the unwed ladies of Meryton or not.

Darcy stood straight and stiff as he followed Bingley through the throng of the assembly. The locals all stared; the mothers licked their chops, no doubt waiting to sink their teeth into his bank accounts or Pemberley. Had the rumours of his income made the rounds so soon? Upon his entrance to a function, someone inevitably made mention of his wealth within his earshot, yet the gauche and too loud whisper of ten thousand pounds had yet to reach his ears.

Upon their arrival, an eager fellow by the name of Sir William Lucas greeted them and introduced them to a selection of the more prominent landowners until they reached a gaggle of women Sir William introduced as the Bennets. Mr. Bennet, whom Bingley had made the acquaintance of the week prior, was absent, though his friend failed to notice.

Bingley's expression was happy as he was presented to each of the daughters in succession, but Darcy's gaze was arrested by the mother's appraising eye as she scanned Bingley's attire followed by his own.

Every muscle in his body tightened as his head jerked towards his friend. Had Bingley just requested the eldest daughter's hand for the first dance? Mrs. Bennet puffed out her chest in pride, and it was all Darcy could do to keep from rolling his eyes. Why had he agreed to this? He should be in London with Georgiana not at some village assembly!

"Do you enjoy dancing as much as your friend, Mr. Darcy?"

He flinched and braced himself so as not to recoil. "No, I do not. Please excuse me." Without even so much as a glance at her daughters, he strode in the direction of the refreshment table.

Mrs. Bennet's indignant huff could be heard as it echoed from the walls. As if he would fall prey to that woman's schemes! He had never liked to dance. It inevitably excited some young lady's expectations, and then, he had to endure their incessant, ridiculous babbling for an entire set as one might tolerate the squawking of a noisy bird. He was in no mood for such torture from any woman—the cacophony of birds was, in fact, preferable!

From the periphery, he observed the dancers and those conversing rather than taking part. Miss Bingley hovered nearby for a time upon her arrival, but he refused as much as a glance to acknowledge her presence. His mere existence was enough to excite her expectations; he would provide nothing further. After a half hour, she disappeared into the revellers, certain to be criticising the local fashion or lack thereof with her sister since there appeared to be no one of rank or circumstance in attendance.

The night was nearing its blessed end when Bingley returned at long last. "Come, Darcy! I must have you dance. I hate to see you standing about by yourself in this stupid manner. You had much better dance."

"I certainly shall not." He continued to watch the unrefined behaviour of those in the current set. "You know how I detest it, unless I am particularly acquainted with my partner. At such an assembly as this it would be insupportable."

"I would not be so fastidious as you are for a kingdom!"

Darcy glared at his friend who continued to give an unaffected grin.

"Upon my honour, I never met with so many pleasant girls in my life as I have this evening and several of them are uncommonly pretty."

"*You* are dancing with the only handsome girl in the room." Darcy gestured toward the eldest Miss Bennet. She was beautiful; although, not at all the look he fancied. Instead, she was society's current ideal: tall, willowy, and blonde with blue eyes—very much to Bingley's preference.

Bingley surveyed the room and gestured with his chin to some unknown object behind Darcy. "One of Miss Bennet's sisters is sitting down just behind you. She is pretty and, if like her sister, very amiable. I am certain my partner would be pleased to introduce you."

"Which do you mean?" He turned to see a petite young woman with auburn curls piled atop her head and sparkling hazel eyes. Their gazes met, and a knot formed in his throat.

"Darcy?"

He gave a small cough, so he could speak. "She is tolerable; but not handsome enough to tempt *me*. I am in no humour at present to give consequence to young ladies who are slighted by other men. Return to your partner and enjoy her smiles. You are wasting your time with me."

Bingley's eyebrows rose to his forehead, but he did no more than grin as he strode back to the eldest Miss Bennet.

With a heavy sigh, he surveyed the room, once again stopping at the young lady, but she was no longer in the same spot. Rather, she was moving toward him. Her light and pleasing figure glided amongst the crowd, and as she passed, she held his eye, raising one brow to give an impish grin.

He stood stock-still. What could she mean by that expression? Could she have heard his response to Bingley? Well, it would not bother him if she had. His frank words would render her less likely to set her cap at him, would they not?

She passed and continued to wend her way until she approached another lady. They began to speak while her eyes found him once more. Her expression was amused and playful, particularly when she began to laugh. Was she laughing at him?

A low groan escaped as he turned his back to them. Would that he and Bingley could return to Netherfield, so he could leave this nightmare behind.

The evening, despite his fervent wishes otherwise, did not come to a swift end. Instead, he was forced to remain until their carriage crept its way much like a snail to the front of the queue, and then, he endured Miss Bingley's unending criticism of the neighbourhood for the entirety of their return to Netherfield.

When he closed his bedchamber door behind him, he leaned back against the dark stained panel and closed his eyes. What a blessed relief to be alone at long last!

Chapter 2

November 12th 1811

Elizabeth Bennet slammed the door behind her and stomped at a swift pace through the back garden of Longbourn, her gloves taking the punishment of having her hands jammed without care into their confines.

"People do not die of trifling colds!" she muttered under her breath. "That has to be the most preposterous notion! How Father could allow her to send Jane on horseback..."

Kitty and Lydia called for her to wait, but she paid them no heed and continued her determined stride toward Meryton. Lydia's loud squeal echoed off the buildings when they reached town, and she peered back as her sisters ran across the road to Captain Carter, who stood in the doorway of a home belonging to one of the officer's wives.

Elizabeth's body continued to tremble, and her breath exhaled in puffs as she made her way towards Netherfield, the rain-soaked earth sticking and clinging to her boots as she trod through the field. She would not be fit to be seen, though what did that matter if she only wished to see Jane?

After she climbed the next stile, a large puddle suddenly loomed before her, and a low growl erupted from the back of her throat.

It would not do to arrive with her walking boots soaked through and her petticoats drenched! A quick survey revealed a dryer path to the side, and she stepped over to follow it along the edge of the wood, continuing to climb stiles and spring over puddles with impatient activity.

As she neared the house, a glance at her feet prompted a soft laugh. Francine Bennet would be appalled at the state of her boots! A wide ring of mud, fallen leaves, and grass had clung to the sides and had made the three-mile ramble with her to see Jane.

Jane! The rain the previous afternoon had been a steady downpour and the temperature had dropped as the storm continued. The poor dear had to be soaked through and frigid upon her arrival to tea with Mr. Bingley's sisters!

Those two ladies' reactions must have been as supercilious as at the Assembly—likely worse. Their spiteful comments and sneers may have been disguised with care, yet they were still evident to Elizabeth. Jane did not perceive their distaste for Meryton society and found the two ladies agreeable; she never did see the ill in people.

Then, there was Mr. Darcy! What could amiable, generous Mr. Bingley have in common with that prideful man? How do such opposites become friends?

"Not tolerable enough to tempt him. Hah! Insufferable man!"

Perhaps Jane would be well enough to travel home once Elizabeth reached Netherfield. She shook her head and sighed. No, Jane would not have sent such a letter as she had this morning if she was well enough to return home. After all, the journey to Longbourn did not require substantial energy or fortitude.

Upon her arrival, she was shown to the breakfast parlour, where all but Jane were assembled. Miss Bingley's critical eye took in her appearance from head to toe with a dismissive sniff.

"Why, Miss Eliza! What could you be doing out so early—and in such dirty weather?"

"I have come to inquire about my sister." She drew back her shoulders and stood firm in response to Miss Bingley's derisive glare. Her courage always rose with every attempt to intimidate her and now would be no different!

"Miss Bennet is resting comfortably, though I believe she passed the night very ill," responded Mrs. Hurst. "I looked in on her myself this very morning on my way to breakfast."

"I thank you for your kindness, Mrs. Hurst." Neither woman appeared inclined to ask whether she would care to visit Jane, and

Elizabeth's nails dug into her palm. She opened her mouth, but it was not her voice that made the request, it was Mr. Darcy's.

"Miss Elizabeth, would you like to spend time with your sister?"

Mr. Darcy's expression was still arrogant, but it mattered not. She could have kissed him! At that moment, he was the kindest, most generous person in the room.

"Yes! I should like to tend to her myself for a time, if that is acceptable."

Mr. Bingley sprang from his chair. "Of course! I do apologise for not thinking of it myself. Please remain as long as you desire. I am certain Miss Bennet will find your tender care more beneficial than that of my sisters or my staff." He narrowed his eyes towards Miss Bingley, but his features softened when they returned to Elizabeth. "In fact, you must stay with your sister for as long as she remains at Netherfield."

Elizabeth's heart leapt for a moment before her stomach sank. To accept such a gesture would be impolite. She could not take such advantage of his hospitality. "As kind as you are to offer, Mr. Bingley, I would not like to be an imposition."

"Nonsense! I insist. I will pen a letter to your father and send a carriage for your trunk straightaway."

The wide smile that overspread her features could not be prevented. "I thank you. I will be much more at ease tending to Jane myself, so your gesture will be appreciated by us both, I am certain."

"Capital!" He motioned to a maid passing the doorway. "You there! Please show Miss Elizabeth to Miss Bennet's room, and inform Mrs. Nicholls that she will be remaining with us until Miss Bennet is well. I am sure she would prefer a bedchamber close to that of Miss Bennet's, if one is available."

The girl curtsied. "Yes, sir."

"Should Miss Bennet feel well enough to spare your company, then, please join us for meals. The staff will notify you when the time nears, so you can prepare or request a tray should you have need of it." With a smile, she thanked Mr. Bingley again, curtsied, and followed the maid to her sister's bedchamber.

Once the door was closed behind her, she crept up to the bed where a fitful Jane rested. A slight touch to her forehead revealed she was indeed very feverish and was too ill to leave her room, much less Netherfield.

A jug of water and soft towelling was set nearby. Elizabeth dampened one of the cloths, laying it against Jane's cheek. With a shiver, her sister's eyes opened and her lips curved upward in exhausted delight. "I am so glad you have come."

"When we received your note, I could not stay away." She sat beside Jane and continued to bathe her sister's face and neck with the wet cloth. "Now, let us tend to your fever; then, I will beg Mr. Bingley to send for Mr. Jones as you appear very ill indeed."

Her sister gave a choking laugh, and Elizabeth cast a glance around the room. "Have you nothing to drink? Has no one brought you even some tea?"

She stood and rang the bell, happening to summon the same maid who had shown her to Jane's chambers. Tea and broth, if it was available, were requested, and she eschewed the luncheon to remain with Jane, only breaking long enough to request the apothecary.

That afternoon, as Jane rested, Elizabeth ventured down to dine in company with the Bingleys, the Hursts, and Mr. Darcy. The ladies were theatrical in their expressions of shock over Jane's diagnosis of a violent cold, and proceeded to have a discourse that lasted throughout the meal about their excessive dislike of being ill themselves.

The urge to roll her eyes towards heaven was tempting, but her manners prevented Elizabeth from affronting her hosts in such a way—even if the ladies were as ridiculous as they were disagreeable.

As the evening progressed, Mr. Hurst overindulged on wine without speaking and, eventually, dozed while the rest of their party conversed or played cards. It was also no surprise that Mr. Darcy had little to offer on the matter of Jane's illness, and ate in silence; however, why did he continue to stare at her so? Was there naught to entertain him but her foibles and flaws?

In contrast, Mr. Bingley's anxiety for Jane was evident and heart-warming, and his attentions to herself were most pleasing, and prevented her from feeling so much an intruder, though the others were sure to consider her a bothersome imposition.

Elizabeth excused herself after dinner to attend her sister. Jane's cheeks were flushed and her brow was warm, but she was in an undisturbed slumber, likely due to the elixir Mr. Jones had left that morning. As her sister required the rest, Elizabeth ventured back toward the drawing room, but halted at the haughty sound of Mrs. Hurst's voice.

"She has nothing, in short, to recommend her, but being an excellent walker. I shall never forget her appearance this morning. She really looked almost wild."

"She did indeed, Louisa. I could hardly keep my countenance. Why must *she* be scampering about the country, because her sister has a cold?"

Elizabeth's eyes widened until they hurt. If Miss Bingley or Mrs. Hurst had even the slightest hint of warmth to their personalities, Elizabeth might not have felt the need to traipse all of the way to Netherfield to care for her sister!

"Yes, and her petticoat; I hope you saw her petticoat, six inches deep in mud!"

"I thought Miss Elizabeth Bennet looked remarkably well this morning," interrupted Bingley. "Her dirty petticoat quite escaped my notice."

A hint of anger tinged Mr. Bingley's voice, and Elizabeth raised her eyebrows. He had never challenged his sisters in public since their arrival in Meryton, but his voice held a distinctive tone of disapproval.

"*You* observed it, Mr. Darcy, I am sure," said Miss Bingley. "You would not allow *your* sister make such an exhibition."

"Certainly not."

She swallowed to keep from commenting aloud. Of course, the high and mighty Mr. Darcy would not condone her actions or wish his sister to emulate them. He only looked upon her to find fault!

"To walk from Longbourn to Netherfield, above her ankles in dirt, and alone, quite alone! Her flagrant disregard for propriety shows an abominable sort of conceited independence."

"It shows an affection for her sister that is very pleasing." Mr. Bingley's voice continued to be laced with disapprobation and had a defensive undertone. "I doubt either of you would go to such lengths for each other."

"I am afraid, Mr. Darcy." Miss Bingley spoke a bit lower, so Elizabeth had to lean in to hear her. "That this adventure has rather affected your admiration of her fine eyes."

Those same eyes bulged wide as saucers. "Fine eyes!" mouthed Elizabeth incredulously.

"Not at all. They were brightened by the exercise."

No! He was staring—looking to find fault. He did not find her handsome and had said so himself! *She is tolerable; but not handsome enough to tempt me.*

Mrs. Hurst's voice brought her back to the conversation within the room. "I have an excessive regard for Jane Bennet. She is a dear, sweet girl. I do wish she were well settled, yet with such a family and such low connections, I am afraid there is no chance of it."

Elizabeth took a step closer to the door and with a light touch, placed her hand upon it.

"I think I have heard that their uncle is an attorney in Meryton." Contempt was evident in the tone of each word that came from Miss Bingley's lips.

Mrs. Hurst gave a small cackle. "Yes, and the other lives somewhere near Cheapside, does he not?"

"That is capital." Miss Bingley and Mrs. Hurst dissolved into vicious giggles.

Darcy glanced to Bingley, who for the most part, was making a concerted effort to ignore his sisters, not that he did not commiserate with his friend. If he made pains to correct all of their conceited ramblings, the poor man would find himself hoarse in but a few hours.

Bingley had, at least, received a response from Caroline's cook, who still manned her post, yet she could not be returned to London forthwith. Bingley still awaited the arrival of Miss Bingley's new companion, which they prayed was no more than a few more days hence!

As her stay grew longer, Miss Bingley had begun insinuating herself closer and closer to Darcy, and it unnerved him. At the Lucas', she made a cloying grab for his arm, but a sudden shift prevented him from falling into her clutches. His patience with her had met a swift end that evening. He would no longer pretend polite conversation or tolerate Miss Bingley!

How dare Miss Bingley presume herself above the Miss Bennets! While the younger sisters and the mother were certainly not models of propriety, they were still above Miss Bingley by birth.

"Yet, they are the daughters of a gentleman while you are the daughter of a tradesman."

Miss Bingley's head spun around to reveal her jaw agape.

"Mr. Bennet has an estate, and though your brother may have a larger income, he has yet to become a part of the landed gentry."

"The Bennets' estate is insignificant," sneered Miss Bingley.

"Nevertheless, it is an estate, which according to Mr. Bennet, has been in the Bennet family for over two-hundred years."

"But their uncles—"

A cringe seized him at Miss Bingley's high-pitched tone. "Their uncles may materially lessen their chance of marrying men of any consideration in the world, but their uncles, at least, have roots in the gentry—unlike you."

Bingley turned and regarded his friend with curiosity. "Do they? I had not heard."

"When I made the acquaintance of Mr. Bennet at Lucas Lodge, he made mention of a prominent Derbyshire family who is well known to me. We spent a portion of the evening speaking of that family and certain members of his."

"Their origins are irrelevant!" Miss Bingley was as red as a beetroot and her eyes were harried. "The Miss Bennets—"

"But you were just deriding their roots," exclaimed Bingley.

Mr. Hurst opened a wary eye, but upon Darcy's gaze meeting his, he returned to feigning sleep.

"You were so concerned with their connections to trade, and while Mrs. Bennet's father was a solicitor, he was a younger brother. From what Mr. Bennet said, the family still owns multiple properties, including an estate in Cambridgeshire and a smaller estate closer to London."

"It matters not, they—"

"Caroline, that is enough!" boomed Bingley. "It is this sort of behaviour that I cannot abide. You have been told on numerous occasions that your disdain will not be accepted in my household.

"Our father, God rest his soul, strove to be a part of the ton, but was unable to purchase an estate before his passing. He was a tradesman. I am not ashamed of that fact, and I will not condone the disparagement of the Bennet family because of an uncle who is in trade. You may as well denounce your own father!"

Darcy nodded. "The eldest Bennet sisters comport themselves with more propriety and dignity in a public setting than you. They do not openly sneer or ridicule others for their lack of wealth or connections."

"I behave no differently than people of fashion!"

Darcy sat forward, bristling on behalf of his family. "My mother never treated anyone with the scorn you display. My uncle, Lord Fitzwilliam, does not behave as such and neither does my aunt, Lady Fitzwilliam."

"Lord Fitzwilliam would never accept—"

"My uncle has been known to lower rents when times are hard and give food, blankets, and coal to the impoverished elderly and young children. He has good understanding and an amiable disposition. He would not abide your company for a second. Not due to your family, *Miss* Bingley, but because of your temper."

Darcy rose from his seat. "I apologise, Bingley. I should retire to my rooms. I fear I will not be good company should I remain."

"Of course." His friend continued to glower at Miss Bingley. "We shall still ride out to survey the field at the north end of the estate in the morning?"

"Yes, I shall ensure Clarke is aware of our plans for the morrow." Without so much as a glance at Miss Bingley, Darcy exited and with a shoulder against the door, he closed it behind him.

A swish of a skirt near the dining room flashed in the corner of his eye. When had Elizabeth Bennet returned from her sister's suite? Her cheeks were pale and her eyes wide as she stared at him. Had she overheard their argument?

What an awkward situation! Did she expect him to speak? He stood straight and tall and clenched his jaw.

Meanwhile, she looked about as if seeking escape, her eyes settling upon the stairs. Her quick stride did not falter as she made her way to the first step, where she paused and turned to him. "Thank you, Mr. Darcy."

Her voice was low, almost a whisper. He gave a nod, and she continued on her way.

Chapter 3

November 13th 1811

Elizabeth finished folding the letter she had just penned to her mother and gave a weary sigh. Jane's rest had become fitful during the evening, and Elizabeth had spent most of the night at her side, tending to her beloved sister.

Her mother needed to see what her conspiring had wrought, not that Jane was on her deathbed, by any means, but her misery could have been prevented. Remorse, however, was not in Francine Bennet's vocabulary. The visit was unlikely to make an impression, but it would appear strange should Jane be indisposed for a period of time and her mother had never laid eyes upon her. That much was certain.

Once Elizabeth sealed the letter, she stepped into the hall and arranged for its delivery, but upon returning to the library, she stared unseeing at the bookshelves, their offerings blurred before her.

Why had Mr. Darcy come to her defence? He was an insufferable, prideful man who only looked upon her to find fault. At least, that was her initial sketch of his character. Could he be more than she presumed? Could his reference to her fine eyes mean he found her more than tolerable?

He was well known in Meryton for his grand estate and income, but the night prior, he had boasted of his uncle's good works and his family's kind manners. What if she was incorrect? He was handsome to be sure, but his manner was offensive at the assembly and not attractive in the slightest. But, what if there was more to Mr. Darcy than any of Meryton presumed? The questions, however, had no answers without further observation of the man himself.

Of course, Mr. Bingley had displayed a new side of himself as well. He was still amiable, yet he had never, in her presence, scolded

Miss Bingley in such a manner as Elizabeth had overheard. He was also more determined than he appeared at a first acquaintance.

"Were you searching for a particular title?"

She gasped and jumped, the hand attached to the thumbnail she was biting dropped to her side.

A small crease formed between Mr. Darcy's eyebrows. "Forgive me if I startled you. You have been standing in the same attitude for a few minutes, and I have no objection to being of aid should you require it."

She bit her bottom lip. "Oh, I am loath to admit that I was wool-gathering, Mr. Darcy. I am afraid my mind wandered, and I ceased to see the books before me."

His brows drew together a bit more. "I do hope your sister has not taken a turn for the worse. I heard the servants make mention of a note dispatched to Longbourn."

"Jane remains much the same. I wished for my mother to visit. She might have some remedy or advice to help alleviate Jane's discomfort."

It was doubtful her mother would have any information that might be of use, yet Jane would be more at ease at Longbourn. Her mother had to agree the three-mile journey home would not be a detriment to Jane's health.

"I am glad she has not worsened. Colds can be nasty beasts. They might seem trifling one day but can progress to something much more serious overnight."

"Jane passed a trying night, but she has not worsened." For the first time since she made his acquaintance, his eyes were kind and concerned. Eyes? Miss Bingley had indicated he found her eyes to be fine—they were brightened by the exercise.

"Miss Elizabeth," he interrupted. "Are you well? You appear a bit flushed."

A gentle warmth suffused her face, and she began to shake her head. "I am a bit fatigued, but I am not ill."

He thought her eyes were fine. They were brightened by the exercise.

She shook her head in a futile attempt to clear it. "Pardon me, Mr. Darcy, but I need to see to Jane." She scooted around him and fled to her sister's chamber, falling back against the door once it was closed.

Her heart stuttered and her stomach fluttered as if she had several butterflies attempting to take flight within. This was ridiculous! Despite his good looks and his defence of her family, he was a disagreeable, insufferable man—or was he?

With a groan, her head dropped into her hands like a lead weight. "I am so confused."

"Lizzy? Are you well?"

She started and began to bob her head with more fervour than was perhaps necessary. "I am, Jane. I just ventured to the library to find a book."

"But you have returned empty-handed." Her sister's wan face wore a crooked smile. "You said you are confused. Why do you not tell me what has you at sixes and sevens?"

"You are ill."

"My sore throat does not render my mind so addled that I cannot comprehend your problem. Perhaps, the opinion of another might provide some much-needed clarity. I could certainly use the diversion after remaining in this bed for the last two days."

Elizabeth's shoulders sagged; she stepped over to the bed, and dropped alongside Jane in a less than graceful heap of muslin. "It is Mr. Darcy."

Jane's nose crinkled. "But you have such a hearty dislike of Mr. Darcy—at least, you did upon your arrival."

"I did! He has been haughty and disagreeable since I first made his acquaintance."

"But." Her sister's lips curved up at the very ends.

"Then, last night happened."

With her eyebrows drawn together, Jane shook her head. "I am afraid I do not recall much of last night, Lizzy."

"No," she responded, a bit exasperated. "You would not, would you? When I looked in after dinner, you were sound asleep."

"So, you came here, and then?"

"I ventured back down to the drawing room. I thought to read while the remainder of the group played cards."

"And?" Jane drew out the word, prompting a half-hearted smile.

"Before I could enter, I overheard Miss Bingley discrediting our family. She was criticising Uncle Philips for being a solicitor and Uncle Gardiner for not only living in Cheapside, but also his status as a tradesman."

"Oh, dear," lamented Jane. "I thought her so amiable. Are you certain you did not misunderstand?"

"No, Miss Bingley was clear in her disdain."

"But how does that affect your opinion of Mr. Darcy? Did he agree with Miss Bingley?"

The conversation she overheard played in her mind as she gave a shake of her head. "No... I mean yes." With a bit of a groan, she covered her eyes.

"Lizzy!" Jane laughed and removed her hands. "You will have to tell me if I am to make any sense of this."

"Miss Bingley seemed to expect him to agree, but all he said was Uncle Philips and Uncle Gardiner would lessen our chances of marrying men of any consideration in the world." She curled her feet underneath her. "Other than that statement, all else he said was in our defence."

"Truly?"

Elizabeth gave a nod of her head in the affirmative to Jane's questioning gaze. "I never would have expected him to come to our aid as he did, but I heard it with my own ears. His words in our favour were not even the most shocking portion of the argument."

Jane rose to a seated position, bent her knees, and wrapped her arms around her legs.

"At one point, Miss Bingley sounded as if she was goading Mr. Darcy, asking if my walking three miles altered his admiration of my 'fine eyes'. He responded by saying that it had not, and that they had been brightened by the exercise."

Jane began thumping her feet against the bed. "I knew it! I was certain he was enamoured of you and this proves it!"

"You will wear yourself out if you continue as you are," Elizabeth retorted drily.

"It matters not. I will simply sleep for most of the afternoon." She bit her lip in an obvious attempt not to giggle with glee. "He did not remove his eyes from you as you performed at Lucas Lodge, and he watched you at the assembly—after his slight, that is. I began to wonder if he was smitten, yet I did not mention it to you since I knew how you disliked him."

"He has been prideful during most of our acquaintance, but I do not know what to make of his statement about my fine eyes. I just made a ninny of myself with him when he asked if I required help locating a particular book."

An indelicate sound that could rival Lydia escaped her prim and proper sister's nose. "He is an exceedingly handsome gentleman, and now you know he is attracted to you. I see nothing unusual about feeling foolish before him. Do you remember when Charlotte was smitten with the eldest Goulding boy?"

Elizabeth grinned. "How could I forget? She could not cease that ridiculous giggle whenever he requested her hand for a set. I still believe the reason he wed Lucy Higgins over Charlotte was because Charlotte was too flustered to speak to him."

Her sister's eyebrows furrowed. "What if his temperament is similar to mine?"

"Pardon?"

"What if Mr. Darcy is reserved in company? Might that come across as prideful?"

"I suppose." The idea was plausible.

Jane took her hand and gave it a gentle squeeze. "He may also not want to excite your expectations. We are not of his standing. What if his family has a match planned for him?"

She started. "I confess I had not considered such a situation."

"If Mr. Darcy is attempting to spare your feelings, he is very considerate to think of it."

Chewing the inside of her lip, Elizabeth gave a nod. Could Jane truly have sketched Mr. Darcy's character accurately and without difficulty? "It does show him in a different light."

She began to recount every encounter with Mr. Darcy since his arrival, searching for nuances that she might have missed in his demeanour.

"Lizzy?"

"Hmmm?"

"Would you ring for some tea?"

Elizabeth sprang from the bed and moved to pull the bell. "Forgive me! I have been so thoughtless. Here I was preoccupied with Mr. Darcy's comment and forgot the entire reason I am residing at Netherfield."

A scratchy giggle erupted from Jane. "Do not scold yourself so. I am not near death, by any means."

The maid responded with haste to the summons of the bell, and after her departure, Elizabeth resumed her place on the bed.

"What are you going to do about Mr. Darcy?" asked Jane.

"There is naught I can do. If you are correct and he is hiding his feelings, he *must* have a reason. Besides, it would be improper to ask him, even if he is aware of my presence last night."

A gasp turned Elizabeth's attention to her sister's shocked countenance. "You did not say he knew you overheard."

"He was furious with Miss Bingley. In fact, he and Mr. Bingley were blunt and unreserved in their reprimand of her words. When he finished upbraiding Miss Bingley, he gave his apologies to Mr. Bingley and departed the room before I could locate a suitable place to hide."

"We know this house so well. Did you forget the cupboard under the stairs?"

"It was locked! I hurried to turn in the direction of the dining room, but he emerged from the drawing room before I could open the door."

"What did you do?"

"I panicked and decided to hurry back to you, but I could not leave without thanking him."

"Did he respond?"

"He acknowledged me, and I hastened up the stairs." She brought her thumb to her mouth and began to chew on her nail. "What do you think?"

Jane stared out of the window for a time. She was quiet, but those closest to Jane would be aware she was considering every option. With a sigh, she gave her shoulders a slight shrug.

"I believe your first instinct is correct. You should behave no differently than in the past—except perhaps be a bit more polite to poor Mr. Darcy. The best advice I can give is to let his behaviour be your guide. If he remains proper and reserved, then do not press for more of a friendship, yet if he is open and amiable, I do not foresee any harm in furthering the acquaintance."

Her sister's hand wrapped around hers and gave a squeeze. "If he does appear to desire friendship, please be careful. He may not intend to pursue more."

"You are one to talk, Jane Bennet. I happen to know that you are well on your way to being in love with Mr. Bingley."

A knock at the door announced their tea had arrived. Elizabeth allowed the maid inside and prepared Jane's cup, returning to her seat once her sister was served.

"I will admit to being hopeful," confessed Jane, "however, I am attempting to guard my heart. I do not wish to be hurt when he departs for town one day in the future."

"I do hope you are incorrect, dear sister. I believe Mr. Bingley would be a good match."

The strident sounds of their mother echoed down the hall, and Elizabeth groaned. "Our mother has arrived."

"She means well, Lizzy."

"I know she does, even if I do not understand her methods."

The door swung open to reveal Mrs. Bennet with her two youngest daughters, and Miss Bingley and Mrs. Hurst just behind them.

"Jane! Why are you sitting? Lie down, girl, before you make yourself worse!"

Perhaps summoning their mother was not such a good idea.

Chapter 4

<u>November 14th 1811</u>

What a blessed relief! Elizabeth's mother had finally departed Netherfield!

Even after hiding in Jane's room for the past hour, the memory of the call still caused Elizabeth to wince. How could she face anyone who had been a party to such a scene? Her mother's lack of manners and discretion were mortifying!

A servant appeared at the door to announce when dinner would be served, and she placed a hand over her stomach. Not that the simple gesture would quell the current churning, but tears would solve nothing. They would only make matters worse as she would then have red eyes and a red nose with which to contend.

Oh, but to cry off; however, the maid had tended the fire not five minutes ago. If they inquired, the residents of Netherfield would know that Jane slept soundly. They would think Elizabeth rude.

With shaky hands, she changed and prepared for the dreaded meal in the company of Mrs. Hurst and Miss Bingley; those ladies were sure to verbally run Elizabeth through over her mother's behaviour. No doubt, they were having a jolly laugh at the Bennets' expense while Elizabeth fretted.

As there was naught that could be done, she brushed her skirt, pinched her cheeks, and started towards the dining room. When she arrived, she was surprised by a new addition to their party.

A squat and stern-countenanced woman occupied the seat beside Miss Bingley, and before the meal was served, Mr. Bingley introduced her as his sister's new companion, Mrs. Langford. Miss Bingley was to depart Hertfordshire in the morning, and Mrs. Langford was to accompany the lady on her return to town.

Elizabeth had not planned on a show with her meal, yet the behaviour of Miss Bingley provided much entertainment. Mrs.

Langford's numerous attempts to rein in Miss Bingley's poor manners were dismissed or ignored, much to her new companion's continued vexation. How diverting!

Jane was still sleeping when she looked in on her after dinner, so Elizabeth returned to join the inhabitants of Netherfield in the drawing room. She took up some needlework, but soon was distracted again by the antics of Miss Bingley, this time towards Mr. Darcy.

The lady, if one could refer to her thus, stood near the gentleman while she fawned over his handwriting, the evenness of his lines, and the length of his letter as her companion endeavoured on several instances to draw her attention. Mrs. Langford placed a hand to Miss Bingley's arm, she attempted a lady-like cough, and even attempted to interrupt; yet, Mrs. Langford was unsuccessful as her charge ignored her companion with apparent ease.

Miss Bingley bent further in Mr. Darcy's direction. Elizabeth cleared her throat to stifle a laugh. The lady would fall into his lap if she leaned any further. Mr. Darcy would, no doubt, view a portion of Miss Bingley's bosom if he were to look in that direction, but his eyes remained fixed to the letter he was writing.

Was Miss Bingley's more brazen behaviour due to her departure on the morrow? Was this her last effort to engage his affections? If it was, then it was a most pathetic display! Her normal manner towards Mr. Darcy was cloying and sure to be annoying, but this was ridiculous!

Had Mr. Bingley been present, he would surely correct his sister's behaviour, but he had excused himself to make final preparations for Miss Bingley's departure. He was not available to chastise her, and Mrs. Langford was obvious in her aversion to creating a scene before company.

"How delighted Miss Darcy will be to receive such a letter!"

He made no answer, but Elizabeth's surreptitious peek at Mrs. Langford revealed the woman rolling her eyes.

"You write uncommonly fast."

"You are mistaken. I write rather slowly."

Elizabeth's teeth dug into her cheek. If Miss Bingley continued, Elizabeth would have to leave the room or dissolve into a most impolite fit of laughter.

Poor Mr. Darcy! Her fawning was absurd, and he was obvious in his wish that she desist her attentions in his direction. His posture was positively rigid, and despite Miss Bingley's attempts, his focus remained upon the paper before him.

"How many letters you must have occasion to write in the course of the year! Letters of business, too! How dull, indeed!"

"It is fortunate, then, that they fall to my lot instead of to yours."

His shoulders dipped as he sighed. He must be frustrated with her present manner, yet neither he nor her brother reprimanded her as they had the night prior. The presence of a guest must have provided Miss Bingley a reprieve.

"Pray tell your sister that I long to see her."

His writing hand dropped to the desk with a thud. "I have already told her so once, by your desire." The impolite tone of his voice was no surprise. He had lost all patience with her.

"I am afraid you do not like your pen." Miss Bingley persisted. "Let me mend it for you. I mend pens remarkably well."

She reached for his quill, but Mr. Darcy halted his activity and levelled an unmistakable glare in Miss Bingley's direction.

"I always mend my own." His arm stretched and pointed towards the settee. "I do not enjoy when people hover about my shoulders as I write, or read, for that matter. Please take your seat."

Miss Bingley's nose became pointier and her lips drew tight as she removed to the nearby sofa. "Tell your sister I am delighted to hear of her improvement on the harp; and pray let her know that I am quite in raptures with her beautiful little design for a table. I think it infinitely superior to Miss Grantley's."

He continued to glower in her direction as he practically bit out through his teeth, "Will you give me leave to defer your raptures till I write again? At present I have not room to do them justice."

Miss Bingley leaned back into the cushion of her own seat as his quill began to scratch against the paper once more.

"Oh! It is of no consequence. I am certain I shall see her in January."

A muttering came from Mr. Darcy, prompting Miss Bingley to sit forward.

"Pardon?"

Elizabeth smothered a giggle and placed a hand to her mouth. Had he truly said, "If wishes were horses, beggars would ride?"

If she had been biting her lips before, her teeth were now digging into the tender flesh in an attempt to restrain her mirth. Under normal circumstances, she did not enjoy finding humour at the insult of another, but Miss Bingley had thus far taken no notice of the subtle cues of Mr. Darcy to cease her overbearing attentions. Judging from the conversation the night prior, she had been disregarding his less than subtle entreaties as well.

"Mr. Darcy, pray how old is your sister?" Elizabeth started. Why? Why had she spoken?

Miss Bingley looked down her nose at Elizabeth with a sneer.

His eyes latched onto hers as he ignored his friend's tiresome sister. "She will be sixteen next month, though she is quite tall for her age."

"And has she played the harp long?"

Mr. Darcy shifted in his chair, his quill forgotten upon the desk. "No, she began with a master but a year ago. She has made significant progress, but I would not say she is accomplished at the art as of yet.

"She is proficient at the pianoforte," he blurted when Miss Bingley opened her mouth to speak.

"Does she have a favourite composer?"

He gave a deep rumbling laugh. "Her preference for composers is alterable, I would say. Last winter, she favoured Handel, and this autumn, she plays nothing but Mozart. By summer, she will likely decide Scarlatti's work has no equal and will not hear a word to the contrary."

With a grin, she shifted forward. "What? No Bach?"

His laugh filled the room with its rich low tones. "Bach was two years ago. She has yet to repeat a favourite."

"Ah, so she *is* fickle."

"How rude!" exclaimed Miss Bingley as she bolted to her feet.

Elizabeth pressed back into the cushions of the sofa as Mr. Darcy speared Miss Bingley with a withering scowl. "May I inquire as to whom you are calling rude, Miss Bingley?"

"Why, Miss Darcy has the sweetest temper and is so accomplished! To call her fickle is to imply she has no loyalty to her friends or to you, her brother!"

Miss Bingley's voice was one of horror, but her expression did not quite match her tone. Why would she pick such a trifling thing over which to feign offence? She was sure to realize Elizabeth was teasing.

"Mr. Darcy, I hope you understood I meant no disrespect."

His lips were drawn into a fine line as he held up a hand in Elizabeth's direction.

"Miss Bingley, I am quite capable of defending my sister when and if the circumstances arise. In this case, Miss Elizabeth was doing no more than teasing, using the word fickle when I used alterable a few statements prior. She has done naught to cause insult."

Miss Bingley gave a huff and dropped into her chair. Her eyes bore into the side of Elizabeth's head, and despite keeping her attention in Mr. Darcy's direction, the heat of Miss Bingley's disapprobation caused an odd sensation on the side of Elizabeth's scalp.

"Caroline, you are travelling in the morning and should retire for the evening."

Mr. Bingley came to stand by his sister's chair and held out his arm. When had he returned? "I will escort you from the room. I wish to have a word with you in the study before you adjourn to your chambers."

A strange whistle came from Miss Bingley when her lips parted but a fraction, and she sucked air through her teeth.

"Come along. I would prefer to remove you before you offend my guests further. Besides, I would not care to stand thus all evening."

She paled and stood, placing her arm upon her brother's. Once they departed, Mr. Darcy relaxed back into his chair.

"I am aware you were teasing and meant no harm, Miss Elizabeth. I was in earnest when I said as much to Miss Bingley. Please do not make yourself uneasy."

"Thank you, Mr. Darcy." She glanced to her hands, clasped in her lap, and back to his face. "I must admit Miss Bingley startled me. I had not expected such an exhibit."

He glanced over from Mr. Hurst, who was still drowsing on the settee, to Mrs. Hurst, who appeared engrossed in a novel.

"Miss Bingley has always insinuated a greater friendship with my sister and myself than what exists. I fear she would have found displeasure in some statement you made, no matter how innocent."

His pen shifted with the movement of his fingers. "May I ask how your sister fares? I have heard no one inquire as to her health this evening."

"She is better, thank you. She was not as feverish and was resting comfortably as of an hour ago."

His lips curved up just a bit. "I am glad to hear it."

She nodded and gestured toward the desk. "I had not intended to interrupt your letter. I am certain your sister will be pleased to receive news of how you are spending your time."

"Oh," he blurted as if he had remembered something. "Yes, I should finish. I had hoped to post it in the morning."

Elizabeth picked up a small book of poetry on the side table and began to stare at the page, though she could not concentrate upon the words.

What had happened tonight? Why had she been compelled to come to Mr. Darcy's aid?

He was full of improper pride, and unpleasant. Was he not? He had come to her family's defence with Miss Bingley, but was his manner altered due to the presence of the insufferable Miss Bingley?

She closed the book with a snap. "If you will excuse me, I will ensure my sister is well and retire for the evening."

Mr. Darcy nodded, and she made her way to Jane's bedchamber where her sister rested. Her forehead was not as warm as earlier, and she slept without agitation, so Elizabeth moved to her own chambers. She changed into her shift and burrowed into the bedclothes, but her mind would not allow her to leave the question of Mr. Darcy alone and let her rest.

She pounded the pillow and dropped back down with a huff. Had she misjudged Mr. Darcy? "No, it just is not possible," she mumbled. His defence of her family had to be the answer. She needed to return the kindness. They were now even—Elizabeth's aid with Miss Bingley repaid Mr. Darcy for his set down of the same lady.

There was no reason he would be any different than he was at the assembly. After all, they were not friends, were they?

Darcy entered his bedchamber and leaned upon the door as it closed behind him. What had happened this evening? Had he done precisely what he swore he would not? Could he have given Miss Elizabeth reason to hope she could win his favour?

"Good evening, sir."

He straightened and propelled himself away from the door. "Good evening, Clarke."

"I hope you enjoyed dinner?"

He ran his hands along his topcoat and pulled Georgiana's letter from an inside pocket. "Yes, of course. Would you see this is put in the outgoing post? I hoped it would be off first thing in the morning."

"Yes, sir." Clarke took the correspondence and placed it within his own coat pocket, walked behind Darcy, and began to help him shed his clothes.

Once Clarke disappeared into the dressing room with Darcy's topcoat and waistcoat, Darcy stared at the floor. *Could* he have incited any feelings in Miss Elizabeth? They had bantered several times since she came to stay at Netherfield. After all, the discussion about composers—she had to be flirting with him!

"Sir?"

"Oh! Forgive me, Clarke." He untied his cravat and handed his clothing to his valet, who provided him with a nightshirt.

"Do you require anything further this evening, sir?"

Darcy glanced down at himself and around the room. "I do not believe so. Thank you."

Clarke bowed and departed the room, closing the door behind him.

A small thud reverberated in the room when Darcy dropped onto the bed, pulling his feet upon the side rails and leaning with his forearms upon his thighs.

He had sworn at the assembly he would not fall prey to Mrs. Bennet and her schemes, but was Miss Elizabeth of the same ilk as her mother? Could she be different? Unlike Miss Bingley and other ladies, she did not attempt to garner his attention at every moment, which was indeed a pleasant change.

Her teasing manner and intelligence also made it impossible for him to maintain his stern appearance. The dilemma now was how to behave in her presence from this point forward. Should he remain friendly and pray it did not entrap him, or attempt to don the mask he wore in public settings in an effort to preserve himself?

The situation was impossible with her residing under the same roof! He needed to regain his equilibrium. He needed Elizabeth Bennet to return to Longbourn.

Chapter 5

"Is there no poetry in this cursed library?" Elizabeth muttered under her breath.

Mr. Bingley had indicated that Netherfield's library had meagre offerings; he had not exaggerated. A few volumes of Shakespeare, a plethora of out-dated books on farming techniques, and a few novels did not constitute a library. At least not in her mind!

She exhaled heavily, the dust on the books flying in every direction, prompting her to cover her mouth with the back of her hand and clear her throat.

"I hope you are not becoming ill, Miss Elizabeth?"

She whirled around. Mr. Darcy stood a few paces back, his posture stiff, his arms at his sides, and a few books in one hand.

"No, I exhaled towards the shelves, and the dust became caught in my throat."

"Ah." He stepped towards the fireplace and sat in a chair, placing his reading on the table beside him. "Have you found anything of interest?"

Was that a smirk upon his face?

"Not unless I desire to learn about wool production or how to produce a plentiful harvest."

His lip lifted on one side. "Yes, the library is rather bare as far as I am concerned." He gestured towards the books on the table. "I only brought a few from Pemberley, but you are welcome to borrow one if it interests you."

She approached and tilted her head in an attempt to read the spines without touching them. "Which are you reading at the moment?"

He pulled the bottom from the pile, and she leaned in an attempt to see the title.

"Marmion?"

"Yes, have you read it?" His head turned, and his blue eyes penetrated hers until she averted her gaze.

"I have. My uncle gave my father a copy Christmas last. I enjoyed it very much."

"As did I." His hand lay with a soft touch upon the cover as his fingers curved around its edge.

She flinched when he lifted the remaining books with his other hand.

"Forgive me, I did not mean to startle you."

With a shake of her head, she reached to take the stack from him, her fingers brushing his as she grasped it. He recoiled, and she dropped his books like a lead weight.

"I am so sorry!" She fell to her knees to gather his property from the rug as he lowered himself across from her; however, she had already organised them and clutched them to her chest by the time he joined her. "Did I pinch you?"

His brow furrowed.

"I thought perhaps when I shifted them, your finger was pinched between the books for you to draw back with such haste."

He waved his hand before him. "It is of no matter."

"I—"

"Well, this is cosy."

Her head swung to the door where Miss Bingley stood, a sour expression upon her countenance.

"I thought I might manage a moment alone with Mr. Darcy before I depart—to make my farewells." Her eyes raked up and down the gentleman in question. "But once again, Miss Eliza, you stand in my way."

Mr. Darcy stood as Miss Elizabeth rose from her seat. "I understand your carriage awaits you, Miss Bingley. I wish you a pleasant journey."

She gave an ungracious smile and peered between Mr. Darcy and Elizabeth as her expression changed to one of scorn. "I have found Meryton intriguing. Would you care to know why?"

Elizabeth gave a slight shrug and glanced at Mr. Darcy, whose face was a mask. He was neither angry, nor happy. Could he be confused by Miss Bingley's behaviour as well?

"Despite your lack of response, I am certain you wish to know, and I am more than pleased to tell you." Miss Bingley gave a malicious-sounding giggle. "Mr. Darcy is such an *honourable* gentleman—well, except when it comes to me, and Miss Eliza, you believe him to be prideful, if the gossip in town is to be trusted. You took such offence to his remark at the assembly."

Oh, but to shrink to the size of a tiny bug and scurry away! Mr. Darcy's eyes blazed at her, but she kept her eyes on Miss Bingley.

"What is the purpose of these reflections, Miss Bingley?" Miss Bingley was certain to have heard the fury in his voice, but she was angry as well, and angry people are not always wise.

"I had an amusing thought last night. Since I could not persuade you to marry me, then it would be such great fun to see you wed to someone who detests you." Her hand moved to the edge of the door as it began to swing towards them.

Elizabeth gasped. "Miss Bingley!" She released the books, which clattered to the floor, as she lunged in an attempt to keep the heavy oak panel open, but it was too late. The latch clicked before she could grasp it, and a key secured the lock with a decisive clank.

Mr. Darcy raised a fist, but Elizabeth yanked his arm back to his side.

"What do you intend to do?"

"I shall call for help. Do you want to be trapped within this room so long that your reputation is ruined?"

"It makes no difference if we are confined for five seconds or five hours. The outcome is the same. I wish to marry for love, and I will be forced to marry no one—especially not you, Mr. Darcy!"

She took a deep breath, covered her mouth with her hands and scanned the room. Think, Elizabeth! This house was almost a second home when she was a child. She merely needed to concentrate.

Her eyes halted upon a far window near the left corner. She almost ran until she reached it, looking through the panes and laughing. A minute was all she required to work the latch and open the sash, but as she reached down to her feet, the boots of her present company invaded her line of sight.

She lifted her head. "I would appreciate it if you would turn around."

"What do you have planned?"

"Something I did often as a child, but have not attempted in a few years.

He remained staring, and she rolled her eyes. "Very well." With a swift turn, she removed her house slippers and tossed them out the window.

Mr. Darcy's eyes widened, and he took a step forward. "Miss Elizabeth! I must object! You might do yourself an injury!"

She ignored his protests and climbed upon the sill, placing her feet onto a limb that ran parallel to the house just below where she made her exit. Once she had a firm grasp on two smaller branches above, she lowered herself onto the limb. Would it still hold her weight? She had been considerably smaller the last time she had made the attempt.

The gentleman launched forward to the window. "You must return to the library. It is too risky!"

She lifted a shoulder as she watched her feet on the branch below her. "Then you should have stopped me before I climbed out."

The way down was quick once the method returned to her. One foot to a lower limb followed by a hand to another. Soon, she was on the ground grinning at Mr. Darcy above. "Now neither of us is forced into an unpleasant situation!"

She glanced in either direction and with no one about, returned her slippers to her feet. "Millie will not appreciate having to clean these!" There was no use for it, however. She could not very well approach the front door of Netherfield with her slippers in her hands.

Mr. Darcy watched Elizabeth stride around the side of the house and drew himself back inside. Once he closed the window, he retrieved the books from the floor, returned them to the side table, and placed a hand upon the back of the closest chair.

He had been inclined to dismiss Miss Bingley's assertions as to Miss Elizabeth's dislike of him, but could it be true? Miss Bingley alluded to a comment he had made at the assembly. He often offended people at balls, but he was uncomfortable in those settings with the mothers and daughters measuring his wealth and seeking introductions. The people he insulted were often those he had no interest in befriending much less maintaining a connection.

Images from the assembly played before him as though he were walking through a gallery, looking at a series of paintings in a specific order. Miss Elizabeth had been present when her mother inquired whether he liked to dance, but his response and exit could not have caused such insult, could they?

Then, he groaned. Bingley had goaded him about dancing with Miss Elizabeth, and what had he said? *She is tolerable; but not handsome enough to tempt me.*

She had been watching. He had caught her eye when he looked to see whom Bingley meant, yet her behaviour afterwards had not been one of a hurt or outraged woman. She had smiled when she passed him, and then laughed with Charlotte Lucas. Could they have found humour at his expense?

The remark was below him, but Mrs. Bennet had been obvious in her designs. He came to Hertfordshire to help his friend and enjoy the sport—not find a wife. He had walked into the assembly unworried of giving offence, and ironically, insulted the one woman he now, in fact, found tempting.

So, did she despise him? If so, did he care? Would he wish to change her view of him? Her opinion of him could not be favourable. After all, she climbed from a window and down a tree to avoid marriage to him! Was falling to her death preferable to life as his wife? Lord, but she must despise him!

He leaned against the mantel and blew out a breath. What did he desire? Did he want Miss Elizabeth with her low connections and vulgar family, or to continue as he had for the past few years, drowning himself in work and caring for Georgiana?

Why did that notion create such an empty sensation in his chest?

Elizabeth set off, rounding the house in no time at all, and was approaching the front just as Miss Bingley stepped forward to enter her carriage with Mrs. Langford awaiting her within.

"I hope you have a pleasant journey, Miss Bingley." Elizabeth wore a grin that likely revealed every tooth in her mouth, but it helped prevent her from laughing, which was a struggle with the dropped jaw and bulging eyes of the lady before her. She made a quick curtsey, then strode inside where she let loose her giggles.

Her amusement was short-lived by necessity—Mr. Darcy was still trapped. Without much of a pause, she made her way back to the library and attempted to open the door, which was, of course, still locked. If a servant were nearby, she would arouse suspicion if she did not try the door first. Fortunately, no more than five steps down the corridor were required before she happened upon Mrs. Nicholls.

"Mrs. Nicholls, do you know why the library would be locked? I hoped to select a book, but was unable to gain entry."

The housekeeper peered around her at the bolted door and lifted her chatelaine from where it was fastened to her waist. "How strange. I am unaware of any reason why it would be locked."

When she opened the door, Mr. Darcy stood with his forearm upon the mantel, staring into the fire.

"Mr. Darcy! Forgive me if I have disturbed your solitude. Miss Elizabeth wished for a book, so I—"

"Please do not worry yourself, Mrs. Nicholls. I am not upset. I was reading with the entry quite open until Miss Bingley locked me in here not five minutes ago, but rather than spend my time pounding upon the door, I calmly waited for someone to notice. Thank you for freeing me, madam."

The housekeeper's eyebrows lifted. "Then I am glad Miss Elizabeth was present to facilitate your recovery. With Mr. Bingley's reading habits, you could have remained undiscovered for hours if not days."

His lip gave a slight curve. "Quite so."

Elizabeth motioned towards the front of the house. "I passed Miss Bingley before she entered her carriage. I imagine she has departed by now."

He nodded. "I am relieved to hear it."

"Well, if you'll forgive me saying it, the staff shall be relieved as well," stated Mrs. Nicholls matter-of-factly. "If you'll excuse me, I have work to do."

Mr. Darcy nodded. "Of course. Thank you again."

The housekeeper gave a dip of a curtsey and departed, leaving them to the company of one another.

"I underestimated your accomplishments, Miss Elizabeth."

She lifted her eyebrow. "I admit to not having practiced that particular skill in some time, but I hesitate to include tree-climbing amongst my accomplishments."

A slight smile graced his lips. "In this instance, I beg to differ. I am certain a few ladies in London might find such a skill useful. The gentlemen would as well if they chose to remember it."

"If I may speak plainly, I believe neither of us wish for a forced marriage, Mr. Darcy. I could not live my life resented for circumstances beyond my control. After all, my dreams would also be forfeit in such a situation."

"But your mother..."

A groan escaped her lips. "My mother may be on a determined pursuit of husbands for her daughters, but how amenable we are to her wishes is another matter. She may push and mortify us to the end of our wits, but Jane and I shall not bow to her demands unless they match the sentiments of our hearts."

"Brave words in today's world. If you do not marry, your life would be changed irrevocably upon the passing of your father."

"Truer words have never been spoken, but my Uncle Gardiner has promised to aid us should that day arrive."

She bit her lip as she considered the man before her for a moment. "Both of us should find spouses we find more than tolerable, I believe."

His shoulders dropped. "Please accept my sincerest apology for my words that evening. I was in a ghastly mood, and after hearing the whispers and titters of the mothers and daughters in the room, became annoyed at Bingley's entreaty to dance.

"You are, in my opinion, a handsome lady. I do not believe I would find marriage to you a hardship, by any means."

Her cheeks burned as she reached down for the books on the table. "Thank you," she whispered. She selected *Evelina* from the pile before her. "May I read this book?"

"Please. I believe Clarke mixed that one into the titles I selected to travel with me." He reached over and opened the cover. "It belongs to my sister." A nameplate bearing the name Georgiana Darcy adorned the inside cover.

"Oh! I can choose another. I had not realized..."

His hand stayed her wrist so she could not withdraw, leaving an unknown frisson in its wake. "Do not worry on my sister's account. She would be pleased to share it with you. She may be painfully shy, but she is kind."

"You are certain?" Her hands clutched the book as she drew it closer and away from him.

"Quite. She will have no objection. I assure you. The remaining two volumes are in my trunk when you have completed the first."

She stared at the fine calfskin binding. Why could she no longer hold his eye? "Thank you. I promise I shall return them before we depart for Longbourn." With a gesture towards the exit, she bit her lip. "I should return to Jane. Thank you again."

Her feet bustled her from the library and up the stairs until she was safe within the confines of her sister's bedchamber.

What just happened? Mr. Darcy complimented her? She drew the book down from her chest. He had loaned her his sister's book!

Who was this man? One moment he was haughty as he was at the assembly, and the next a perfect gentleman.

Whoever he was, she had to maintain some distance. Her responses to him were a mystery, but she could not afford to form an attachment to him. He would depart Netherfield one day and she would not be going with him. He was a risk she could not afford!

Chapter 6

Darcy woke the next morning, tired and agitated from the constant dreams he endured the night prior. Clarke, bless him, brought coffee directly, which revived him a bit before he descended to the dining room for breakfast; however, another cup or two was required.

Miss Elizabeth sat silent across from him as she took great care in spreading jam on her toast. He took a drink from his latest cup and examined her while her attention was occupied elsewhere. Dark lines framed the undersides of her eyes as she sipped her own coffee. Had she been required to remain awake for the sake of her sister? She would make herself ill should she not rest from time to time.

"You appear worn, Miss Elizabeth. I hope your sister has not taken a turn for the worse?"

She lifted her eyebrows. "You do know how to compliment a lady, sir."

His eyes closed. How could he have phrased it in such a fashion! "Forgive me."

"I knew you meant no harm, but I could not let the opportunity pass." Her lip lifted on one side, prompting his to follow suit. "Jane is much improved, thank you. Mrs. Hurst requested trays for Jane and herself and offered to keep Jane company for a time. My sister shooed me from the room, claiming I required some fresh air and solitude."

"And do you? Require solitude, that is?"

Her teeth nibbled at her bottom lip as her eyes narrowed just a bit. "Not necessarily, but I do appreciate the opportunity to do as I choose."

"The weather is agreeable for this time of year. I would be pleased to escort you around the gardens when you have finished your meal."

The smile fell away from her lips, and she stared at him, her eyes wary. "I confess I had hoped to walk before I returned to Jane, but if you have business, I do not require your presence. I often ramble about Longbourn without a chaperon."

Did she not wish for him to accompany her? She appeared as a deer when it notices a hunter's rifle aimed in its direction.

"Miss Bennet, I feel you and I have misjudged one another on a frequent basis since our first acquaintance. After the events of the past few days, I would welcome the opportunity to ask a few questions, and since I know you overheard us speaking of your family, I feel certain you would appreciate the opportunity as well."

"I confess I have attempted to sketch your character, yet you have puzzled me exceedingly." Miss Elizabeth tilted her head as she appraised him. "I thank you for your invitation. I should be pleased to have you as my escort."

"Splendid." This was nonsensical. What was he doing? He continually vowed to avoid Miss Elizabeth's company, but upon drawing near to her, his resolve vanished into the mist.

When she had sipped the last of her coffee, they left the house for the gardens where they began to walk side by side.

"Am I free to ask any question I wish, Mr. Darcy?"

He grinned. "You may ask, but I may choose not to answer."

"Touché." She turned so she walked backwards. "Why did you defend my family to Miss Bingley? I am still amazed Mr. Bingley did not object. You were hardly complimentary of his family, his roots."

He stopped, and she halted after one more step. "The answer is simple. Miss Bingley was impolite and insulting. She has a decided contempt for anything related to trade, yet her father was a tradesman, which Bingley has never denied or scorned. Her false sense of superiority has infuriated her brother for years, but other behaviours in the last two years have prompted him to take measures to restrain her."

"Restrain? I do not understand."

He shifted on his feet. "At one time, I was unfailingly polite to Miss Bingley. Out of respect for her brother, I would have never raised my voice or corrected her behaviour, yet she attempted to force me into a marriage with her. Bingley, rather than lose my friendship, formed Miss Bingley her own establishment. Since she failed at her attempt to entrap me, Bingley has ensured she is unable to use a connection to either of us, and she is not allowed to reside within the same home as her brother."

"Yet, she came to Netherfield."

He scuffed the bottom of his shoe along the ground. "She ignored her brother's express instructions not to journey to Netherfield."

She lifted her eyebrows. "I am amazed he did not send her back directly."

"Bingley did try, but she travelled without a maid or a companion. They both left her service in the month prior to her journey here." A bark of laugher escaped his throat. "Miss Bingley is in for a shock as she comes to know her new companion. I have it on good authority that she does not accept nonsense. Bingley was almost giddy with excitement when he read her references."

"You make her sound more of a governess than a companion." She shook her head. "I would never have imagined Miss Bingley venturing to such lengths! May I inquire of Mrs. Hurst? Was she a part of her sister's machinations?"

"Mrs. Langford may be a companion by title, but by Bingley's direction, she is to ensure Miss Bingley's proper decorum by whatever means available to her. As for Mrs. Hurst, she has been told not to support her sister's schemes. The Hursts did convey Miss Bingley to Netherfield, but Mrs. Hurst claims to have had little choice in the matter since she felt she could not leave Miss Bingley without a maid and a companion."

"Do you believe her?"

He lifted a shoulder. "No, though I feel Mrs. Hurst should have sent an express warning her brother of Miss Bingley's pending arrival. Matters were poorly handled in my opinion. Miss Bingley could have remained in the Hurst's home, which has more servants, but Hurst does not allow her to live with them either."

Miss Elizabeth plucked a vivid amber leaf from a nearby hedge, spinning it in her hand. "I appreciate your defence of my sudden appearance here at Netherfield. I confess I was distressed upon hearing of my sister's illness, and wished to determine her condition for myself. The horses could not be spared for the carriage."

"Miss Bennet is a fortunate lady to have such a devoted sibling. I know my own sister has oft times indicated a desire for such a sister, and I have oft thought of how it might be beneficial to her, especially now."

Her attention returned to his face, and her eyebrows drew together. "I do hope she is well."

"She has had a difficult time as of late. I pray she will rally, but I am, as of yet, uncertain."

"With such a devoted brother, I believe she will be well."

His cheeks warmed. "You are too kind. I failed to protect her when it mattered. It is why she…"

The sympathetic eyes of Miss Elizabeth stopped his tongue. He could not reveal Georgiana's secrets! He might find Miss Elizabeth irresistible, but could he jeopardise his sister on such a short acquaintance?

"Should you need to speak of your sister, you can be assured of my discretion."

"I thank you for your consideration, but I cannot—not yet at least. Perhaps…"

Her hand upon his garnered his attention. How long had he been twisting his fingers? "If you have the need or feel you can speak of it, you know where to find me. I will not push or pry."

A nod was all he could manage before he gestured toward the path. Miss Elizabeth took the place at his side as they walked in silence for a few moments.

"It must be difficult to be apart from your sister at such a time."

He swallowed hard. If only the dreadful lump in his throat would disappear. "I found it particularly trying when I first arrived, but my aunt, Lady Fitzwilliam, has been of great aid to Georgiana, who requested to stay with my uncle and aunt while I was away."

"It must be a comfort that your sister can confide and trust in your relations."

How true her statement was! Aunt Charlotte's care and concern had been irreplaceable!

"I must confess my aunt has been of great help. Since my mother's passing, Lady Fitzwilliam has been more of a mother to us than an aunt."

"In some fashion, my Aunt Gardiner is the same." Miss Elizabeth wore a warm smile as she watched two squirrels frolic under a tree. A laugh bubbled from her lips at the pair's antics, sounding like the happy tune of a rambling brook. Did Miss Elizabeth not have one trait he would find unappealing?

"This is your uncle and aunt in London?"

"Yes, though Miss Bingley did not realize that the local gossip of my uncle is not all it appears."

His eyebrows rose. "Your statement stirs one's curiosity. Will you share the information the local matrons lack?"

She grinned and peered at him from the corner of her eye. "You must understand my mother is also unaware of this information."

"Then this must be quite the tittle-tattle if your mother does not know."

With a roll of her eyes, she stopped and turned to face him. "You mentioned to Miss Bingley that my mother's father was a younger son."

"Yes, I believe Mrs. Philips boasted of it at the assembly."

"I would not be shocked if she did," she said with a sigh. "But what is not commonly known around the neighbourhood is that my grandfather's estate was entailed. My Uncle Gardiner inherited my grandfather's properties and possessions five years ago upon the death of my cousin, but has maintained his residence in Cheapside to continue his business. Since he does not use the estates, they are leased for additional income."

"Your uncle owns Netherfield?"

"Very good, Mr. Darcy. Yes, though he has not mentioned as such to my mother, as she would bemoan the fact that my uncle does not give up his business and move to Netherfield. My uncle finds matters simpler to keep secret rather than give an ear to my mother's protests."

"He is prudent to maintain his investment."

"My uncle has two young sons and would like to have the estate to leave to his firstborn without leaving his younger son penniless to make his own way."

"Quite prudent, then."

Her forehead crinkled. "I am unsure why I confided my uncle's business to you just now. I have never mentioned it to a soul outside of Jane, who was told by my aunt and uncle." She shook her head and began to walk once more. "May I ask how you realized I spoke of Netherfield?"

"Your knowledge of the tree to the library as well as a comment that you were younger when you attempted that manoeuvre last. You are far more familiar with Netherfield than one who only visits."

"I should not have told you."

"Do not trouble yourself. I shall not jump in my carriage and travel the county, spreading word to all of the rumour-mongering ladies of the neighbourhood."

With a hand to her mouth, she giggled. "Forgive me. I had this image of you sitting with my mother and Aunt Philips as they gossiped."

He feigned insult. "Would I not fit with such company?"

Her laughter echoed through the trees. "Not at all! You would give them the scowl you usually do me."

"Scowl?" He caught himself watching Miss Elizabeth often, but scowling? "I hope you have not thought me to be stern or angry with you?"

Her cheeks reddened. "I should not have mentioned it."

"Do not apologise when I seem to owe you one."

"When I have found you staring in my direction, I thought you looked to find fault."

"Dear Lord, no!" He ran a hand across his mouth. "I have found I enjoy listening to an intelligent lady speak. My cousin, who is a colonel in the Regulars, has oft told me I appear cross in situations when I have concerns of the mothers matching me with their daughters."

"Ah, so you hide behind a forbidding expression." She walked around a tree, trailing her fingers along the bark. "Your family must expect much from your marriage."

"They do. My aunt, Lady Catherine, wishes me to wed my cousin, Anne, though neither of us wishes for such a travesty. We are more brother and sister than cousins. I could never..." A shudder ran down his spine.

"So you are still searching for the correct lady?"

"I would not call it a search." Her eyebrow lifted, and he smiled. "Lady Fitzwilliam introduces me to eligible ladies at balls and parties; I speak with them for a few minutes, I become impatient, and I excuse myself with haste."

"You become weary? Can none of them hold a proper discourse on fashion or the weather?"

Her lips twitched, and his hands clenched at his sides. How he wanted to tickle that laugh from her lips!

"You are terrible, Miss Elizabeth."

An improper sound escaped her nose, and she covered the bottom of her face with her hand, peeking from the corner of her eye to ascertain if he noticed. She cleared her throat. "All of them are wanting in some manner, then?"

"They are insipid and do not interest me in the slightest."

"Perhaps your aunt is introducing you to the wrong ladies?"

"I fear she has had me make the acquaintance of every young lady the ton has to offer."

Miss Elizabeth pursed her lips. "Oh dear."

Oh dear, indeed!

He stepped around her, so he would not claim her lips in an impulsive gesture. He could not kiss her! Matters became more challenging with every look and every discussion. What was he to do?

Chapter 7

November 19th 1811

Elizabeth made haste from the front door, walking ahead of her sisters to avoid the insufferable company of her cousin. His voice was behind her, but she would not look! She could not risk him taking it as encouragement!

As of that morning, he had begun to trail her around the house. He spoke of Lady Catherine—was that not the name of Mr. Darcy's aunt?—Rosings Park, and his own parish at Hunsford in that order of priority. He prattled on and on without a care for the thoughts of others or of how tedious his conversation was. She could take no more!

When she first returned to Longbourn, she was pleased to be home. Sure, her mother ranted and raved that they should have remained longer at Netherfield, but Elizabeth needed to separate herself from Mr. Darcy. She required a clarity she could not obtain with his constant presence.

The gentleman had been kind and gracious, but that was the problem. He had become everything for which she could hope in a husband, yet he could never consider her. Their conversation in the back garden at Netherfield revealed as much, and explained why he behaved so at the assembly—at least her vanity was restored.

She had heard rumours of his wealth and bachelor status whispered about the assembly that night. The sound likely carried to his ears as well. Include her mother in the fracas, and the night was a disaster in the making to his sensibilities.

"Elizabeth Bennet, wait for your cousin and your sisters!"

She turned back. When had her mother ventured to the portico? With a low growl, she tempered her pace a bit, though not enough for Mr. Collins, whose shoulders heaved up and down as he panted like a dog to reach her side.

As she rounded the corner and was no longer in sight of her mother, she pressed forward despite the calls from the obsequious parson.

"Cousin Elizabeth!"

Lydia pranced alongside her. "Just wait until I tell Mama you abandoned Mr. Collins! She will not be pleased."

"You will not say a word. Lest I tell her *you* wish to be the object of our cousin's attentions."

Lydia's jaw dropped. "You would not dare!"

"Oh, but I would. I do not appreciate his fawning so do not provide more to persuade me."

With a huff, Lydia sauntered back to Kitty. Her words were unintelligible, but the tone of her whining was certainly discernible.

"What did you say to Lydia?"

She startled. Jane had managed to make her way to Elizabeth's other side.

"She threatened to tell Mama that I was avoiding Mr. Collins. Speaking of our cousin, what is he doing?"

Jane peered back. "He continues to look at you, but he is speaking with Mary."

"I daresay she has more in common with him."

"That is ungenerous, Lizzy." Her words rebuked, but Jane's lips were drawn tight. She was suppressing a smile.

"You would not wish to wed Mr. Collins any more than I."

Jane shook her head. "No, I would not, but I believe Mama indicated I was soon to be betrothed to Mr. Bingley."

"Are you saying, she offered me in your stead?"

Her sister fidgeted with her fichu. "I entered the drawing room this morning as they were concluding their conversation."

Elizabeth peered back to Mr. Collins as he steadily spoke with Mary. "Well, he cannot expect me to accept if he never has the opportunity to speak with me."

"You cannot avoid him for a se'nnight!"

"I can try!"

They entered Meryton but had not gone far when Lydia and Kitty began to giggle and point; however, before Elizabeth could reprimand them, her youngest sisters ran ahead to greet Mr. Denny and a young man whom they had never seen before but who had a most gentlemanlike appearance.

Elizabeth lifted her eyebrows to Jane, who gave an almost imperceptible shrug, before they followed their youngest sisters. Lydia was in high animal spirits as she tittered and batted her eyelashes. Her behaviour was shameless and mortifying. Could she not control herself?

"Lizzy! You must come meet Mr. Wickham! He is to join the militia. He will be so charming in regimentals, will he not?"

Jane approached Lydia's other side and whispered in her ear, though their youngest sister ignored Jane's gentle and subtle chastisement.

"Oh la! I would never have any fun if I listened to you and Lizzy!"

Elizabeth closed her eyes. Her father needed to step out of his book room and take Lydia in hand before she was forever a younger version of their mother, or worse.

As her eyes reopened, Mary approached with Mr. Collins, both giving Lydia disapproving glares. Not that Lydia noticed. On the contrary, she continued on as though nothing had been said at all.

"Miss Elizabeth and Miss Mary," said Mr. Denny when Lydia broke for air. "I would like to introduce Mr. Wickham."

Elizabeth curtsied as the young man gave a bow. "So, if my sister is to be believed, you have just joined the militia?"

"Yes, I happened upon Denny while he was in London, and he convinced me of the militia's worth. I must say that if everyone is as welcoming as you and your sisters in Meryton, I will be quite well pleased with my situation."

"I hope you will."

A horse neighed and a movement in the corner of her eye caught her attention. Mr. Darcy and Mr. Bingley rode down High Street, but upon taking notice of the Bennet sisters, steered their horses in their direction.

As they drew closer, Mr. Darcy exhibited a peculiar change. His face, which had been calm and collected, became inflamed and his lips all but disappeared they thinned so. What had come over him? Her eyes traced the gentleman's line of vision to that of Mr. Wickham, who paled but wore a smirk. When Mr. Wickham took notice of Elizabeth's examination of him, his expression shifted to become more neutral.

Mr. Bingley dismounted and strode forward. "I was on my way to Longbourn to inquire after the health of Miss Bennet and here you are. Most fortuitous, I would say."

After he stepped down, Mr. Darcy drew beside Elizabeth. "Quite. Bingley, why do we not accompany the ladies on their return to Longbourn?"

A weak clearing of the throat came from the direction of Mr. Collins, who had raised his hand, but Mr. Darcy must not have heard. Of course, that gentleman's eyes were boring into Mr. Wickham without so much as a blink.

"But we have not yet stopped at Aunt Philips'!"

With a firm grip to Lydia's elbow, Elizabeth gave her a pull. "I will send a note when we arrive home. I am certain she will understand."

"But *I* do not understand," she continued to protest, attracting the notice of others on the street.

"Hush, Lydia!" She kept her voice low in the hopes the gentlemen did not hear. "You are being rude to Mr. Darcy and Mr. Bingley. Mama will be displeased if she learns of it."

Her youngest sister jerked away from Elizabeth's grasp. "*I* wish to remain in Meryton."

"Well, we are returning to Longbourn. You are well aware you are not permitted to remain in Meryton without one of us."

Lydia growled and flounced to Kitty, whom Jane had already begun to usher back towards home.

"Please forgive our hasty departure, Mr. Wickham, Mr. Denny. We had not anticipated company at Longbourn. Our mother will expect our return."

Mr. Wickham bowed, not removing his eyes from Mr. Darcy, while Mr. Denny bowed to Elizabeth. "We shall be sorry to lose your company, but we do understand. Do we not, Wickham?"

Mr. Wickham jolted. "Yes, it was a pleasure making your acquaintance, Miss Elizabeth."

Elizabeth dipped a brief curtsey and turned, Mr. Darcy's boots stomping the ground as he followed behind her. What was that all about? Would Mr. Darcy explain or was she to assume Mr. Wickham was not to be trusted?

"Cousin Elizabeth," Mr. Collins panted as he jogged alongside her. "One of my other cousins mentioned the gentleman behind you is none other than Mr. Darcy of Pemberley. Is that true?"

"Yes, I believe his estate is called Pemberley. Why do you ask?"

Mr. Collins bounced on his toes as his entire face lit. "His esteemed aunt, Lady Catherine de Bourgh, is my patroness. I must make myself known to him!"

With a grasp to Mr. Collins forearm, she halted his movement toward the object of his latest raptures. "Mr. Collins, you must not—"

Her cousin shook her hand from his arm. "My dear cousin, you must trust me in this, as you one day will trust me with all."

He stepped back and Elizabeth continued walking, grinding her teeth as she awaited the storm that was sure to come.

"I could not help but overhear that your name is Mr. Darcy!"

"I beg your pardon?" The gentleman's voice was lower than was his wont, and menacing.

"*You* are Mr. Darcy, nephew of my patroness Lady Catherine de Bourgh." There was not even a moment's pause. "I am pleased to report your aunt and betrothed Miss Anne de Bourgh were in—"

"What pray is your name?"

Elizabeth could take no more and turned. Mr. Darcy had halted and glared down upon the much shorter Mr. Collins, who was undaunted and stared at the wealthy gentleman with a look of pure adulation. Mr. Darcy's entire bearing, however, was stiff and unrelenting. His eyes were hard, his jaw clenched.

"I am Mr. Collins, sir." Her cousin was too occupied bowing before Mr. Darcy to take notice of his displeasure.

"Mr. Collins, I feel I must disabuse you of the misinformation you have received. I am not now, nor have I ever been betrothed to my cousin, and as both of us find the idea abhorrent, we shall never be so. Do you understand?"

"B... b... but your aunt?" Mr. Collins shrank some with each stutter.

"My aunt cannot accept my cousin's current betrothal and has been attempting to change her mind for the past year. Spreading the rumour of my attachment to her daughter is the final ploy of a woman desperate to alter a situation she dislikes. You will spread such lies no further. Do I make myself clear?"

"Y... yes, sir."

"Now, the youngest Miss Bennets are walking ahead without escort. You must go ensure they are not endangered on the remainder of their way home."

"I was told by Mrs. Bennet to accompany my cousin Elizabeth."

"Miss Elizabeth is not walking ahead, and I can provide her protection while I lead my horse. You must run ahead and escort Miss Lydia and Miss Kitty."

Mr. Darcy continued to stare down at her cousin until the man bowed and scurried to the front of the group where Lydia and Kitty sulked as they complained of the unfairness of their being forced to return. No doubt, when they reached Longbourn, they would tell their mother how horribly Elizabeth treated them.

"Is he truly your cousin?" came Mr. Darcy's incredulous voice from beside her.

She sighed. "Unfortunately, yes. He is set to inherit Longbourn when my father passes."

"And your mother has offered you as the sacrificial lamb?"

"I have reason to believe she has." With an arm, she gestured before her as she began walking. "I cannot imagine marriage to such a man, but my mother is more concerned with her security."

"Shall we have a bit of fun at your mother's and Mr. Collins' expense?"

She grinned. "What did you have in mind?"

"Nothing scandalous," he said with a laugh. He leaned in her direction and offered his arm. "Perhaps just enough for her to think you might find a betrothed elsewhere."

Her stomach dropped. "I could not ask that of you as I know what great lengths you go to avoid such conjecture."

"I do not mind if it saves you from the fate of Mr. Collins."

A laugh bubbled from her lips. "He is not unattractive."

Mr. Darcy's head jerked back with his jaw agape. "He is an imbecile."

"That he is." She placed her hand upon his elbow. "I hope I do not live to regret this."

"What damage could arise?"

"You will one day leave, and I shall be forced to endure Mama's laments that I have failed to secure your hand."

A lop-sided grin appeared upon his face. "But you will not be wed to Mr. Collins."

"Very true!"

"Miss Elizabeth." All trace of humour had disappeared and his features were hardened. "I must speak with your father as soon as we reach Longbourn. Can that be arranged?"

She nodded. "I shall take you to his study immediately."

"Thank you. I must apologise for forcing your hasty retreat from Meryton. I had no intention of being rude to yourself or your sisters."

She gave a gentle squeeze to his arm. "I gathered by your expression there has been some disagreement between you and Mr. Wickham. I did not believe you would rush us from the village without good cause."

"I have the best of reasons, and your trust at that moment was greatly appreciated. I had no wish to cause a scene."

As Longbourn came into view, Lydia and Kitty ran ahead, calling for their mother the moment they entered. Jane and Elizabeth waited as Mr. Bingley and Mr. Darcy handed their horses to a groom, then followed Mr. Collins and Mary inside and into the drawing room.

"Mr. Bingley! It was so kind of you to see my daughters home. They can walk to Meryton anytime." Her mother's eyes fell upon Elizabeth's hand and its placement upon Mr. Darcy's arm. Elizabeth snatched it away as though his topcoat had scalded her. Those same eyes bulged a hairsbreadth before she resumed her fawning attentions to Mr. Bingley.

"Mama?" As she spoke when her mother drew breath, Elizabeth was heard. "Mr. Darcy requested to speak to Papa. If you will excuse us, I shall show him to my father's library."

"Oh, yes, of course," she dismissed with a wave of her handkerchief. "It is not as though your father would deign to leave his study to receive callers." She peered at Mr. Collins and back. "You will return directly. Mr. Darcy can have nothing of interest to say to you."

"Actually," came the low voice from beside her. "I had some information to impart to Mr. Bennet, and it is of great importance to Miss Elizabeth as well. I am certain she will be asked to remain."

Her mother's jaw opened and closed as Elizabeth pressed her lips together. Do not grin!

"A... as you say, Mr. Darcy."

Elizabeth dropped her head and made her way into the hall, Mr. Darcy's boots thudding across the wooden floor behind her. When she reached the library, she knocked. A moment later, her father bid them to enter.

"Papa, Mr. Darcy requested to speak with you."

Her father's eyebrows rose upon his forehead. "He did? I cannot imagine why, but please show him in."

With her step to the side, Mr. Darcy made his way before the desk and bowed to her father as he stood to greet the visitor. "Thank you for agreeing to see me, sir."

Her father nodded. "I must admit to a significant amount of curiosity at your application to speak with me." He gestured to a pair of chairs set before the desk. "Please."

She closed the door and took her usual spot as Mr. Darcy seated himself in the chair beside her.

"I hope you do not mind, Mr. Bennet, but I requested Miss Elizabeth join us. I fear I was quite rude in Meryton in hastening your daughters' departure, and I wished to explain myself to her."

Her father leaned forward and rested his forearms upon his desk. "I did not imagine my interest in the reason for your call could increase, yet you have piqued my curiosity. Pray sir, continue."

"Bingley and I departed Netherfield with the intention of calling upon Longbourn since my friend wished to be certain Miss Bennet had regained her health. When we arrived in Meryton, Bingley noticed your daughters to one side of the road speaking to a member of the militia—I believe I heard him called Mr. Denny—and an acquaintance of his."

"Lydia and Kitty would be responsible for such an endeavour," stated Mr. Bennet lifting his eyes to the ceiling. "I must say I am growing weary of the talk of red coats in this house."

"Mr. Bennet, it is the man who accompanied this Mr. Denny that concerns me. I am loath to share private family business, but I feel I must if you are to understand why I have come to speak with you today."

Her father's brow furrowed and drew down over his eyes. "Of course."

"The man, Mr. Wickham, was the son of my father's steward, who was a very respectable man, yet the son is not of the same ilk as his father. Wickham and I were educated together at my father's expense—he even attended Cambridge with me."

"Quite generous of your father, if I may say."

Mr. Darcy nodded. "My father had a great respect for the elder Mr. Wickham, and I never disabused him of the notion that the son deserved a similar affection." The gentleman stood and stared through the nearby window. "I could not pain my father, especially as his health declined."

Elizabeth turned to keep her gaze upon Mr. Darcy. "If the son was so different from his father, may I ask his sins? I assume those are why you desired us return to Longbourn without delay."

"Mr. Wickham has several vices, but the most worrisome is his interest in the fairer sex. I was aware of him persuading quite a few young women into activities usually reserved for marriage, but after my father's death, the plight of a maid and a tenant's daughter came to my attention.

"While Wickham was at Pemberley for the burial, he forced himself upon these two women. One beget a child by him, the other is now buried in an unmarked grave outside of the Kympton churchyard."

A gasp escaped her throat. "Those poor women!"

Mr. Darcy closed his eyes and sighed. "Please forgive me for speaking in such a blunt fashion, Miss Elizabeth, but I cannot think of a more palatable way of describing his treachery."

"You stated it in as gentle a manner as you could." Her voice was weak. How could such a man appear so charming at a first acquaintance? She had witnessed his pallor and shock at meeting Mr. Darcy, but he had such an appearance of goodness prior to the arrival of the gentleman before her.

"Of all my daughters, you have chosen the correct daughter to enlighten. Lizzy visits our tenants and ensures those who are sick are tended. She has also read most of the contents of my library in her short years. Evil may not have touched her personally, but she is better equipped than the rest of the girls to be aware of the truth."

Mr. Darcy ran his hand through his hair. "I wish I could claim those two cases were the only ones, but there have been several more. One was a young gentlewoman, who he preyed upon. She was not yet sixteen years old."

Her gut clenched and a knot rose to sit in her throat. Dear Lord! His sister! Had he not said she had been hurt? Could the young gentlewoman be her?

"If you will forgive me for saying, Mr. Bennet. Your youngest daughters are free spirited and would not recognise the danger they faced until it was too late. No family should suffer ruin for his depraved actions."

Elizabeth's eyes burned, and she swallowed in an attempt not to cry. "You mentioned other vices."

"Yes, he is fond of gambling. He inherited one thousand pounds from my father and was paid three thousand in lieu of a living, which he squandered in three years."

"That is quite a sum to waste!" her father exclaimed. "He could have lived well enough for quite some time had he managed his funds in a more careful fashion."

"Yes, he has never been a prudent spender. Wickham also leaves substantial debts in his wake." Mr. Darcy took his seat once again. "I paid those in Lambton and Kympton, with the understanding that I would cover no more of Wickham's spending. As a result, he is no longer extended credit in the villages around Pemberley."

Elizabeth turned her attention to her father. "What shall we do?"

Her father removed his glasses and rubbed his eyes. "I shall never have a moment's peace for this, but I will ban the militia from Longbourn. If Mr. Wickham is now a part of their ranks, I cannot ban him without calling attention to him. I am unaware if he is of a resentful temper, but I do not wish to tempt him."

Mr. Darcy sat forward in his chair. "One of the reasons I have not exposed him publicly is his propensity to seek revenge. Your plan is wise."

"I shall speak with Sir William Lucas on the matter of this Mr. Wickham's debts. The businesses in Meryton might be safer to refuse all of the militia any sort of credit. Several of the merchants cannot afford losses of any significant amount, yet a problem could arise if Colonel Forster or any of his men take insult to the refusal."

"Are you familiar with Temple of Muses in London?"

"Yes, Mr. Lackington extends no credit to anyone and runs the most popular bookstore in town." Her father gave a shrug. "I do not know if it will prevent them from taking offence but it is worth a try I suppose. Some may offer credit regardless."

Elizabeth sat forward. "Other young ladies of Meryton should be protected from him as well."

"I would hope..." Mr. Darcy's voice was anxious.

"I shall not mention your name, sir, though if this Mr. Wickham discovers we have been warned—"

"He will know it was me. I do understand." He glanced at Elizabeth. "I could not allow him to harm another lady when I could prevent it."

Her father's eyes shifted between them. "I laud your sense of honour, and I assure you I will take every precaution."

Chapter 8

Elizabeth escaped from Longbourn not long after the sun rose the next morning. When she stayed at Netherfield, Mr. Darcy's horse could often be heard galloping away from the house at such a time, and if she was lucky, she would happen upon him today as she took her morning walk.

Her mother's displeasure at her father's decision had resonated through the walls of Longbourn the evening prior. Her laments were voiced in the loudest and most vehement terms at dinner and after, even when her father departed for his library. The house was not silent until her mother had at last taken laudanum to find sleep after being so cruelly ignored by her husband.

Lydia's wails of displeasure were also grating to Elizabeth's ears. She joined her mother as she ranted and railed the entire evening. Of course, her youngest sister had no idea of the reason for the militia's banishment from Longbourn, but it was doubtful she would care. Lydia would never believe something evil could befall her— particularly within the sleepy environs of Meryton. Lydia's potential response to the idea was obvious: "La! What a joke!"

Elizabeth walked through the well-worn trail in the direction of Netherfield. Unlike the day when she journeyed to tend to Jane, today, she took a trail that bypassed Meryton. When the edge of Longbourn's property was reached, she climbed the stile, and began to scan the countryside for Mr. Darcy. The sound of a neigh from beside her caused her to jump with a hand to the fencepost.

"You startled me!"

Mr. Darcy sat atop his bay stallion as it emerged from some trees and approached where she stood, a large grin upon his face. "I noticed, but you should be more aware. My horse's footsteps are hardly silent."

With a huff, she stepped down one board so she was face to face with the tall gentleman on his sizable mount. "I confess I hoped to happen upon you."

Something flickered in his eyes. Was he surprised, pleased, annoyed?

"And why is that?"

"I hope I am not presumptuous, but I wished to say how distressed I was to hear about your sister yesterday."

His jaw clenched and released. "I should have been more circumspect when I mentioned a young gentlewoman. I had not intended to divulge so much."

"My father is unaware, and you can be assured I shall not tell. She does not deserve such censure when she has already been violated in so cruel a manner. I hope she finds the strength to put Mr. Wickham's evil behind her."

His eyes remained upon his hands, which gripped the reins with such force his knuckles were certain to be white under his gloves. "I *wish* I could call him out! It was all I could do to prevent my cousin from pursuing Wickham and killing him." His eyes met hers. "My cousin Colonel Fitzwilliam shares guardianship of my sister with me." He looked into the distance. "I could not allow him to incite gossip. Georgiana's reputation would be damaged if anyone even suspected or conjectured as to why we challenged Wickham. I could not—I cannot take such a risk."

"No, you could not. She would not only have to bear what he did, but endure the sneers of those who do not care or understand what she has suffered. And what if either you or your cousin were killed? She would mourn your death as well. She requires both of you to help her through this ordeal."

His eyes lifted to hers with such sorrow, her chest pained her. "I have felt such guilt leaving her these past weeks."

"I believe you said she is staying with her aunt?"

"She is. My aunt felt she could be of more help to Georgiana than two bachelors, and I had made a promise to Bingley prior to Ramsgate that I would come."

"Your sister was in Ramsgate when this occurred?"

His Adam's apple bobbed as he swallowed hard. "Yes, we formed an establishment for Georgiana, and she was to spend the summer by the sea. Wickham followed, by design it seems, and conspired with my sister's companion. Mrs. Younge encouraged Georgiana to think of Wickham as a suitor."

Elizabeth gasped. "I am aware that Lydia is a similar age and is out, but both she and your sister are far too young for courtship and marriage. I would not have desired a husband at such a tender age."

"Georgiana found herself uncomfortable with Wickham's attentions and wrote to me, divulging Mrs. Younge's persuasion and Wickham's idea that they should marry. I hastened to Ramsgate, but Wickham, in an attempt to convince Georgiana they should elope forced himself—"

"You do not have to say it." Her eyes blurred with tears at the sadness and shakiness of his voice. "Her aunt must be such a comfort to her at this time and would, no doubt, write should your sister have need of you."

Mr. Darcy dismounted, stepped around his horse, and held out his hand to help her alight from the stile. "Might I accompany you on your walk? It would ease my mind to know you are safe."

As she stepped down, she peered in the direction of Meryton. "Do you believe it unsafe for me to walk as I always have?"

"Wickham is unpredictable, but I would rather you are unharmed."

She placed her hand upon his proffered arm. "I am unaccustomed to such worry. We are a small community, so my father never saw a reason to curtail my ramblings." They proceeded away from the village as Mr. Darcy led his horse.

"When such happenings seem so far away, one does not always see the danger to themselves." He cleared his throat with a gentle cough. "Forgive me."

With a slight tug at his arm, she stopped him, and he turned slightly to face her. "As I said before, I am a willing ear should you require it, but please do not feel you must divulge anything to me."

His eyes searched hers. "I have never spoken in such an unguarded manner with another person. I cannot explain why I seem to trust you as I do."

A fluttering erupted within her belly and her chest was light. "I am honoured by your trust, sir. I just did not want you to feel forced to confide in me."

"I have kept this inside for the last few months. To be honest, it is a relief to speak of it. Your kindness towards my sister's situation gives me hope."

His eyes held hers with such intensity that she could not tear hers away until he gave an abrupt turn and began to walk towards Longbourn.

"I should be returning to Netherfield soon, but I would like to see you safely home."

"Longbourn is not far. Nothing untoward should happen in the short time it would take to return."

"Regardless, I shall escort you as far as the back garden. I shall brook no arguments on the matter either."

With a grin, she looked up with a raised brow. "You should be aware that I do not take commands well."

"Perhaps you should learn."

A crooked smile she had never seen before lit his face, revealing a dimple on one side. Was there one on the opposite as well? She would have to make him give a full smile! He was definitely a handsome man when he wore a pleased expression, and who knew he had a sense of humour?

They walked in silence for the remainder of the path bordering Longbourn's back garden. There, Mr. Darcy removed her hand from his arm and encased it between his palms.

"Thank you for today. I am in your debt, Miss Elizabeth."

His lips grazed her knuckles. Why did it feel as though he had kissed her bare flesh? His warm breath tickled the back of her wrist as her chest began to feel as though it would burst. She needed air!

"There is no debt, Mr. Darcy." She curtsied, and before he could discern her heated cheeks, she ran to the door of the kitchens. As she slipped into the house, she did not look back lest her heart break if he had departed before she was inside.

Darcy leaned around the hedge to watch her enter Longbourn. Were her cheeks pinker just before she dashed in the direction of the house? Had she truly blushed?

When the door closed behind her, he led Boreas far enough from the house that they would not be seen with him atop, mounted, and turned his stallion towards Netherfield.

What had happened? He had intended to meet Miss Elizabeth, though when he first set out, it was only to ensure her safety. He had lied to himself! For the duration of his stay at Netherfield, he had fought an overwhelming attraction to Miss Elizabeth—a battle he was losing by the day.

He had never spoken so openly to anyone. His cousins, his aunt, and even his father would never have been told of his grief or his feelings of culpability in Georgiana's situation. They would listen and keep his counsel, yet he was not comfortable with the intimacy of the gesture—until Elizabeth.

Was he beetle-headed not to consider Elizabeth as a potential wife? Her connections were not as poor as some, and she likely had little or no fortune, but had he a need for such considerations? Would he be more willing to take her for a wife if she were higher born and still penniless?

He was not a spendthrift and had saved a considerable sum since he began receiving an allowance at Cambridge. He could afford to take a wife who came with little but herself to the marriage, so why was he not considering that very situation?

He had no need for more connections or money, so the circumstance of the utmost concern was her family's behaviour; however, they would not be in the company of her family often as his responsibilities required him to be at Pemberley or in London for most of the year.

She would be an excellent sister for Georgiana—understanding, compassionate, kind. Georgiana could not ask for a better relation. Elizabeth had cared for Jane with such diligence at Netherfield, she would certainly do the same for Georgiana.

He was a numbskull! A low growl left his throat as he spurred Boreas into a gallop. He had offended the one woman he should have considered from the beginning of their acquaintance! He had made an amends for the gaffes at the assembly, but now, how to proceed?

Should he request a courtship? Should he call upon her at Longbourn and see how matters progressed?

What a nightmare! How did you court a lady? He had run from the women pursuing him for so long, he now had no idea how to woo one. The situation was hopeless!

He pulled his stallion to a halt atop the last rise before Netherfield and gazed back at Longbourn's roof in the distance. What was Elizabeth thinking at that moment? Was she as conflicted as he? Would she welcome him as a suitor?

Boreas shifted beneath him, impatient to reach the stables. "Easy," he soothed.

It was settled! He would meet her for her walk on the morrow and see how their friendship progressed. Bingley had a ball planned for Tuesday next. If all went well over the next week, he would request a courtship.

His family might be disappointed in his choice initially, but they would have to welcome her. Once she accepted his hand, they would have no choice.

Chapter 9

"Mr. Darcy!" Elizabeth's hand flew to her heart when she rounded the hedgerow and almost collided with his chest. "I thought you would be near the stile."

"Then my company is not unwelcome?" He pinched his lips together to prevent a smile.

"You are well aware that your company is most welcome." Her cheeks crimsoned, and the cool breeze of the morning dried his gums and teeth as he grinned.

"I am pleased to hear it. Otherwise, Boreas missed his daily run for naught." He presented his elbow and a certain satisfaction rushed through him when her small fingers pressed against the thick wool of his great coat.

"I could not deprive your horse of his exercise."

"Bingley and I plan to ride to the south end of Netherfield's property when I return. He will stretch his legs and enjoy a race while he is out of his stall."

"Ah, then I shall not worry that he is neglected."

Her lips curved a mite on the ends. She appeared pleased at his presence, yet she had every morning this week when they met at the stile. When he awoke, he was all anticipation until he set eyes upon her, picking her way through the trail. His palms itched until she placed her petite hand in his as he helped her descend the stile.

Their conversations had also expanded to consist of more than just Georgiana. Discussions of books, current events, and even Pemberley filled their mornings. As they spoke further of different subjects, he increasingly admired her fine eyes and the steadfast opinions she professed as they debated—even when she later confessed she had altered her opinion for the sake of the argument.

"You have become quiet. I hope there is naught amiss."

He started and gazed down. Her brows were drawn and her teeth wore at her lip.

"I am well. I meant to ask how the party at your Aunt Philips' passed as I forgot to ask yesterday."

"I have never been so eager to return to Longbourn."

Good Lord, what could have transpired to warrant such a reaction? "You did not have difficulties with Wickham, did you?"

"He was present, and I felt as though he watched me a great deal. I cannot explain, but I was uncomfortable most of the evening with him present. It might have been my imagination, but—"

"But it may not have been. My actions in Meryton would not have gone unnoticed. He knows I do not usually extend my protection to just any lady."

She looked off to the right. The brim of her bonnet blocked his sight, so even should he lean forward, he could not see her reaction.

"My father caused a maelstrom within the house by pronouncing Lydia and Kitty were not attending. I have never heard such wailing and complaining, but he stood his ground."

"I am surprised your mother did not object."

A wry laugh escaped her lips. "Oh, she objected with much enthusiasm. My father merely informed her she would remain at Longbourn with her youngest daughters should she not cease her complaints."

"He did?" He had underestimated Mr. Bennet.

"I have never witnessed him put Mama or my youngest sisters in their place. Jane, Mary, and I were informed we were not to converse with any of the militia alone, and he remained nearby for the entirety of the evening. Mr. Wickham never had an opportunity to approach me, much less speak without my father or one of my sisters nearby."

"I am relieved to hear it." Her father's actions in this situation were wise. The man could not be too careful when protecting Elizabeth.

Darcy filled his lungs to quell the quivering in his belly. "I hoped you would reserve the first set for me on Tuesday night?"

Her head whirled around to reveal her slightly open mouth. "You want my first?"

He halted and turned to face her. "And the supper, if you are willing."

"Mr. Darcy, you will have the neighbourhood tongues wagging."

"Would you object?"

Her eyes widened. "I..."

"Please say what you will. I must confess I have met you every morning in the hopes of learning whether I would gain a favourable answer to a request of courtship."

"I did not expect..."

He removed her hand from his arm and held it between his own. It fit so well, her buff kid leather glove encased in his palms. "You did not expect me to request a courtship?"

"No, I convinced myself you merely sought kindness after the horrible events in Ramsgate. My connections and my family's wealth are not enough to warrant such attention from you."

Her voice was faint. Was she displeased? Could she be upset by his revelation? His thumb began to caress her knuckles as his mouth became dry. He tried to swallow, but it was as though a brick had lodged itself in his neck.

"I have wanted so much to prove I am not the insulting man of the assembly. I have no need of a large dowry or grand connections through my wife. I desire more—because of you. I desire a wife who will care for me and not my property or my relations, so how can I not search for a lady whose desires match my own?

"You proved in the library at Netherfield that you care naught of material considerations. You have shown sympathy for my sister's plight, and I know you would care for her as though she were born a sister and not merely a sibling through marriage—your generous heart would allow no less."

Her head shook. "I do not deserve such praise, Mr. Darcy." A tear dropped from her eye upon her cheek, and he brushed it away with the tips of his fingers as she released a shaky breath. "I told myself at almost every meeting that you sought someone with whom to speak of your troubles. I told myself that I could not form a tender regard for you, lest I be broken-hearted when you depart Hertfordshire. I reminded myself time and again, yet I failed miserably."

Something in his chest jumped as his hands gripped hers. Did she say what he thought she had? "You failed?"

"Yes, I have come to realize that I care for you, but I continued to tell myself that you could not pursue me. I had to make some attempt to protect my heart."

His hand cradled her cheek. "You will allow me to court you then?"

"Yes," she whispered with shiny eyes.

He removed her gloves and pressed kisses to the backs of her hands. How his lips ached to claim hers! But it was too soon. Her whispered, tremulous voice and her timidity indicated she was overwhelmed by his request. She would need some time to accustom herself to their new relationship; he could not rush matters.

"May I go to your father?" He put her gloves in his pocket and removed his own. His fingertips skimmed against the soft flesh of her wrist and through her palm.

"You may, though I shall require my gloves before I return."

"I had not planned on keeping them, but I have longed to touch you without the impediment." She trembled. "Are you cold?"

"A little."

He helped her replace her gloves and placed his great coat upon her shoulders. A smile lit his face at its length as it dragged the ground. "I never thought of men's attire having trains."

She glanced behind and giggled. "They could be quite fashionable. Perhaps someone should make one for Beau Brummel, then all the men of London would rush to their tailors for their own."

How he adored her wit! She was never speechless and always voiced her opinions with intelligence and humour, never professing to be something she was not. Elizabeth Bennet was Elizabeth Bennet. Her nature was without artifice, which drew his notice more than any other attribute she possessed.

Her free hand kept the hem of his coat from grazing the carpet of leaves upon the ground while she took his proffered arm.

"When would be best to speak with your father?"

"What is the time now?"

His pocket watch was retrieved and opened. "Almost ten o'clock."

"He will have just finished his breakfast. I suggest just after eleven. Hill brings him tea near that time while he sees to the business of Longbourn, though I am certain he would welcome the interruption. He is not fond of estate business and attends to it swiftly in order to enjoy his books."

"That should give me adequate time to retrieve Boreas and exercise him before I arrive at Longbourn."

"I was surprised you did not ride him today."

He covered her hand with his free one. Why had he replaced her gloves?

"I rode him from Netherfield to the copse of trees near the stile where I tethered him to a low branch."

"He could not be happy to be deserted for all this time."

Darcy gave a small shrug. "He is well-trained, and I shall give him ample time to run before my arrival at Longbourn."

Too soon, the familiar hedgerow that separated Longbourn's garden from the fields appeared, and Elizabeth removed her hand from his arm to return his greatcoat. He shrugged himself into it and grasped her hands, entwining his fingers with hers.

"I shall see you soon."

Her head gave a slight bob, yet she was silent as he bestowed kisses to her knuckles.

"Do not accept Mr. Collins before I arrive."

One side of her lip curved into an impish smile. "Then, perhaps you should not tarry."

Elizabeth backed from Mr. Darcy. His expression at her retort was quite amusing. She would derive a great deal of enjoyment from surprising him in the future. His eyebrows lifted and a wide grin stole across his face. There was the other dimple!

When they met at the stile, both dimples were visible, and showed themselves with a frequency she had not seen in the past; however, she would not tire of their appearances. They gave her a pleasure she had not the words to explain.

As soon as she rounded the hedgerow, she ran to the rear door and hastened inside. How she appreciated the warmth of the kitchen on a chilling day. Mr. Darcy's coat had certainly helped, and it smelled of him as well. Who knew a gentleman's scent could be of such comfort?

She peeled her gloves from her fingers, so she could untie her bonnet. Once she removed her pelisse, Hill entered and started.

"Miss Lizzy, you have returned." Hill took the garments from her arms. "I shall bring these to your chambers. Food is laid out in the breakfast parlour, and I just put a fresh kettle of tea on the table."

"Thank you, Hill."

When she reached the breakfast parlour, she stared at the offerings before her. How could she eat? Mr. Darcy would be here in less than an hour to speak with her father, a part of her trembled at the notion. She was to be courted by Mr. Darcy. It could not be real!

Her nerves were unequal to sitting idly until he arrived, so she departed to play the pianoforte, which was always of benefit when she was anxious or unhappy. Her fingers fumbled and slurred through the short etude she selected, and Elizabeth sighed when it was completed.

"You must be at sixes and sevens to forgo breaking your fast for practising."

Her heart leapt as her head jolted in the direction of the doorway where her father stood, appraising her over his spectacles.

"Join me in my study, Elizabeth. I believe we should have a talk."

She bit the inside of her cheek as she followed. Once she was seated in her usual chair, her father passed behind her before he walked around to his own seat.

"We have not had a chance to speak since Mr. Darcy called. I cannot say what shocked me more—the confessions and gentlemanly bearing of Mr. Darcy or your acceptance and behaviour towards the man."

"I had the opportunity to sketch his character more fully when I stayed at Netherfield and found him to be the opposite of my initial perception."

"Indeed. By my observation, Mr. Darcy is not an outgoing man. I would imagine the assembly, the neighbourhood ladies, and your mother were overwhelming to one of his reserved disposition."

Her fingers found a small pull in the fabric of her skirt, and she stared at the misplaced thread as she scratched at it. "He has indicated as much."

"Are you aware that Mr. Hill witnessed him walk you to the edge of the park yesterday?"

She gave a sharp inhale as her eyes jerked to her father's. "Mr. Darcy accompanied me on my walk, and when I was to return home, he escorted me to the hedgerow to ensure my safe return. I swear we do nothing more than talk.

"You are well aware Mr. Hill would never tell a soul other than you. My reputation is safe."

His lips drew tight. "I know that Mr. Hill will not breathe a word, yet we cannot discount the possibility of your being seen by another servant who is not as discreet or a Meryton gossip.

"Mr. Darcy is a wealthy man, and while he may appreciate your wit and intelligence, it is unlikely he would make an offer of marriage. If he were forced by idle conjecture, he might come to resent you, and you him. It would pain me to see you trapped so in marriage."

"Mr. Darcy will call at eleven o'clock to request a courtship."

Her father's face paled. "Truly?"

"Yes, sir. He claims to have considered the situation for the past week and has no need of a dowry or further connections."

As the colour returned to his face, her father cleared his throat. "I did not think you could shock me as you just did. You are certain of your acceptance?"

She clasped her hands in her lap. "Since Netherfield, I have told myself time and again that he could not offer for me. I attempted with all I have to protect my heart, but as of late, those reminders have become painful. My heart is engaged, Papa."

"I am sure you will be pleased to forgo the attentions of Mr. Collins."

He smiled as she groaned. "I shall be satisfied if our cousin found a new object to shower with his compliments. I confess his efforts are wasted upon me."

A knock at the front door could be heard in the silence. Her father glanced at the clock on the mantel. "Your young man is early."

"Perhaps it is not him."

Low tones could be discerned through the door and her father smirked. "He could wait no longer, I suppose. His impatience counts in his favour, but if he has seen your worth, I have no choice but to think highly of him."

"You will not tease him?" A wicked grin was her answer. "I shall remain then. I would not have you scare him for some sort of a joke."

He waved his hand in her direction. "I would not go that far, Lizzy."

A knock sounded upon the door of the study, and Hill entered. "Mr. Darcy has called, sir."

Elizabeth and her father rose as Mr. Darcy entered. He stood tall and his face was dour—much as it had been at the assembly. How did she not realize earlier that his taciturn expression was a mask? He was ill at ease. Could he be nervous?

"Please have a seat, Mr. Darcy." After their initial greeting, her father resumed his place in his favourite chair, while Mr. Darcy remained standing. "My daughter and I have been having an enlightening discussion prior to your arrival."

Mr. Darcy's questioning eyes met hers, and she gave a slight shake to the head that was hopefully, not noticeable to her father. Would Mr. Darcy understand?

"Lizzy, Mr. Darcy and I shall get along well enough without you. You might take your breakfast while we talk."

"If it is all the same, Papa, I shall remain."

Her father gave an amused bark. "She means to protect you, sir."

Elizabeth's cheeks burned. "Papa! Perhaps it is that I worry you will exercise your wit upon Mr. Darcy when he is not equal to it."

"I shall be well, Miss Elizabeth." His lips curved upwards at the ends, and his eyes crinkled at the outside edges. "Though I do appreciate your defence."

"Do you object to my remaining?"

"I have nothing to say which you cannot hear."

Her shoulders, which had tensed during their exchange, relaxed as Mr. Darcy came to stand behind the empty chair.

"Mr. Bennet, I have come to enjoy your daughter's company immensely. She is witty, intelligent, and has a compassion lacking in many of society. I have requested her permission for a courtship that she has granted. I now seek your permission."

Her father waved his hand. "Take a seat, young man. My daughter came home from her walk this morning, did not partake of any breakfast, and began to play the pianoforte, an indication she is either out of sorts or anxious. She revealed the intention of your visit prior to your arrival.

"First, I do give you my permission, and I wish you luck. My daughter can be formidable when she is in high dudgeon. You are a brave man to consider her for a wife."

"Papa!" How could he!

"You opted to stay, remember? Since you will not allow me to tease your young man, I shall exercise my wit upon you."

A glance to Mr. Darcy revealed the end of a fist to his mouth as he restrained his laughter. "I thank you for your protection, Miss Elizabeth."

She crossed her arms over her chest. "I have a long memory, gentlemen."

Her father leaned and placed his forearms upon his desk. "I must confess that I am most concerned with your morning walks."

Mr. Darcy paled and opened his mouth.

"Before you say a word, Mr. Darcy, I believe you to be an honourable man, yet I do have concerns. I do not want either of you pressed to wed before you are certain of one another. One of my servants saw you with Elizabeth behind Longbourn." Before Mr. Darcy could speak, her father continued. "Fortunately, Mr. Hill can be trusted to keep quiet. If another person witnessed one of your meetings, I could not guarantee matters would remain silent— especially if the news reached my wife's ears.

"In the past, I have tried to no avail to temper my wife's tongue. The ruin of her own daughter would not concern her if Franny thought she could have Lizzy married."

"I should be loath to lose our morning discussions, but I understand your concern, sir."

Her father's stare moved to her. "At one time, Jane walked with you. Do you think you could persuade her to adopt the practice once more?"

Her heart leapt. A courtship under the ever-present watch of her mother would be a nightmare. If Jane would agree to chaperon, they would not lose the time together she had come to anticipate.

"I shall ask."

Mr. Darcy sat forward in his chair. "Sir, are you saying…"

"As long as Jane accompanies Lizzy, you are free to walk with my daughter in the mornings. I can understand her wish to speak without the interference of her mother, and I daresay, you will not miss the experience either."

"I thank you for your consideration, sir."

As they had spoken, her sisters and mother arriving in the breakfast parlour created a din that carried into the book room.

"Have you eaten, Mr. Darcy?"

He shook his head. "Not as of yet. I departed Netherfield early this morning."

Her father rose, and slapped Mr. Darcy on the shoulder. "Then why do you not join us. We are a noisy lot, but my wife does set a generous table."

"I thank you for the invitation. I shall be pleased to accept." Mr. Darcy's shoulders were rigid. Despite his polite words, he likely did not relish a meal in company with her mother and sisters. Even to the most patient man, her mother's enthusiasm was difficult to tolerate.

Upon their entrance, those assembled stopped to stare.

"La! What is *he* doing here so early?"

"You may choose to sleep the day away, Lydia," chastised their father, "but there are people who rise with the sun.

"Before you return to your plates, Mr. Darcy has requested to court Lizzy, and I have granted my permission. I hope one day he will not rue the moment he made this decision."

"Papa!"

"Oh, Lizzy, let an old man have some fun."

"Congratulations, Mr. Darcy." Miss Bennet stood beside her mother, whose mouth was agape. "I am pleased for you, Lizzy."

"Thank you, Miss Bennet." Mr. Darcy gave a slight bow. "Mrs. Bennet, I hope you are well this morning."

Her mother's mouth shut with a click, and she swallowed. "Yes." The tone was not normal for her mother; it was quite faint. "Mr. Bennet," she whispered loudly, "I have promised Mr. Collins—"

"Mrs. Bennet, you are not head of this household. I have not given Mr. Collins *my* permission, so Lizzy is free to be courted by Mr. Darcy. Am I understood?" Her mother made to speak again, but her father held up his hand. "I said no more, Mrs. Bennet."

"But Mr. Darcy is betrothed to Miss de Bourgh!" Mr. Collins stood at the opposite end of the table. His mouth was full, which made understanding his words a challenge.

Mr. Darcy tensed. "Mr. Collins, this is not the first time I have been forced to censure you for spreading rumours and idle gossip. Though it has not been announced, my cousin is attached and betrothed to another. I happen to know my uncle is to intervene and an announcement should be in the paper before the end of the month, so I insist you desist in your errant proclamations at once."

Mr. Collins' mouth snapped shut as Mr. Bennet gave a hearty laugh. "If my presence is no longer needed, I shall return to my book room. Mr. Darcy, should you require an escape for some sensible conversation, you and Lizzy are welcome to join me when you have concluded your meal."

"Thank you, Mr. Bennet."

Darcy held out a chair for Elizabeth and took the seat beside her. The table was quiet when one considered the usual behaviour of the Bennet girls. Miss Lydia whispered and tittered into the ear of Miss Kitty. Miss Mary returned to the book she had been reading when they entered, and Mr. Collins, who had stuffed his remaining food in his mouth, hastened from the table and up the stairs upon begging to be excused.

"He is sure to be penning a letter to Lady Catherine," whispered Elizabeth. "He has made a point of telling us how he keeps her apprised of all his activities."

He rolled his eyes. "I can well imagine based on my aunt's personality. She enjoys declaring herself attentive to all matters. His subservient behaviour is identical to that of her previous parson."

"Oh dear!" Elizabeth's hand covered her mouth as she giggled.

What was it about her laugh that soothed him so? The manner in which it bubbled from her lips and the tone could bring an unbidden smile to his face in but a moment. When her eyes regarded him with that twinkle of humour, his troubles disappeared—he was happy.

"What is it that amuses you so?"

She bit her fingernail as she stared for a moment. "It is just that your aunt's choices of parson do not speak well of her. Please forgive me for my blunt assessment. I should have refrained from laughing in the first place."

"Do not fret. I happen to be of the same opinion." His attention was captured by Mrs. Bennet, who gaped in their direction.

Elizabeth turned and pressed her lips together when she took note of her mother's expression. With a quick movement, Elizabeth took a piece of toast and began to eat.

Miss Lydia and Miss Kitty soon were back to their usual high spirits, joking and braying, while Miss Bennet and Elizabeth pinked at their youngest sisters' antics and brash statements.

As they were rising from the table, Mr. Collins entered and bowed to those assembled. "It has occurred to me that I have been remiss in requesting a set from each of my lovely cousins for the ball." He turned to Elizabeth, and Darcy's fist clenched. "Cousin Elizabeth, might I request your first set?"

"I thank you, sir, but that set is taken."

The snivelling parson's face fell for but a second. "Then, might I request the supper dance?"

Elizabeth cleared her throat. "I am afraid that set is spoken for as well."

Mr. Collins' nose crinkled and his lips pursed. "May I inquire as to what sets you have available?"

Darcy cleared his throat. "I have claimed the first set and the supper set. My cousin Colonel Fitzwilliam is to arrive in time for the ball and asked that I reserve Miss Elizabeth's last dance of the evening."

"Has he?" She peered up with a mischievous glint in her eye. "I suppose I shall have to agree. I would not wish to snub the son of an Earl."

Mr. Collins eyes widened. "Of course you would not!"

Thank goodness! The last thing he could bear was Mr. Collins claiming any set that might have some significance. The little toad had to be put in his place. Whether Mr. Collins liked it or not, Elizabeth would not be his.

The youngest Bennet girls stepped closer. "A colonel?" asked Miss Lydia.

Miss Kitty stepped in front of Miss Lydia. "Is he handsome?"

Elizabeth ignored her sisters. "My card is free for the remaining dances of the evening, Mr. Collins. When you have decided which set you would prefer, I shall reserve the spot."

"Very good of you, cousin." He scanned each of the Bennet daughters and turned to Miss Bennet. "Might I have the honour of the first set?"

Poor Miss Bennet was gracious in her acceptance, yet the manner in which her eyes shifted to Elizabeth during her answer and how she adjusted her shawl bespoke of her awkwardness.

Elizabeth took his elbow and squeezed. As they began to stroll towards the drawing room, she leaned closer. "Thank you!"

When she lowered from her tiptoes, she lost her balance and her breast grazed his upper arm. A hand to his chest helped her to right herself while he held his breath. How could he observe propriety when accidents such as this tested his will power! Lord help him!

Chapter 10

<u>November 26th 1811</u>

Elizabeth secured one last curl and rushed through the door that connected her bedchamber to Jane's. When she entered, her eldest sister turned her head as Elizabeth fastened the back of her gown.

"Where is your spencer?"

"On the hook," Jane said with a laugh. "Lizzy, calm yourself. I am certain Mr. Darcy will be there when we arrive."

"But we are late!" She held out her coat, which Jane buttoned, and passed Jane her reticule and her shawl.

"I do not require both my shawl and my spencer."

Elizabeth threw up her hands and departed, hurrying down the stairs with the sound of Jane's boots just behind her. She snatched her bonnet from a peg and donned it as she rushed out the rear door of Longbourn.

"Lizzy! Slow down! I cannot keep your pace!" With a heavy footfall, Elizabeth stopped and awaited Jane while her fingers fumbled with the ribbons of her bonnet. When her sister approached Elizabeth's side, Elizabeth forged ahead.

Mr. Darcy came into view when she rounded the hedgerow. He was pacing back and forth, his shoulders tense as he whipped his crop against the trunk of an apple tree.

"Has the tree offended you in some fashion?"

He halted and stared with furrowed brows.

She pointed to his hand. "You struck the trunk."

"Oh!" He glanced down and then back to her. "No, my mind is occupied by a number of issues, and I was not attending until you spoke."

"We can postpone our walk if you require time for business?"

He stepped forward. "No! I would not miss this time with you for anything."

She took his arm but resisted the urge to pull it closer. "I hope you have not waited long."

With a glance behind her, he gave a dip of his chin. "Good morning, Miss Bennet."

"Good morning, Mr. Darcy"

After clearing his throat, he began to lead her towards Grayson's Pond. "To answer your question, no, I arrived perhaps five minutes ago."

"I told you he would not leave without seeing you," called Jane.

Elizabeth's cheeks burned as she pivoted and widened her eyes. *"Thank you, Jane."*

Her sister grinned.

"You must know I would wait. Even should I have business to attend, I would not have departed for Netherfield without speaking to you."

Were her cheeks to be warm for the entirety of their morning? "Is your distress due to your sister? She is well?"

His hand covered hers. "I received a letter from her yesterday. Her spirits seem improved, and she has expressed a desire to meet you. I am content that my aunt's company and counsel have proven beneficial, so no, Georgiana is not the source of my disquiet."

"A trouble shared is a trouble halved." Why had she used that singsong voice? She must have sounded ridiculous, though not any sillier than one of Mary's favourite proverbs!

He looked at her askance. "Pardon?"

"Mary uses that saying frequently."

"Ah." He paused. "I am concerned about Wickham."

"But Sir William Lucas and Papa have had some success in Meryton. The owner of the local inn and several shopkeepers have decided not to extend credit to the militia, and as a result, the officers remain closer to their camp. I have seen very little of Mr. Wickham since my Aunt Philips' party, and when I have, it is at a distance while I am in the village."

"Do you remember when I mentioned my cousin might journey to Netherfield?"

"Colonel Fitzwilliam, correct?"

He nodded. "He is not in London at the moment, but on an errand for his commander. I hoped he could have Wickham moved elsewhere. Without Richard, I am unsure how to proceed."

They stopped at the edge of the water. "Then we must go on as we have. I am certain your cousin will respond when he returns to town."

"I suppose you are correct."

"You suppose?"

His lips slipped to a sort of half-smile. "Do not be impertinent, Miss Elizabeth."

She placed her hands on her hips. "I live to be impertinent, Mr. Darcy."

A horse's neigh startled her, and she glanced to where a familiar stallion was tethered on the other side of the pond. "Boreas appears to have noticed you."

"He is an impatient beast."

"But that is your preference, is it not? Do you not desire a horse who will run without fear or restraint when you race or hunt foxes?"

"There are some excellent mounts who are not as spirited, yet I learned on an animal with a similar temper. Boreas was born at Pemberley a fortnight after I finished Cambridge. I helped train him."

"He is dear to you." His deep laugh brought gooseflesh to the back of her neck.

"In a fashion, yes, though not as dear to me as some."

Unable to maintain his gaze, her eyes shifted beside him to watch a small flock of pheasants pecking along the opposite bank of the pond.

He pulled out his pocket watch. "I am loath to leave you, but I have letters to post before this evening."

"I am sure Mama will be bemoaning our lack of compassion for her nerves should we not be home by breakfast."

He gestured behind her. "I believe your sister is attempting to give us a moment alone."

Elizabeth turned, but Jane was not nearby, as was her wont. Instead, she stood at the edge of some trees, facing the trail towards Longbourn. "I shall have to accuse her of becoming Mama."

"Do not do Miss Bennet such a disservice." His bare knuckles grazed a tingling trail down her temple. "I am thankful for her consideration. She has been an agreeable chaperon."

"She follows a few steps behind, she does not listen, and she does not speak." Her voice was incredulous, but his notion of an agreeable chaperon was laughable.

"Quite right, she allows me all of your attention."

Elizabeth made to push his chest, but his hand grasped hers and tugged her forward. His warm palm cupped her face as her breath hitched. He was coming closer! His exhalation warmed her cheek and she closed her eyes just as his lips pressed against hers.

What should she do? Should she just stand there? Why was every hair on her body standing on end?

He withdrew and whispered her name in a voice that made her toes curl. Then, he kissed her again.

His lips were so soft and full as they cradled hers, and she used the hand upon his lapel to balance as she lifted to her tiptoes. His colour was high when he drew back, trailing his fingers through a few curls that had fallen from her bonnet, and she covered her mouth. How could she meet his eyes now and remain composed?

His lips brushed her forehead before he released her and stepped away. A sudden chill was a cruel reminder of the comfort she had found in his arms.

"I shall meet you in the hall tonight. I wish to escort the loveliest lady into the ball on my arm."

Her palm remained over her mouth as she nodded. He pulled it away and placed a kiss upon her knuckles. "I look forward to being in your company once again."

She tried to speak, but no sound came from her lips. What was wrong with her? All she could do was watch him walk to his horse. When he mounted, he lifted a hand to wave before he rode away.

Once he was cantering up the hill, Jane rushed over. "Lizzy! Did Mr. Darcy just kiss you?"

Elizabeth threw her arms around her eldest sister. "Oh, Jane! I do not know when it happened, but I am in love with him. I want to marry him!"

She withdrew and began to bite her thumbnail as Jane placed her hands upon Elizabeth's shoulders. "I am overjoyed for you, dear sister. How long before he offers you his hand, do you think?"

"I do not know." She began to bounce in place. "I do hope he will not tarry too long."

Jane giggled and looped her arm through Elizabeth's, pulling her in the direction of Longbourn.

Elizabeth halted. "What if he changes his mind?"

A tug from Jane propelled her back in the direction of home. "Mr. Darcy is besotted. Something truly dreadful would have to occur for him to abandon you now—even then, I believe he would attempt to move heaven and earth if it were to be of aid to you."

"You exaggerate, Jane."

Jane squeezed Elizabeth's hand. "I have seen how Mr. Darcy looks at you. He even observes you when you are not attending him. The softness in his expression at those times is noticeable to anyone who is looking."

"You are in earnest?"

"I would not lie to you, Lizzy. I only pray a gentleman will regard me with such affection one day."

Elizabeth wrapped her arm around Jane's shoulders. "You are so beautiful and kind. I am certain it will not be long before Mr. Bingley bestows adoring gazes upon you."

Her dearest sister was quiet for a moment. "Tell me what it is like to be kissed?"

Elizabeth almost tripped she made such a quick halt to glare at her sister. "No!"

Jane began to laugh. "Lizzy! We share everything. You know I shall not speak of it to a soul."

"No, I cannot." She began to head toward Longbourn once more, but as fast as her legs could carry her without running.

"You will tell me eventually!" called Jane.

"Never!"

"Lizzy, wait! I shall not press further. I promise!"

When Jane approached, she wore what was for her a mischievous smile. "Just answer one question."

Elizabeth placed her hands upon her hips and waited.

"Does he have good breath?"

She dissolved into peals of laughter as Jane followed. When she regained some of her equanimity, Jane pushed her towards Longbourn.

"When you have sufficiently recovered, I do expect an answer. In the meantime, we should hasten home before Mama sends all of Meryton to find us."

Darcy reined in his horse at the top of the rise and looked down towards the pond. Elizabeth slowed from a run to a walk as Miss Bennet strode at her usual sedate pace, following behind. The sisters knew to keep one another in each other's sights, but he would remain until they disappeared into the trees. They would be almost to Longbourn by that point, close enough to ensure their safe return.

When Miss Bennet's pale green gown faded into the forest, he cued his horse towards Netherfield. His hands still held a tremor from when he kissed Elizabeth, so he gripped the reins to avoid losing control of Boreas. The feel of her lips beneath his was exquisite! She trembled and held her breath, which spoke of her nerves, but she did not slap him for his attempt.

He had kissed Elizabeth Bennet!

How he wanted to shout it from the top of the tallest hill in Hertfordshire! He loved her—that much was certain. Now, he had better propose, but when? Did she require more time to be certain of her own feelings?

He took Boreas to a gallop and allowed the favourite activity to relieve his anxiety. Tonight would be important. He would do his utmost to discover what was in Elizabeth's heart, so he would know when to reveal his.

When his mount was worn, he entered the stable, handing the horse over to a waiting groom. Without tarrying, he entered the house and followed the sound of Bingley's voice to the ballroom.

"It looks wonderful, Louisa. I hope tonight will be a grand occasion. Meryton has been welcoming to me, and I wish to repay them for their kindness."

"I doubt their amiability was a struggle, Brother. There have been quite a few eligible ladies thrust into your presence."

"Bingley's desire to welcome the people of Meryton is a mark in his favour. When he becomes master of an estate, such an attitude will win him the loyalty of his own neighbourhood." Darcy held out his hand. "I congratulate you on all you have accomplished in the last month. You have worked diligently with the steward to understand the estate, and I am certain the dedication you have displayed will serve you well."

Bingley grinned as he took Darcy's hand. "That is quite a speech from you. You have adopted a measure of Miss Elizabeth's outgoing nature." With a tilt of his head, Bingley appraised him. "This morning's walk must have been encouraging."

"Careful, Bingley. We are always chaperoned by Miss Bennet, so do not insinuate—"

"I meant no disrespect." Bingley's hands were held in front of him. "You are not as stern since you began this courtship with Miss Elizabeth and appear more content than I have ever seen. I am pleased for you, my friend."

"I need to speak with Mrs. Nicholls." Mrs. Hurst glanced between the two of them. "If you will excuse me."

When she had left the room, Darcy looked to Bingley. "Should I be concerned?"

His friend's forehead creased. "Are you asking if she will cause you problems?"

"Well, yes. She and Miss Bingley are not so dissimilar."

"Hurst will not allow his wife to sabotage your friendship with me. He may lay about after a night of heavy drinking, but when he is sober, he boasts of keeping your company."

Darcy rubbed his face with his hands. "I had no idea."

"There is more to Hurst than you realized?"

"It would appear so."

"He and Louisa have their fair share in common," said Bingley with a smile. "Do not let them fool you."

"As long as they do not interfere with myself and Miss Elizabeth, they can claim a connection to their heart's content."

A grin overspread Bingley's countenance. "Things are going well then?"

"That is none of your concern." Darcy strode through the doors and towards the stairs.

"You will tell me nothing?"

Darcy did not answer, but continued directly to his rooms. His personal time with Miss Elizabeth was not something he wished to share. Those memories were too close to his heart to divulge to just anyone. His feelings would be revealed to Elizabeth when he found the perfect moment. He only hoped he would not have to wait too long!

Chapter 11

Mr. Collins' incessant prattle during the ride, and a few instances of Lydia's elbow to her ribs were enough to prompt Elizabeth to alight the moment the Bennet's carriage came to a halt. The cold night air was a welcome relief! Once she had smoothed her gown, she lifted her skirts to prevent them from becoming soiled, and did not allow them to fall until she placed her foot upon the first stone step where she paused until Jane was by her side.

"Are you well, Lizzy?"

She clasped her hands into fists. "I feel as though I am being pulled in a hundred different directions at once, I am shaking, and I feel a bit sick."

"Tonight will be wonderful. You will see." Jane took her hand with her usual serene smile and held it in her firm grasp as they climbed their way to the front doors. Jane was always so calm, which was unnerving. How did nothing ever disturb her equanimity?

Her parents led their group into the receiving line until they greeted Mr. Bingley as well as Mr. and Mrs. Hurst, yet once Elizabeth gave her curtsey, her eye was arrested by the broad-shouldered gentleman waiting behind their host.

"Ah! There you are, Darcy," exclaimed Bingley. "I thought you might appear to whisk Miss Elizabeth into the ballroom."

Jane placed a hand to Elizabeth's back and pressed her forward as Mr. Darcy approached. He bowed as she curtsied and held out her hand, which he gave a chaste kiss since they were in such a public setting. If only they were alone! If only Mr. Darcy did not wear those gloves!

"Mr. Bennet, Mrs. Bennet, I hope you are well tonight."

Her father smirked. "I know you have no wish to remain and make idle chatter with us, young man. I am certain you have secured my daughter's hand for the first set, so be off with you."

Mr. Collins opened his mouth, and Elizabeth's shoulders stiffened. She could take no more!

"Thank you, sir." Before her cousin could utter a sound Mr. Darcy took her hand, placed it upon his arm, and led her through the hall towards the ballroom, leaving Mr. Collins and his sermon far behind.

Mr. Darcy was so handsome in his formal attire. As he made his way through the guests milling around them, he stood confident and tall, his well-tailored topcoat and trousers accenting his dignified bearing and handsome figure. A curl of his dark hair fell upon his forehead and the grey in his waistcoat accented his crystal blue eyes. The ladies all observed him as he passed, but she could hardly blame them. She would as well if he were not her escort.

She drew in a long breath, releasing it slowly, in an attempt to calm her roiling insides. An entire night of this incessant quivering would make her mad. Not only that, but with her hand upon Mr. Darcy's arm, he was certain to take notice of her tremor. In the past, her courage always rose to the occasion when she required it—yet where was it tonight?

"You are very silent, Miss Elizabeth."

"I..." She peered from side to side at the matrons whispering behind their fans. Her courtship with Mr. Darcy was certain to be prime gossip, and her mother, who had been reluctant at first to accept such a disagreeable man over the security of Mr. Collins, had changed her opinion when she had more time to consider the wealth Elizabeth could obtain by becoming Mrs. Darcy.

"I confess I am nervous."

His hand covered hers, and he brushed her knuckles with his thumb. "Then, I must find some remedy for your anxiety. I had hoped to pass the evening with the bold Miss Elizabeth to whom I am accustomed. Is she to be hidden from me tonight?"

"I do not believe so, sir, but I fear I may require some time before I am my usual self."

"Perhaps some wine?"

He ushered her to the refreshment table where he handed her a glass. She took small sips lest she drink too much too fast. Her wits could not abandon her as had her courage at that moment!

Mr. Darcy remained by her side until the musicians were ready to begin, when he escorted her to the floor to dance. The small ensemble played the introduction of the first piece and when the moment came, his hand took hers.

Mrs. Goulding leaned in the direction of Mrs. Long and began to whisper as Elizabeth passed, staring at her and Mr. Darcy as they spoke.

"I believe you have shocked some with your willingness to dance this evening and you have taken a significant gamble, sir, by standing up with me tonight. I suspect you will find yourself pursued by the eligible ladies of the room since you have proven yourself more agreeable than at the assembly."

He grinned. "There is my Elizabeth." His voice was deep and soft—intimate.

She stumbled over her own toes, but Mr. Darcy caught her with his arm before she could fall. "Forgive me. I am never so clumsy!"

"Do not beg forgiveness since your near tumble allowed me to embrace you as much as I can without violating propriety or disgracing you before all of these people."

She bit her lip and looked away as she took a turn with the gentleman to her side. Upon her return to Mr. Darcy, his dimples appeared. She lifted her eyebrow.

"You appear pleased with yourself."

"I am dancing with the loveliest lady in the room, and I plan to spend a significant amount of time in her company. I am quite content."

She looked from side to side. "And who is this lady? Do I know her?"

He gave a bark of laughter, and several nearby guests stopped to stare. "You know very well I refer to you, Miss Elizabeth."

"I do not know how I should react to such flattery. You will render me a vain creature should you continue."

"You are teasing me."

The dance required them to separate and partner others, and the lieutenant who now stood across from Elizabeth peeked down at her chest. With a cringe, she looked to the ceiling as she awaited Mr. Darcy to re-join her.

As she progressed through the pattern, her outstretched hand caught her attention. When had she stopped shaking? At some point between Mr. Darcy taking her wine glass and settling into the dance, her nerves had subsided. Perhaps the familiar tune or the pattern of the movements helped to steady her?

His hand grasped hers again before they parted when the dance ended. "You are no longer shivering."

"I do not know why, but yes, I seem to have regained my composure."

"You could confide in me what disturbed you. I would welcome the opportunity to know more of you."

She peered at him out of the corner of her eye. "With the long talks we have had, you should know me almost as well as Jane."

His shoulders lifted. "I am content to know what I do, but you speak little of your feelings."

Her cheeks became warm. "I share those with a select few, but you can be assured I have no reservations speaking of my heart to you."

The music for the second half of the set began. "Truly?"

"Oh, I am not saying it would not fluster me, but I know you would treat me with kindness. I can trust you."

Their dance ended much too soon, and Elizabeth was claimed by her cousin, who ushered her back into the line. Between the local gentlemen and the militia present, Elizabeth remained engaged until the supper dance, when Mr. Darcy approached her as she spoke to Charlotte Lucas.

"Mr. Darcy," acknowledged Charlotte as he approached.

"Miss Lucas, I hope you are enjoying the evening."

Charlotte lifted her eyebrows at Elizabeth. The entire neighbourhood found themselves astounded by Mr. Darcy's changed demeanour, and had laid the transformation at Elizabeth's feet. Only the cheer of such a lady would cause such a proud man to make polite conversation with those he once deemed insignificant. The question was whether he would remain sociable once the inevitable wedding occurred or whether he would revert to his once disagreeable behaviour.

"The evening has proven itself diverting indeed."

"Ah." He glanced to Elizabeth. His expression was neutral, but there was something in his eyes. "We should take our places."

"If you will excuse us."

Charlotte acknowledged Elizabeth with a dip of her chin before Mr. Darcy whisked her back into the line. When the music again filled the ballroom, he leaned his head in her direction.

"I must confess I am pleased to have you returned to me."

She lifted her eyebrow. "Had I been stolen away?"

"Yes, most cruelly by Mr. Collins, and I have had a terrible time trying to find an opportunity to reclaim you."

She turned away with a grin. "Did no one teach you to share, Mr. Darcy?"

His finger brushed against her wrist. "I know how to share, but I do not appreciate the practice when it separates me from you."

Her cheeks burned. "I..."

At that moment, Sir William Lucas, who intended to pass through the set, halted when his eyes lit upon Mr. Darcy. "I am most highly gratified indeed, my dear sir, by such superior dancing. You must allow me to observe that your fair partner does not disgrace you, and that I hope to have this pleasure repeated when a certain desirable event, my dear Miss Eliza, occurs."

With a flinch, her eyes darted to Mr. Darcy. He did not seem at all disturbed by Sir William's loose tongue and appeared to take the assumption of their eventual marriage without surprise.

Sir William then glanced at Jane and Bingley. "And let us not forget another greatly anticipated union! What congratulations will once again flow in!"

Upon Sir William's conjecture of Jane and Mr. Bingley, Mr. Darcy paled and his visage altered. He peered down the line to where his friend danced with Jane, his jaw pulsed as he clenched his teeth and released several times in succession. He said naught, but Sir William took no notice.

"But let me not interrupt you, sir. You will not thank me for detaining you from the bewitching converse of that young lady, whose bright eyes are also upbraiding me."

Elizabeth's entire being burned in mortification. "Mr. Darcy, do you require a moment?"

He gave a slight jump as she regained his attention. "No, forgive me."

They resumed dancing, yet Mr. Darcy did not speak. Instead, he searched for Mr. Bingley and Jane as they turned down the line from them.

"Are you disturbed by Sir William's conjecture regarding us?"

Again, his eyes darted to hers. "No! I would not have requested a courtship if I had reservations. You must know I would never pain you in such a way."

His manner was open, so the idea of Mr. Bingley and Jane had been what discomposed him. Had he not noticed his friend's partiality? The entirety of the neighbourhood was aware of it, so how could he have escaped the knowledge?

The set soon ended, and Elizabeth was seated at Mr. Darcy's side while dinner was served. Lydia and Kitty's periodic whines reached her ears, but they could not do much more than complain under their father's relentless supervision.

Despite Mr. Wickham's obvious absence, her father had kept his youngest daughters under tight rein. They were allowed to dance, but each partner was to deliver them directly to him. At present, they were seated beside him as Lydia batted her eyelashes at a captain down the table. Mr. Bennet whispered in his youngest daughter's ear, which prompted her to huff and cross her arms over her chest. Elizabeth snickered.

"What amuses you?"

"Oh! My father has taken a stricter stance with Lydia and Kitty as of late. He just corrected Lydia for attempting to flirt. I must admit to a certain amount of vindictive glee in his taking the pains to control her. Jane and I have made attempts for years while he ignored her embarrassing behaviour."

"I would not call you vindictive. I am certain it is a relief to no longer bear that responsibility."

Her eyes met his. "I do not know if you are aware, but I credit the change to you."

"You do?"

"Yes, it was your mention of Mr. Wickham." She kept her voice soft. "He began taking control of her then and has continued. I just pray he does not cease his efforts after the militia departs Meryton, else she will revert to what she was. She has not changed—not in essentials."

He glanced in the direction of her parents. "Your mother does not appear pleased with his corrections."

Her mother was chastising her father, and by the expression upon Lydia's face, taking Lydia's part. Papa could not let her mother succeed! She would have them chasing the officers before the next course was upon the table.

"Mama views Lydia as a young version of herself and sees naught amiss with her behaviour. My sister could prance through the dining room flirting with the officers and waving a sabre, and Mama would see nothing improper in it."

Without fail, Mr. Darcy remained attentive as they conversed during the meal. He was witty, charming, and ensured she wanted for nothing, yet he was distracted. While in such a public setting, she could not inquire as to his disquiet, which frustrated her. At least, she had discerned it was not her or their courtship.

Dinner progressed as a formal meal often does until they were served the final course, and Elizabeth turned just as her mother's mouth opened.

"I had planned for Mr. Collins to wed Lizzy, but she will be so much richer as Mrs. Darcy! Why that man would take to Lizzy is a mystery! My Jane would be more appropriate to a gentleman of his station than Lizzy. Jane is so beautiful! Of course, I expect Mr. Bingley will be requesting a private discussion with my Jane within a fortnight!

"Mary will do for Mr. Collins, I suppose, but he continues to follow Lizzy and Jane, despite being told they are both soon to be betrothed. I tell you, my poor nerves cannot take much more of that man!"

Elizabeth dropped her head, covered her mouth with her hand, and swallowed the sick that rose in her throat. Her other hand was clenched into a fist, her fingernails digging into the tender flesh of her palms.

"With Lizzy and Jane so advantageously married, they will be able to throw their sisters into the paths of other rich men! With my Lydia's amiable personality, she is certain to attract a greater man than even Mr. Darcy."

She choked and made to rise, but large fingers entwined with hers. "Breathe, Elizabeth," he whispered in her ear.

"You must be horrified." Elizabeth's head remained down as she shook it. "How could you wish to have her for a mother?"

Mr. Darcy leaned towards her. "We shall be in Derbyshire while she will remain in Meryton. I imagine we shall visit, but perhaps I shall find a nice cottage nearby to purchase or lease for those occasions. Please do not be offended when I confess that I thought small doses might be easier to tolerate."

She pursed her lips in an attempt not to giggle. "I do not believe I would be averse to your suggestions."

His hand squeezed hers, but his eyes darted to something behind her. "Please excuse me. I need to speak with Bingley." Before she could acknowledge his statement, he was gone.

After Mr. Darcy's departure, she remained in her seat until the pianoforte was opened, and Mary took the invitation to play. After one line of her sister's fumbling concerto, Elizabeth required air.

Her determined pace took her to the ballroom where the musicians prepared for the second half of the dances. She scanned the decoration, admiring Mrs. Hurst's efforts. The house had never been so lovely.

She approached some flowers from the orangery and bent forward to smell their fragrance.

"How pleased your Mr. Darcy must be to be free of Wickham for the evening."

Elizabeth retreated a step back from the sneering voice of Mr. Denny. "I beg your pardon?"

"Has Mr. Darcy not wronged my friend enough? He also had to ensure Wickham was not in Meryton for the ball as well. Saunderson has even heard Wickham might be moved to another regiment."

Her spine went rigid as she stood as tall as she was capable. "I can assure you, Mr. Denny, Mr. Wickham has not been injured by Mr.

Darcy. It is, in fact, quite the opposite. Mr. Wickham is who should not be allowed amongst polite society."

Mr. Denny's hand shot out as though he would grab her arm, and Elizabeth pulled away, darting through the door to the hall and down a corridor before she could consider where she was going.

When she stopped, the library was just ahead and appeared to be lit. She only wanted a place to gather her thoughts for a moment. Mr. Bingley would not mind.

She stepped forward, but halted once she stood in the doorway. The room was not empty.

"You are well aware that you cannot marry Miss Bennet!"

Her heart sunk to her toes as Mr. Darcy's unmistakeable voice emanated from the man whose back she was facing. Mr. Bingley stood to the side, staring into a glass of brandy.

"I tell you, Darcy, I have given her no encouragement! I have enjoyed speaking with her and a dance this evening as well as at the assembly."

"You stood up with her twice at the assembly."

Mr. Bingley held out his arms. "So, I danced with her twice that evening, but I have done nothing else! I have done naught to excite people's expectations!"

Mr. Darcy's fingers combed through his hair. "Regardless, it is assumed you and Miss Bennet will become betrothed. You *must* avoid her for the remainder of the evening and depart for London on the morrow." His voice was calmer, but still emphatic.

"How am I to avoid Miss Bennet's company without being rude? You truly think of the most preposterous solutions!"

A high-pitched bark came from Mr. Darcy. "You would risk everything. After all that I have done for you!"

Elizabeth gasped and stumbled. Her shoulder hit the wall, the painting beside her rattled, and her eyes widened as Mr. Darcy spun around.

"I was looking for quiet. Forgive me!" Without another word, she ran.

Chapter 12

Elizabeth held one side of her skirt, so it did not impede her hasty stride. She required a door! She had to leave and leave now!

How could she be so cork-brained as to believe Mr. Darcy cared for her? Was his offer of courtship nothing more than a terrible joke? Well, he would have quite the laugh at her expense when he departed Meryton because she had fallen for his act of sincerity. How could she have been so gullible?

A sob tore from her throat when she came to a stop. The chill of the night prickled her skin and rent at her lungs as she pulled in great gulps of air. She swiped the damp from her cheeks with rough motions.

How could he? How could he profess to have feelings for her when he intended to hurt her dearest sister? She was a fool!

"Elizabeth!" His hand touched her upper arm. She wrenched herself away.

"Do not address me so informally, sir. I have given you no such permissions, and after tonight, I never shall!"

"You must allow me to explain."

"Explain?" She placed a hand over her heart. "Explain how you claimed to care for me while you injured my dearest sister? Why would you do it? How could you do it?"

"Elizabeth—"

"I told you not to address me as such!" Her voice was shrill and harsh even to her own ears.

"I have never told you a falsehood, and I never shall. You must believe me!"

"I may have believed your flattery and pretty lies before, but how can I trust what you say now? I have witnessed your true self, Mr. Darcy."

"Miss Elizabeth, please."

"Was every word from your lips meant to deceive me?"

His head shook. "No, I have only spoken the truth. You *must* give me a chance to tell you—"

"You have a sister, who you love and protect. Would you be pleased to discover she was to be hurt in this fashion? Would you not defend her?"

"I would be Georgiana's greatest advocate, and I would expect no less from you when it comes to Miss Bennet. I swear to you—"

"I *heard* you! I know what you said!" Her knuckles ached from the relentless grip of her hand on the front of her gown. "You cannot change what you told Mr. Bingley. You cannot pretend you did not just forbid your friend from proposing marriage to my sister."

"It is not I who forbids him."

Her hand shot out before her and pointed at his chest. "You ordered him to depart Meryton!" She covered her face with her hands until she jumped away from a light touch to her forearm. "If Jane's dowry and connections are not good enough for your friend, how are mine sufficient for you?"

"I have explained that I do not require money or connections, and if Bingley—"

"I do not want to hear any further excuses! You can have nothing to tell me that will alter what you have done!"

She needed to go home—to Longbourn. Her tear streaked face and swollen eyes would draw attention if she returned to the ball, so she peered above her. The clouds of that afternoon had subsided, leaving a bright gibbous moon to light the inky black sky. She could make her way home through the fields.

"I have to leave." With an abrupt pivot, she began to stride away, but a firm grasp to her elbow spun her around. She ripped herself away from Mr. Darcy. "I can walk to Longbourn. Please leave me be."

"I cannot allow you to endanger yourself by walking those three miles."

She opened her mouth to protest.

"Before you object, I shall arrange for a carriage to bring you to Longbourn, but I beg you to hear my side."

Her head pounded as memories and thoughts swirled in her mind. She could not do this! She could take no more! "I cannot. I just need to go home. Please."

His hands were clasped tight at his sides as his shoulders slumped. "I shall have my carriage prepared." He held out an arm in the direction of the stables. "I merely want to ensure your safety."

Leaving a wide berth, she made her way around him, remaining several paces ahead. The damp chill of the evening combined with her emotions caused her to shake while she blinked to clear her tear-blurred vision. Mr. Darcy's steady stride thudded through the grass behind her, reminding her of his presence.

"Miss Lizzy!"

Elizabeth's head shot up and her body sagged when she spotted Mr. Hill. "Mr. Hill, would you take me home?"

The elderly brother of their housekeeper studied her from her feet to her face. "Are you well, Miss Lizzy?"

"I am not injured, but I have found little enjoyment at the ball. I would prefer to go to Longbourn than remain."

"What of your parents and your sisters?"

"You could come back for them since they will stay until the very end."

Mr. Hill peered around her to Mr. Darcy. "You will inform her father, then?"

"Once I know she is home, I shall tell Mr. Bennet. If it would be an inconvenience for you, I could have my own carriage readied."

"Won't be necessary, sir. I have Mr. Bennet's just there." He pointed to one side, and Elizabeth grasped her skirts as she hastened towards the equipage. Mr. Hill passed her as he ran ahead to open the door, and she jumped in without a hand from either of the men.

When she took her seat and turned towards the door, Mr. Darcy's foot was lifted in an attempt to enter, so she sprang forward. "What are you about?"

"I want to ensure your arrival at Longbourn."

"No." She clenched her jaw. He could be so infuriating! She did not desire anything from him—not anymore. Could he not just leave her be?

"Please," he pled. "I could explain what you overheard."

"Have you not heard me? I beg of you to importune me no further. I free you of any obligation you feel towards me."

His countenance became white as chalk. "You cannot mean that."

Her tears tickled as they flowed like rivers down her cheeks, pooling at her chin until they dripped onto the ivory muslin of her gown. "I do. I want nothing more to do with you."

"Sir," interrupted Mr. Hill. "I would welcome your company if you wish to be assured of Miss Lizzy's well-being. Once my sister has the lady's charge, I can convey you back to Netherfield."

Elizabeth was stock-still as the two men discussed the arrangements before her. Whether he remained or rode with Mr. Hill, she cared not, only that he was not inside with her.

The servant nodded towards a crate under the seat. "You might offer her a rug before we set off, sir."

Mr. Darcy pulled the box forward, removed a quilt, and held it aloft. "You are trembling. I would place it around your shoulders, but I fear you would object."

The blanket was snatched from his grip and clutched to her chest. "Please leave."

His eyes were shiny as he closed the door, and she collapsed back into the squabs. She shook the rug and draped it over herself. She was frozen! The chill permeated her gown, her flesh, and down to her bones. Would she ever be warm again?

Darcy climbed atop the equipage and took the seat beside Mr. Hill. He did not look at the man or acknowledge him at that moment. He could not. If he spoke or allowed himself an emotion, he would be unable to maintain the façade he erected when the carriage door closed.

Elizabeth was unreasonable. She was hurt, and with time and clarity, she might agree to listen to his part—but that would not occur tonight. He heaved in a gulp of stinging night air—a struggle with the sensation of an anvil resting upon his sternum. The heaviness would not subside, either, but intensified with each laboured breath.

If she would but listen! Nothing was the way it sounded, and the story behind his argument with Bingley would exonerate him. The tale was not exceedingly long or tedious, yet she did not know, because she would not hear him.

"The two of you had a disagreement, I take it."

He stared down to his hands clasped in front of him.

A crack broke the silence as Mr. Hill whipped the reins down upon the horses' rumps. "You don't have to answer if you don't want to."

The sound of a sob came from the inside, and Darcy grasped the edge of the seat.

"Miss Elizabeth misunderstood a conversation she overheard. She will not allow me to set her mind at ease."

"Hmm..." was all the man said.

Darcy placed his head in his hands and remained in such a position until they pulled to a stop before the front door of Longbourn. As Mr. Hill climbed down, the entry opened and the

Bennet's housekeeper, Mrs. Hill exited. "Horace? What has happened?"

He opened the equipage at the same time Darcy's feet hit the ground. Darcy extended his hand, but Elizabeth clutched the rug around her as she reached past him for Mr. Hill's shoulder.

"Miss Lizzy wasn't enjoying the ball. She wished to come home."

Mrs. Hill took one glance at Elizabeth and opened her arms, allowing Elizabeth to fall into her embrace. She made soothing noises in his beloved's ear while Elizabeth sniffed against the old woman's shoulder.

When Mrs. Hill ushered Elizabeth inside, the old man gestured up towards the driver's seat. "We should be returning."

Why was he to ride atop the carriage? Without Elizabeth, would he not sit inside?

Mr. Hill climbed back into his place, and squinted down to Darcy in the dark until he followed. Once they were moving, Mr. Hill cleared his throat.

"Did you know that Miss Lizzy once had a huge row with Miss Bennet?"

His head darted to Mr. Hill, who did not look at him, but continued to watch the dark road ahead.

"Miss Bennet and Miss Lizzy have always been close. If you've never seen them together and alone, Miss Bennet is a different girl with Miss Lizzy than with others. She shows more of herself.

"Well, none of us, to this day, know what their argument was about, but Miss Bennet just had to leave Miss Lizzy be for a few days. Once Miss Lizzy got over her temper, the two girls could resolve matters."

"Are you suggesting I give Miss Elizabeth time?" His voice came out raspy and altered.

The older man nodded. "I've known Miss Lizzy since she was a wee thing, and that girl's always had a fearsome temper. I think that's why Mrs. Bennet never took to her as she did Miss Jane, but that's beside the point."

Darcy's nails dug into the wood of the seat at his sides. "May I ask why you are telling me this?"

Mr. Hill laughed. "I've watched that lady grow up. She spent a great deal of time in the garden and in the stable at Longbourn from the time she was a wee thing. I never married or had children, so she became the closest thing I would ever have to a child of my own.

"I taught her to ride, I helped her out of that big oak tree behind Longbourn when she was stuck and couldn't get down, and I took her out to the stables when a cat had kittens or one of Mr. Bennet's hunting dogs had pups.

"She was a curious, kind, but mischievous child. In time, she grew up, and she gives me a small gift every Christmas and for my birthday."

Darcy's lip curved. "Miss Elizabeth has a generous heart."

"That she does." He cleared his throat. "I've also seen the way that girl looks at you and you her. She may think you've done a terrible deed now, but when her head's cleared, I wager she'll change her mind. I'd hate to see her broken-hearted."

He gazed into the pitch-black darkness of the trees. Would Elizabeth listen if he gave her but a few days to calm her ire? Allowing the situation to wait was problematic since an express he had received that afternoon required his removal to London. Elizabeth was to be told before they departed the ball that evening, yet he had never had the chance. He would have given assurances of his swift return, but the summons of his uncle could not be ignored.

Perhaps if he departed for London, but hastened back at his first opportunity to explain? Elizabeth would learn in time, yet he needed to make clear that he would never harm her sister in such a way.

"Mr. Darcy?"

He startled at the lights of Netherfield before them. When had the carriage come to a stop?

"I thank you for your advice and allowing me to see Miss Elizabeth to Longbourn."

Mr. Hill bobbed his head. "You remember what I said, young man."

Darcy climbed down and strode inside, hastening to his room before any of the guests could delay his errand. He twisted the ring on his pinkie a few times, fidgeting before he pulled a sheet of paper from his belongings, and dipped his pen in the inkwell. Now, what to write?

"Mr. Bennet."

The gentleman turned with an eyebrow raised that was eerily familiar. "I have wondered where you and Lizzy disappeared but was unable to leave Lydia and Kitty in the sole care of my wife."

With a tug at his cravat, Darcy struggled to gain a good breath. "I followed Bingley from the dining room near the end of dinner. I had an urgent matter that begged to be discussed with him." He kept his voice low. It would not do to be overheard.

"I fear Miss Elizabeth followed and listened to a portion of our conversation, which she misconstrued. She became furious. I attempted to explain, but—"

"She would hear none of it?"

"I attempted to reason with her, yet she would not relent. She insisted upon journeying to Longbourn. Until I forbade her, she was intent on walking as well."

Mr. Bennet gave a low laugh. "You forbade her? When she was still young, I learned that was a fool's errand. She does not take kindly to orders."

"I did not use the word forbid, but offered to have my carriage readied. As we made our way to the stables, we happened upon Mr. Hill, who was concerned by Miss Elizabeth's upset and offered to take her home. He even permitted me to ride atop with him, so I might ensure her safe journey."

"So she is now at Longbourn?"

"Yes, Mrs. Hill ushered Miss Elizabeth inside the moment she alighted."

Darcy reached into his inside pocket and removed the letter he had just penned. "Business necessitates my travel to London in the morning. I do not wish to depart with Miss Elizabeth and I on such bad terms, but I have no other choice."

Mr. Bennet placed a fatherly hand upon his shoulder. "Son, it is likely for the best. My Lizzy is more apt to end your courtship if you press. A day or two will give her time to calm, then she might be willing to hear your explanation."

He held out the missive. "I have prepared this in the event she changes her mind before I can return." With raised eyebrows, Mr. Bennet glanced down at the letter. "You may read the contents if you feel the need. I have also included my direction in London. Should Miss Elizabeth wish to speak with me, I shall travel to Longbourn on but a day's notice."

Mr. Bennet peeked around one of the guests to check on his youngest daughters as he pocketed Darcy's hopes. "I warn you I am not much of a correspondent, yet I shall do my best."

"Please inform Miss Elizabeth I shall not surrender my wishes. We are still courting, and I *will* return to seek her hand."

His beloved's father smirked. "Then I look forward to your next call at Longbourn."

Chapter 13

Light penetrated the fine slit between her eyelids, and sent a searing pain to her skull. Elizabeth groaned. What time had she finally fallen asleep? Her family returned some time after the clock struck three, but she had not ventured downstairs when they arrived. Instead, she cowered inside her bedchamber with her head tucked under her pillow.

Jane had given a light knock upon the door, but Elizabeth had not been equal to company. She had no desire to disillusion her dear sister, much less reveal her own doomed romance. How she struggled to maintain her composure as it was! She certainly could not be expected to recount the night before with any equanimity to another.

She rubbed her fingers against her temple in an effort to relieve the throbbing of her head. The thought of food brought a foul taste to her mouth, but perhaps some tea would set her to rights.

A light rap prompted her to sit and draw her legs close to her chest. "Come in."

The door opened a fraction, and Jane peeked through the resulting crack. "Are you feeling better? Papa said you departed the ball early because you were ill."

"My head still aches, but I would welcome your company."

Her sister entered and made herself comfortable on the end of the bed while Elizabeth pulled the coverlet around her shoulders. When they were both settled, Jane brushed a curl from Elizabeth's brow.

"You are a bit peaked and your eyes are swollen. Have you been crying?"

A folded piece of paper was in Jane's hand. Elizabeth pointed to it. "What do you have?"

"Oh! Mrs. Hurst sent a letter early this morning. The visitors at Netherfield have all returned to London. Mr. Darcy must have informed you of their planned departure."

Elizabeth was faint. Mr. Darcy left? "What did Mrs. Hurst say?"

Jane proffered the letter, which Elizabeth took with the utmost care. Why was she so timid? The letter would not burst into flames upon her touch.

> *Miss Bennet,*
>
> *I apologise for not taking my leave as I should have done, but my brother awoke determined to depart for London. He claims to have business to attend, and is most eager to settle his future. Unfortunately, we are not certain if his obligations will allow him to return to Hertfordshire before the end of the year.*
>
> *Mr. Darcy, who travelled with my brother at first light, is eager to return to town. He has missed his sister, and anticipates being reunited with her. I hope I am not too forward when I say that I am certain he will conclude his affairs in a swift fashion in order to return at his first opportunity.*
>
> *I do not pretend to regret anything I shall leave in Hertfordshire except your society, my dearest friend. I do hope we might find ourselves in company together sometime soon, and in the meanwhile; we may lessen the pain of separation by frequent and unreserved correspondence. I depend on you for that.*
>
> *Yours ever,*
> *Louisa Hurst*

Her vision blurred. Mr. Darcy had departed Netherfield. What was wrong with her? Why was she crying? She had begged him to leave her be, and he left. Was it not what she wanted?

"Lizzy?"

She used the bed sheet to wipe her eyes. "Do not mind me. I am being ridiculous."

Jane's eyes narrowed. "You are not telling me all that occurred last night."

"Please do not ask it of me, Jane. I do not feel capable of reciting the tale. I am afraid it would do neither myself nor Mr. Darcy credit."

"The two of you had a disagreement, and you did not let him explain."

Elizabeth crossed her arms with a huff. "I do not require his excuses. I am certain of what he intended."

"Oh, dearest." Jane placed an arm around Elizabeth's shoulders. "Mr. Darcy spoke with Papa for a time last night. He appeared so dejected and tired. Are you sure you know what you are about?"

"I know what I heard." She blinked several times in rapid succession. She would not cry again!

"He loves you, and you love him. I know you do."

She rose and stepped over to where her day gown hung upon a hook. "I shall have to overcome such silly sentiments. He was not worth my time and is not worth my tears."

The sound of Jane's sigh rang in her ears, but she paid it no heed as she dressed for the day. Once Jane fixed her hair, Elizabeth led the way to the dining room where, upon their entrance, Mrs. Bennet began waving her handkerchief.

"My poor Jane! Mr. Bingley has used you very ill—very ill indeed! How could he have departed without a hint of an understanding? It is beyond my comprehension!"

Elizabeth bit her lip to prevent a retort from escaping her lips. There was a lot beyond her mother's comprehension!

"And he took Mr. Darcy with him! Just when he was beginning to become agreeable!"

Elizabeth seated herself at the table and began to prepare her tea. When she looked across from her, Mr. Collins gave a simpering smile to both her and Jane. Oh no! He did not believe them to be eligible, did he? Granted, they both had no offers of marriage or betrothals, yet neither would divulge as much to him!

"It is all your fault, of course!"

Her head jerked to her mother as she almost spilled the milk.

"Why you had to depart the ball last night when matters were going so well between you and Mr. Darcy! He needs a wife to bear his heir! He does not desire a sickly woman for his mate! He must have found you pretty enough, though he might have preferred Jane had Mr. Bingley not shown his preference first."

A lump rose in her throat. She swallowed hard, though it was difficult.

"But then Mr. Darcy might have enjoyed my Lydia's company. A man as reserved as he is might favour a lively wife."

"Lizzy, would you please join me in my book room?"

Her head spun to her father, who stood in the door. What a blessed relief!

"Bring your tea."

The sound of a chair scraping against the wooden floor sent a shiver down her spine. "My dear, Mr. Bennet," said Mr. Collins, "I hoped to speak with Cousin Elizabeth this morning—privately. If such a meeting can be arranged." Mr. Collins gave a condescending smirk as he rose from a short bow.

"Mr. Collins, I have informed you on more than one occasion that Lizzy is being courted by Mr. Darcy. Regardless of your information, which Mr. Darcy refutes, I shall not allow her to become betrothed to another. Even should Mr. Darcy indicate he wishes to end their courtship, I would still not allow such a quick betrothal. The gossip that would arise from such a hasty alliance would not be in my family's best interest."

Her mother's eyes were wide with a hand pressed to her chest. "But Mr. Darcy has deserted Lizzy. He will not return! I am certain of it!"

"Well, I happen to know Mr. Darcy would disagree with you, Mrs. Bennet. He spoke with me at length last night in regards to his return and his intentions towards our second daughter. You would not wish to displease a gentleman of ten thousand pounds a year by betrothing the lady he is courting to another, would you?"

Her mother's jaw opened and shut several times, but not a sound emerged.

"Come, Lizzy." Her father held out his hand. "I must speak with you."

Without argument, she sprang from her chair and held her breath until the door of his study was closed behind her. She sank into her favourite spot and set her cup and saucer upon the desk.

"Thank you, Papa."

While I agree you required aid, we do need to have a conversation in regards to Mr. Darcy and your courtship."

"Nothing can be gained by repeating the happenings of last night. Our courtship is at an end, though I am not at all averse to pretending otherwise until our cousin returns to Kent."

Her father eyed her over his spectacles as he pulled a book from the shelf, moved to his well-worn chair, and sat. "I loathe disagreeing with you, but I believe Mr. Darcy will not accept defeat without argument. He is a determined young man, and he appreciates your worth, which renders him more agreeable in my view."

"He cannot have a reasonable excuse!"

"Yet he claims he does."

Righteous indignation spurred her from her seated position to pace to and fro. "He would see Jane broken-hearted by forbidding Mr. Bingley from offering her marriage. After all, Mr. Darcy insisted Mr. Bingley depart for London this very morning."

He rose and placed his hands upon her shoulders, halting her in her tracks. "Has it occurred to you he has good reason? Perhaps Mr. Bingley never intended to offer for Jane?"

"If that is the truth, then Mama is correct, and he has used her very ill indeed."

"Lizzy, how long have Mr. Bingley and Jane been acquainted?"

An incredulous chirp of laughter erupted from her lungs. "You know the answer to that question as well as I do."

His steady gaze remained serious. "Humour me. How long?"

"Since the assembly, so the eighteenth of October."

"That is just over a month, is it not?"

"Well, yes, but sufficient time for one to develop feelings for another."

"I agree, yet when has Mr. Bingley pursued your sister? When has he taken more than a friendly interest in her?"

"He stood up with Jane twice at the assembly!"

Her father gave a sad smile. "They had just met and dance partners were scarce, as I recall your mother's lament. The action was careless on his part, but hardly a prelude to a proposal."

"The concern he showed for her while she was ill!"

"May have been indicative of his care for any guest who ailed while residing in his home."

She knocked his hands from her shoulders. "You are determined—"

"To be realistic," he interjected. "Mr. Bingley may have preferred Jane to the other ladies in Meryton, yet I saw no symptoms of partiality on his part. I daresay he found her to be agreeable company."

"If you are correct, Jane will be heartbroken."

With a wave of his hand, he made a dismissive sound. "Next to being married, a girl likes to be crossed in love a little now and then. It is something to think of, and gives her a sort of distinction among her companions." He stepped around his desk and relaxed into his chair. "I daresay you are fancying yourself crossed now."

Her back became rigid. "I am hardly finding this pleasurable, Papa."

He placed a letter upon his desk. "Then read his explanation. Mr. Darcy detested the idea of departing Netherfield today. He did not want to leave matters with you unresolved, but he had no choice. He is a man of consequence and has responsibilities beyond what I could fathom with merely Longbourn in my charge."

Her eyes traced his flowing script. How her fingers itched to rip the missive open and absorb the words written within, but could those sentiments be trusted? She stood and stared until the clock on the mantel chimed the hour. She jumped. Her blurry vision moved to her father, she shook her head, and departed without a word.

December 3ʳᵈ 1811

What had he meant by returning? Had she not made her wishes clear when they quarrelled but a week ago? A sharp pain in her thumb made her draw the nail she had been biting back. She was not bleeding, so she began to gnaw upon the nail once more.

What was that sound? Her father would not bring Mr. Darcy to her room, would he?

When she had recognised his familiar form, approaching the house on horseback, she had run for her bedchamber, despite her mother's loud remonstrations. Jane had attempted to cajole her to see Mr. Darcy, but Elizabeth could not. Setting eyes upon his face would be too painful. Nothing had changed. No explanation could right his wrong.

A door opened below and gave a long creak; Mr. Hill never had greased the library door. The low tones of Mr. Darcy's voice resonated through the floorboards, and she drew her legs up to her chest, wrapping her arms around them and resting her forehead upon her knees.

She closed her eyes as the timbre of his voice soothed the ache in her chest—the ache that had remained since the night of the ball. If only she could run into his arms and relieve her suffering!

The front door closed, and she scrambled across the bed to the window. Eager eyes peered around the draperies and watched him climb astride his mount. When Mr. Darcy's gaze roved over Longbourn's façade, she jolted back; he could not know she was watching him.

"Just leave," she muttered under her breath. He would have left eventually, so it was better for him to depart now. Perhaps the pain would not be as long-lived this way.

The sound of hoof beats indicated he had begun his return to wherever he was going, and she again, peered forward, watching until his broad shoulders disappeared around the bend in the road.

She closed her eyes as a warm, wet droplet landed upon her cheek. She did not want to cry again! Her hands covered her face, but a loud wail from below startled her from her own grief.

With a rough swipe at her face, she darted out of the door, down the stairs, and slid to a stop in the doorway of the parlour. Her mother was fanning herself frantically as Jane stood at one shoulder and her father at the other, holding a paper where her mother was able to read it.

"My salts! Hill!"

Her father straightened and made his way to her. His lips were pressed into a fine line, and his eyebrows drawn in the middle. "Perhaps you should read the gossip column as well."

Wary fingers wrapped around the proffered sheets of paper, and pulled them forward until the words were legible. No recognisable name, yet how could they be familiar when they were the initials or vague descriptions of gentlemen from that county and ladies from this county. It was useless! She made to return the paper, but her father thrust it back and pointed to a specific passage.

It is now rumoured that a certain lady from Kent was whisked from town a year ago when her understanding with a certain wealthy tradesman from Yorkshire was revealed to her family. The latest word is that the lady, Miss AdB, has returned to London with her beau to finally plan the long-awaited nuptials.

Her eyes widened. "Mr. Bingley?"

"Yes, and Miss Anne de Bourgh. Do you not remember when Mr. Darcy corrected Mr. Collins about his betrothal to his cousin? He indicated she was promised to another, who did not have the approbation of Lady Catherine."

"He did say as much, but he never indicated it was Mr. Bingley!"

"He could not very well reveal such matters when Mr. Bingley did not yet have the approval of her family. According to Mr. Darcy, Lord Fitzwilliam agreed to consider Mr. Bingley if he made further strides towards becoming a landed gentleman while Lady Catherine was adamant the union would never occur."

"Which is why Mr. Bingley took the lease on Netherfield?"

Her father nodded. "Lord Fitzwilliam felt if Mr. Bingley continued and remained true to Miss de Bourgh, he was not marrying her for her fortune."

"If rumours are to be believed, Mr. Bingley has five thousand pounds per annum. He is no pauper."

"But he is not gentry, and she is the heiress of Rosings."

Her eyes blurred. "This was Mr. Darcy's explanation?"

"Yes," he replied with a disappointed tone. "One you would not allow him to deliver in person or even perhaps by letter." Her father held out the missive Mr. Darcy offered her the day after the ball at Netherfield. Trembling fingers took the proffered note and traced her name written in a neat, concise hand.

"I never dreamt—"

"You did not give him a chance."

Elizabeth stepped past her father. "Jane, are you well?"

The once overwhelming wails of her mother ceased. "Is she well? Of course she is not well! Why would you ask such a ridiculous question?"

Jane squeezed her mother's hand. "Mr. Bingley was pleasant company, but he made me no promises. He never gave any hint of regard for me."

"He indeed showed you preference!" cried their mother. "He stood up with you *twice* at the assembly! He requested the supper dance at the Netherfield ball."

With a sigh, Jane knelt before her mother. "He may have enjoyed my company, but he was amiable and pleasant. He never looked at me in the same manner Mr. Darcy gazes upon Lizzy. I want the man I marry to love me as I love him. I do not wish for a gentleman who merely feels polite affections."

"Affection?" Her mother's eyes were wide as she stared at Jane aghast. "He has *five thousand pounds a year*. I would be pleased to tolerate amiable and polite affections for such a sum."

"Then it is truly a shame that he did not like you best of all." Their father leaned against the doorframe behind them. Had he not returned to his book room?

"Papa!" Jane gave an incredulous laugh.

Her mother's shoulders began to shake as though she were crying a river, yet not a tear fell from her eyes. "What good are Mr. Darcy's gazes if Lizzy will not see him?"

"That is enough of your caterwauling, Mrs. Bennet. You will not alter the outcome of either situation with your laments, so I do expect them to cease."

Jaw agape; her mother stared at her father, speechless for once, yet she would not remain as such for long. The note in Elizabeth's hand scraped against her palm as it begged to be opened. Her grip tightened around it, curling it within her grasp. If she was going to escape, the time was at hand.

"Please excuse me."

Elizabeth's hurried steps aided her withdrawal. Her outstretched hand ripped her bonnet from its peg and she ran until she reached the pond where he had kissed her. A misty rain fell from the sky like the tears she now wished to God she could shed. They flowed like a river earlier. Why would they not do so now?

She took refuge under a tree; however, the overhanging branches did little to shield her from the damp. The droplets were too small.

She broke the seal, unfolded the paper, and took a bolstering breath.

> *My dearest Elizabeth,*
>
> *I have just returned to Netherfield after seeing your safe return to Longbourn, and I know not what to do. The sounds of your sobs as we journeyed rent my heart into pieces, yet you gave me no opportunity to explain. The situation is not as simple as you would believe. I have never been at liberty to discuss such matters, but I now understand I must tell you all. I only pray you will read this letter before you close your heart to me entirely.*
>
> *Two years ago, my aunt, Lady Catherine, journeyed to London to give her daughter, Anne, a season in town. Lady Catherine always hoped for a match between her daughter and myself, but we rebelled against such a notion. Fortunately, my aunt heard our vehement protests, and the season was to give Anne an opportunity to meet eligible young men.*
>
> *Bingley and I had become acquainted a few years prior due to some of my investments, which are rooted in trade. Due*

to his early completion at Eton, Bingley had just finished his studies at Cambridge and was eager to fulfil his father's desire of their family becoming gentry.

I acquired an invitation to Lord and Lady Fitzwilliam's Twelfth Night Ball for Bingley, and over the course of the evening, he made my cousin Anne's acquaintance. As the season continued, Bingley and Anne danced at balls, attended several of the same dinners, and happened upon one another when paying calls to my London home, yet never did we suspect any partiality on either of their parts.

You cannot imagine my surprise when Bingley approached me in regards to his proposal of marriage to Anne. I was astonished—to say the least! He had broached the subject at a ball the night before and Anne had accepted him. Bingley's demeanour is typically joyful, but you have not witnessed him as elated as he was that morning.

I accompanied him to my uncle, who was sceptical, but willing to consider Bingley a suitable candidate for Anne's husband. Lady Catherine, on the other hand, was incensed. She claimed Anne to be ill and hied her away to Rosings where she has remained, except for a Christmas she passed with Lord and Lady Fitzwilliam.

Bingley was morose, but my uncle gave Bingley hope. Should Bingley continue on his path towards becoming a gentleman and remain faithful to Anne, my uncle would grant his permission and arrange the marriage. Lady Catherine is aware of Lord Fitzwilliam's decision, but has reverted back to her original delusion that I shall wed Anne, which explains your cousin's misinformation.

Since then, I have taken pity upon Bingley and Anne. I have enclosed correspondence between the pair within my own—else they would have been parted all of this time.

Bingley has accomplished much in the past two years. He has done all he could to prove himself to Lord Fitzwilliam, and a few days prior to the ball at Netherfield, we received word of his success. My uncle wrote that he would sanction the match. My uncle was to journey to Rosings to retrieve Anne from my aunt, and Bingley needed to return to town to finalise the arrangements.

I assure you that no matter what was perceived from Bingley, he never considered being more than friendly with your sister. Since his arrival in Hertfordshire, he enjoyed her company, but did not intend to mislead her. In fact, he was stunned when I informed him the neighbourhood expected a betrothal to be forthcoming.

I do pray Miss Bennet has not been injured by his gregarious nature. I assure you Bingley is a different person when he is in Anne's company. If only you could see the comparison, you would understand.

I can only hope you do not find me culpable of any wrongdoing as I would be loath to commit any sin that would cause your disapprobation. You must know my heart is irrevocably yours and will be until the last breath leaves my body. I cannot imagine a life without you, and I do not desire such a bleak existence.

You are my heart. You are my soul. I have never needed any person as I need you. I was desolate, wallowing in my own despair over my sister's misfortunes, when I met you, and you rekindled a part of myself I thought lost.

I do not accept that you have released me from our courtship, as I have no such wish! Instead, I shall await your acceptance of my hand with as much patience as I can muster, but I shall not surrender my hopes and desires over a misunderstanding.

A word to your father will have me at your side as swiftly as I can ride to Meryton. Do not keep me waiting long, my love.

Yours,

Fitzwilliam Darcy

Her free hand covered her mouth, and she dropped to her knees. The damp soaked through her skirts, the frozen ground stung her flesh, and the cold made her tremble; she had forgot her pelisse. Those discomforts were trifling, however, to the pain in her heart.

Mr. Darcy had done naught but attempt to save Jane's feelings as well as those of his cousin's. He was the best man she had ever known, and she had behaved like a child. How could she possibly ever face him?

Chapter 14

After stopping by his house to refresh himself and change clothes, Darcy stepped up to the front door of Clarell House as the butler opened the door to allow him entry.

"Good day, Mr. Darcy. Lord Fitzwilliam and Lord Milton are at their club, Lady Fitzwilliam is in her study, and your sister is in the music room. Would you like me to announce you?"

"That will not be necessary, thank you."

"Fitzwilliam?" called his aunt's voice, as she peered into the hall. "Would you join me for a moment?"

He followed her to the parlour where she gestured to a chair. "I understand from Georgiana that you travelled to Hertfordshire this morning."

With a tug to the bottom of his topcoat, he took the offered seat. "Yes, I had some unfinished business to attend."

She tilted her head and appraised him. "You refer to your courtship of a young lady as business?"

He turned to the window and feigned interest in the back garden. "Georgiana told you?"

"I wished to speak of Miss Elizabeth Bennet when you arrived in town last week, but we had other more important matters to discuss." She sat in a seat beside him and placed a hand upon his forearm. "Georgiana is concerned for you, Fitzwilliam, as am I. You returned with your friend, and we expected a much different man when you did. Your letters to your sister were happy, as though you were letting go of what happened and moving forward. Though she was ill during that time, she was content. Her life may have been disrupted, but she does not wish for you to remain despondent over it. She needs you to be strong for her so she can heal."

"Miss Elizabeth and I had a disagreement before I left Hertfordshire. She declared our courtship at an end, but I cannot accept it."

"She sounds as though she knows her own mind. What reason did she give?"

"That is the problem, Aunt. She misunderstood me chastising Bingley, became insulted, and ended our understanding on misinformation."

Lady Fitzwilliam lifted her eyebrows. "Now I am all curiosity. You must tell me what grievous sin Mr. Bingley has committed."

"He was his usual self in Meryton, but Miss Elizabeth's mother is not unlike many mothers of our station. She saw Bingley as a match for Miss Bennet. The first time Bingley was in company with Miss Bennet was at a local assembly where there was a scarcity of suitable dance partners. He must have enjoyed Miss Bennet's company as he stood up with her twice and conversed with her for some time."

"Were they any sets of significance?"

"No, but I assume Mrs. Bennet crowed to the neighbourhood, though I heard none of the gossip at the time. Then, Miss Bennet became ill while having tea with Miss Bingley and Mrs. Hurst."

His aunt's nose crinkled. "I can hardly blame her for taking ill in the company of those two ladies."

"She became feverish and resided at Netherfield for a week. Miss Elizabeth stayed as well for the express purpose of nursing her sister."

"Which is when you became better acquainted?"

"Yes, I requested a courtship approximately a se'nnight after her return to Longbourn." He heaved in a breath and blew it out. "A fortnight later, as Elizabeth and I took part in the supper dance at the Netherfield ball, Sir William Lucas alluded to our future wedding as well as Bingley's betrothal to Miss Bennet."

"Oh my! Had Mr. Bingley not realized?"

"No, he had not. When I had the opportunity, I spoke to him alone in the library. He was astounded that the entire neighbourhood expected a proposal from him to be imminent. Unfortunately, Elizabeth approached as I scolded Bingley and insisted we return to town as soon as arrangements could be made."

His aunt closed her eyes. "Oh dear! She assumed you were forbidding Mr. Bingley from her sister, but knew naught of his prior betrothal."

"Precisely! I tried to explain, but she was so angry she would not listen. All I could do was ensure she returned home without incident and speak with her father. Today, I journeyed to Longbourn with yesterday's gossip column, but Elizabeth would not see me."

"Mr. Bingley needs to be more observant and restrained. Anne will be of great help in those matters, but he may have hurt Miss Bennet's feelings with his recklessness." She rested her elbow against the arm of the chair as she leaned forward. "Once your Miss Elizabeth realizes her error, she will be embarrassed. She may find it difficult to face you."

He shifted in his seat. "If I can gain her acceptance of my hand, will I have the support of you and my uncle? She is a gentleman's daughter, but her father's estate is entailed to none other than Lady Catherine's parson."

"There is no son?"

He shook his head.

Her nose crinkled. "I do hope the parson is a distant relation?"

A small bark of amusement escaped. "Yes, a distant cousin."

"Thank goodness for that!" She reached out and covered his hands with hers. "Your uncle and I trust you to choose a lady who would do the family credit. If she has gained your approval, she is likely intelligent, handsome, and does not suffer fools gladly."

"You have forgotten witty, charming, and has the most beautiful eyes."

His aunt gave an affectionate grin. "You fell in love with her eyes?"

His cheeks grew warm, and he gave a one-shouldered shrug. "I tried to fight my attraction to her, but she manages to surprise me whenever we are in company. I decided I did not require money or connections from her. I just wanted her."

She stood and cupped his cheeks with her hands. "Then do not allow her obstinacy to keep the two of you apart. Fight for her."

"I had no intention of doing otherwise."

With a succinct nod, she removed her hands and clasped them together. "I am pleased to hear it. Now, Georgiana has awaited your call all morning. I do not know what you have told her of Miss Elizabeth, but she is bursting at the seams."

"All that Georgiana knows is from my letters. I mentioned I was courting Elizabeth, but nothing more." He stood and took a few steps towards the door. "I shall go speak with her."

"Fitzwilliam?"

He turned to find a mischievous smile upon his aunt's countenance. "When you speak to Georgiana, do remember to refer to Miss Elizabeth as *Miss* Elizabeth. You are not betrothed or married yet."

Had he forgotten the Miss? The offence was one he committed in Elizabeth's presence as well, so it was possible he referred to her thus in their conversation. "Yes, of course. Thank you for the reminder."

His shoes clicked upon the marble tiles of the corridor, and when he reached for the handle to the music room, the broad oak panel swung open.

"Brother! You have returned!"

Georgiana wore a huge smile as she pulled him inside, but her eyes betrayed her as dark circles below her bottom lashes revealed her lack of sleep. Had she been having nightmares again? His aunt had not mentioned, but neither his aunt nor his sister wished to trouble him more than necessary.

"A short time ago. Aunt wished to speak with me when I arrived."

Her face fell. "She promised she would not tell."

He saw her seated and pulled a stool before her, taking her hand in his. "What did our aunt promise not to tell?"

Her shoulders slumped. "It is of no consequence."

"If you are asking our aunt to keep your confidence, then I disagree." He brushed her dark curls from her eyes. "Is it that you are having nightmares again?"

With wide eyes, she swallowed. "She told you."

"No, you appear exhausted, Georgiana. You must rest."

Tears welled in her eyes. "I have tried. You must believe me. Last night was the first time I have had bad dreams in a few weeks."

He rubbed his hand over his mouth. "Were they as dreadful as before?"

"No, when I was ill, I had the worst of them."

He could throttle his aunt for keeping such a thing from him! Georgiana had not had courses prior to Wickham, but upon his return, his aunt confided that his little sister had suffered them at last; however, they were far worse than what a lady would expect for her first time—at least, according to his aunt they were. He had limited knowledge of such feminine happenings and had no desire to become acquainted with them—at least in relation to his little sister.

Lady Fitzwilliam believed Georgiana had lost a child, yet they did not impart the knowledge to her. The poor dear had endured enough. Hopefully, she would never discover the truth!

She turned her hands over and squeezed his. "Please do not make me speak of it. I have told our aunt, and I cannot bear to talk of it again. I have waited all day to hear of Miss Elizabeth, and I hope you will not disappoint me." Her manner was subdued, but she blinked and leaned to the side to catch his attention.

"I have told you of her."

"You mentioned her wit and her kindness in your letters, yet you have not spoken of her since your return from Hertfordshire. I know you journeyed to Meryton today, and I assumed you were to propose."

He sighed. "Matters are complicated between us, Georgiana."

"Then uncomplicate them."

"I wish it were so simple." He had already told his aunt. It would not do to divulge his heart to his much younger sister!

"Why will you not confide in me?"

"You do not need to fret over me when you already have so much to cause you grief." His voice cracked. Why was he having such a difficult time concealing his struggles?

"I shall worry whether you tell me or not, Fitzwilliam."

His head dropped to his hands, and he combed his fingers through his hair. After one last appraising look at his sister, he capitulated. Was there naught he could keep for himself? Though he wanted nothing more than to keep matters to himself, his entire history with Elizabeth poured forth from his lips like a rushing river forged over a waterfall while he paced before Georgiana. When he concluded the tale, he dropped back into his chair.

"Poor Miss Elizabeth! And Miss Bennet! Mr. Bingley should have been more careful!"

"I agree, but situations are always clearer after they have occurred, are they not?" Georgiana had indicated many times over the past few months that if she had only behaved differently at Ramsgate, Wickham would never have had the chance to harm her. She, of all people, should understand the sentiment.

"Yes, that is true," she agreed in a soft tone. "What do you plan to do now?"

"I shall give her more time. Mr. Bennet has my direction in London. He agreed to notify me should Miss Elizabeth indicate a desire to see me."

"Do not wait too long. Miss Elizabeth makes you happy. I may not have witnessed your interactions, but your letters spoke of your improved spirits while you were in Hertfordshire."

"As I informed our aunt, I do not intend to let Elizabeth go."

Georgiana smirked. "So, it is Elizabeth, is it?"

First his face was warm when he spoke with his aunt, and now again. When had he become such a lady? He was certainly blushing like one!

A giggle came from Georgiana and his heart swelled. She so rarely laughed these days that the sound was a welcome one.

"I forget myself at times."

"Well, do not forget yourself during dinner. Richard and Charles will tease you mercilessly for it."

"Of that I am well aware."

"I thought I heard my name." Their heads darted around to Richard who stood in the doorway. He returned to London a day after Darcy and had been his usual insufferable self.

Darcy winked at Georgiana. "You were dreaming."

"Then go wake me, else Mother will have a fit when I am late to dinner." He moved as if leaving, then peered back around the doorframe. "Are you going to join me?"

Darcy grinned, stood, and offered his arm to his sister. He was lucky to have such relations. If only he could trade Lady Catherine for someone more docile, his family would be ideal!

When he returned to Darcy House, he went directly to his rooms, and after handing over his topcoat and waistcoat, dismissed his valet.

The knots in his cravat... blast! Would they never come free? When the cloth loosened, he managed to remove the garment and flung it across a chair by the fire.

Darcy had been careful not to drink too much while dining with his relations, but now he was blessedly alone and could drown his sorrows to his heart's content. He filled the glass to the brim and took a large gulp.

Was Elizabeth as miserable as he was?

He removed a small box from his dresser and took a seat before the fire, propping his foot on the table before him. With one more significant swallow, he popped the lid on the case to reveal the ring within and his hand dropped to his thigh.

A long inhale was an attempt to control his emotions, but it was for naught. Instead, he took another swig of scalding golden liquid and stared at the line of five pearls with tiny diamonds placed around them.

The piece was not the most ornate or the most valuable of the Darcy jewels that could grace Elizabeth's finger, but the ring called to be hers. The five oval-shaped pearls brought to mind the pale alabaster of her skin, and she was sure to favour the floral repoussé of the band. She would not desire a huge or ostentatious show upon her hand. No, the simple arrangement suited her—this one was perfect.

Now, if only she would agree to be in the same room with him!

"You asked to see me, Papa?" Elizabeth stood in the door as her father glanced up from his papers.

He peered over his spectacles and leaned back in his chair. "I did. Why do you not come in and close the door behind you?" Once she was seated in her usual chair, he picked up a paper to his side. "A few days after the ball at Netherfield, I penned a letter to your Aunt and

Uncle Gardiner, requesting you stay with them in London for a time."

What was she to say? Her aunt would be a welcome relief from her mother's laments over the loss of Mr. Darcy, but she could not hide from the world in London. Her aunt would not tolerate it.

She opened her mouth to speak, but he held up his hand. "I felt your aunt's counsel would be beneficial. I became more convinced of the usefulness of my plan yesterday when you refused to even set eyes upon the poor man."

"I know I must face him. I have attempted to pen a letter, but I do not know what to say. I cannot find the words..." Her chest constricted when his eyes closed for a moment and he frowned. His disappointment had always been difficult to bear.

"I pray your aunt might break through what is holding you back before you destroy the affection that man carries for you. He is everything I could have hoped and dreamt for your future—intelligent, honourable, and loves you beyond reason. I know you harbour deep feelings for him. Do not wait until it is too late. You do not want to be left wondering what if."

Her chest was heavy and made it difficult to get air. "When do I leave?"

"Early tomorrow. Our carriage will take you as far as Waltham Abbey where your uncle's coach will meet you and convey you the remainder of the journey to London."

Her father stood, came around his desk, and, taking Elizabeth's hand, made her to stand. "I daresay you will not miss your mother's wailing in London, but I shall find this house lonesome without you." He enveloped her in his arms. "I want what is best for you, Lizzy. I would not part with you unless I found it necessary."

She rested her chin upon his shoulder. "I am no longer angry."

"I am glad of that, but you need to speak with him."

"I know, Papa." She choked down a sniffle. "I know."

Chapter 15

Elizabeth gave her gown a last straightening before she peered around the corner into her aunt and uncle's parlour. The children's voices floated into the hall, and brought a smile to her lips.

"Will Cousin Lizzy be much longer, Mama?" whined Madeline.

"She will read us a story, will she not?" Grace's voice was excited, yet when was that girl not exuberant about something?

"As soon as she has refreshed herself and has had dinner, I am certain Lizzy will spend time with each of you, as well as your baby brother."

"But James does not understand that it is Lizzy!" objected four year old Lewis, who sat beside his mother. "He is too young!"

Quietly, Elizabeth stepped into the room. "I happen to enjoy babies, and *I* shall know I have spent time with little James."

"Lizzy!"

Before she could move, she was almost toppled over by the three children and had three sets of arms wrapped around her waist.

"If you knock her to the floor, she might not do any of your bidding while she stays with us." Her aunt's tone was gentle but held a warning.

Elizabeth laughed. "They know me better than that."

Her aunt pursed her lips. "I know, but you could play along."

"Will you read us a story?"

"Lewis, you are aware your dinner awaits you in the nursery. If Lizzy is not too tired after her trip, she can read to the three of you *and* James before bed."

"Will you?" Madeline's big brown eyes were filled with such happiness. How could she say no?

With a nod, Elizabeth stroked the six year old's head. "Yes, of course."

Her aunt rose from her chair. "Go on with you. Your nurse awaits." Lewis, Grace, and Madeline ran from the room with tremendous smiles upon their faces. They were the sweetest children. Perhaps they would lighten her mood while she remained at Gracechurch Street.

When she turned, her aunt examined her with a crease between her eyes. "Your father was not exaggerating when he said you have been unhappy."

"Papa does not typically exaggerate."

"No, he does not, but I did not expect your melancholy to be so evident upon your countenance."

She gave a rueful laugh. "Why thank you, Aunt."

"You were not made for sorrow, dear." She gestured to the sofa and rang for some tea. "We have time before your uncle returns home. Will you not tell me what has you so upset?"

Elizabeth sat and clenched her hands in her lap. "What has Papa told you?"

"He wrote from his perspective. I wish to hear yours."

She glanced to the window, even though not much could be seen through the panes as the sun had already set. Her stomach clenched, and she shifted in her seat. "It is a painful recollection that I fear does me no credit."

Aunt Gardiner sat beside her and placed a hand upon Elizabeth's, halting its fidgeting. "Yet perhaps speaking of it will provide comfort."

Her chin dropped to her chest. "I have been so foolish. I do not even know where to begin." Her voice cracked as she spoke, and she swallowed hard.

"Your father indicated you and Mr. Darcy had a disagreement at the ball. Why do you not start there? What began the argument?"

"I... he..." She shook her head.

Her aunt's arm came around her shoulders. "You may not believe so now, but it will do you good to tell someone."

With her aunt's gentle coaxing the dam broke and the entirety of her acquaintance with Mr. Darcy poured from her lips—their initial meeting, their being confined in the Netherfield library, the morning walks, and finally the ball. She finished her tale as she dabbed her eyes with her handkerchief.

"My goodness, Lizzy," whispered her aunt. "I confess I had hoped you were wrong when you said the quarrel did you no credit."

Elizabeth nodded and sniffled.

"You do understand that you must see him. You must discuss what has transpired between you."

"I miss him, but I am afraid to face him."

Her aunt took Elizabeth's hands in her own. "What has brought on such a lack of confidence? The Elizabeth Bennet I know is fearless."

Aunt Marianne's forehead creased while she studied Elizabeth's eyes. "I certainly hope this has nothing to do with your mother."

"Pardon?"

Her aunt stood and faced her in a whirl of skirts. "Your mother has belittled your beauty and worth in comparison to Jane and Lydia for years. While the criticism never appeared to bother you, you have never before had a gentleman take a serious interest in you."

"Mama's comments never upset me because they are the truth. I am not handsome like Jane or as amiable as Lydia. I have never appreciated her voicing those opinions aloud, but I learned to roll my eyes and ignore her."

Her aunt sighed. "You learned such indifference from your father, but do not pretend you are as unaffected by such statements as you seem. I shall not believe it of you. Not anymore."

Elizabeth's heart began to pound against her ribs, and her mouth became dry. "I do not understand what you believe me to be hiding."

"While Mr. Darcy courted you and showered you with attention, you gave little thought to much else. I think you were too overwhelmed by his notice. After your misunderstanding and his departure, you had a moment to sit back and question why a man of his consequence would choose you. I also suspect that it was your insecurities which drove you to refuse his explanation the night of the ball."

With a few rapid blinks, Elizabeth shifted upon the sofa. Her aunt was reaching close to the mark, and she could not bear to hear another person say it!

"You have allowed your mother's untrue and biased words to influence you. If only your father had checked your mother years ago." She shook her head. "There is no use weeping over spilt milk now." Aunt's Marianne's arm wrapped around Elizabeth's shoulders. "How I wish you had spoken to Jane or your father before you turned Mr. Darcy away! They would have told you, without question, that your mother's words are falsehoods."

A warm dampness rolled down Elizabeth's cheek. "I do see myself in the looking glass. I am not blind."

Her aunt lifted her chin. "You have allowed your mother to colour what you perceive. You are a beautiful young lady inside and out, and neither your uncle nor I were surprised Mr. Darcy showed a preference for you. I admit we were a bit stunned he acted upon the inclination, since his family is certain to have expectations of wealth and connections for his marriage."

She gulped. Her voice was sure to crack! "He indicated he has no need for further wealth or connections." Her shoulders relaxed. Her voice wavered, but did not falter.

"Then you are truly a fortunate lady. He seeks your hand for nothing other than admiration and love."

"Yet, I have driven him away."

Aunt Marianne took the seat beside her once again and clasped Elizabeth's hands within her own. "We do not have any reason to believe he has abandoned hope. Perhaps you should compose a small note, indicating you wish to see him, and your uncle will enclose it in a letter of his own. We shall ensure he understands he is welcome here."

"What if he does not come? I refused to see him but two days ago."

With a soft touch, her aunt brushed a tear from her jawline. "Then we shall do our best to cheer you. We have been invited to a ball, and you will accompany us. Lewis and Madeline will lure you into all sorts of games and stories, and do not forget James' big grins and happy chatter."

Elizabeth put her hands over her face. What had she done? She had suppressed the voice in her head that whispered she was not enough for a man such as him for a time, but during their argument, the whisper became more pronounced. Her fears had been her worst enemy.

"For what it is worth, I believe he will appear at our door the moment he discovers your presence in London."

"Oh, Aunt!" Elizabeth placed her head upon Aunt Marianne's shoulder as the older lady took her in her embrace.

"Your father has likely already written to Mr. Darcy and informed him of your journey here."

She sat straight, wiped her eyes, and gave an unbecoming exhale by noisily blowing out her mouth. "I need to think of something else. What of this ball?"

Her aunt smiled and squeezed Elizabeth's hand. "It is two days hence and is given by a new friend of your uncle's. Edward made the gentleman's acquaintance when Oswald Gardiner, your grandfather's nephew, passed, and he inherited his estate. The man was a friend with your late cousin, as they had attended school together, and he wished to maintain the friendship between the families."

"He does not mind Uncle's roots in trade?"

"He has invested in your uncle's business, so I would think not. He has also indicated an understanding for why Edward has not sold his business."

"Papa said you would be moving in the new year?"

"Yes, the house in Mayfair is not let at the moment, and we have reason to believe we may require a larger home in the near future."

Elizabeth covered her mouth with her hand and placed her palm to her chest. "Truly?"

With a smile, her aunt bobbed her head. "I have not felt him yet, but the sickness is beginning to wane. He should not leave me wondering for too much longer."

"I am so pleased for you and Uncle, though I shall miss this home since it has contained so many happy memories."

"We shall make memories just as dear in the larger house. It will not be as convenient for your uncle, but he has worked more at home and less at his warehouse as of late. He is fortunate to have a good man to oversee the employees while Edward handles documents and other work that arises."

"I had no idea Uncle was so busy."

"Not much more than he was prior to the inheritance. Leasing the estates has helped quite a bit. He has excellent stewards in place, and is mostly notified when his advice is required or there is information Edward has requested."

"Where is my lovely wife?" came a booming voice from the front door. Uncle Edward was an excellent man, and his obvious affection for his wife was one of his most endearing attributes. Even after nearly ten years of marriage, he was still besotted.

He stepped into the doorway and grinned. "There she is, as well as my favourite niece!"

Elizabeth laughed as she stood. "Poor Jane!"

After a wave of his hand, he hugged Elizabeth and then kissed Aunt Marianne upon her cheek. "She is aware she shares the title with you."

"Yet, you did not say 'one of my favourite nieces.'" She lifted her eyebrow.

Her aunt giggled. "You know Lizzy will argue with you just for the sport of it."

"I must admit I am glad she is willing to quarrel with me."

His wife placed a hand to her uncle's arm. "You will need to pen a note to Mr. Darcy later, inviting him to call upon Lizzy."

"Why am I not surprised you sat her down and forced her to unburden herself before she had time to unpack?"

Elizabeth laughed. "She was not as forceful as you imply, Uncle."

"After your father's letter, I am happy to hear you laugh. We have been quite concerned."

"I did not intend to cause so many such disquiet." Their attention was drawn to a maid, who poked her head through the servant's door.

"Pardon me, ma'am, but when you are ready to eat, the cook has dinner prepared."

"Why do we not go into the dining room?" suggested her aunt. "We can discuss matters further while we eat."

Her uncle rubbed his slightly rotund belly. "I confess to requiring some sustenance before we begin discussing suitors and courtships. I do hope it will be another thirty to forty years before I need speak of it again."

With a grin, her aunt looked to the ceiling. "You know well that our daughters will marry long before that."

"They are my little girls. They will not leave me."

His pouting bottom lip and drawn eyebrows caused Elizabeth and her aunt to erupt into gales of laughter. Elizabeth hugged her uncle. "Regardless of who they wed, they will always be your little girls."

He offered her and her aunt each an arm to lead them into the dining room. "Well, perhaps I can practice my fatherly skills while you are here, Lizzy. Someone should ensure this young man is worthy of your hand."

"He is too good for me, Uncle."

His eyebrows rose. "Now that I find difficult to believe."

Elizabeth sat in the window seat. An open book rested upon her lap, but her eyes were staring unfocused through the panes of the window. People, carts, and carriages all blurred by but none of it was of interest.

He had not come.

Uncle Edward had enclosed her letter within his own inviting Mr. Darcy to Gracechurch Street and travelled to Grosvenor Square personally to deliver the missive. Unfortunately, Mr. Darcy had not been at home, so her uncle had been forced to leave it without so much as setting an eye on the gentleman in question.

Tonight was the ball, but she was not in the correct frame of mind for such an outing. The desire to remain at home and sulk overwhelmed, yet she had no choice. Her best gown was pressed and ready—if only she could render herself so with as little effort.

A wave from the pavement snapped her from her thoughts. She gave as much of a smile as she could muster when she recognised her aunt, who had left an hour prior to pay a call on a friend. Voices were heard in the hall as she entered the house, and but a moment later, her aunt entered the parlour.

"Have you left your perch at all today?"

Elizabeth leaned her head against the wall behind her. "Not since luncheon. I attempted to read, but I could not focus."

Her aunt sat upon the edge of the window seat and took her hand. "You know how these important men can be. I am certain he had business which could not be delayed else he would have been at our door at first light." She smoothed a curl from Elizabeth's forehead. "We do not know if he even received your uncle's letter. It may have been put aside with other correspondence. Do not fret just yet."

"Perhaps you and Uncle should attend the ball without me."

"Elizabeth Bennet. You need to get out and away from your thoughts. You will accompany us to the ball and do your utmost to enjoy yourself. You cannot continue to wallow about this house for the entirety of your visit. I do not keep those gowns in the cupboard to collect dust."

From the time Elizabeth and Jane were old enough to join their aunt and uncle on outings, her aunt had always ensured they had a few gowns at Gracechurch Street in the event they were needed.

"We shall also need to make a trip to the modiste in the next few days."

"I do not require any further gowns."

Aunt Marianne leaned forward to, no doubt, ensure she had Elizabeth's eye. "Once Mr. Darcy realizes you are in town, he will wish to escort you to an event or two."

"He has to appear at the door first."

Her aunt's hand cradled her cheek. "I wager he will appear before long. I am certain of it."

Elizabeth looked back out the window as a few droplets of rain streaked their way down the glass. "I hope your instincts are correct, Aunt."

"They are, dear girl. He would be a fool to let you go."

Chapter 16

December 7th 1811

Elizabeth stared, bewildered at her surroundings upon entering the opulent hall. Gilded mirrors and enormous portraits hung upon the wall, a large bouquet of roses and other out of season flowers was set upon a shiny mahogany table in the middle of the room, and marble tiled floors gleamed in the candlelight.

What sort of friend had her uncle made?

Uncle Edward's arm pulled her closer as he stepped forward in the queue to greet the hosts of the event. By the looks of the carriages and the crowd inside, the ball would be a tremendous crush. She had never attended an affair such as this, and the idea caused a frisson of excitement as well as trepidation. How would those in attendance treat her? Would they be rude since she was not a part of high society or would they be curious?

As they made their way to the ballroom, she spotted the hosts near the wide doorway, greeting guests. Two grown men stood to either side, presumably their sons. The elder gentleman was tall, distinguished, with some silver in his hair and dressed in a fine black suit. He was neither garish in his dress nor foppish, but conservative, and his appearance spoke of money.

His wife was tall for a lady and wore a beautiful ivory silk gown with a sheer overlay. Pearls and rubies adorned her neck, ears, and wrists, and even trimmed her gown. Upon her head she wore a small tiara of matching jewels, but it was not ostentatious. She was tasteful and elegant.

Before Elizabeth could examine the sons, they stood before the regal couple, so she and her aunt curtsied as her uncle bowed.

"Gardiner," the gentleman exclaimed, "Mrs. Gardiner, you are acquainted with my wife, Lady Fitzwilliam and my sons, Charles and Richard. I am so pleased you could attend."

Uncle Edward shook the man's hand. "The pleasure is ours, Fitzwilliam. I appreciate you including my niece when we indicated she would be visiting."

Did he say Fitzwilliam? Could this be Mr. Darcy's uncle? How many Fitzwilliams could there be in England? Her fingernails dug into her palms as she perused the guests milling about her.

A hand between her shoulder blades pressed her forward. "May I present my niece, Miss Elizabeth Bennet. Elizabeth, this is the Earl and Countess Fitzwilliam and their sons Lord Charles Wentworth-Fitzwilliam, Viscount Milton and Colonel Richard Fitzwilliam."

She started and gave a small dip of a curtsey. "I am pleased to make your acquaintances." When she lifted her eyes, Lady Fitzwilliam's eyes skimmed from Elizabeth's feet to her face, pinking when she realized she had been caught.

"I hope you enjoy the ball, my dear." The countess' expression was open and kind, not that it quieted the rush of thoughts whirring in her mind. "I do expect we shall have a crush, but the musicians I have arranged are quite talented and my cook has been working on tonight for the past month."

Her uncle placed a hand to his stomach. "Then, I anticipate the offerings at supper."

Lord Fitzwilliam gave a rumble of a laugh. "You are similar to my son in that regard. His assessment of any ball has nothing to do with the music or the company, but the food. He never misses a meal at home when he has the time. If he is not at our table, he is dining with his cousin Darcy. I believe he is looking forward to the meal as well."

Elizabeth flinched. They were relations! Would Mr. Darcy be in attendance this evening or would he spend time with his sister? She was staying with Lord and Lady Fitzwilliam, was she not?

"Lizzy?" She startled and looked forward. Aunt Marianne held her arm outstretched for Elizabeth to join them. With a quick dip of a curtsey to their hosts, she followed. Hopefully, she had not missed any information of import while she was wool-gathering.

When she came side to side with her Aunt, Elizabeth wrapped her arm around her aunt's. "Were you aware of their relation to Mr. Darcy?"

"Dearest, there is not a soul in London who is unaware of the connection between the Fitzwilliams and the Darcys. Forgive me if you feel deceived, but we worried you either would not come if you knew or you would fret from the moment you were told until the end of the evening."

"I feel ill." She swallowed with difficulty. "I would have much preferred to have our first meeting without all of society bearing witness."

"I have no doubt, but he has not responded to your uncle's letter as of yet. We planned to attend prior to your coming to London, so the opportunity to reunite you with Mr. Darcy was a fortuitous circumstance."

Uncle Edward trailed behind as they entered the ballroom. People milled about from wall to wall, squeezing through the crowd to obtain drinks or find acquaintances. As they waited, a conversation behind them caught Elizabeth's ear.

"Viscount Milton cut a dashing figure, but I do hope Mr. Darcy will be in attendance."

"Why is that, Thea?" asked a condescending voice.

"My mother believes he will finally seek a bride during this upcoming season, and *we* intend to ensure he chooses me."

Another voice laughed incredulously. "How do you intend to succeed in such an endeavour? Mr. Darcy is known for his refusal to dance unless Lady Fitzwilliam cajoles him, and he does not speak more than a few words to most ladies. I believe 'Please excuse me' is the phrase he uses most often."

"That was before I came out." The original voice became haughty. "My mother and Lady Fitzwilliam are friends. My father is also of great political import to Lord Fitzwilliam. They will promote the match if I wish it."

"I would not be too convinced of myself if I were you. I have heard rumour he is courting a lady from the country."

One of the ladies scoffed. "As if Mr. Darcy would lower himself to consider such a woman. He will wed a lady of standing. Lord and Lady Fitzwilliam would not allow him to choose otherwise."

The voice was the first. The one who was certain she would become the next Mrs. Darcy.

"Lizzy?" Her aunt pulled her from her eavesdropping, so her uncle could introduce her to a gentleman, who requested her first set. He was polite, but had a certain air about him that was not hard to place—he thought well of himself. As she settled into the familiar pattern, her nerves dissipated until she was returned to her aunt and uncle.

Several gentlemen followed. One short and squat, who trod upon her toes, another tall with a thin frame and large stomach. He appeared as though he would fall forward at any moment with his disproportionate appearance, his stomach resembling the shape of a punch bowl without the stem. Withholding her laughter became a necessity after such a revelation.

Her next partner required a bath in the worst of ways; his cologne did not help matters either. Would it be rude to hold one's handkerchief to one's nose while dancing? Perhaps a vinaigrette? He smiled before she moved to the gentleman beside her. Eww! Was that cabbage in his teeth?

When she was delivered back to her aunt and uncle, she took the first good, deep breath since the last set began.

"Miss Bennet?" Her insides jumped. Colonel Fitzwilliam stood before her, his red uniform striking in a room of men in black topcoats and trousers. "Would you dance the next with me?"

The glint in his eye was off-putting, but she could not say no. What if Mr. Darcy suddenly appeared and requested a set? She could not refuse in the event he arrived. "Yes, I would be honoured."

Her thankful nose appreciated he had not the body odour of her previous partner as they made their way to where the set was forming and took their places.

He tilted his head and took her measure. "I am familiar with your name. I believe you are acquainted with my cousin Darcy and my soon-to-be cousin, Bingley."

"Yes, I am. Mr. Bingley is leasing the nearest estate to that of my father's, and when my sister Jane fell ill at Netherfield, Mr. Bingley was generous enough to allow me to stay until she was well. The last ball I attended was the one he gave at Netherfield." The dance began, and he held out his hand as she scanned the room.

"Bingley is in attendance with his betrothed, my cousin Anne de Bourgh. They are at the end of the line, there." He gestured with his head. "I am certain he would be pleased to greet you. Bingley is always a jovial fellow."

She attempted a smile. "He is very amiable."

He appeared to take no notice of her unease. His demeanour was sociable and without artifice. "Darcy was visiting with his sister and should be joining us soon." He chuckled. "Just look for the dour, scowling face standing to one side of the room. You cannot miss him."

Her heartbeat quickened and pounded against her ribs. Mr. Darcy would be there! What would he say when he took notice of her? Would he be angry? He would not cause a scene, yet would he ignore her in order to discuss their disagreement in private?

"But if you attended the Netherfield ball, you should know his habits in society well."

Something within her bristled. "On the contrary, Mr. Darcy was a complete gentleman last we were in company together. He stood up with me twice, my friend Miss Lucas once, and also partnered my elder sister for one set."

They parted due to the pattern of the dance, but the colonel's grin was unmistakeable when he approached her once more. "So I was correct."

"I am afraid I do not understand. What do you believe you have deduced?"

The colonel leaned towards her. "You are the Miss Bennet he is courting." His voice was low, but his words burned her ears. Her mouth became dry, and she averted her eyes.

"My cousin is too fastidious to partake of more than one set unless he had designs upon the lady in question." An impish expression lit his face. "You have no idea the number of ladies here tonight who would maim or kill for such notice from him."

Her eyes looked to the ceiling for a moment at the ridiculousness of his last statement; it was certain to be a gross exaggeration.

"He did not mention you were coming this evening. By his morose demeanour upon his return, I would have thought you remained behind in Hertfordshire."

"I arrived but two days ago to visit my aunt and uncle." She would not comment on Mr. Darcy. She needed to speak *to* him, not about him.

Colonel Fitzwilliam's eyes bulged, and he gave a guffaw. "He does not know you are here. Oh! I shall enjoy this ball immensely! His reaction when he sees you will set the tongues of the matrons and their daughters wagging. Be careful for the claws, Miss Bennet. I am certain some young lady will attempt to sharpen hers upon you."

She took a sidelong glance around the room. More reason to fret was all she needed! "I sincerely hope your prediction proves false."

"It depends upon Darcy, of course. He does enjoy that mask he wears in public—the disapproving one in particular, but can he disguise his shock upon meeting you in my father's house? I would wager the Major General's horse he cannot maintain his stern and frightening visage." A gleeful cackle came from the colonel.

As the first half of the set ended, and the colonel's incessant amused expression was beginning to wear. He was so determined to find humour at Mr. Darcy's expense. Why would he wish Mr. Darcy to be disturbed so?

When they began again, he took both of her hands and stepped to the music. "You must understand. Most of the ladies under five and twenty in this room have vied for Darcy's attentions as well as some of those who are older. Some want his money and position and some just want..."

She stepped over and turned with the gentleman beside her. When she returned to Colonel Fitzwilliam, she lifted an eyebrow. "They want?"

A frown now graced her partner's face. "Forgive me. I have come to the realization that I should not be so frank. I have been too free with my information."

She took the hand of the gentleman beside her and worked her way through the pattern until she again reached the colonel.

"I would beg you finish your statement. I do not know what to make of how you ended it."

He groaned and leaned a hairsbreadth closer. "They do not want him for his mind or his friendship. Does that answer your question?"

If they do not want his money, his mind, or his friendship, what... "Oh!"

He gave a guttural exhale and closed his eyes for a moment. "Darcy is going to kill me."

She bit her lip and suppressed a giggle. Her first impression of the colonel was intrusive and annoying, but he began to strike her as humorous.

"You have no need to mention what I have told you tonight, do you?" The dance ended, and he held out his arm. "Darcy is like a brother to me. Since we are so close, I could discern his improved spirits in his correspondence from Hertfordshire. I have no wish to cause mischief—I assure you."

He glanced about the room. "Let me return you to your aunt and uncle, and then I shall pretend we never met. I will also deny any charge that I informed you of inappropriate intelligence."

Biting back a grin, she tilted her head. "You did not say if he accepted those ladies." The words had been meant as a tease, yet... she stopped short and her eyes hurt they bulged so wide. "Did he?"

Colonel Fitzwilliam pivoted and looked her directly in the eye. "I cannot say."

"Cannot or will not?"

He rubbed his hands up and down his face and stepped forward "I honestly do not know. For what it is worth, I have never known him to dally with the ladies and never had rumour of such an arrangement or assignation spread. Does that satisfy your curiosity?"

With a bob of her head, she placed her hand once again upon his arm. "Thank you, Colonel."

"Miss Bennet!" Lady Fitzwilliam pushed through the crowd around them and glanced at her son. "Good grief, Richard. What more could you possibly have to say to her? I do not think you ceased babbling for the entire set!" She wrapped her fingers around Elizabeth's elbow. "Now, Miss Bennet, if you would accompany me for a moment."

Without ceremony, Lady Fitzwilliam pressed through the revellers with an efficiency that displayed her experience at such events as Elizabeth struggled to stay close. A few ladies stopped the countess for a word, but never requested an introduction. Lady Fitzwilliam was polite and cordial, yet managed to excuse herself with alacrity.

Elizabeth peered about the ballroom. "I should find my aunt and uncle. They will worry if I do not return."

She waved her hand. "Do not fret about Marianne. I mentioned I wished to have a word with you, and she did not object."

"You did?" Her aunt was on such intimate terms with Lady Fitzwilliam that they used their given names?

"I have been in your aunt's company a mere handful of times, but I know her to be a conscientious woman. She has kept a steady eye on you during the ball; I am certain of it. I would never dream of removing you from her watch without due warning."

They passed the punch table, and the countess steered her towards the back corner of the room.

"Here we are," she exclaimed.

Elizabeth was pulled to the side and brought to a halt in front of a tall gentleman. Her eyes shifted from his cravat to the face of... "Mr. Darcy!"

Chapter 17

Elizabeth's stomach jumped to her throat, the sound of her heart pounded in her own ears, her mind was blank. What could she say in front of a contingent of revellers? Was *Mr. Darcy, I was a fool. I hope you can forgive me because I want to be your wife* appropriate under such circumstances?

Mr. Darcy stood straight and tall, but his eyes did not leave hers. He did not speak, but stared until he flinched.

"Do not just stand there, Fitzwilliam. Greet the lady and request a set!"

Elizabeth's palms grew damp in her gloves, as he did no more than continue to gape.

"You have always been a quiet young man, but this is preposterous!" With a tug of his elbow, Lady Fitzwilliam placed Elizabeth's hand upon it before whispering in his other ear. He made to turn towards her, but she gave his back a push. This was mortifying!

Without a word, he stepped forward and led Elizabeth to the edge of the dancers. His expression was rigid, like stone, and his arm was just as unyielding. Was he displeased with her appearance?

Her eyes burned and blurred as she blinked back tears. She would not cry! A deep breath was sucked into her lungs in an attempt not to retch at her feet. Why was she so weak when it came to him? Nerves never plagued her until she met Mr. Darcy. Now, she resembled her mother more than her usual self. What a nightmarish thought!

The current set ended, and he led her to the floor. When they were in their places, the tingling from his stare prickled her skin.

"I apologise for not greeting you properly."

Without delay, her gaze whipped to his face.

"Please understand I am stunned to find you here. I was unaware you were in town."

"I arrived two nights ago." Her voice was a bit scratchy, so she cleared her throat in as gentle manner as possible. "My father thought some time with my aunt would be beneficial."

The music began, so he bowed while she curtsied. She was back to holding a conversation in parts. How could they resolve matters in such a fashion and in such crowded company?

"And is it? Beneficial, that is." She followed the line between his eyebrows to the dark circles under his eyes. He was sleeping as poorly as she.

"Yes, quite. My aunt has a great deal of good sense. I have found her counsel invaluable as of late, but then, her advice has proven useful in the past as well."

The dance forced them to take one another's hands, so she grasped the opportunity to trace her thumb along his knuckles. Would he know she caressed him on purpose or would he believe her thumb slipped? Before she could catch a glimpse of his expression, he pivoted in the opposite direction, and she was forced to continue, passing through the pattern.

When she made the circuit and returned to him, she drew herself up as tall as she could. She required every ounce of fortitude she possessed and would draw upon it! If they could not resolve their differences on the dance floor, she would endeavour to keep him in conversation. If she succeeded, he could not believe her still angry when the dance concluded.

"My uncle delivered a letter to your home."

"When?" His forehead crinkled and his jaw was set.

"Not long after I arrived. He hoped to put it in your hand, but was told you were not at home."

"I have spent most of my time as of late with Georgiana."

"I hope she is well."

He swallowed. "She is better."

Better? When they spoke before the Netherfield ball, he had confided that his sister's spirits, by the tone of her correspondence, seemed improved. She must have suffered some sort of emotional setback.

"I had not the pleasure of receiving your uncle's missive, but I have had little time to sort through my post in the past few days. The note may have been mixed with the invitations and business correspondence awaiting me on my desk."

He had not known she was in town. She had waited, assuming he would abandon everything and rush to see her. His note indicated he would, but she had not taken the happenings in his life into account. He was a busy man. His business affairs frequently occupied his time at Netherfield, and he had been away for some time. His desire to spend time with his sister was understandable and laudable. He had no way of knowing that she awaited him.

She turned and caught a glimpse of Colonel Fitzwilliam, who stood along the edge of the dance floor, wearing an insufferable grin. When she pivoted once more, Mr. Darcy was rolling his eyes.

"Your cousin takes great amusement at your expense."

"You have met Richard?"

"I made his acquaintance when we entered, and we danced before your aunt brought me to you."

His hand gripped hers as they turned. "How did you find my cousin?"

"I am not certain."

Mr. Darcy lifted his eyebrows.

"He seems to enjoy the sound of his own voice."

A bark of laughter from him startled those around them. "I suppose that is a polite way of saying he talks too much."

"I believe while you tend to be more circumspect, he says what comes to mind regardless of the audience. I was unsure what to make of him, to be honest." She again wove her way through the dancers in their group until she reached him once more.

"Do not be disturbed by Richard. He may be loquacious, but he is loyal to a fault. Forgive me for not enquiring sooner of your family. I hope they are well."

"They were all well when I last saw them, thank you."

When they came to stand face to face, she started. The set was complete. She had been either caught up in conversation with him or in her own thoughts. What would happen now?

He offered her his arm and escorted her from the dance floor. "Where are your aunt and uncle?"

"They were near the statue of Dionysus in the corner."

His lip curved to one side. "You believe that to be Dionysus?"

"Who else would be bedecked in grapes?"

He gave a low chuckle. "I confess I had not given it much thought."

Her aunt and uncle were missing upon reaching the spot where she last saw them, but when they turned, her eye lit upon a familiar smile. "They are dancing." She could not help but admire the adoring glances her aunt and uncle bestowed upon one another.

"Where do you see them?"

She pointed discreetly in their direction. Once he noted their location, he turned. "Miss Elizabeth—"

"Darcy," interrupted a voice. They both turned as Viscount Milton approached. "My father is requesting to speak with you."

Mr. Darcy's lips thinned. "Please inform him I will attend him when I have a moment."

"He knew you would say as much and insisted you come now. I believe he wants to introduce you to one of his political connections. I whispered in his ear that you could care less. Well, you are aware how well he listens."

"I do not mind waiting for my aunt and uncle here." Elizabeth had to bite her lip at the comical expression of horror that crossed Mr. Darcy's face.

"I shall not leave you unaccompanied."

His cousin made to speak but Mr. Darcy held up his hand. "Miss Elizabeth's aunt and uncle are dancing, but let me ascertain if your mother would welcome her company. Tell your father I shall be there as soon as I am able." With a huff, the viscount pivoted on his heel and was gone.

She took Mr. Darcy's proffered arm, so he could guide her across the ballroom to the countess, who was stepping away from a group of ladies when they came upon her.

"Aunt, your husband sent Milton to drag me into the card room, but Miss Elizabeth's aunt and uncle are dancing. I hesitate to bring her into one of Uncle's—"

Lady Fitzwilliam smiled. "Say no more. The poor dear would be overwhelmed and bored in one fell swoop. Besides, I would be pleased to know her better."

"If only I could cry off with such ease." He gave Elizabeth a short bow. "Please excuse me."

Without another word, he hastened through the nearest door and a hollow sensation in her chest reappeared. How was he so essential to her in such a short period of time?

"Are you enjoying the ball?"

Her head jolted towards the countess. "I am, though I must admit I have never seen the like."

"I do not hold the most ornate events, yet I never have had a complaint."

Elizabeth surveyed the room and the revellers. "And why should you? Everything is lovely."

As her eyes completed the circuit of the room, two ladies came into view, who were whispering behind their fans and staring at her. Lady Fitzwilliam leaned towards Elizabeth.

"Do not mind those two." The older lady drew a bit closer. "They are catty and insufferable. If their husbands were not so important politically, they would not be extended an invitation, I assure you."

The walls began to draw closer. Why could she not take a deep breath?

"Have you greeted Mr. Bingley? I believe you made his acquaintance in Hertfordshire."

"I have not had the opportunity." Her voice was faint and shaky. What was wrong with her?

"Miss Bennet? Are you well?"

Would Mr. Darcy return? Was that to be their only interaction of the night? Would he come to Gracechurch Street now he knew the existence of the letter?

She clutched the fabric on the stomach of her gown. "Air. Might I go outside on the terrace?" Her hand motioned towards a nearby door as she stepped forward.

"This way, my dear." Lady Fitzwilliam grasped her elbow, led her into a room, through a panelled door, and up a flight of stairs. "My first lesson to you about London society. Never use a terrace open to all guests without a chaperon. You never know what sort of rake might importune you."

After following the lady through a corridor and a dimly lit room, the countess opened a door, allowing Elizabeth to step through before her. She stepped forward onto the stone balustrade as the cool night air nipped at the flesh not covered by her gown.

"I cannot be away long."

Elizabeth whirled around. "How silly of me! I did not think."

Lady Fitzwilliam placed a calming hand upon Elizabeth's forearm. "Do not upset yourself. The heat of the ballroom may have been the culprit of your sudden pallor, which has already made a marked improvement."

"If I could have but another moment."

"I shall fetch a maid to escort you to the ballroom when you are ready."

"I thank you for this. I know it must be an imposition."

With a wave of her hand, the countess scoffed. "'Tis nothing. If my other guests were pleased with such ease, I would be the most celebrated hostess of the ton. Do not make haste. I am certain your aunt and uncle will seek me out when they have completed their dance."

The countess departed, and Elizabeth peered down at the garden below. There were indeed a few people partaking of the air on the terrace, one couple walking in the garden, and a few gentlemen enjoying a smoke in the night air.

She tilted her head towards the sky, but it was a starless night. The cloudy November weather had given them nothing but rain and ensured they could not see the twinkling stars overhead. Tonight, the wet weather had subsided, yet the clouds remained.

Eventually, she would be required to return to the ballroom. How was she to remain composed in light of the situation? Mr. Darcy was in attendance yet could not remain by her side due to familial obligations, and she could not pout like an overindulged child who could not have her favourite toy.

"Lord, but I am a silly creature," she breathed.

As he weaved through the crowd in the card room, Darcy grumbled under his breath. Why did his uncle never fail to issue a summons at the most inopportune moments?

Elizabeth was here! She was in his uncle's home, and he was in the card room. The cruelty, the impolitic cruelty! With a firm step, he halted before his uncle, who stood with a man unknown to him, and Richard.

"Ah, Darcy. There you are." He nudged the man beside him with his elbow. "Carlisle, I would like to introduce you to my nephew, Fitzwilliam Darcy. Lord Carlisle is an old school chum of mine. He and I were much like you and Richard, always getting into scrapes of this sort and that."

"A pleasure to make your acquaintance, sir."

Lord Carlisle gave a dip of his chin in acknowledgement. "I was just telling your uncle how you need to meet my wife and daughter during supper." He looked around him and gestured in the direction of a servant. "Of course, if you remain, you could meet Althea when Milton returns her from their set."

Darcy glared at his uncle, who lifted his eyebrows. "I would be pleased to meet them, my lord. I am certain Miss Elizabeth would also be happy to make the acquaintance of other ladies in town. She knows so few."

The portly gentleman's smile fell. "Miss Elizabeth?" His uncle began coughing as he placed a hand upon Darcy's shoulder.

A smug smirk appeared upon Richard's face. "Are we speaking of Miss Elizabeth Bennet? I must say I envy you, cousin. She is a lovely young lady, but I am at a loss as to how you persuaded her to accept an offer of courtship from you."

"Courtship?" Carlisle's brow knitted.

"I would attribute her acceptance to luck." His eyes shifted to Lord Carlisle. "I hope to be so fortunate as to call Miss Elizabeth my betrothed very soon."

His uncle's grip was firm as he regarded Darcy over his spectacles. "You have made your final decision, then."

"I entered into this courtship with the full intention of making Miss Elizabeth Bennet my wife. My choice was fixed from the moment I laid eyes upon her."

While his aunt had introduced him to lady after lady, his uncle had always ensured Darcy met his political allies, who would push their daughters in his direction. They meant well, but he needed to be clear. Their aid was no longer necessary.

"Then I wish you well." The earnest gaze of his uncle relaxed the tense muscles in his upper back.

"Say, where is Miss Bennet?"

"The card room would not be to her liking, so I left her speaking with Lady Fitzwilliam. I hope you gentlemen will excuse me, I promised to hasten my return."

Richard gave a chuckle. "Besotted and not yet betrothed!"

Darcy exhaled and looked to the ceiling. "Has your mother not taught you to never keep a lady waiting?"

"I have known that lesson since I asked for Lady Fitzwilliam's hand. You should return before my wife teaches your young lady to lead you about by the nose." The men at a nearby table turned to stare as his cousin brayed with laughter.

"At least Darcy has found a woman he wishes to wed, unlike my sons." A pointed glare from his uncle quelled Richard's amusement. "Might I remind you that you would not be in danger of returning to the Peninsula if you wed. Have you met any young heiresses?"

Before Richard could speak, his father gestured in the direction of the ballroom. "Find your mother. She will arrange some suitable young lady for you to partner."

Richard opened his mouth.

"Go on with you," his father interjected.

Darcy took his cousin by the arm. "Please excuse us, Uncle. Lord Carlisle."

As they stepped, Richard rent his arm from Darcy's grasp. "He never asks if I desire marriage." He turned and jabbed himself in the chest with his fingers. "Perhaps I enjoy the army!"

"No you do not. I do give you credit for knowing your limitations and not choosing to take orders."

"Ha!" he cried with a jolt. "That was my mother's brilliant plan. Not that I could explain why I would not consider the life of a vicar. Could you imagine that conversation?

"*I could never forgo women until marriage, Mother.* My face would have stung with the force of her hand to my cheek. I had enough of my parent's discipline as a child. I have no need of it now."

Darcy smiled. "Yet you were just disciplined by your father."

"Do not forget I carry a sword, which I have no qualms about using."

"There are dozens of reasons why you will never raise a fist or your sword to me."

Richard stopped and pivoted to face him. His ginger-blond hair appeared redder somehow. "And what are those?"

"Why, the contents of my wine cellars."

The smug grin fell away from Richard's face. "Right you are." With a slap on the back, his cousin propelled Darcy in the direction of his aunt. "I do not see your betrothed."

"I have not yet requested her hand, Richard."

His cousin sniggered. "You have been despondent without her, and she was more than curious about you when we danced. You may as well ask. She will say yes."

He grabbed the epaulette of Richard's coat and tugged him back. "Do you truly believe that?"

"Yes, I do." As he shifted to adjust his uniform, he shook his head. "I assume the two of you had some disagreement since when you returned you were as bluff as bull beef[1], and she is insecure. That said, she appears as downtrodden as your pathetic countenance the last fortnight, and when I discovered who she was, she listened with rapt attention to every word I said about you."

"I wonder if I should—" he whispered.

"Shackle yourself?" He picked at his fingernails as though he were speaking of the weather. "She will make you miserable, but you have been a pathetic prat without her. Cannot see there would be much of a difference."

He gave a low growl as he turned, but Richard grabbed his arm and pulled him back. "I know she is not the eldest, but her elder sister is not here, which makes her Miss Bennet. You might want to watch your address."

Darcy gave a steady glare. "Whether Miss Jane Bennet is in attendance or not, she is Miss Bennet to me, and I shall not refer to Miss Elizabeth by the name of her sister."

Richard made to speak, but Darcy did not wait to listen. Instead, he made his way to his aunt, who was speaking with a footman. Elizabeth was nowhere to be seen. "Did Miss Elizabeth's aunt and uncle retrieve her?"

"No, she needed air."

His eyes shot to the terrace doors. She was outside by herself?

"She is on the balcony off my sitting room." She struck his arm with her fan. "You should know I would not allow her to venture out there without an escort."

"Should I?"

One side of her lips curved. "I would be disappointed if you did not. The privacy will provide the perfect opportunity to talk."

As he made to pass, she caught his hand. "Do not dismiss the maid, Fitzwilliam. I insist she remain to chaperon the two of you."

"Yes, ma'am."

His heart was in his throat. Could they resolve what stood between them? Elizabeth did not appear angry or upset with him. She was not comfortable, but after their misunderstanding, her unease was understandable. His disquiet was certain to be noticeable as well.

The dark circles discernible under her eyes grieved him. Sleep had become a fickle friend for them both it seemed. He, at least, had the luxury of a brandy or two; Elizabeth, however, was not one to drink more than a glass of wine with dinner.

His eyes remained on the floor as he strode from the room. His name was said by a few as he passed, but whether they were calling him, he knew not. A lady tittered as he slipped up the servant's stairway and through a hidden panel to the family corridor.

The maid, who stood inside the room as she awaited Miss Elizabeth, dipped a curtsey. "Sir?"

"Lady Fitzwilliam requested you stay while I have a private conversation with the lady."

The girl's lips curved upwards to one side. "Yes, sir."

He put his hands over his mouth and nose. God help him to say nothing to cause offence!

With a shaky hand, he turned the handle and pushed. The door did not make more than a slight noise when it opened and closed just as quietly. The brisk night air bit at his cheeks. How was she not cold? She stood at the edge of the balcony, staring at the garden, with her hands upon the stone railing and wearing no pelisse, spencer, or shawl to keep her warm. How she was not trembling was a mystery.

He stepped behind her as the rigid control he had been attempting to maintain broke and his forehead rested upon her shoulder. "You are too generous to trifle with me. If your feelings are still what they were at the Netherfield ball, tell me so at once. *My* affections and wishes are unchanged; but one word from you will silence me on this subject for ever."

[1]"bluff as bull beef" "Bluff—Fierce, surly. He looked as bluff as bull beef."
Captain Grose et al. 1811 Dictionary of the Vulgar Tongue

Chapter 18

"You are too generous to trifle with me. If your feelings are still what they were at the Netherfield ball, tell me so at once. *My* affections and wishes are unchanged; but one word from you will silence me on this subject for ever."

Elizabeth's gloved hand rested upon his cheek. "I was such a fool. I should have allowed you to explain rather than allowing my abominable temper to overrule any good sense I might possess." She sniffed and turned, placing her palms upon his chest. "Can you find it in your heart to forgive me?"

His hands grasped hers, holding tight. "A trifling misunderstanding is not enough to separate me from you." A fervent kiss was placed upon each set of her knuckles.

"I hesitate to call our disagreement trifling. My temper was unyielding. I know better than to behave so, yet I feared what you might say."

"You need never be afraid of me. Your heart is dearer to me than the pitiful organ which beats within my chest. I could not break yours without causing irreparable damage to my own. I have been a miserable beast without you."

"A beast?" She raised an eyebrow. "Have you been feasting upon your poor servants and attacking unwary family members?"

"No, but Georgiana would not rest until I divulged all of our acquaintance. My aunt managed to elicit a confession as well." She shuddered; he removed his topcoat and wrapped it around her.

"I did wonder about Lady Fitzwilliam. I thought she might know who I was when we first met, and after our dance, I questioned her excuse of introducing us to one another."

His hands rubbed up and down her arms. "When I asked if I should come here to speak to you, she said she would be disappointed if I did not."

"My aunt and uncle are aware of your connection to Lord and Lady Fitzwilliam. I believe we have been manipulated."

"I have no complaints," he confessed. "Do you?"

"No. On the contrary, I am indebted to them for their aid. I do not know how long I could have waited to resolve our quarrel without becoming fit for Bedlam."

"I planned on attending to business on the morrow. I would have found your uncle's letter and rushed to your side." The light from the windows below was sufficient to reveal the sparkle in her eyes. She was exquisite. Her dark curls were piled upon her head, spilling from the pins in a becoming fashion. Her ivory gown was a better quality than what she wore to the Netherfield ball and enhanced the creamy complexion of her skin as well as the blush of her lips and cheeks.

Her lips! His head dipped, but before he touched her, she placed a hand to his chest. "Your aunt stationed a maid just inside the door."

He peered behind him where the girl stood with her back to them. "She is not watching."

Her tongue peeked out to moisten her lips, and he bent to press a chaste kiss to her irresistible mouth. Her palms pressed against his chest as she rested against his form. They were not alone. They were not alone. He had to keep repeating those words lest he forget himself!

He made to withdraw, but her mouth opened and the warmth of her breath fanned against his face. Lord help him! A guttural noise came from his throat as he claimed her lips with a desperation borne of a fortnight's longing.

Elizabeth did not balk or step away, but responded in equal measure. She did not even flinch when his tongue invaded the warmth of her mouth or grazed her tongue, but mimicked his actions, rendering him senseless. His mind could not form a coherent thought as he clenched the silken fabric of her skirt.

The fingers that combed through his hair now tugged at his curls with a painful pressure, dragging him back to the reality before him. He gently took her top lip between his then bestowed a final kiss to her forehead.

"I should not have lost control."

She lowered from her tiptoes and peeked around his side. "She still faces the other direction." The tinkling laugh he adored rang in his ears. "Lady Fitzwilliam's maid is not much of a chaperon."

"And I am grateful for it." Her entire body shook as she buried her face in his cravat. "Perhaps we can arrange for her to accompany us at all times until we are wed. Your family will be satisfied that propriety is upheld, but we can misbehave to our heart's content."

"Until we are wed?" She pulled back and tilted her head. "I do not remember a proposal of marriage."

He was a leather-headed git! Not that he objected to proposing, but he had yet to do it! Without a word, he dropped to one knee. A tear dropped to the swell of her cheek that she brushed away with her fingers.

"If you kneel, you will ruin your trousers! Please stand."

He chuckled, but did as she asked, stepping closer to her as he rose.

"I have always dreamt of finding a lady who had a distinct preference for my company rather than my pocket book. I searched the crowded balls and dinner parties of the season and did not find her. I tortured myself by attending Almack's, but that plan was a failure as well. I never thought I would find the lady I wished to marry in the wilds of Hertfordshire."

She hiccoughed a laugh and covered her mouth with her hand.

"I have been a reserved man all my life. I prefer a quiet life at Pemberley to the pandemonium of the London season, I prefer to sit in the library before the fire with a book to a ball, and I have only ever required the company of my closest friends and family to ensure my happiness. Since I made your acquaintance, I now require more. I need you. I love you."

He cleared his throat. "Elizabeth Bennet, would you do me the honour of accepting my hand in marriage?"

Her hands wrapped around the back of his neck as she lifted onto her toes and touched her forehead to his. "Yes," she whispered.

His heart leapt at the word—the one simple word that ensured his happiness and made his soul sing. He wrapped his arms around her. "Thank you. I swear you will never regret it."

"Wait."

She drew back, but his hand kept a firm hold of her wrist. She would not change her mind, would she?

"Until we parted at Netherfield, I never knew myself. I thought I did, yet I never let myself acknowledge the full extent of my feelings for you. After I misunderstood you so abominably and you left, I realized a part of my heart remained with you."

He removed his handkerchief from his pocket and began to dab her cheeks. "Elizabeth—"

"No, I want to say this. You deserve to know." She blew out a heavy exhale. "I love you, Fitzwilliam Darcy. I am not whole unless we are together. We shall quarrel in the future and—"

"Hopefully far into the future."

With a chuckle, she stepped back into his embrace. "But I promise to be more reasonable than I was a fortnight ago. I fear my recalcitrance was more an issue with my own confidence than with you."

"What could you possibly have to doubt about yourself?"

"When we were courting, I was lost in the moment and excitement, but after overhearing your conversation with Mr. Bingley, I gave my mother's criticisms and comparisons to Jane more credence than I should."

"Is this the ridiculous notion that you are not as handsome as Miss Bennet?"

"I have heard it all my life."

"And you will never hear it again if I have a say in the matter!" His voice came out as a growl while he pulled her to him and kissed her temple. "With your mother's insufferable proclamations at an end, as well as Bingley wed and off the marriage block, let us hope we have no reason to misunderstand one another as we did at Netherfield."

She shook her head. "You are terrible, Mr. Darcy!"

He brushed a curl from her eyes. "You called me Fitzwilliam earlier. I rather liked it."

Her cheeks turned a becoming shade of pink as she whispered, "Fitzwilliam."

"Oh!" He stepped back, unbuttoned his waistcoat, pulled his fine lawn shirt from his trousers and began to search for what was hidden beneath his collar and cravat. He had to bend at an uncomfortable position, but it paid off when the flesh of his fingertips brushed against the gold chain. With fumbling fingers, he unclasped it, holding the precious piece of jewellery suspended from it so it would not fall.

When he removed the item he needed, he tucked in his shirt, but Elizabeth wore a bewildered expression. "Forgive me, but I have wished to place this on your finger for some time. Now that you have accepted my hand, I find I do not want to wait."

"Even if you remove your clothing to do so?" Her eyebrows lifted upon her forehead.

"I do not have the talent of tying my cravat as intricately as my valet. I do not know if anyone would notice, so I thought to remove this the best way I could."

Once he finished fastening his waistcoat, he took her hand and pulled her closer, removing her glove. "This ring belonged to my mother. It is not the grandest of the Darcy jewels, but the lustre of the pearls reminded me of your complexion." He spread her fingers enough to slide the band into place as her intake of breath drew his eyes to her face.

She tilted her hand to better see the jewels. "It is beautiful. I shall wear it always."

After a quick glance around him and into his aunt's sitting room, she pulled his head down for a kiss he was quite happy to give.

A clock chimed within the house, and she startled. "I should return before my aunt and uncle worry."

"Elizabeth?"

She handed him his topcoat, which he donned without delay.

"Did you read the letter I left with your father?"

"I did, though I must confess not until after I saw the reference to Bingley and your cousin in the gossip column." She closed her eyes. "I cannot apologise enough for my stubbornness."

His thumb grazed her temple. "No more apologies, no more regrets. We begin again tonight."

"Think only of the past as its remembrance gives us pleasure?"

"Precisely." He took her hand and kissed the ring upon her delicate finger. His mother wore it upon her index finger, but Elizabeth was more petite. The band fit her middle finger with ease, yet did not slip from its place.

As he entered his aunt's sitting room, he retained possession of Elizabeth's hand despite the presence of the maid. "Thank you for remaining, but Miss Bennet will be returning to the ball directly." After a curtsey, the girl disappeared through the servant's door as they exited to the corridor where he paused.

His palm pressed against her cheek. "I wish we did not have to return."

Her fingers toyed with the top button of his waistcoat. "I…"

A creak sounded from behind, and Elizabeth dropped her hands. When they both turned, Georgiana's head peeked from the door of her chambers.

"Fitzwilliam?"

He removed his pocket watch and flipped open the cover. "I thought you would have taken your draught by now? Are you well? Could you not sleep?" With a quick stride, he drew up to where she stood, peering around her. "Where is Mrs. Annesley?"

"She is fetching my draught. While I waited, I heard your voice." She glanced towards Elizabeth, who had remained behind. "I would be honoured to make her acquaintance."

"Oh!" He extended his arm and Elizabeth stepped forward with an air of uncertainty. "Please forgive me. I had not meant to abandon you."

"I thought you might require a moment of privacy." Her regard for the feelings of others did her credit, though in this instance, her consideration was not necessary.

"Miss Georgiana Darcy, I am proud to present Miss Elizabeth Bennet."

His sister's eyes bulged. "*The* Miss Elizabeth Bennet? My goodness! Neither my aunt nor my brother indicated you were to attend this evening." She started. "I am exceedingly pleased to make your acquaintance. Surprised, but pleased."

Elizabeth's lip quirked to one side. "I have heard a great deal of good about you, Miss Darcy. I am happy to meet you as well."

Georgiana smoothed her dressing gown. "Please pardon my attire. I had not expected guests."

"Which is understandable. I required air, so your aunt was kind enough to escort me to her sitting room balcony. Otherwise, I should have remained in the ballroom with the rest of the rabble."

His little sister pursed her lips in an attempt not to giggle; however, the tell-tale jolt of her shoulders gave her away. Georgiana was not accustomed to such a sense of humour or teasing unless it was from Richard.

"I do not believe your aunt and uncle would appreciate being referred to as rabble." His tone remained light.

"When we return, we shall join the rabble, shall we not?" Her head tilted as she watched his reaction.

He chuckled. "My aunt's guests would protest being referred to thus."

"You did not have to stand up with them."

"You could have refused."

"Then I could not have danced with you." Her eyebrow arched, and he clenched his hands to refrain from pulling her into his arms. If only he could kiss that mischievous grin from her lips!

A noise from inside Georgiana's room drew their attention, but his sister's expression held his gaze. The largest, most genuine smile he had seen since before Ramsgate adorned her face.

She stepped forward and took Elizabeth's hands. "I must retire for the evening, but I..." Georgiana's fingers traced the pearls down the centre of the ring. "This was my mother's." Her voice was no more than a whisper, but her words and amazed tone were easily discerned. "You have accepted my brother?"

Elizabeth nodded. "I have." Her eyes darted to him and back to his sister. "I hope you have no objections, Miss Darcy."

"No! Of course not! But you must call me Georgiana as we are to be sisters."

"My sisters call me Lizzy if you would care to join them."

Tears welled in Georgiana's eyes, but did not fall. "I have always wished for a sister."

His hand wrapped around Elizabeth's elbow and gave a gentle squeeze. "Now you will have Elizabeth and her sisters. Have I mentioned she has four?"

"I look forward to making the acquaintance of them all." Georgiana kissed his cheek and hugged him. "I am delighted for you, Brother."

"You will return to live with us once we are married?" He had not spoken of the possibility with Elizabeth. She would not object, would she?

"Yes," Georgiana responded with a sniff. "Yes, I will."

He gave her his handkerchief to dab her eyes as she stepped back into her room.

"Lizzy, would you have tea with me one day this week? I hope to know you better before you wed Fitzwilliam." A glint appeared in her eye. "Mrs. Reynolds has told me stories from when my brother was a young boy. I do not mind sharing."

"Georgiana!"

Elizabeth laughed. "I would have come without such temptation, but now that you have mentioned them, I shall hold you to those stories."

"Time for you to retire." His sister would not be telling those tales if he had anything to say about it! After a quick farewell, the door closed.

"She is lovely, Fitzwilliam."

"Her manner is reminiscent of my mother. She was the gentlest of souls." He offered his arm. His heart satisfied when her fingers wrapped around his elbow. "I fear after Ramsgate she will never marry."

"Then I would be content for her to remain with us."

He bestowed a kiss to her curls. Why had he been concerned? "I love you."

"She is the nearest relation you have in this world. I could do no less for you or for her. Home and family are what will help her endure this ordeal. I would be heartless to keep her from such comforts."

"When we next have a moment to ourselves, I must tell you more."

Her eyes closed. "Why do I dread what you must say?"

"She will be well. We shall ensure her future health and happiness. Dread nothing, for I do not wish to dwell on it once it is said. I must forge ahead, and everything in me screams that Georgiana must do the same. She will not heal otherwise."

"I agree."

Every muscle in his body tensed at the notion of their return, but avoiding the throng of people below was not an option. Despite the green-eyed monster within wanting to keep Elizabeth to himself, Darcy led her down the servant's stairs to the corridor off the hall. "I shall go first and await you just inside the ballroom."

He slipped through the door with ease. No cloying mothers or preening young ladies were about, so he purposefully strode through the entry, pausing by one of the large Greek statues along the wall.

Elizabeth had recognised Dionysus. Who was he standing near now? With an upward glance, the lion's skin and head upon the man revealed the statue's identity—Hercules. He stifled his laughter. With any luck, the remainder of the evening would not be a Herculean task!

A woman and her two daughters came to stand nearby. Blast! He spoke to soon! The mother nudged him with her elbow a few times— once painfully as she fiddled with her reticule. She attempted to apologise as an excuse to begin a conversation, but he pretended he did not feel or hear her. Where was Elizabeth?

When she appeared in the doorway, he all but ran to greet her. "Miss Elizabeth, may I escort you to your aunt and uncle?"

Her face lit with happiness. "Why yes, thank you."

Once she took his arm, he leaned a tad closer. "Do you see them?"

"Head in the direction of the refreshment table. Perhaps they are near your aunt."

They wound around those who milled about the edge of the dancing until they spotted his aunt. She stood with a well looking couple—certainly people of fashion.

"Darcy!" cried Richard. "How did you find Miss Darcy? I assume she has retired for the evening."

Why was Richard speaking for all to hear? He was standing close enough to be heard and Darcy was by no means deaf.

"My sister is well and has indeed retired for the night."

His aunt steered him closer by the arm. "Mr. Fitzwilliam Darcy, I would like you to make the acquaintance of Mr. Edward Gardiner and his wife Marianne. Mr. Gardiner inherited his cousin's estates, Dawley Court in Cambridgeshire and Netherfield Park in Hertfordshire."

"I have heard a great deal of you from Miss Elizabeth." He shook Mr. Gardiner's hand. "Please forgive me for not responding to your recent letter. My butler must have placed it with my business correspondence, which I have not yet had the opportunity to sort."

Mr. Gardiner waved his apology away. "Think nothing of it. In fact, I informed Lizzy myself of the likelihood of such a circumstance as similar mistakes have occurred within my own business."

"Thank you for your understanding."

"I do hope we will have your company soon." The softer and higher pitch voice drew his attention to Mrs. Gardiner. "You are welcome to call at your earliest convenience."

"I look forward to it." Elizabeth's hand squeezed his arm. "I shall need to travel to Longbourn within the next se'enight, but I do expect I shall call often."

Richard rolled his eyes, stepped around, and gave a small bow. "I requested the next set from a young lady, so if you will excuse me." He lifted Elizabeth's hand but did not complete his farewell as he gaped at her finger.

"You actually asked her to marry you at a ball, Darcy?" With a snicker, Richard kissed her hand. "I knew he was eager, but I thought he would wait at least a day or two."

His mother slapped his wrist with her fan. "Go see to your partner and stop goading your cousin. You would do well to follow his example."

Mrs. Gardiner pulled Elizabeth aside, examining her ring and speaking in hushed tones as Richard stalked off with his mother following close behind. In the meantime, Mr. Gardiner took Richard's closer spot to Darcy.

"Lizzy's father sent a note with her to London in which he gave his permission for your betrothal. If you do not wish to journey to Longbourn, it is not required of you."

"For the last fortnight in London, I kept myself occupied with the usual estate matters, but I also had Miss Elizabeth's settlement prepared in the event she agreed to speak to me again."

"You were rather confident," stated Mr. Gardiner with a teasing grin.

"On the contrary, I was clutching for some shred of hope that she would absolve me of guilt—that she would make me the happiest of men."

"I have no doubt she will do just that, Mr. Darcy."

He peered to the side where Elizabeth gazed at him from the corner of her eye. "She already has."

Chapter 19

Elizabeth stretched as the morning sun filtered through a gap in the bed curtain and gasped. With haste, she drew back the heavy fabric blocking the light and lifted her hand to ensure the stunning ring Mr. Darcy placed upon her finger truly existed.

In the early morning light, fresh from sleep, her memory of the night prior was a beautiful dream, but she wanted it to be more. She pinched her thigh and hissed at the piercing sting. Definitely no fantasy!

With a gentle touch, she fingered the pearls to further solidify the night before in her mind. What a broken-hearted creature she would have been had she awakened to find their reconciliation and betrothal no more than a creation of her own mind.

A soft rap came from the door. Betsy peeked inside. "I come to replenish the fire, miss."

"Of course." She rose and donned her slippers to prevent the chill of the floors from freezing her toes. As Betsy worked, Elizabeth sat at the small escritoire in the corner and penned a quick letter to Jane, sealing it as the maid finished her chore.

"When you are ready, a late breakfast is laid out in the dining room. Mrs. Gardiner is in the parlour."

"Has Mr. Gardiner left for his warehouse?"

"Yes, miss. He left before sun-up this morning."

Elizabeth peered down at the missive for Jane. Hopefully, her father would not mind the expense of such a short note; she could not bear to wait until she had more time. After all, Fitzwilliam would be here...

She glanced at the clock. Oh my, he would arrive in less than an hour!

"Betsy!" The girl paused at the door. "Please see this is put in the post?"

"Yes, miss." With a quick dip, she disappeared through the door.

Elizabeth rose and opened the cupboard, sorting through the gowns within. Her fingers brushed against a pale green she had always favoured and pulled it from the peg to hold it by the shoulders. "I think he will like this one."

As she took a seat before the dressing table, another knock startled her. "Come in!"

Aunt Gardiner bustled in with her maid in tow. "Millie will help you prepare for the day." Elizabeth opened her mouth, but her aunt held up a hand. "I know you are capable of doing for yourself, but like last night, you will be expected to look and dress to a certain standard. I do this to aid your acceptance into the ton. Lady Fitzwilliam may have callers today, and you must look every bit the gentleman's daughter rather than that of a simple country squire."

She lifted her chin and sat taller. She wanted to appear at her best for no one other than Fitzwilliam, yet her aunt was likely correct. Fitzwilliam would also expect her to have a lady's maid once they were wed. Perhaps she should become more accustomed to the practice now rather than later.

Even with Millie's help, preparing for the day was more time consuming. Hairstyles were more intricate; stays were cinched tighter. When she took in her appearance in the looking glass, she balked. Her attire and coiffure were supposed to be more elaborate last night, but for the day, she was overdressed, and her stays were digging into her ribs. Why was she not allowed to breathe?

"Do you not like the hair, miss?"

She tilted her head and studied herself in the glass before her. "I do, but I am unaccustomed to such finery for a simple call."

Aunt Gardiner placed her hands upon her shoulders. "Yet that is how people of fashion behave."

"Does Mr. Darcy truly expect this?"

Her aunt excused the maid. "You adored this gown when we purchased it for you, and never took issue with wearing it before today. Why are you questioning matters all of a sudden?"

"I feel different."

"You do not regret accepting him?"

"No!" Elizabeth fidgeted with the wrist of the long sleeve. "I suppose I am concerned with the differences between being Miss Bennet and Mrs. Darcy; how I shall change."

"Lizzy, he will expect you to dress to his station once you are wed, though I doubt he has given it much thought as of yet. Every person who enters the state of matrimony alters, but though you may change, you will remain the same in essentials—what he loves about you will not disappear."

Her aunt turned Elizabeth around to face her. "I can tell you from my experience that both of you will find more to love about one another as time passes. What I adored about Edward when we first wed still exists but is not the attribute I hold dearest at this moment." She shook her head. "I do not know if this makes sense."

The slight concern, which had begun to become louder as the morning progressed, quieted. "I believe I understand."

Aunt Gardiner's expression brightened. "That is good since I do not know how else to explain it." She pointed to the dressing table. "Do not forget your reticule. You will not have much time for breakfast before Mr. Darcy arrives."

She reached back and grasped her bag, hurrying down the stairs after her aunt, who drank tea and chatted with Elizabeth while she ate. When a knock sounded at the door, they had only just situated themselves within the parlour.

Voices from the hall grew louder until the housekeeper bustled inside. "Mr. Darcy to see Miss Bennet, ma'am."

"Thank you, Mrs. Henderson."

Mr. Darcy moved around the servant as she exited, and bowed. "I hope I find you ladies well this morning."

With a nod, her aunt curtsied. "Quite, Mr. Darcy. Thank you."

"I am pleased to hear it." His intense gaze settled upon Elizabeth, and a fluttering erupted within her belly. "I did locate Mr. Gardiner's letter as well as one from Mr. Bennet once I returned to Darcy house early this morning."

Elizabeth's breath caught in her throat. "You conducted your search when you returned from the ball?"

"I did. We may have come to an understanding without the correspondence, but I wished to read them myself—in particular the words you wrote. I also penned a response to your father. I do need to travel to Longbourn for the settlement, though I confess to desiring a day or two in your company first."

Her aunt's raised eyebrows were visible out of the corner of her eye, but she would not turn lest her face burn crimson.

Madeline, Grace, and Lewis burst through the door and halted as if they had hit a stone wall. "Lizzy!"

The children took a sudden step back as Aunt Gardiner moved around Mr. Darcy. "The three of you know better than to burst into the parlour, not to mention running within the house." She continued to glare at her children. "Please excuse them, Mr. Darcy. They adore Lizzy and attempt to claim as much of her time as their father and I shall permit. I daresay they did not realize we had a guest."

"I can hardly blame them since I would hope to have as much time with Miss Elizabeth as you will allow." Elizabeth swallowed a giggle and placed her palm over her mouth as Fitzwilliam knelt before her young cousins. "And what is your favourite activity with Miss Elizabeth?"

Lewis looked to the ceiling for a moment in thought and then grinned at Mr. Darcy. "Lizzy is the best at Conkers!"

"Is she?" His lip curved as he peered in her direction.

"She is! She always wins."

With a huff, Madeline stepped forward. "Conkers are a bore! You always complain when you lose, too." His sister placed her hands upon her hips. "Lizzy is the best at reading aloud. She pretends to be all the characters in the story."

Elizabeth covered her cheeks with her palms, allowing them to cool her heated face.

Mr. Darcy leaned towards Madeline as though sharing a secret with her young cousin. "What is your favourite story?"

"Any tale by Mother Goose." The young girl's eyes glowed as she mentioned the tales she begged Elizabeth to read. Thank heavens there were multiple stories, lest Elizabeth beg for a new book!

He stood and tilted his head towards her. "Do you read from the original Perrault?"

"I have read Perrault, but my uncle has a version of Samber's translations. If it is not their bedtime, the children will read along with me. Madeline has just begun to learn French, so I am certain we shall read Perrault together when she can understand them better."

"Your plan is a sound one. Her prior knowledge of the stories should aid with the vocabulary she lacks."

When they were not attending, Lewis had stepped forward and now pulled at Fitzwilliam's sleeve. "Who are you?"

Aunt Gardiner gasped. "Lewis!"

Fitzwilliam gave that low chuckle that made her knees wobble and turned to face the children. "I am Fitzwilliam Darcy."

After a swift glance at his mother, Lewis narrowed his eyes at the interloper. "Why are you so interested in *our* Lizzy?"

"Lewis!" Elizabeth bit her lip as she and her aunt cried out at the same moment. His mother should be the one to reprimand him for his behaviour rather than Elizabeth, but how could he be so impolite?

"Apologise to Mr. Darcy this instant, young man."

Lewis stared at his shoes as his body almost caved into a hunched position. "Please forgive me, Mr. Darcy."

Fitzwilliam maintained a serious mien though a twinkle in his eye betrayed his amusement. "I believe the fault is mine. I should have introduced myself more fully." He held out his hand, at which Lewis frowned, but took. "My name is Mr. Fitzwilliam Darcy. I am betrothed to your cousin, Elizabeth."

Lewis peered around Fitzwilliam. "You are leaving?"

"Not today." She stepped just behind Fitzwilliam and placed her hand on his shoulder. "In fact, we have not yet set a date, but once I am married, I shall still spend time with you."

"You could also journey to Pemberley to visit," suggested Fitzwilliam in a hopeful tone. "We have lots of places for you to play out of doors, a stream begging for an able bodied fisherman to pluck a few trout or pike from its waters, and a stable with horses to carry you around the peaks near the estate."

Lewis' wary eyes transformed as Fitzwilliam spoke, and he began to bounce as the description of Pemberley continued. "Can we, Mama?"

"Not today. Mr. Darcy and Lizzy must wed first." Her son's lip protruded in an excessive pout. "But I want to go now."

Her aunt folded her arms across her chest. "I believe you should return to Mrs. Bunting for your lessons, or I shall have Nanny Kate put you down for a nap."

Young Madeline's eyes bulged. "Yes, Mama." She stumbled as she curtsied. "It was a pleasure to make your acquaintance, Mr. Darcy." Without another word, she slipped through the door.

Her brother, however, was not as prompt at taking his leave. "But I want Lizzy to read to us."

"If you behave, she will read to you before bed tonight. As it is, Lizzy will be late for the call she is supposed to make today."

Hopeful blue orbs turned to her. "Do you promise?"

"As long as you are a good boy for Mrs. Bunting and Nanny Kate." His body sagged before he shuffled from the room.

"I apologise for their manners. Lewis has never been so forward."

Using a nearby chair, Fitzwilliam pushed himself to his feet and shook out his leg, which must have ached from kneeling for so long. "Please do not make yourself uneasy. They love Elizabeth and wish to spend time with her. I can hardly blame your son for his possessiveness. After all, it was I who threw propriety to naught and introduced her as my betrothed last night."

"My father sanctioned the match through my uncle. You did nothing scandalous."

A giggle escaped his aunt's lips. "By the expressions of a few of the ladies, Mr. Darcy's betrothal alone was a scandal. In particular the one... I do not remember her being introduced to us."

"I confess to not listening as my aunt was making the introduction."

"I believe the daughter's name was Althea." Elizabeth shrugged.

Fitzwilliam grimaced. "I do remember her mother painfully elbowed me in the ribs several times while I awaited you near the entrance. Her terrible attempt to garner my attention gained not even a glare in her direction, I am afraid."

"Did she really?" Elizabeth's tone conveyed her astonishment.

"Yes, she did." He pulled his pocket watch from his coat. "I do not mean to be rude, but we shall not be at Clarell House by eleven if we continue to talk."

Aunt Gardiner helped Elizabeth, who had just retrieved her reticule and pelisse from a side table. "You need not fret about offending me. You indicated last night you would bring a maid?"

"Yes, Ruth awaits us in the carriage."

Her aunt gave a satisfied nod as she adjusted Elizabeth's collar. "I appreciate your willingness to provide the service. I intend to hire more help for the move, but I admit to being behind. We have had so much to prepare in advance with the new house."

"It is no bother. If you require any aid in the endeavour, I can introduce you to my housekeeper. She might know of some worthy candidates."

Elizabeth placed her hand upon his sleeve. "What a wonderful idea!"

"I would appreciate any help she might offer." Aunt Gardiner walked with them to the door, and once they were within the plush interior of the carriage, waved and closed the door.

While his maid stared out of the window, Darcy shifted in his seat. How he wanted to whisper in Elizabeth's ear! He wished to tell her how happy he was they were betrothed, how pleased he was to be spending the day with her. Well, a myriad of nothings that were everything. His heart was so full of her, yet he could not express such sentiments. How could he speak of his feelings with a servant present? They were not for all to hear—only Elizabeth.

"I look forward to having tea with Georgiana."

His eyes darted to Elizabeth. "She has been desirous of meeting you for some time, so I know she is anticipating today as well."

"Have you had an opportunity to speak with her since last night?"

"I slept later than is my wont and came directly to Gracechurch Street for you."

She laced her fingers together, set her hands upon her lap, and tilted her head as she appraised him but did not say a word. He wished to touch her—nothing scandalous, mind you. A touch to her fingers or wrist would satisfy, but with the presence of the maid, he swallowed his disappointment and held her gaze instead.

A hint of a smile graced her lips as they rode to Clarell House. Was her pleasure from being in his presence, or was she amused? Where was Miss Bennet when she was needed?

Upon their arrival, he alighted to the pavement and waved away the footman. Any excuse to take her hand, whether they wore gloves or not, would be seized without delay; however, before she exited the carriage, the driver climbed down and approached.

"I beg your pardon, Mr. Darcy, but I need to speak with you."

Kirby had never behaved as such. What could not possibly wait until their return to Darcy House?

"Now?"

He nodded with his entire upper body as he held his hat before him. "Yes, sir."

A squeeze of his arm redirected his attention. "I shall await you here."

"Are you certain?"

"I shall be well for a few minutes. I do not think he would request a word were it not important."

After a kiss to her knuckles, he followed Kirby a few feet away while the driver shifted his hat in his hands.

"As I said, please forgive the interruption, sir, but I thought it important to tell you that I believe someone has been following us."

He took a step closer and leaned forward. "Following us? You are certain?"

The driver dropped his hands to his sides. "Yes, sir. I remember seeing his horse this morning as we prepared to depart Darcy House. I noticed him again in Cheapside while I awaited you and Miss Bennet. I asked young Leonard to keep an eye out since he rides on the back, and he watched the man follow us from Gracechurch Street to here."

"Do you know who this man is?"

"No, sir. Never seen him before."

Darcy's eyes swept the street for any sign of someone familiar. "Is he nearby?"

"When I stopped, he continued into the park on the corner."

Who would want to follow him and why? No one was visible at the moment in the trees on that side of the park. "Please inform me if you see this man following us again. I cannot imagine how this could be a coincidence, but I want to be certain you did not simply see two similar horses."

"Sir, I have worked with horses since I was a wee lad. I *know* the horse was the same. Had a wide blaze down his nose that covered one eye, which was blue. He's also a tall one—at least sixteen hands—with a white sock and hoof on the front left leg."

His driver could not be mistaken with such a detailed accounting of the mount. "Very well, I know not of what I can do at the moment, but I want to know if this continues. Do you understand?"

"Yes, sir."

"Thank you for informing me so swiftly."

Kirby gave a bow and climbed back atop his spot as Darcy returned to Elizabeth. The butler awaited them at the door, so he offered his betrothed his arm and followed the butler to the drawing room where all in attendance stood. When had this become a family affair?

Bingley stepped forward with a joyous countenance. "Miss Elizabeth, no, you are Miss Bennet at the moment! I am pleased to see you again. I hope you are well."

Elizabeth's eyes sparkled and danced in amusement. "I am, thank you."

"And your family?" Darcy suppressed a roll of his eyes as Bingley rolled up and down on his toes. Bingley was the only person he knew who bounced when he was cheerful.

"They were well when I departed Longbourn three days ago. I was pleased to hear of your betrothal. I wish you great joy."

"You are very kind." He started. "Oh! But you have not met my betrothed, have you? I thought I noticed you at the ball, but by the time I was certain it was you, I fear we could not break away to greet you."

"Do not trouble yourself, Mr. Bingley. Never have I been in such a crowded ballroom. It is a wonder the guests were able to find their friends much less speak to them."

"But you happened upon Darcy." He drew a young lady to his side. "Miss Elizabeth Bennet, may I present my betrothed, Miss Anne de Bourgh."

Anne stepped forward, without any of the usual formalities, and embraced Elizabeth, whose arms remained outstretched as she gaped at Darcy. "I am thrilled to make your acquaintance, Miss Bennet." She drew back but clasped her hands before her. "Forgive me. I am not typically so forward, but you must understand. Just this morning, my aunt informed me of your understanding with Fitzwilliam, and I could not be more satisfied by the announcement. I do not know if you are aware, but with the exception of a season in town, my mother has insisted Fitzwilliam and I were to marry. Your betrothal means Charles and I have less of an argument with her over ours."

Elizabeth glanced from Bingley to him. "I thought Lord Fitzwilliam's permission for your marriage ended your mother's wish."

Anne gave a laugh. "You have never met my mother, have you? She will campaign for my uncle to call off our wedding until the vicar pronounces us husband and wife. Your understanding with Fitzwilliam, however, removes some of her ire from us."

The pink faded from Elizabeth's cheeks. "I am glad we could be of assistance."

The door opened, and Georgiana hastened towards their group. "I hope I am not late." She peered at Anne. "You have not done what you said you would at breakfast this morning?"

"Why should I not?" Anne held her chin a little higher than was her wont, making her resemble her mother more than she would prefer.

Georgiana crossed her arms over her chest with an amusing huff. "We are pleased for their betrothal for better reasons than yours."

Loud voices came from the hall, prompting them all to turn as his Aunt Charlotte and Uncle William entered with Lady Catherine.

Lady Catherine halted upon her notice of Elizabeth and raised her cane. "And who is this upstart?"

Darcy pulled his arm closer in an attempt to draw Elizabeth nearer to him. "Lady Catherine de Bourgh, may I present my betrothed, Miss Elizabeth Bennet."

His imperious aunt walked forward, her cane thudding with each step. "You are to wed Anne."

"Mother, no more! Uncle has signed the marriage settlement and the official announcement will appear in tomorrow's paper. I shall be Mrs. Charles Bingley this season whether you approve or not."

Lady Catherine's cane struck the floor. "Such insolence! And from my own flesh and blood! I have told you on repeated occasions, including the ball, that I shall never sanction this marriage. Are the shades of Rosings to be polluted by a tradesman?"

Anne stepped closer Bingley. "Then perhaps you would prefer to reside in the dower house."

A shrill whistle came from Lady Catherine as she sucked air between her teeth. "You would not *dare!*"

"Charles and I do not wish to spend our days listening to your diatribes. If you cannot accept our marriage or even my cousin's betrothal to Miss Bennet, then I shall see you removed from Rosings."

"It is her right, Catherine." The resonant voice of his uncle carried with ease through the large room. "Rosings has belonged to Anne for the last two years. She may do as she desires. Many women are moved to the dower cottages without choice, yet Anne allows you to decide where you will live. If you find yourself unhappily installed in Rose Cottage, you will have no one to blame but yourself."

His obstinate aunt straightened her spine as her eyes moved from her brother, to him, to Elizabeth, to Anne, and finally to Bingley where they narrowed. She gave a huff and dropped into the nearest chair.

"Do you have nothing to say?" asked Anne in an incredulous voice.

"You do not desire me to speak my mind, so I shall not say another word."

Anne rolled her eyes, and Bingley whispered, "If only we could be so fortunate."

A stifled laugh came from Darcy, and he gulped in an attempt not to make a sound as Anne swatted her betrothed's arm with her fan. They were indeed fortunate that Lady Catherine gave no indication she heard his remark.

Maids began to deliver the tea service, so Darcy sat upon the sofa with Elizabeth between himself and Georgiana. With the exception of a quiet and resentful Lady Catherine, his family took a great interest in Elizabeth, enquiring of her preferences and her family. None of their interactions were forced or stilted as Elizabeth was accepted as a part of the Fitzwilliam clan.

That evening, once Darcy had returned his betrothed to Gracechurch Street, he poured a glass of brandy, sat at his desk to review the day's correspondence, and allowed his mind to wander to the day's conversations.

Elizabeth did her best to become acquainted with all present, in particular Georgiana, who observed Elizabeth with a rapt fascination and attempted to make conversation with his betrothed at every opportunity. In the meantime, Elizabeth managed, with grace, to give his sister as much attention as she could without being rude to the remainder of his family, which was gratifying.

A rap at the door prompted him to jolt from where he stared at the fire. "Enter."

Without ceremony, Richard strode through the entry, swinging it closed behind him, and made his way to the liquor tray. "I have had a devil of a day, Darce! You have no idea how I would have preferred to sit around in my mother's drawing room and sip tea rather than deal with miscreants."

Darcy took a long drink from his glass. "What *are* you blathering on about?"

"When I returned to London but a few days after you, I ensured Wickham was transferred to a regiment nearer town. A few pounds in the right palms, and I not only had his commission transferred to the regulars, but also had him leaving for the continent in January."

The chair squeaked as Darcy sat forward. "I shall reimburse you the expense."

Richard swallowed and stared into his glass. "I daresay you will since I have not told you all yet."

Darcy lifted his eyebrows.

Richard downed the rest of his brandy, swore, and stood to refill his glass. "The unit to which Wickham is now assigned is comprised of troops in training to be sent forward, locate enemy camps, and fire upon them."

His blood ran cold. "You intend for him to be killed in battle."

"He deserves it and do not dare tell me he does not. I wanted to call him out at Ramsgate, but you prevented it for fear of damaging Georgiana's reputation beyond repair. In hindsight, you were correct, but I want the bastard to pay!" He had not poured more than a gulp that was downed in a swift movement before the glass was hurled into the fire. The flames bloomed from the remnants of the alcohol on the glass and then steadied.

"I want retribution as well." Darcy's tone was calm and steady. Richard could not be inflamed more than he was already. "I know this is not as calculated as murder, but in some way, it feels the same. He was my father's godson. We were raised—"

With a violent movement, Richard's arm shot out as he pointed. "Do not get sentimental! Do not! I can guarantee he has no affection or loyalty towards you. He has proven he would do anything to revenge himself upon you and claim any Darcy money he can get his thieving hands upon." The crystal decanter clinked against the glass as he filled another to the top.

"I know." Darcy put the heels of his hands to his eyes. His head was beginning to throb. "I just worry."

"You fret like a woman." He bared his teeth as he swallowed. "You also expressed concern about Wickham in such proximity to the Bennet family—a valid consideration with five daughters, I might add. Now that you are betrothed to Miss Bennet, Wickham would make sport of them just to hurt you."

"Has he been removed from Hertfordshire yet?" The thought of Wickham using his evil to harm him through the Bennets was not new. He needed the blackguard away from Meryton before the announcement of his betrothal made the papers.

"Wickham journeyed to London yesterday, reported to his new commander, and has since disappeared."

"Disappeared?"

Richard gave a mirthless laugh. "Wickham always was chicken-hearted. I would wager he learnt what his new assignment entailed and took French leave."

"You believe he deserted?"

"He was given no time away and his new commander has no tolerance for such behaviour. As it has only been a few days, I received a note from his commanding officer this morning. His desertion will be official if Wickham does not appear before tomorrow morning." His cousin raised his eyebrows with a hint of a wicked smile upon his lips. "Do you want to know the best part?

"I want you to tell me all, so yes." Why did Richard ask such exasperating questions?

"One of the officers with whom Wickham shared quarters was missing a substantial amount of money after Wickham's disappearance."

Darcy shifted forward. "How much?"

"Almost fifty pounds, it seems. Lieutenant Denny had saved part of the money, but had also had a lucky night at cards as well. It is believed Wickham stole the funds to facilitate his departure."

A knock startled them. Darcy took a deep breath and ran his fingers through his hair. "Enter."

"I beg your pardon, sir," said the butler as he entered, "but one of Lord Fitzwilliam's footmen, a Matthew Thacker, has appeared at the servant's entrance. He claims Colonel Fitzwilliam expects him."

Richard nodded as he gulped down his last mouthful of brandy. "Yes, please bring him up."

"What is this?"

"Matthew came to me after the ball with information he happened to overhear. I thought you should know and asked him to meet me here this evening."

"You could have simply forwarded what he heard. Did you think I would not trust you?"

"It is not a matter of trust, but that Matthew can give a first-hand account should you have questions."

A skinny young man still dressed in his livery was ushered into the room, and the door closed behind him. With a bob at Richard, he shifted his hat in his hands. "Sir, I came right on the hour, just as you said."

Darcy stood, walked around his desk, and leaned back upon it. "I understand you overheard gossip of me. I assume it must be damaging for my cousin to have you excused from work to come here."

"'Twas no rumour, sir."

No rumour? Darcy folded his arms over his chest. "Nevertheless, please tell me what you witnessed."

He looked between Richard and Darcy and cleared his throat. "As the last of the guests were leaving Lady Fitzwilliam's ball, I waited behind the servant's entrance to the front hall. Mr. Wilson had told me to go through and gather punch cups and wine glasses, but he was adamant I not enter the hall until all the guests had left. As I stood there, a lady and her daughter were putting on their coats and hats while they awaited the rest of their party.

"The young miss was whining because her mother promised her something—well, promised her you. She heard or was introduced to your betrothed during the ball and was right angry you weren't to marry her."

He was going to beat Richard. Incidents such as this were not unexpected, so why would he drag this young man to his home to recount idle chatter.

Richard held out his glass. "Just wait, Darcy. There is more."

"As I recall," continued Matthew, "the mother said, 'Mr. Darcy may be betrothed, but he is not married yet. We shall rid Mr. Darcy and ourselves of the little bunter.'

"I peeked through the door to see the daughter grin. She said, 'I can see to it he rips my gown at an opportune moment.'

"Her mother did not seem to like that idea. I believe her words were 'We shall not sully your reputation to win him—such methods may not bring us the success you desire, but leave you ruined. I believe Mr. Darcy to be one of those men who would leave your reputation in tatters should you succeed in your attempt. I have other ideas.'"

Richard's eyebrows lifted. "What do you think?"

"To be honest, I am unsure." He looked to Matthew. "Can you describe the young lady?"

"She had brown hair. Her gown was white but had a..." He gestured down his sides with his forehead furrowed. "Slight fabric in blue covering the white. You could see the white through the blue. I do not understand women's fashions. I am no abigail."

Darcy set his hands before him on the desk and looked to Richard. "He means an overlay, but how many ladies attended the ball in a similar gown?"

Richard shrugged. "Or had brown hair?"

"I don't often work above stairs, so I don't know the guests by name. I also didn't see the mother's face. I'm sorry."

The young man's slight body shook when Richard clapped him on the shoulder. "Do not distress yourself. We may not know the identity of the ladies, but we have some warning of their intentions. You have helped us immensely."

Darcy withdrew a sovereign from his pocket and passed it to Matthew, whose eyes widened upon seeing the reward. "If you hear anything further, please tell the colonel or you can come to Darcy House to inform me. Do you understand?"

"Thank you, sir!"

Richard spoke in a softer voice as he escorted Matthew out of the door. Once they had their privacy once again, he retrieved his glass from the mantelpiece. "What do you think?"

"It could be naught but an angry mama venting her frustration."

Richard plopped into a chair by the fire and adjusted his sabre at his side. "You cannot deny that it might be a valid concern."

"It is unfortunate Matthew did not know the identity of the ladies."

"He is young and not of a similar height to the rest of the footmen. At dinners, Wilson uses footmen of similar height so they appear uniform as they stand along the wall. Matthew polishes a great deal of silver or is stationed in the corridors when needed. He is not amongst company often."

Richard took a drink from his glass. "How do you intend to proceed?"

"Not much can be done unless they act." He gave a shuffling kick to the floor in front of him. "Women of the ton scheme and brag about who they intend to wed or ruin, yet it is not commonplace to hear of one of these machinations amounting to anything. I doubt we have cause for concern. We must wait and hope their threats are no more than idle words."

"I do not like to wait," groused Richard.

He could not blame his cousin. Waiting was never something Darcy did well, and a threat to Elizabeth riled every bit of him to act. But what could one do when the threat may not be legitimate and the identity of the ladies was unknown? He took a burning gulp of his own brandy.

"Do you intend to tell Elizabeth?"

"No, I am certain it is idle talk. I see no reason to spoil this time by speaking of a circumstance I doubt will take place."

Richard cocked his head to one side as his eyebrows rose to near his hairline. "I hope you are correct, cousin."

Darcy studied the pattern on the carpet below. "I hope so, too."

Chapter 20

December 14th 1811
Longbourn

My dear Lizzy,

I do not have the words to express my happiness at the news of your betrothal. Mama has not ceased offering your praises since Mr. Darcy's arrival this very morning. She is ecstatic and speaks of nothing but the pin money, the jewels, and the gowns you will have. Her priorities are misguided, but she is proud of you, which must be gratifying. She ordered the carriage readied as soon as Mr. Darcy set foot in Papa's library, and I venture the entire neighbourhood will be aware of your betrothal by luncheon if she has her way.

Dearest Elizabeth, I want you to know I hope and pray for your joy with as much fervour as Mama's gossip. I may not be as vocal as my mother, but it does not diminish my feelings on the matter. I am ecstatic for you. You desired a marriage based on love, and your dream will be fulfilled. I can think of no better way to ensure happiness in your future life.

In light of your betrothal, I must make a confession, so you do not feel you must protect me from future encounters with Mr. Bingley. If asked when Mr. Bingley first departed, I might have claimed his return to the neighbourhood with his new wife would bring me pain, yet his name does not disturb me as it ought—not if I truly cared for him as I once believed. Since you departed Longbourn, I have had time to think and realize that neither the mention of his name nor the thought of his appearance bring me so much as an ache in my chest. His notice flattered me, but I was not attached. Please believe me sincere in this matter as I would not wish for such a trivial matter to prevent us from being in company in the future.

This morning, when Mr. Darcy was shown into the parlour, Mama inquired directly if Mr. Bingley intended to return to Netherfield, and I felt naught but an idle curiosity on the subject. At least until Mama said, "If he does not intend to return, then he should quit the place altogether." I was mortified, Lizzy. Her tone was so rude! I am certain you would have scolded her had you been present. I must admit that your Mr. Darcy bore her improper declaration with aplomb, which is a testament to his love for you.

Yet, I digress. I am in earnest in regards to Mr. Bingley. I anticipate attending your nuptials and do not have a concern of meeting the gentleman again. After reading your account of a London ball, I have no desire to be a part of that society. I would not deflect their barbs and harsh words with the ease and wit you display on a daily basis. I fear I would be made a fool and my feelings injured in the process. A smaller society, such as Meryton, would serve me better. I only hope I can convince Mama of my wishes.

A footman was just sent to prepare Mr. Darcy's horse, so I must conclude this letter in order to place it in his hands for his return. He is too kind to deliver this missive, and I am indebted to him for his generosity.

> *Yours ever,*
>
> *Jane*

Elizabeth shifted in the window seat, folded the letter with care, and ran her finger across the folds. The honesty of her sister was in most cases absolute, but was Jane diminishing her feelings for Mr. Bingley? Her elder sister might if she felt Elizabeth would worry for her heart during the wedding.

"Jane must have had some interesting news for you to read her note again," observed Aunt Gardiner as she embroidered.

She blew her fringe out of her eyes. "She spends the greater part of the correspondence claiming she feels naught for Mr. Bingley, entreating me not to have concern over them meeting again. I cannot decide whether she means to prevent my fretting, or if she is in earnest."

"You have no way of divining the accuracy of her statements without being in her presence. Even then, her serenity may be deceiving. My advice is to take her words as truth and enjoy this time of your life. You will only wed Mr. Darcy once."

She could not help the smile that overspread her face. With the exception of the day he spent traveling to and from Longbourn, Fitzwilliam had called daily. He never appeared without flowers or a book from his library for her to read. He was too good to her.

"His small gifts and obvious regard do him credit. His love for you knows no bounds. Your uncle and I enjoy seeing his adoration for you so freely displayed upon his countenance. If we have not told you before, we like him very much."

"I am pleased you approve."

Aunt Gardiner placed her needlework in her lap. "As long as he was suitable, we could never disapprove your choice. We are just overjoyed to find him as in love with you as you are with him."

A movement on the street drew her attention to the Fitzwilliam carriage that pulled before the house, its crest unmistakeable to all who passed. As they expected Lady Fitzwilliam and Georgiana for tea, Elizabeth tucked Jane's letter into the book of poetry she brought from her bedchamber and stood.

Lady Fitzwilliam stepped down and glanced around her while she awaited her niece, who joined her a moment later, though not as composed. Georgiana fidgeted with her reticule as Lady Fitzwilliam put a hand to Georgiana's elbow to steer her up the steps.

"Lizzy?"

She turned and joined her aunt at the sofa as Lady Fitzwilliam's voice was heard in the front hall.

The housekeeper entered and stood against the open door. "Lady Fitzwilliam and Miss Darcy."

Georgiana hurried over to Elizabeth and took her hands. "I am thrilled to be here. Thank you for inviting me." Despite her words, Georgiana eyes darted about the room, and she shifted from foot to foot.

"Please take a seat." Aunt Gardiner motioned to the sofa and chairs, but Lady Fitzwilliam stayed her aunt with a touch to her aunt's forearm.

"I hope I am not being presumptuous, but if you have no objection, I thought we might have our own tea and give the girls a chance to become better acquainted."

Her aunt's face lit with a smile. "I think it a marvellous idea. I have a small parlour we can use. You girls enjoy your tea." Without ceremony, Aunt Gardiner led Lady Fitzwilliam from the room as Georgiana and Elizabeth situated themselves before the fire. Georgiana wore a thin-lipped smile. Why was she so tense?

"I hope you are well."

Her future sister twisted her hands in her lap. "I am, thank you."

Elizabeth leaned over and placed her palm upon her wringing fingers. "I know we have known one another for a short time, but if you are uncomfortable, you can tell me. I would like to help ease your distress."

"I have not left Clarell House in some time. I am afraid the experience has quite discomposed me."

Elizabeth shifted as close as the chair would allow. "My aunt and I would have travelled to Lord and Lady Fitzwilliam's for tea. You need not agitate yourself to this extent to spend time with me."

"But I wanted to!" Her eyes filled with tears. "Please forgive me. I was not like this before..."

Elizabeth pulled Georgiana from the chair and brought her to the sofa where she sat directly by the young lady's side. One arm wrapped around her while she maintained a firm hold on Georgiana's hands. The poor girl!

"Should you ever need to talk, I shall listen. You can depend upon it."

"I cannot speak of it again." Her voice came out as a tortured whisper. "I have spoken to my brother, Mrs. Annesley, Aunt Charlotte." She shook her head. "I want to put it behind me, yet I relive the experience anew whenever I speak of it. Would you mind terribly if I give Fitzwilliam permission to tell you?"

"Would you be angry if he already has done so?"

Georgiana looked up from her lap and searched Elizabeth's face. "He did?"

"Do not be upset with him. He needed to relieve himself of it as well. Your experience tormented him and created a burden of guilt he needed to have absolved."

"But he is not responsible! He could not have known!"

Elizabeth dabbed Georgiana's cheeks with her handkerchief. "He is your elder brother and your protector since your parents' death. I believe his reaction is natural even if he is mistaken."

"He and my aunt attempt to shelter me more than they should since Ramsgate."

"I am certain they believe it to be for your own good."

Georgiana covered her face with her hands and shook her head. "I love them for their efforts to protect me, but I do not want to be treated as a child. I need to be told the truth." She grasped Elizabeth's forearm. The anguish in her young eyes tore at Elizabeth's soul.

"I was ill last month. Did you know?"

"Your brother may have mentioned it."

"Did he tell you why?" she whispered.

"No, before I journeyed to London, your brother was satisfied because your spirit seemed improved by your letters. We have never had the privacy required to speak of your illness since my arrival."

"When my brother first returned from Hertfordshire, I was terribly excited to hear about Mr. Bingley's ball and his evening with you, so I hurried from the music room to my aunt's sitting room. I heard them before I could knock upon the door. The butler must not have closed the door tight as it was open just an inch—enough to allow me to hear what they discussed."

Elizabeth rubbed Georgiana's clenched hands. "What did they say, Georgiana?"

"My aunt concealed the true reason for my illness from me, but I listened to every detail as she enlightened my brother." A strangled sob tore from her throat. "I heard him cry, Lizzy. I have never heard much less seen him express himself in such a way."

How Elizabeth wanted to grip any object without mercy until her knuckles were white. Fitzwilliam indicated he had news of Georgiana to share with her, yet as she had told his sister, they had not found the opportunity.

"Did you not tell Fitzwilliam or your aunt what you heard?"

"No, I did not know how. I feigned sleep when he sought me out an hour later. I needed time to think." One of the girl's hands pulled from hers to rub back and forth across her stomach as she rocked in her seat. "I never slept that night, but my aunt's revelation was not what kept me awake. Once I accepted what happened, I was so ashamed, Lizzy."

Georgiana looked to Elizabeth wide-eyed and desolate. "I lost a child. I lost a child and God forgive me, I was relieved."

Elizabeth's palm rubbed Georgiana's back. "Oh, dearest."

"I could not live with such a reminder. I wanted the ordeal done and finished. I could not have a baby."

"Your feelings are understandable."

"I am selfish," she spat.

"You are still young, you were violated in the worst of ways, and you did nothing to cause the loss of the child. You have done nothing to draw censure. Your relief is not shameful or selfish."

"I wish I could believe you."

Elizabeth cupped Georgiana's face in her hands. She appeared so young, yet so old at the same time, her eyes reflecting the torment within. "You *are not* to blame, and I shall repeat those words daily until you accept them. Do you understand?"

"What if I never believe them?" Her agonised whisper rent Elizabeth's heart.

"Would I lie to you?"

Georgiana's eyes searched hers. "I do not believe you would. Despite our brief acquaintance, I trust you."

"Good, then I shall tell you often for I cannot have you place confidence in such false notions."

"What have I done!" With a swift movement, Georgiana stood and hastened to the mirror. "I told myself I would not unburden myself upon you, and I have done just that. I have ruined our afternoon."

"You have done nothing of the sort." She turned Georgiana by her shoulders. "Do you not know that sisters confide in one another? We share our deepest, darkest secrets because we know we can trust our truest friend. You have not shocked me, I shall never think less of you for what you have revealed, and you will seek me out should you require this service in the future. I shall brook no opposition on the subject. I am quite decided you see."

Georgiana hiccoughed as Elizabeth drew her into a hug. "You do not have to endure this alone. Your brother, the colonel, your aunt, and I shall not allow it."

She held Elizabeth tight. "I do not deserve such kindness."

"You are wrong, dearest. You deserve our love and more."

A noise drew Elizabeth's attention to the door. Lady Fitzwilliam peered inside, but before she could enter further, Elizabeth gave a slight shake of her head.

"Are you certain?" mouthed Lady Fitzwilliam.

Elizabeth did not respond other than to place her palm upon the back of Georgiana's head as she rocked her from side to side while Lady Fitzwilliam backed from the room without a sound. "Why do we not get your face washed and dried? By the time we return, the maid will have brought tea."

The girl took in her appearance. "I look affright! What will my aunt say?" She dabbed at her face with her handkerchief.

Elizabeth tugged Georgiana towards the stairs, but the young lady pulled back. "While I feel safe in my uncle's home, I need to be able to live in the world again. I want to shop on Bond Street, I want to enjoy the theatre, and have Fitzwilliam take me to art exhibits. I do not wish to hide behind my relations and in my uncle's or brother's house for the rest of my life."

"You will do all of it and more. We will make sure of it."

Georgiana's posture relaxed as she wrapped her arm around Elizabeth's. "I am fortunate to be gaining you for a sister. Since I have not made mention of it before, thank you for marrying my brother."

Elizabeth smiled as the girl's head rested upon her shoulder. "I am the fortunate one. I shall be gaining a wonderful man for my husband and you for my sister. I shall certainly have no cause to repine."

A rag with cool water aided Georgiana's tear streaked face, and when folded and placed upon her eyes, helped reduce the swelling. The redness, however, would linger for a time.

Their tea was laid out when they returned to the parlour, and they took places on the sofa to enjoy the repast. Georgiana ate little, but did take a second cup of tea while Elizabeth began a discourse on music. Since Georgiana adored the subject, she might not dwell on topics which were unpleasant and discomposed her. The ploy was successful as they spent the next two hours in a discussion of composers that, as good conversation often does, wended its way into other subjects.

Eventually, Elizabeth entreated Georgiana to play the pianoforte. She was reluctant at first, but relented since Elizabeth was her only audience. Fitzwilliam's young sister may have been meek and mild in person, but what a transformation occurred before the pianoforte! Her insecurities disappeared, and she commanded the instrument and its keys as though she had played since birth. Her fingers danced with a light touch as they moved nimbly across the instrument while she was engrossed in the tune she knew from memory.

The most beautiful rendering of Bach's Fantasia in C minor flooded the drawing room as a movement at the servant's entrance gave away the cook and housekeeper, who peeked from a crack in the door to listen. Even they recognised the young lady's talent.

Her aunt and Lady Fitzwilliam entered without a sound and seated themselves where they could watch as well as enjoy the music. With the exception of the pianoforte, the room was silent.

When she completed the Bach, she moved on to Scarlatti without much pause while Elizabeth watched, enraptured, until a hand rested upon Elizabeth's shoulder. With an abrupt jolt, she about jumped from her chair as her palm flew to her chest. She looked up to find Fitzwilliam and frowned as he pursed his lips to restrain his mirth. A shaking finger pointed to the nearest chair, yet the insufferable man shook his head and remained where he was. Of all the nerve!

When Georgiana released the final note and returned from the music, her eyes lifted to Lady Fitzwilliam and started. "I did not hear anyone enter." She then scanned the room to find Fitzwilliam, and her expression shifted to happy surprise. "Brother! I did not expect you to join us." Her hurried steps rushed her forward to hug him.

"I finished my business early and wished to call upon Miss Elizabeth. I hoped I might join you before your return to Mayfair. Is that acceptable?"

Aunt Gardiner nodded. "You are always welcome. Is he not, Lizzy?"

"He is, indeed. I am pleased you could come, Mr. Darcy."

"I shall have the maid bring fresh tea." Aunt Gardiner made to pull the bell, but Lady Fitzwilliam moved beside Georgiana.

"None for us, Marianne. We have spent several lovely hours in your company and should be returning to Clarell House soon."

Fitzwilliam stepped forward. "I wanted to invite all of the Fitzwilliams, the Gardiners, and Miss Elizabeth to attend church with me on Sunday. After, we could dine at Darcy House and spend an afternoon in company." He looked to Aunt Gardiner. "Your children would be welcome should you not wish to be separated for the day. The nursery has not been used in some time, but I am certain it should suffice."

"I would be pleased to accept your invitation, Mr. Darcy. My husband and I do not yet take the children to services, so they will remain behind."

Lady Fitzwilliam reached for her reticule and passed her niece her own. "We shall see you at church, but your uncle and I have a previous engagement that afternoon with Catherine, Anne, and Mr. Bingley. Georgiana might welcome a day at home rather than alone at Clarell House. What do you say, dear?"

"I *would* like to come."

"Even to church?" Fitzwilliam's tone rang of his concern.

Georgiana shifted and swallowed. "It is the last Sunday before Christmas, and I have not been once. Yes, I shall go to church."

His brows were still drawn and his lips tight, but he nodded. "Then you can come with Aunt and Uncle to the chapel, and depart with us."

"Thank you, Brother." Georgiana stepped up on her toes to kiss his cheek and gave a quick hug to Elizabeth.

"Allow me to walk you to the door." Aunt Gardiner followed Lady Fitzwilliam and Georgiana from the room, leaving the door ajar.

"Georgiana either slept very ill, or she has been crying," observed Fitzwilliam.

"She confessed the cause of her illness last month. She knows."

He paled, closed his eyes, and dropped into the closest chair. "I cannot bear to have you say it. Did she mention how she is aware of such matters? My aunt has taken great pains to conceal—" His voice broke as he attempted to rein in his emotions.

"Georgiana, in her excitement to welcome you back from Hertfordshire, unintentionally eavesdropped on your aunt revealing the information to you. It is my opinion that she required time to come to terms with it on her own. She has no wish to cause you further upset, so she has remained silent."

"As of late, I have done all I could to hide my anger and hurt at Wickham's actions. How could she be aware of my struggles?"

She knelt before him and took his hands. "Your sister is neither blind nor deaf. I have noticed your sadness not only when you speak of her, but also when you look at her. She also heard you cry when your aunt told you of the child's loss."

His forehead rested upon her knuckles. "I do not know how to help her."

Elizabeth stroked his dark curls. "You can do no more than be her brother—offer her a shoulder on which to cry when she requires it, protect her from further harm, listen to her troubles. You are not infallible and keeping secrets will cause her more anxiety than your honesty."

He lifted his head, turned over her hand, and kissed her palm. "Why did we set a date six weeks hence?"

"So as not to take away from Mr. Bingley's wedding to Anne." Elizabeth rose to her feet as she placed a kiss upon his forehead.

After a glance at the door, he pulled her forward into an embrace and rested his forehead against her belly. "We could have set a date prior to theirs." His tone was a bit petulant.

"For shame, Fitzwilliam. After the length of time they have been betrothed, they deserve the right to be wed first." She peered through the door. "We cannot let my aunt find us thus." Her palm rested upon his cheek with her thumb stroking his temple as he sighed.

"I know, but I wanted to touch you. I miss our walks... and Miss Bennet as a chaperon."

She bent and pressed her face into his locks to bestow one last kiss. My, but he smelled divine. His cologne was like Longbourn's kitchen at Christmas, smelling of nutmeg and cloves. Her father wore scents with tones of evergreens and cedar, which never appealed, but when Fitzwilliam placed his topcoat upon her shoulders at the ball, she had to resist the urge to never give it back.

As it would appear ridiculous to remain with her face in Fitzwilliam's hair, she kissed him and straightened. A movement in the corner of her eye caught her attention.

"My aunt is standing outside of the door with her back to us."

His laugh vibrated against her flesh. "We now know where Miss Bennet acquired her chaperon skills." He released her and ran his fingers through his rich brown curls. "I love you."

"I love you, too." She leaned back. "Aunt, will you not join us?"

As her aunt bustled to her usual seat, she lifted her eyebrows to Elizabeth. "I would have entered in a moment." She retrieved her needlework. "Lady Fitzwilliam has proposed an outing for us ladies in order to purchase a trousseau for you, Elizabeth, and Miss de Bourgh."

"Did my aunt mention a date?"

"No, she needed to speak with Miss de Bourgh, but as she has yet to make an appointment with Madame Guiard, I would speculate after Christmas."

Fitzwilliam adjusted his jacket. "My aunt has been busy as of late. She may have forgotten Christmas is next week."

Elizabeth peered at the clock. "I promised the children a story before dinner."

As she rose, Fitzwilliam stood as well. "I should be leaving."

"You just arrived. Can you not spend the evening with us?" She looked to her aunt. "He is welcome at dinner, is he not?"

"You are very welcome to dine with us this evening, Mr. Darcy."

He picked up his hat and gloves. "I regret that I cannot. While you promised the children a story, I promised Georgiana my company this evening. I have no desire to disappoint her, though she would, no doubt, understand."

Aunt Gardiner set aside her embroidery and stood. "Please know that you are always welcome."

"I thank you, Mrs. Gardiner."

Elizabeth took Fitzwilliam's proffered arm. "May I walk Mr. Darcy to the door?"

With a nod, her aunt gave an indulgent smile. "Yes, you may."

Fitzwilliam stopped and faced her when they reached the front hall. "I have some early morning business, but I shall call after it is completed."

"I look forward to it."

"We have had rather mild weather for autumn. If the day is fine, would your aunt permit us to take a walk in the park?"

"She might require a maid to accompany us, or the children, but I shall ask this evening."

He brushed his lips across her knuckles. "How I wish I could take you home with me."

After a quick glance around the room, she lifted to her tiptoes, wrapped her arms around his neck, and whispered into his ear. "I desire the same, but the day will come."

His hands slid around her waist as he held her close and buried his face in her neck. His warm breath fanned against the exposed skin; she closed her eyes at the prickling sensation and heat that overspread her body.

She indulged herself but a moment, taking one last deep inhale of his scent before she withdrew. "Any of the family or the servants could enter."

"And I must go before I throw you over my shoulder and carry you to the carriage." He opened the door, but turned when he stepped outside. "Goodnight, Elizabeth."

His low voice caressed her without a touch; she shivered.

"Goodnight, Fitzwilliam."

Chapter 21

Without ceremony, Richard walked through the door of Darcy's study, threw it closed with a careless motion, and dropped into a chair before Darcy's desk. "What do you mean summoning me at all hours of the night?"

Darcy glanced at the clock upon the mantel. Half seven was an early morning for his cousin, which explained his foul temper. "I sent a message at ten—not late when one considers your usual habits. I had no response, so I sent another note this morning as I consider the matter to be of some import." He opened the door. "Jobbins, would you see to it coffee is brought to us, please?"

"Of course, sir."

Once they again had privacy, Richard dropped his head back into the cushion of the seat. "So what has your feathers in a dither?"

He strode to his desk, picked up a letter, and thrust it in Richard's face. "This arrived yesterday while I was calling on Elizabeth."

"A piece of paper seems rather innocuous to me."

"Yet you know I would not send for you without reason. Blast! Stop being a right bastard and read it!"

Richard rubbed his eyes with a growl. "You do not have to yell, Darce."

"You should not have been in your altitudes last night, else you would not be in such a terrible temper."

"I thought to see what sort of mettle your friend Bingley is made of. I would not have thought the cub could drink so much and remain standing."

Darcy took his seat as he chuckled. "Simple. He did not consume all you gave him."

Sitting up straight, Richard stared hard at him. "What do you mean?"

"Since Bingley began moving in society, some gentlemen thought it a great joke to put him in his cups. They would purchase the liquor and then entice him to gamble; however, such schemes were first tried at Cambridge, and Bingley learnt after a few bad evenings how to avoid the trap without giving offence."

"Why would he give offence?"

"Because the peers and other young men would purchase his brandy or port. Bingley refused once, and a viscount thrashed him for it. After that evening, he learned to use distractions to his favour. When the barmaid came around, he would pour his glass into theirs, at times even splitting the contents between more than one glass." With a chuckle, Darcy placed his forearms upon the desk and leaned forward. "How were you distracted last night?"

Richard made a fist and struck the arm of his chair. "Milton kept pestering me about going to White's." His jaw dropped. "I shall horse whip him next I see him! He knew!"

Darcy grinned. "Why would you think so?"

"When I refilled Bingley's glass, Milton laughed like one of those blasted hyenas at the Royal Menagerie. I was duped!"

"I shall make a bargain with you, Richard. You read that letter, and I shall help you get revenge."

"What sort of revenge?"

He lifted his shoulder. "We do not want to exact any sort of retribution so soon after their fun. We have time to consider a plan to execute when they least expect it."

After a light rap, a maid entered with the coffee, which was placed on a clear side of the desk before she departed with haste.

"You know, I would read this regardless," his cousin confessed, holding the letter between his fingers."

"I do, but I have a bit of a grudge to settle with Bingley after his behaviour in Meryton. If he had been more circumspect, he would not have caused such a rift with Elizabeth."

Richard scratched his stubbly chin and nodded. "While Bingley did not intend any harm, I can understand your desire to enact a little revenge."

"Good! Since we have settled your issues, would you read the correspondence!"

Darcy poured his cousin a cup of coffee and set it on the edge of the desk as Richard unfolded the paper, pulled it back and then forwards before he settled to reading; however, before Darcy could pour his own cup, his cousin was out of his seat and pacing.

"That shit sack!"

"Thank heavens your mother was not here to hear that appellation."

"Wickham is not worth the flesh that binds him together. When did you say you received this?"

"It arrived yesterday while I was calling at Gracechurch Street."

"Did Jobbins have a description of who delivered it?"

"The letter was mixed in with the post."

"He did that on purpose. A messenger or delivering it himself would have simplified our efforts to locate him, but sending it through the post makes it nigh on impossible. We can see by the mark where it was posted, but I find it unlikely he sent it from the closest post station."

Darcy blew the scalding liquid. He had no wish to burn his tongue. "We cannot doubt the sincerity of his threat."

"No, after what he did to Georgiana, I would believe his every vicious word. The best way to rid ourselves of this blighter is to have him sent to the gallows, but a life of conscription or transportation is a tolerable substitute. He must be found and turned over to the army."

"I sent a request for a meeting to the Bow Street Runners last night. I do not know if I shall receive a reply as it is Sunday and so close to Christmas, but I hope to by the morrow."

"Did your father keep a miniature of Wickham here?"

"No, but when you mentioned his desertion, I sent to Mrs. Reynolds for the likeness at Pemberley in the event you should require it. I should have it within the week."

Richard returned to his chair and sipped his coffee as he stared at the letter. "He makes no direct reference to Georgiana, but I shall alert Father to the threats. I would not underestimate him if I were you. He is angry. We must pray his ire impairs his judgement, and he makes a foolish decision."

"He makes mention of you."

He gave a bark of a laugh. "Oh yes. '*No mystery surrounds my sudden transfer to a new regiment. Your cousin, the good colonel, has done your bidding well. I am certain he also desires to have me pay for the affair at Ramsgate, yet I shall give neither of you the satisfaction. Your plans for me will come to naught.*'" Richard held the note before him. "Did the idiot not understand that he needed pay for someone to take his position? He also stole a fellow officer's money. If he is found, he will have consequences."

"Wickham has never lacked arrogance. He intends some form of revenge, and I am certain plans to flee the country once he feels he has accomplished his task."

Darcy stood and moved to the side of the window. Yes, he was still there; his shadow was discernible, even in the fog. What could he want and for whom did he work? "You should also know I am being followed."

Richard's head shot up with an unusual swiftness considering the amount of brandy he had consumed the night prior. "Who? When?"

"I know naught. Kirby noticed the horse during the journey across London to retrieve Elizabeth for tea. When we returned to Darcy house that evening, he informed me the man had not only followed us to Clarell House, but also had trailed us home. Since that day, I have noticed him in the square on several occasions."

With a leap from the sofa, Richard pushed Darcy from the window. "Is he watching now?"

"Under the trees on the opposite side of the square."

He turned and began to stride by as though he had a purpose, so Darcy placed a hand to his chest. "Where are you going?"

"To discover what he wants."

"No."

"No?" Richard's voice was raised, his tone incredulous.

"I intend to have the investigators look into him as well. They can discover whether he is alone or whether he is employed by someone."

Richard's hand clenched and struck the palm of the other. "But I can beat it out of him."

"If he is working for someone, they would then replace him. No, we wait."

A strange growl came from his cousin's throat as he settled back into his chair. "I do not like to wait." He grimaced, swallowed, and shifted. "Since you will not let me take care of him, I may as well tell you how Colonel Forster sent a man Thursday to find Wickham."

After one last glance outside, Darcy returned to his desk. "Was he seeking money to cover Wickham's debts?"

"Wickham left debts of honour with his men, yet I was surprised to learn he owed no money to the local inn or other merchants."

"I mentioned Wickham's gambling habits as well as his usual practices with tradesmen to Mr. Bennet. It seems the discussion he had with Sir William Lucas and their subsequent warning of the local businesses was not in vain."

Richard sat back in his chair. "I am impressed. I know you would not endanger Georgiana's reputation, yet you did not allow him to wreak his usual havoc. I do wonder what prompted this course of action. You have never been so forthcoming."

He shifted as his finger found a notch in the solid top of his desk and began to pick at it. "I happened upon Wickham on his first day in Meryton. He was being introduced to Elizabeth and her sisters."

At the sound of his cousin's chortle, Darcy stiffened. "Elizabeth is too intelligent to fall for his schemes, but I could not chance that Wickham would not force himself upon her. There is also the matter of the youngest Bennet girls. They are flighty and immature. The youngest, Lydia is her name, would flirt with any man in a red coat if afforded the opportunity."

His cousin's eyes narrowed. "Were you courting Miss Bennet at that time?"

"No, I did not ask permission to court her until the week following."

"You felt protective of her quite soon in your acquaintance, then. I hope you are aware, she is likely the easiest target when it comes to Wickham's schemes."

With a push up on the arm of his chair, he shifted so he sat straight and rigid. "When I began to admire Elizabeth has no bearing on this conversation. I shall see her protected at all costs, Richard. I was unable to protect Georgiana, for which I shall always bear some responsibility."

"You had no way of knowing until Georgiana sent the express that she was in danger."

"She should not have been on her own as she was."

"No more, Darce. My mother approved, I found naught amiss in the endeavour, and you had no reason to suspect Mrs. Younge. We must put this in the past and concentrate on Wickham's current threat. Georgiana rarely leaves Clarell House, so she should remain safe. Our primary concern should be to ensure Miss Bennet's protection."

Darcy rubbed the back of his neck. "I have no wish to alarm her or the Gardiners."

"You may not want to ruin today with speaking of this, yet it must be done. If you insist on enjoying the day first, tell them after luncheon." He held the letter aloft. "The announcement was in yesterday's paper, and Wickham mentions your betrothed. He has knowledge of your relationship with the lady, and you know as well as I do how he will make use of such information." His cousin tossed the letter upon the desk in a haphazard motion. "Do not underestimate him."

He rubbed his eyes. A clock chimed. Why did it sound so far away? His fingers combed through his hair.

"The carriage will be ready soon. I must leave in order to meet the Gardiners and Elizabeth at St. George's."

"You must tell them."

"I know," he groaned. "I know."

Fitzwilliam leaned towards her as he led her from the pew. "Your fingernails do not need to grip my arm so. I shall allow no one to harm you." Once Georgiana took her place on his other side, he stepped forward but did not move.

With a start, Elizabeth looked ahead where a familiar woman and her daughter stood before him. The muscles under her palm grew taut as his entire body stiffened.

"Mr. Darcy! We have not been in your company since Lord and Lady Fitzwilliam's ball. We have received invitations to several Christmas parties and of course the invitation to Viscount Meere's Twelfth Night masquerade. Do you have plans to attend any of the season's festivities?"

The mother smiled in a practiced fashion as the daughter's eyes ran from Fitzwilliam's dark curls to his eyes, and on to the span of his broad chest. The nails of Elizabeth's free hand dug into her palm.

How dare she! Fitzwilliam was taken! The prior day's paper announced their betrothal to the world. Even if these women were unable to read, they were certain to have heard it in the drawing rooms.

"I shall save you a dance, Mr. Darcy."

Elizabeth glared at the tilted head and flirtatious bat of her eyelashes. The vulgar little hussy! Her efforts were brazen indeed and not appreciated.

"It is a pleasure to see you again, Miss Darcy," prattled the mother as she directed her attention to Darcy's other side. "We met in October, I believe, when Thea and I called on your aunt."

Something was not right about Georgiana's expression, but the girl pulled herself a bit taller. "I do remember, Lady Carlisle." Her voice had an edge when she answered. "It is agreeable to see you again, Lady Althea."

"You must convince your brother to bring you to the Grantleys' dinner party this week. Mother and I would enjoy the addition of your company."

Fitzwilliam cleared his throat. "I do not believe you have made the acquaintance of my betrothed." He drew Elizabeth forward a step. "Miss Elizabeth Bennet, may I present Lady Carlisle and her daughter Lady Althea."

The two ladies had not requested an introduction and did not seem best pleased by Fitzwilliam's initiative. Lady Althea turned to Georgiana. "The Grantleys have such superb parties. You should—"

"My sister is not yet out, Lady Althea. When she is ready to attend such events, Miss Bennet and I shall decide which functions she attends. Now, if you will excuse us, we have plans for this afternoon. My cook will not forgive us if we are late for luncheon."

Lady Carlisle and her daughter eyed Elizabeth, the former giving a disdainful sniff, but upon returning her attention to Fitzwilliam and Georgiana, Lady Carlisle's unnatural smile returned. "Mr. Darcy, we do hope to have your company soon. Miss Darcy, you must join your aunt the next time she calls at our home."

"We must greet Lady Fitzwilliam, Mother."

"Oh yes, we must. Please excuse us."

With a slight tug, Elizabeth followed Fitzwilliam to the doors of the chapel where Colonel Fitzwilliam awaited them. Aunt and Uncle Gardiner had given her permission to ride in the Darcy carriage after the services, so they wended through the parishioners until they were able to climb inside. The door closed and the equipage lurched forward.

"The nerve of those women!"

Elizabeth turned where a visibly angry Georgiana Darcy sat beside her.

"They snubbed you, Lizzy! Oh! And I noticed that Lady Althea's eyes roving over my brother." She shuddered. "If I did not like them when they called at Clarell House, I certainly do not care for them now. They are rude, vulgar—"

"Georgiana!"

The colonel burst into laughter. "Do not correct her for speaking her mind. I daresay she learned it from Mother while she has lived with her, and I am glad to see a bit of the old Georgiana returning to us." He grinned so wide his teeth were on full display. "Besides, I may have been standing near the rear of the church, but I noticed a vibrant green emerge in Miss Bennet's complexion."

Elizabeth jerked her gaze outside of the window. The colonel had noticed her jealousy? How mortifying! The side of her face tingled, so her eyes darted to where Fitzwilliam stared at her with a smug curve to his lips.

"I, for one, do not blame Lizzy in the slightest. If she followed the conniving harlot's line of sight, she would have a vast deal of complaints against the so-called lady."

"I do not care for your language, Georgiana. You sound of Lady Catherine and not Aunt Charlotte."

"Aunt Charlotte would not have countenanced such a display, Fitzwilliam, or did you not notice *Lady* Althea's blatant perusal of your lap?"

The colonel began to cough, turning the colour of a beetroot as the fit continued, while Fitzwilliam's jaw dropped. "Georgiana!"

Elizabeth whipped around. "She did not! I saw her look from his hair and across his chest, but never lower."

"I had been so nervous the entire service, but forgot my fears when she began to ogle my brother."

The colonel's cough had subsided into a hoarse chuckle. "This is not his first encounter of that nature, but I pity the lady who attempts it in the future. With the looks the two of you gave Lady Althea, the culprit might not survive. I never thought Georgiana would be one to protect your virtue." He gave a raspy chuckle.

"Richard, you are being nonsensical."

"*You* did not see your sister's eyes bulge or your betrothed's murderous glare. I am just glad Georgiana managed to school her features before Lady Carlisle turned her attention to her."

"Brother, how could you not notice?"

"I ignored her unless I had to respond." He tugged at his waistcoat. "I have never enjoyed the machinations of ladies like Lady Carlisle and Lady Althea."

Elizabeth leaned her temple against the squab. "I never fawned or sought your notice."

"No, but I did attempt to keep you at bay during the assembly. Do you remember?" His voice was low and a touch softer. "You did not react in the manner to which I am accustomed. You laughed as though what I said made no difference, yet the look in your eye I could not forget. No malice or avarice lay in their depths—only joy and beauty."

The colonel cleared his throat; she started, glancing to Georgiana, who beamed as she looked from her brother to Elizabeth. How could she forget Georgiana and the colonel were present? Her eyes sought Fitzwilliam's and she held his gaze until the equipage pulled before Darcy House.

With Fitzwilliam's aid, Elizabeth stepped to the pavement as she gaped at the pearl white façade before her, ending at the dark wood door with flanking columns. The house was large for London—and the windows! On top of the kitchen and servant's portion below street level, three floors stood proud and tall before her with five windows glinting in the late morning sun across each of the upper two levels.

"What do you think?" His heated breath fanned against her ear, and she forced her eyes to remain open and straight-ahead.

"I think it very handsome. How long has it been in your family?"

"My grandfather had a substantial windfall from a mining venture about five years prior to his death. This house had just been completed when the new owner's debts became too much for him to pay and agreed to sell the property to my grandfather for less than the original purchase price."

"How lucky for your grandfather."

"The man required funds in a desperate way. My grandfather had the money and was prepared to sign the papers quickly. We still possess the home we owned previous to this one, which we now lease. I shall show it to you sometime, if you wish it."

"Where did you spend most of your childhood?"

"In London?"

She nodded.

"I was still in short pants when my grandfather purchased this property, so most of my time in London was spent in this home."

"Then I would not mind seeing the other house, but I prefer this one."

A slight pink tinged his cheeks as his steady gaze held hers.

"Would the two of you stop cooing at one another and come inside!" Her head shot forward where Colonel Fitzwilliam and Georgiana stood inside the front hall, the colonel beckoning them onward with his outstretched arm. "'Tis cold outside and Jobbins will not close the door until you enter!"

A sigh came from beside her as Fitzwilliam offered his arm. "Come, before I am tempted to compromise your reputation on the street."

She put her palm to her chest and gasped in feigned shock. "I am scandalised, Mr. Darcy. What could you mean by such a statement?"

"Merely that I am tempted to kiss you when your aunt and uncle's carriage could arrive at any moment." A rattling and plodding of horse hooves behind them indicated his equipage pulled away from the kerb.

Her lips pursed. "My uncle would not be amused."

A stiff, austere looking man stood beside the open entry. "Sir, as you requested, Mrs. Rowley has prepared the drawing room and Cook will have luncheon ready to be served in a half hour."

"Very good," responded Fitzwilliam, handing over his hat.

Elizabeth removed her best white kid leather gloves as a maid stepped before her, and then fumbled with the buttons of her pelisse while she scanned her surroundings.

Fitzwilliam approached her side, and pointed to a closed door. "My study is through there." Once the maid curtsied and departed, he escorted her to the side of the stairs and gestured to the next. "The library is not as large as Pemberley, but has a good selection."

He led her through a set of double doors to a lovely room decorated in muted shades of blue with white trim. "This is the drawing room, which is where we entertain callers and guests. When it is just Georgiana, Richard, and I, we tend to use the parlour upstairs.

"Should you wish to redecorate, you need only ask. I desire your comfort when you are in residence with me."

Her eyes flitted from one piece of furniture to another as well as the decor. How could any sane person find this wanting? The furniture bespoke of money, yet appeared comfortable. The colours soothed her nerves and were tasteful rather than garish. The overall effect was pleasing rather than uselessly fine.

"Elizabeth?"

She gave his elbow a squeeze. "I have no desire to change even one vase upon a table. The room is perfect as it is."

"But perhaps other rooms will require—"

"Fitzwilliam." His crystal blue eyes met hers. "I wish to wed you for you. Not to upend your houses or spend your money."

"I do know that, but I would have you comfortable."

"I shall be."

He leaned closer as her aunt and uncle entered. "And they are *our* homes."

Elizabeth set her teacup on the table before her and peered at the other occupants of the room while Georgiana played Handel on the piano. Her aunt, her uncle, and the colonel held a quiet conversation where they were seated near the fire—likely in regards to Georgiana's mastery of the instrument since they watched her a great deal as they spoke. Fitzwilliam remained near her side.

His knee tapped hers as he shifted in his seat. "Pardon me," he whispered.

She pressed her lips together, restraining her laughter. Poor Fitzwilliam had taken every opportunity to touch her as the day passed. His hand brushed hers as they sat beside one another at luncheon, he offered her his arm for the arduous journey from the dining room to the drawing room, and this was the fourth time in the last hour he had bumped either his hand or his knee against her person.

The sound of the pianoforte ceased and the compliments of the others returned her attention to the room rather than the tingling sensation of his surreptitious touches. "That was exquisite, Georgiana."

Fitzwilliam adjusted and fidgeted with his sleeve. "Well done, indeed."

As his sister returned to her music, the sound of the door opening turned her head as Mrs. Rowley entered.

"I beg your pardon, sir, but I thought now would be a good time for Miss Bennet to view her suite."

Elizabeth rose and looked to Aunt Gardiner. "I have no objection. Aunt?"

"I am certain you are curious, Lizzy. I am amenable to joining you now should you wish it." Her aunt stepped forward. "Come, Mr. Darcy. Though it may not be the usual practice, I know you are eager to join us."

His eyebrows furrowed, yet he followed, his palm pressing the small of her back as they ascended the stairs. "Mrs. Gardiner, how would you know I desired to join you?"

"My husband and I have been vastly amused at your attempts to touch Lizzy without our knowledge. I made a guess based on your behaviour. Was I incorrect?" Aunt Gardiner continued on as she spoke in a cheerful tone without missing a step.

Fitzwilliam first blanched, then appeared that of an overgrown child being punished. "I meant no disrespect to your husband, to you, or to Elizabeth."

"Though Edward and I have been married for close to ten years, we were once in the same situation. I admit to finding a bit of humour at your expense, but I would not have you uneasy. As far as viewing

Lizzy's future rooms, I see no reason you should not join us. With the presence of a chaperon and your housekeeper, the situation is not scandalous."

When the housekeeper ushered them through the door, Elizabeth took a few steps inside the small sitting room and stopped. The furniture was in good repair, though the fabric was worn and faded.

"These rooms have not been used since my parents' deaths. They will require work."

She pivoted to take in the rest of the décor. "Nothing too terrible. A bit of fabric for the furniture."

"Some new draperies," called her aunt from the window.

"And perhaps a new carpet for the floor? This one is dark for my tastes."

Mrs. Rowley stepped over to the escritoire, uncorked the ink, and made a note on a piece of paper. She did the same with the few alterations for the mistress' bedchamber while Elizabeth looked in the dressing room, and walked into a small room that housed an enormous copper tub, a chest, and a small cabinet.

Fitzwilliam stepped around her and leaned against the chest. "Please tell Mrs. Rowley the scents you prefer, so she can have them stocked. We do not keep much in this room, but the chest to store towels and the close stool. My father liked the idea of the pot being concealed, so he purchased one of Mr. Sheraton's designs for each bedchamber in this house and at Pemberley."

"At once?"

"No, over several years."

Why were they discussing chamber pots? With a last glance at him, she returned to the empty bedchamber. Where had her aunt gone?

Her fingers pulled the sun-damaged fabric aside as she peered into the back garden. Nothing bloomed at present, but if the arbours and the cleared beds were any indication, the view would be quite the colourful palette come spring.

Two hands snaked around her waist as soft lips pressed where her neck and shoulder met and a shock travelled from the point of his lips through her body. "I cannot go without touching you. Without the presence of another, I have no restraint."

Her eyes fluttered closed. "You must find some. My aunt will soon return."

His lips grazed up the flesh of her neck until he nuzzled behind her ear. Gooseflesh erupted down her neck and her heart began to flutter madly. How did one remain standing with such sensations coursing through them?

"Just one taste of your mouth is all I ask." His words burned her ear, and her resistance crumbled.

Her head turned so her lips could touch his. It was not enough, so her palm cupped his cheek as she rotated in his arms. His tongue tasted of honeyed brandy and caressed hers like silk. How was she to pull away? Her body revolted at the notion while her fingers found their way under the base of his waistcoat.

His hand pressed against her backside, drawing her hips against his, as his warmth permeated her flesh. How she wished to cup his rear and squeeze! What would he think of her if she did so? Would he be horrified? No, she could not be so bold.

"Fitzwilliam." Her voice sounded so strange and rough, but the thought disappeared as he trailed feather soft kisses along her shoulder. Instead, she smothered a moan into his shoulder.

The sound of someone clearing their throat penetrated the incessant pounding in her ears, and she propelled back against the wall, her knuckles pressed to her mouth. Fitzwilliam took one long look at her and, without a word, disappeared into the dressing room.

"Aunt?"

Aunt Gardiner peeked around the door, and upon noticing Fitzwilliam's absence, entered. "I thought to give you a moment to hold hands or steal a small kiss. I had no idea you would throw propriety to naught." Her aunt's words were firm and her lips in a fine line. "You have weeks until you are wed. Do not give your uncle reason to force march the two of you up the aisle."

Her aunt's gaze narrowed at the base of Elizabeth's neck. "We must cover that before your uncle sees it." She removed her fichu and reached for Elizabeth, but Elizabeth ducked around and hurried to the mirror.

She did not appear much different than the usual. Her eyes were a bit harried, but other than... she leaned forward as her fingers touched the small bruise at the base of her neck. "What is this?"

Her aunt placed the fichu around the back of her neck, and they both began to tuck it in place. "*That*, my dear, is from Mr. Darcy's attentions to your neck."

"But all he did was kiss!"

A giggle erupted from her aunt before she clamped her mouth shut. "Forgive me for laughing."

Fitzwilliam entered, his forehead wrinkled when he noticed the addition to her gown. "Why is this necessary?"

"I shall await you by the door," interrupted Aunt Gardiner, "but I will not leave the two of you alone again. While we may be a bit lenient, Mr. Darcy, our values are not so lapse as to allow the display I interrupted. I request you please mind your behaviour."

Elizabeth pulled the fichu aside. His eyes widened, and he stepped close. "I barely pulled. I do not understand how?"

"If my uncle sees it, he will not be pleased. My aunt will not keep a secret from him, but I am certain she does not want him to become angry while in company." A noise came from below where the toe of his shoe kicked against the plush carpet.

He watched his foot with great concentration. "I am sorry. Now that we are betrothed, my restraint disappears in your presence."

"I am not hurt, Fitzwilliam. Embarrassed, but not injured, by any means." She pressed her palm to his chest and raised her eyebrows when he lifted his head; however, before he could respond, her aunt cleared her throat and peered to a small clock on a side table. "We should return to the drawing room, but please be assured I am not offended or upset with you."

"I shall accept your pardon, though you should have slapped me for my actions."

"Would you regret the kiss had I done so?"

A line formed between his eyebrows for a moment before one of his dimples appeared. "No, I doubt it."

With a chuckle, he held out his elbow for her to take, and her aunt fell into step behind them as they entered the corridor. Elizabeth paused near a window overlooking the street to study the houses and the square when a familiar figure startled her.

"Fitzwilliam? I am certain I have seen that man before today."

He glanced over her shoulder. "The man at the edge of the square, standing near the tree?"

"Yes, he passed the carriage on horseback this morning when we arrived, and I am certain he did so when we went to Clarell House for tea. He rode by on his horse just after you stepped to the pavement."

"Are you certain, Lizzy?" Aunt Gardiner stepped closer to the window to peek around the draperies.

"I am positive. Could he be following us?" She looked up to Fitzwilliam. "If he is, why?"

Fitzwilliam's entire body tensed as he clenched and released his jaw. "I might know. We should return to the drawing room and alert Richard and your uncle." His entire body stood rigid as he narrowed his eyes towards the corner of the square.

"You are scaring me, Fitzwilliam."

"I hope you have no reason to fear, but I shall take no chances."

"But why us?" Her aunt's eyes darted between them.

"I have reason to believe he is following me and not you. I shall explain when we have joined the remainder of our party."

Why would anyone wish to watch Fitzwilliam? What did they hope to accomplish by the action? Did they wish to frighten him or were their intentions more sinister? Her head spun as her heart beat in a furious cadence that made her body throb.

Aunt Gardiner placed an arm around Elizabeth's shoulders. "I hope this is a misunderstanding and you are mistaken, sir."

Fitzwilliam's warm palms enveloped her icy fingers. "I shall not fail someone I love again. Regardless of what arises now or in the future, I shall protect you, Elizabeth. You believe me, do you not?"

She searched his fixed gaze, which never wavered. He was tense but composed and radiated strength. How could she not depend upon his assurance of her safety? If only she could be as sure of his own well-being.

"I trust you, Fitzwilliam."

Chapter 22

December 22nd 1811 continued...

Elizabeth's hand still held a slight tremble when they entered the drawing room, so Darcy maintained his firm hold upon it despite the presence of the others. Georgiana no longer sat before the pianoforte, but with Mrs. Annesley near the fire. How would she cope with the possibility of danger? Would it be more prudent to conceal this situation from her as well?

Before he could decide one way or the other, his sister looked up, glanced between him and Elizabeth, and frowned. "What has happened?"

Their entire party turned to face him and a weight settled upon his chest. He could no longer avoid the confession, but needed to tell all.

"Darce?"

His eyes darted to Richard. "I require your help."

His cousin's brow furrowed, and he propped his hand upon the sabre at his side. "You will always have any aid you require, but I am afraid I need you to be more specific in this instance."

His betrothed squeezed his hand. "Perhaps we should sit and discuss the matter. You indicated you have information to share with us, and once we are all acquainted with the situation, we can decide the best course of action."

"Sounds a deuce of a plan." Richard sat in the chair closest to him and stared at Darcy with his eyebrows raised. "Well, should I assume you are to tell them what we discussed this morning?"

"Yes, I cannot delay the matter any longer." Darcy pinched the bridge of his nose. "Georgiana, I—"

She drew herself up as tall as she could in her seated position. "I will not go take a nap or read in the library, Brother." Her eyes never wavered from his as she spoke. "I am determined. You will not change my mind."

He stood, mouth open. He never had a chance to utter a word before she spoke. Even now, she sat rigid. Did she think he would try to remove her bodily from the room? She wanted to control her own life, so no, he would not argue. Not this time. His silence in regards to Wickham had cost her in ways she might never recover. He could not take a chance of repeating his mistake.

After he escorted Elizabeth to a place on the sofa, Darcy moved to the table set with brandy, sherry, and port. "I fear I require a fortifying drink. Would anyone care to join me?"

"You do not need to ask me twice," called Richard. Mr. Gardiner requested a brandy, which Darcy delivered with his cousin's. He brought the ladies all glasses of sherry and took his place beside Elizabeth.

"I believe it best to start at the beginning as it might help to have the opinions of others. The day after the Fitzwilliam's ball, Richard arranged for me to meet with one of the footmen who worked that evening. He overheard a mother and a daughter discuss their disappointment at the announcement of my betrothal—"

"Hah! It was more than a trifling disappointment. They were conspiring."

He levelled a glare in Richard's direction. "Would you prefer to tell the story?"

Richard took a gulp of his brandy and shook his head. "No, you are doing well. A masterful job, I would say."

Georgiana gave an abrupt giggle at Richard's antics before she covered her mouth with her hand. "Forgive me."

"As I was saying, these ladies expressed their displeasure and spoke of planning to end my betrothal and to ensnare me with the daughter."

Elizabeth gasped. "Have they no shame?"

Mrs. Gardiner set her glass upon the table. "Apparently not, my dear. It is not unheard of for a man betrothed to one lady to be forced into matrimony with another. I would not say it is a common occurrence, but it has happened."

"The footman could not provide the identity of the ladies in question. I have heard such matters spoken of before, which, as Mrs. Gardiner said, have been on rare occasions, so I dismissed the young man's information."

He looked to Georgiana. "Are you certain you wish to hear the entirety? I warn you the next may cause you a great deal of upset."

Her hand sought Mrs. Annesley's, which the lady took without reservation. "I shall not be kept in the dark. Continue your story."

With a nod, he gulped at the knot in his throat. "Yesterday, I received a letter from George Wickham."

His sister blanched but remained composed as he told them of Wickham and the Darcy family while omitting the entire affair at Ramsgate. He had to make them see Wickham's vices as well as his propensity towards leaving debts and ruined young ladies in his wake.

"The letter congratulated me on my recent betrothal. He mentioned making Miss Elizabeth's acquaintance in Meryton as well as a few descriptions of her I shall *not* repeat." Darcy put his forearms on his knees and rubbed his hands against one another. "When I first noticed Wickham in Meryton, I spoke with Mr. Bennet, warning him of Wickham's nature, and we took measures to protect the ladies and tradesmen of the area while I contacted Richard to have Wickham reassigned. In his letter, Wickham accuses me of having him removed from the militia in Meryton and moved to another regiment."

Richard gave a low growl and re-situated himself in his chair. "Once I received Darce's letter, I contacted a few friends and had Wickham transferred to the Regulars and a more dangerous assignment where he would be sent to the continent in the next few months. Wickham has always been white-livered. He reported to his new commanding officer, learned of his consequences, and deserted."

The bushy eyebrows of Mr. Gardiner lifted. "Did he think his chances better with conscription or transportation?"

"I doubt Wickham had a sensible thought in his head," quipped Richard.

Darcy stood and stepped to the fire, placing his elbow upon the mantel. "Wickham has vowed revenge."

"He is always bent on vengeance for naught but being the steward's son rather than that of George Darcy's." Richard took the last gulp of his brandy and rose to refill his glass.

"Is that truly his complaint?" Elizabeth's eyes studied his.

"We played together as boys, but as we grew, he became a different person when we were not in the company of my father. Wickham was mean spirited and resentful. I found myself in trouble several times through Wickham's schemes."

Elizabeth set her sherry on the table before her and clasped her hands. "But what could he have hoped to gain?"

A disdainful laugh came from Richard. "He desired my uncle's notice. After his father's death, Wickham was handed an education and the possibility to be more than his own father, yet he scorned the notion of working for his reward. He desired it handed to him on a silver salver. My uncle left Wickham a thousand pounds and a living—not that Wickham should be the spiritual leader of any congregation—yet, Wickham considered the living beneath him and requested compensation in lieu of the position."

"Did you agree?" asked Mrs. Gardiner.

Darcy dipped his chin. "I did. I wanted Wickham away from Pemberley. The money seemed a good way to rid myself of him, and he claimed a wish to study the law. I hoped rather than believed him to be sincere.

"His initial demand to compensate him for the living was an outrageous sum. I refused to give him a shilling more than three thousand pounds, which he eventually accepted."

"Four thousand pounds between your father's gift and the funds you provided were not a pittance." Mr. Gardiner leaned against the arm of his chair and extended his legs. "A prudent man could live a lifetime on such a sum. Careful investments could have provided a substantial return as well."

Richard scoffed. "If there is one thing Wickham is not, it is prudent. He squandered the lot in three years and returned to Darcy to demand the living."

Mrs. Gardiner put her hand to her chest. "To waste such a sum! He was also quite bold to insist upon what he had refused a mere few years prior. I hope you denied his request."

"I did, and he became angered. His temper was so unyielding I required two of my footmen to remove him from the house."

"If he was as furious as you say, he has enacted some form of retribution before now." Mr. Gardiner's eyes narrowed as he looked between Darcy and Richard, who both stared into their drinks.

"He satisfied his spite through me." Georgiana's small voice in the silence overpowered the room in as efficient a manner as a deafening blast.

Richard's head jerked in her direction. "Georgiana, no!"

She stood and stepped to Darcy, placing a hand upon his arm, but looking at Richard. "Thus far, you have done all you could to protect me and my reputation. If telling the Gardiners about Ramsgate will protect Lizzy, they should be told." Her eyes were wide, but open and honest. She had no qualms about informing Elizabeth's aunt and uncle.

But how could he allow such knowledge to be revealed? Would the Gardiners treat his beloved sister differently as a result of Wickham's actions? Her words showed her courage, yet the more people aware of that time, the more chance of it being revealed to society. Every person they told was a risk.

"Fitzwilliam?" Elizabeth stood beside Georgiana, holding her hand. "They can be trusted."

"I do not..." His voice cracked, so he swallowed. "I do not know how..."

Richard held up his hands. "I cannot."

Georgiana squared her shoulders, took in a shaky inhale, and placed her free hand on her stomach. "Last summer, my brother and Richard, who are both my guardians, removed me from school and formed an establishment for me at Ramsgate.

"I was excited to spend the summer at the seaside, and Fitzwilliam travelled with me to see me settled, remaining a fortnight before he departed for London and later Pemberley. A week after my brother's departure, Mr. Wickham appeared one morning during my walk along the sea wall. He was charming and pleasant company. I did not think he would continue to meet me while I took my exercise, yet he did. I saw no harm in it. After all, we were never without Mrs. Younge."

Georgiana's voice was soft, yet she remained composed. She had found it so difficult to relate those memories in the past, how would she manage?

"My companion, Mrs. Younge, spoke well of Mr. Wickham on many occasions. She considered him a gentleman, amiable and handsome, but it was not until she mentioned him as a suitor that I became alarmed. To me, he was a carefree elder brother. I had fond memories of him from when I was a child. I had no wish to call him husband.

"I wrote my brother and informed him of Mr. Wickham's presence and Mrs. Younge's comments, which were becoming more frequent, and requested he hurry to Ramsgate. I had no one else to contact. I did not know Richard had returned from the continent.

"As Mrs. Younge's entreaties that I accept Mr. Wickham became more frequent, I grew more distrustful of her. I longed to flee Ramsgate but could not depart without a companion. I considered taking my maid, Lucy, and departing on the post. Lucy, once apprised of the situation and my concerns, was willing to undertake the scheme, so we plotted our course, taking great care not to alert Mrs. Younge or Mr. Wickham to our plans.

"The night before we were to make our escape, Mrs. Younge insisted I give Mr. Wickham a private audience. Lucy was not within the house. She had gone to verify the time of the post coach we wished to use for passage, so I was forced into meeting him... alone."

She shifted upon her feet as the Gardiners stared; their drinks forgotten in their hands. Mr. Gardiner's brows were drawn down in the middle. Mrs. Gardiner's eyes were shiny and appeared damp. They had to suspect where Georgiana's story was leading, as they remained silent as the grave.

Elizabeth rubbed Georgiana's back and whispered in her ear, but his sister shook her head in response.

"Upon Mrs. Younge's quitting the room, Mr. Wickham professed himself violently in love with me and proposed marriage. He made an eloquent speech that two people who loved one another with as much passion as we did should not be made to wait for interminable weeks to make our vows, and insisted we should make haste to Gretna Green.

"I thanked him for the compliment of his offer, but declined. I explained I did not love him as a wife loves a husband but as a sister to a brother. We both deserved better from matrimony than what I could offer him.

"He insisted I would grow to love him, but I would not relent." She clasped her hands before her and gave a strange strangled sob. "He became furious. He grasped my gown by the shoulder and ripped to—"

Mrs. Gardiner jumped from her seat and wrapped Georgiana in a motherly embrace. "We need hear no more, dearest. Should you require unburdening yourself, I suspect you have those who you would prefer to reveal such personal recollections. If you want to continue, we shall listen and keep your confidence, but please do not feel you must."

While Mrs. Gardiner soothed his sister, Mr. Gardiner's jaw clenched and a slight crunch sounded, as his teeth must have ground upon themselves. "This man still walks the earth. I do not believe I would have your forbearance were I in a similar situation."

"Please excuse us," interrupted Elizabeth. "We are going to accompany Georgiana to her chambers." Mrs. Annesley appeared with the rest of the ladies, who hastened from the room.

Once the door was closed behind them, Richard took the seat across from Mr. Gardiner. "I wanted to run the bastard through, but Darce feared Georgiana's attack would be discovered. Wickham always returns like a bad penny, so I thought I would find my moment when he least expected it and without any link to Georgiana. His joining the militia was a gift I had not expected. I confess I prayed he would find his death upon the continent without sullying my hands in the process."

Darcy rubbed his face. "Richard, I—"

"No!" Richard pointed his brandy towards Darcy. "He deserves it. If he is gone from this earth, perhaps Georgiana can finally have a decent night's rest, and you won't have to look over your shoulder."

"I am not a bloodthirsty man, but I agree with the colonel." Mr. Gardiner sighed and shrugged his shoulders. "You have given this Wickham every opportunity. I doubt he will ever disappear if he thinks he can best you in some way or extort money in some fashion. Should he hurt my wife, my daughter, or even one of my nieces, I would not show the mercy you have bestowed."

He was weary of Wickham! At present, however, another could, through him, cause harm to Elizabeth. But what if the threat was, in fact, Wickham? How was he to know whom the real danger was?

He sat in a chair near Mr. Gardiner. "We have another problem. It could be related to Wickham or the women from the ball. I am unsure."

Mr. Gardiner sat forward. "What has happened?"

"I believe I am being watched."

Mr. Gardiner's head gave a slight jerk back. "What has given you such an idea?"

"My driver, Kirby, took note of a man on horseback when I retrieved Elizabeth for tea at Clarell House. Since that afternoon, he and my postilions have seen the same man during my travels around London as well as when I call on Gracechurch Street. Though I cannot see him well enough to verify it is the self-same man, an individual watches my house from different locations around Grosvenor Square."

"Today, Elizabeth noticed a man watching this house from an upstairs window. She recognised him as having passed the carriage on two previous occasions."

Richard stood and motioned for Mr. Gardiner to follow him. Once they were before the window in Darcy's study, he stood against the draperies, narrowed his eyes, and scanned the street. A minute later, he walked around the desk rather than in front of the glass, and searched the opposite end of the square.

"There he is."

Mr. Gardiner joined Richard and squinted. "My eyesight is not adequate to distinguish his features, but I believe you."

"He was behind a tree on the opposite end earlier." Darcy moved behind Richard and glanced over his shoulder. "That is him."

Richard again strode around the desk, but made for the servant's hallway.

"Where are you going?"

"I know you forbade it this morning, but I *am* going to determine what he is about."

Mr. Gardiner grabbed his cousin's coat as he passed. "If you alert him, and he has been hired by someone, might the employer replace him?"

"But what if we can discover the employer?"

"We might do that with the investigator I wish to hire." After stepping away from the window, Darcy leaned against his desk. "I should have an answer to my letter to the Bow Street Runners on the morrow. In the meantime, I have sent for some of the larger sons of tenants for additional protection.

With a weary demeanour, Mr. Gardiner sat in a chair by the fire. "As he has followed you to Gracechurch Street, I feel we should move to the new house sooner than I had planned. I will take no chances with my family."

"I cannot blame you." Darcy joined Mr. Gardiner by taking a place on the sofa. "What of Elizabeth? You would not return her to Longbourn, would you?"

"Her mother would never forgive me. She wrote Marianne, insistent we were to help Lizzy purchase the finest trousseau her father's funds could purchase—even if she only came to you with one gown. Do not worry. We intend to give her a piece or two for Christmas as well as a wedding gift."

"I am not worried. Anything Elizabeth lacks, I do not mind purchasing."

Richard put an elbow upon the mantel. "She could stay with Georgiana for a time at Clarell House. Darce could call on her and there are few places the addle pate could hide around my father's home."

"Addle pate?" Mr. Gardiner's voice shook with laughter.

"He was noticed by not only Darce's driver, but by Miss Bennet. He is piss poor at his job; you must admit."

Mr. Gardiner bobbed his head to one side and the other. "My main concern is that we had not planned to move to Mayfair until after Christmas. The house is prepared, waiting empty, but Marianne has not hired enough servants as of yet."

"As I mentioned to your wife, my housekeeper might be of some aid. She may know of people seeking work or be able to lend you a few of ours, depending upon what you require."

Richard gestured towards the window. "Or I could threaten and beat the man on the corner until he confesses if he works for Wickham or not."

"I doubt Wickham hired him; he is dressed better than any scoundrel Wickham could afford."

Richard rolled his eyes and made for the liquor tray, calling over his shoulder, "He may owe Wickham money. This may be to settle his debts."

Mr. Gardiner disagreed. "I am inclined towards Mr. Darcy's point of view. From what you have said of Wickham, he is more apt to deal with this himself—as he did in Ramsgate. I would also venture his ploy with Miss Darcy was to gain access to her dowry as much as it was to cause you pain."

"Blast!" swore Richard, as he struck the table. "You have a point. And if they change the spy, we may never know who his employer is, as his replacement may be more competent."

Richard stalked to the sofa and dropped onto it, his fist bumping his mouth. He was deep in thought until suddenly, his countenance changed and he straightened. "Say, have you considered Lady Catherine?"

"I do not understand what she would have to gain."

"She is unhappy Anne is to wed Bingley and that you are to wed Miss Bennet. We might inquire whether Bingley and Anne are being followed as well. Neither may have noticed, or they may not recognise what it means until they are made aware of your situation."

"I have some men whom I employ to investigate possible investors and at times, employees. I shall pen a letter to them when I return home. They may be of help."

His cousin's head gave an abrupt jerk back. "You investigate potential employees? What sort of men do you hire to require such scrutiny?"

Mr. Gardiner pointed to the brandy as he looked at Darcy. "May I?"

"Of course."

As Mr. Gardiner rose and filled a fresh glass, he gave a one-shouldered shrug. "I run an import business. Money changes hands, and merchandise is delivered to shops or individuals purchasing my wares. In the past, I have suspected an employee or two of theft, and these men were of great help. They now investigate any man who is to take a position in which they handle money."

Darcy moved to the other chair. "What information do they seek for you?"

"Debts can be important. A man who owes a substantial sum is eliminated from consideration for those positions. I prefer to know of the worker's reputation with his neighbours.

"I had one employee who stole money and purchased a myriad of items his friends and those who lived nearby coveted. When the men went to the local pub, these people all complained of what this man bought and wondered how he could afford such items. Greed and envy can be useful to my cause as well."

He took a swallow of his brandy. "I have also had gentlemen who claim to have money to invest when they do not possess the funds at all. Delays in shipments can cost me dearly. These investigators are worth their fees as far as I am concerned."

"If you bring in your men, will you keep me abreast of their investigation? By sharing our information, we can cover more ground in a timely fashion."

Darcy turned to Richard. "Please let me know when you have word of Wickham."

"I shall. I shall also speak with Father and nose around Lady Catherine's house. The servants have always liked me. Perhaps I can discover if she has had any unusual guests or been tending to more correspondence than is her wont."

Mr. Gardiner stared into his now empty glass, his forehead creased. "If this is Lady Catherine, an early wedding could eliminate this possible threat."

A lop-sided grin lit Richard's face. "I am shocked he is not rushing her to the church even now."

An abrupt laugh from Mr. Gardiner diverted their attention to him. "I agree with your cousin."

Darcy's insides jumped. He could be married to Elizabeth without a long betrothal, but his stomach sank as quickly as it had risen. He had not applied for any license as of yet, and Elizabeth deserved a trousseau and her family around her. They needed to try to wait. "I admit to being an impatient bridegroom, but I would prefer Elizabeth have a wedding worthy of her, not some rushed affair. If it becomes a necessity, I will not hesitate to take her as my wife."

With a crack of a joint, Mr. Gardiner stood and placed his glass upon the table. "I am certain you will."

Chapter 23

January 7th 1812 – Clarell House

"Good morning, Mr. Darcy. Lord Fitzwilliam, the colonel, and Mr. Gardiner await you in his lordship's study."

"Thank you, Sykes." Darcy passed his coat, hat, and gloves into a footman's waiting hands before the butler led him to his uncle's private library.

Sykes entered ahead of him and positioned himself against the door. "Mr. Darcy, sir."

"Darce!" exclaimed Richard as he stood. "We expected you a half hour ago. Where have you been?"

"I stopped at Doctor's Common before making my way here. I applied for a special license after we spoke of the possibility of an early wedding, and I thought it might be ready by now." He took a chair near the fire and stretched his feet closer to the heat. The carriage had not prevented him from becoming chilled with the morning's frigid weather.

His uncle removed his spectacles and began to wipe them with his handkerchief. "Licenses from Doctor's Common take a week or a fortnight at most, yet you sound as though yours was not completed."

"I was certain it would be prepared, but they cannot even locate the paper I left with the proctor. I submitted another request, and fortunately, I was remembered so I did not have to pay another fee."

"I have never heard of a similar circumstance." His uncle hooked the ends of his glasses around his ears as he spoke in an incredulous voice. "Either you receive the license or they deny the petition, but I do not trust this explanation. I shall visit the Archbishop on the morrow on your behalf."

Darcy shrugged. "I thought it possible my petition would be denied since I am not a peer, but I wanted to try. I hoped to marry at Darcy House, and her mother would enjoy bragging of it."

"She will crow for a year at least, Darcy." With a quiet laugh, Mr. Gardiner laced his fingers and rested his hands upon his rounded stomach. "Lizzy loves her mother, but Frances has not treated Lizzy as she should. I would not go to such an expense for her alone."

"I assure you I am not. Since we are still unaware of who is following me, I have come to believe a special license to be imperative, in the event we are required to wed expeditiously."

Richard stared into the fire as though he did not hear a word around him. "Could a few pounds in the right hands have caused the application to disappear? Perhaps this is the work of whomever is having you followed."

The earl nodded. "It is possible, and I believe probable. Whether this is Wickham or another party, we know they want to disrupt your betrothal and wedding. What better way than to prevent the ceremony itself? They cannot, however, prevent you from purchasing a common license in your own parish or even Miss Bennet's."

A common license was a solution, but they would be required to wed in the church as opposed to Darcy House. They could also not marry at the time of his and Elizabeth's choosing. The reading of the banns was an impossibility as well. They would be required to wait three weeks and could draw the attention of whoever was scheming against them. A special license was still the best option.

"You could wed from St. Clement's," interjected Mr. Gardiner. "Mr. Pye has always been fond of Lizzy. He would perform the ceremony, and no one would expect you to be married in Cheapside." All of the men laughed as a knock came from the door. At the earl's summons, a maid entered with a coffee service, prepared each of them a cup, and promptly departed.

His uncle rubbed his chin. "Gardiner is correct, you know. You could wed Miss Elizabeth and most of this would no longer be an issue. We could concentrate on locating Wickham and be done with it."

Darcy rose and paced before the fire. "I do not want to consider my wedding to Elizabeth as something to be done with. We shall only wed once, and while I am anxious for her to be my wife, I want Elizabeth to have the gown she desires and her family present. I know Mr. Bennet would be hurt if he could not give her away."

Two hands to Darcy's shoulders halted his strides and brought his attention to Mr. Gardiner, who now stood directly before him. "You need to remember that Elizabeth cares for people, not frippery. The most important thing to her will not be whether she wore a new gown or whether her trousseau was ornate and prepared before she wed. Her favourite memories of the day she becomes Mrs. Darcy will be the look in your eyes as you recite your vows and her joy at joining her life to yours. Just remember, I can have her father and Jane brought to London in a day."

"We discussed this prior to your arrival, Darce. The Bow Street Runners were unable to begin until Boxing Day, and Mr. Gardiner's men have discovered precious little. We do not believe this is Wickham, but another party who for some nefarious reason of their own is making a pest of themselves."

With a jolt, Darcy whipped his head to Mr. Gardiner. "You have heard back from your men?"

He gave a guttural exhale and returned to his seat. "One of the men came to the house late last night with his first report. They have found three individuals who have watched you in the last week. You have noticed the one since he has the watch during daylight hours. With the early setting of the sun this time of year, the second and third are certain to be indistinguishable since both of their shifts are after dark."

With a knot in his stomach, Darcy began to walk back and forth before the fire at a more sedate pace than earlier. "I agree, that this cannot be Wickham. He would never find the funds to pay three men for work of this sort." But if it was not Wickham, then who else could it be? The women from the Fitzwilliams' ball or Lady Catherine were suspect, yet how did they discover whom? "Have they followed these men when they depart their post?"

"I had a man do so two nights ago," responded Mr. Gardiner. "He traced the man who watched you all day back to a pub in St. Giles where he met with someone. The meeting was brief and occurred last night as well."

"What of the man at the pub? Has he been followed?"

"My man left his partner at Darcy House to go to St. Giles. Tonight, they both intend to go in order to do just that. None of my men relish venturing to that part of town, and they never do so alone—until that night, that is."

Richard pointed to Darcy's empty chair. "Would you sit! I cannot think when you march to and fro in that manner!" A knock from the door gave them all cause to start.

"Come in!" called his uncle.

The door opened as Bingley peered inside. "Am I intruding?"

"No, you are welcome." Lord Fitzwilliam stood and clapped Bingley on the shoulder. "I apologise if I sounded harsh a moment ago."

Once he situated himself in Darcy's empty seat, Bingley glanced around at each of them. Richard still stared into the fire as Mr. Gardiner poured himself another cup of coffee.

"Have you discovered any new information on the gentleman standing in the park on the corner?"

Darcy's hand clenched at his side. "You saw him as well?"

"He is hardly being discreet. I suppose he feels the distance from the house makes him so, yet he makes no effort to appear as though he belongs." He took a biscuit from the tray on the table before him. "I managed a moment alone to speak to Anne. She has noticed nothing unusual in her mother's associates or meetings as of late but will continue to keep an eye on her. Neither of us has someone watching us that we can tell, but if we do, they are more skilled at their occupation than that standing budge[1] of yours."

"I want to accompany your men this evening, Mr. Gardiner." All in the room looked at Richard, whose jaw was set and his eyes hard.

"Son, I do not believe this is a good idea. These men watching Darcy House might recognise you, and St. Giles can also be a dangerous place."

"I have faced Bonaparte's troops. Do you not think I can hold my own in St. Giles? If I join the investigators, we can outnumber him three to one, or one might stay behind to keep watch here. I shall stay out of their sights."

Richard stood and straightened his coat. "I must speak with my commander. I requested leave, so I could be of use during this time."

"The men from Pemberley arrive tomorrow, and your father has been kind enough to allow the use of some of his larger and more trusted servants. I appreciate your willingness to be of aid, but if you cannot be spared from your duties—"

"I do naught but train troops at the moment down at Horse Guards, with a half dozen other men. They can spare me for a fortnight or so." He extended his hand to Mr. Gardiner. "Leave word with my father about where to meet your investigators, and I shall be there." Mr. Gardiner nodded and Richard strode from the room.

"Do you think this is wise?" asked the earl. "He can be impetuous when those he cares about are threatened."

Mr. Gardiner leaned back into his seat. "We have had little success with our current tactics. A more aggressive approach might be useful. I can hardly fault his desire to be of aid when I would do the same were I in his place."

His uncle was correct. Richard could be hasty, ill tempered, and impulsive at best when his family was in danger. Should they now convince Mr. Gardiner to renege on his agreement with Richard? He walked to the window and gazed down the street to the park on the corner. The man had moved to a different spot, but was still watching. No, they needed to know what he was about and who employed him regardless of Richard's methods or temper. He could not chance that Elizabeth would come to harm because of him.

When Darcy turned, Mr. Gardiner, his uncle, and Bingley all stared at him. "Richard should go if for no other reason than to perhaps bring this to a close. I intend to escort Elizabeth to visit the modiste on Monday with Anne, Georgiana, Mrs. Gardiner, and my aunt. While they appear to be interested in me, I desire her safety and do not put it past Wickham to make an attempt on her if I am not in her company."

"We all share the same goal."

Mr. Gardiner's voice was sympathetic and calming, but it did nothing to assuage the restlessness of his limbs. He needed to move. No, he needed Elizabeth.

Without a word, he hastened from the room. His name was called from the study, but he continued without stopping until he reached the drawing room and entered.

"Darcy!" His aunt stood and made her way before him. "I did not expect you to join us." Her arm extended to his right. "You remember Lady Carlisle and her daughter Lady Althea, do you not?"

Behind Lady Fitzwilliam, Elizabeth's eyes rolled toward the ceiling, and his body relaxed. She was well.

He faced the guests and gave a curt bow. "Lady Carlisle, Lady Althea, it is agreeable to see you again."

Once they curtsied, Lady Carlisle stepped forward. "We are most pleased to be in your company again, Mr. Darcy. Are we not, Althea?"

His teeth ground together as the daughter tilted her head in a flirtatious manner. "Quite pleased indeed."

After he cleared his throat, Darcy withdrew his hand and rushed to take a seat beside Elizabeth. Just her proximity was enough to alleviate the remaining tension from the earlier talk with the men.

The conversation, as long as the Carlisles were present, was tedious to say the least. Despite his aunt and Anne attempting to steer them towards the theatre and the upcoming season, the two ladies were insistent on the latest gossip they had gathered at their previous calls.

"I have heard that Miss Bingley anticipates moving into her brother's home once he is wed and residing at Rosings." Lady Carlisle's brows were raised as she fiddled with the rings adorning her chubby fingers and smirked.

Anne frowned. "Even though Miss Bingley has made such assertions, I can assure you Mr. Bingley has no plans to alter his sister's arrangements. In fact, we intend to use his London home during the season so my mother might have the use of her own."

"Ah, I see. I shall have to inform Miss Reddington when I next see her. Miss Bingley, by all accounts, hired a hackney to make a recent call on Miss Reddington. Can you imagine?"

Lady Althea tittered. "I would be mortified to approach the door."

A feather light touch brushed his hand on the cushion of the sofa as Elizabeth shifted, which he continued to feel long after her hand returned to her lap. Would these women ever leave?

Elizabeth pressed her lips together to keep from laughing. Lady Althea was ridiculous with her preening—not that Fitzwilliam noticed or perhaps he did. His stiff posture was far from relaxed. At the moment, he was staring at the hand in her lap as Lady Althea's lips pursed tightly. How could she have been jealous of this girl a mere few days ago?

"We should depart," announced Lady Carlisle as though a parade should be held in her honour. "We are to call on the Duchess of Albany this morning as well." Lady Carlisle's shoulders and chest were puffed, making her appear like a bird who had ruffled its feathers.

As Lady Carlisle stood so did Lady Fitzwilliam. "I had not heard she was in town."

"I hear the duke has been rather poorly, so they journeyed to London for the doctors."

Elizabeth rose with Fitzwilliam suppressing a shake of the head at Lady Carlisle's gossipy whisper. Those who thought her mother was a gossip should travel to town. Her mother could tittle-tattle with the best of high society if skill were taken into account.

Lady Althea sidled closer to Fitzwilliam and tilted her head as her eyes raked up to his face. "You should come to Durham House for tea, Mr. Darcy. You would be welcome. Would he not, Mother?"

"Oh, yes, of course. You may come when you wish. Althea would be pleased to have your company."

Anne, who had the fortunate position of standing behind the two ladies, covered her eyes with her hand and shook her head.

"We shall have to call on Lady Catherine soon as well." With a start, Anne dropped her hand before Lady Carlisle turned. "It has been too long since I called on her."

"We have not spent much time in London until recent events returned us to town. I shall inform my mother of your intention to call. I am certain she would enjoy your company."

Lady Catherine enjoy company? Elizabeth had yet to see the woman smile much less show true pleasure in an activity. Instead, Lady Catherine professed an appreciation of a great many things, none of which she possessed as an accomplishment. No, precious little amused Anne's mother—or her stays were too tight, which could render any woman of sense peevish.

Once Lady Fitzwilliam managed to usher Lady Carlisle and her terror of a daughter from the room, they all relaxed and took their seats.

"I have oft times wondered why men of sense take silly wives," observed Anne, "and does the daughter believe her flirtations will make you leave Lizzy and offer her your hand? I thought Lizzy would claw her eyes out at church, but today you appeared to find her comical."

"I did, but she was not eyeing my betrothed as though he were a pudding she wished to savour." Fitzwilliam shuddered and they laughed until Lady Fitzwilliam returned.

"I do not mind Lord Carlisle, but I detest having to be polite to that woman, and if it were not for her father, that daughter would not step foot in my house! I pity the poor man who she lures into her trap!"

Anne snickered. "As she is still spinning her webs for Fitzwilliam, perhaps we should take pity on him."

"How could you prefer Elizabeth to Lady Althea, Fitzwilliam? Such an amiable creature should not be cast away." Lady Fitzwilliam tilted her head as she appraised her nephew, who gave a huff, took Elizabeth's hand and pulled her from the sofa towards the door.

"I was teasing," called his aunt as Elizabeth trotted at his side to maintain his pace. "I promised Marianne that Elizabeth would be chaperoned in your company!"

Fitzwilliam slowed when he reached the hall, but took the corridor to the right while he wrapped her arm around his. His thumb traced her knuckles as he slowed to a more sedate pace.

"Your aunt was not serious. You should not have walked away while she spoke."

"I shall apologise, but I could not bear another minute of them laughing at my expense."

She clutched his arm closer to her. "You are well aware they were making sport of Lady Althea and Lady Carlisle more than you."

They reached a small conservatory where he led her inside, but before he could close the door behind them, Anne squeezed through the opening. "Aunt Charlotte insisted I play chaperon. I am sure you have confidences you wish to share, and I would be in your way should I remain. I shall stand just outside the door where I can see you through the glass."

"Thank you, Anne." Elizabeth nudged Fitzwilliam in the ribs.

"Yes, thank you."

Anne pointed to Fitzwilliam. "You owe me for this, but do not put me in a bad position with our aunt. I do not want to be rebuked by her since she allows me to escape my mother and see Charles every day." She pivoted and proceeded back to the entrance.

Fitzwilliam lunged forward a step as Elizabeth's hand slid down his arm and into his. "Anne!"

She turned in the doorway to glance back.

"I apologise if I am in an ill humour. I do appreciate your willingness to act as chaperon."

Her shoulders rose and fell as she breathed. "I understand your frustration. I may not have had the trials you face at present, but my mother has stood in the way of my happiness for too long. Lizzy confided that part of the reason you have waited rather than marrying with haste is due to Charles and myself."

"One of several reasons, but yes."

Anne's attention wavered to a rose at her side. She grazed the silken red petals with a finger before she looked back to Fitzwilliam with a determined glint in her eye. "I believe I speak for Charles and myself when I tell you to seize your happiness when you can. We do not require all of society talking of our wedding to be content in our situation. Our desire is to begin our lives together as I believe yours is as well."

She glanced between the two of them. "If I were you, I would not tarry. Our aunt and uncle support a swifter wedding in an effort to see if it resolves the issues at hand. Lizzy's aunt and uncle would not object either since you cannot restrain yourself, dear cousin. Nothing stands in your way except yourselves, so what is preventing you?"

Elizabeth lay her forehead against Fitzwilliam's arm as the click of the door signalled Anne's departure. "She has told me we should plan according to our wishes and not with deference to her and Mr. Bingley."

Her head shifted from the rough wool of his topcoat to the silky fabric of his waistcoat as he took her in his arms. With the uncertainty that lay outside of Clarell House, his arms were of great comfort and security. As a child, her father's embrace gave a similar gratification, yet Fitzwilliam's arms now replaced Longbourn and her father. She was home. With a deep inhale, the scent of his cologne invaded her senses and her body relaxed.

"I have never seen her so adamant and insistent, though I must admit that I can understand why." His lips brushed her temple as he caressed the bare skin of her neck above the hooks of her gown.

She felt as though a feather was tickling from his fingertips down the length of her spine and down to her toes. His warm breath prickled against her scalp and the thumping of his heart filled her ear. How was she supposed to think? "I know you want to wait for the date we set."

His hand slid to her cheek and his thumb lifted her chin. "I would marry you wrapped in a burlap sack in the mews of Seven Dials if that was your desire, but I want you to have a wedding you will not regret."

"As long as you are the bridegroom, I shall have no regrets, Fitzwilliam, though I would prefer more than a burlap sack."

His chest shook with the low rumble of his suppressed laugh. "You would not mind the mews of Seven Dials?"

She scrunched her nose. "A church would be my choice."

"With the unanswered questions of who is following me and why, I thought the drawing room of Darcy House. The ceremony would not be accessible to any party with nefarious motives."

"Such a ceremony requires a special license, does it not?"

"I am attempting to procure one, but I shall not know for a few more days if I am successful."

His eyes fixated on the embroidery of her gown, tracing it with his eyes. Why was he not looking at her?

"Have you had difficulty procuring one thus far?"

His gaze returned to hers. "Why would you assume I have?"

"You avoided my eye when you spoke of it."

His fingers had long since returned to her back where they wreaked havoc on her ability to form a coherent thought. She removed his meandering hand and held it tight. "Will you not confide in me?"

"I applied for a special license after you noticed the man at Darcy House. This morning, I returned to Doctor's Common, and the request appears to have been misplaced. Lord Fitzwilliam intends to confirm the replacement is not lost on the morrow." He buried his face in her hair. "I want nothing more than to marry you as soon as possible. I cannot bear waiting, yet I fear I might put you in harm's way when we wed."

She lifted her face and threaded her fingers through his dark curls. "I want to be your wife. I know you have concerns, but I do not want to wait."

"You are certain?" Her gown bunched in the back where he gripped the gathers as he studied her face.

"I am."

His lips stroked hers once, twice, three times before he opened her lips to his tongue and pulled her flush to his body. "When?" He trailed kisses down her neck as she could do naught but rest her forehead against his chest. Her knees wobbled, but his arms about her kept her upright.

"When what?"

He paused at her shoulder and lifted his face with a huge grin. "When do you wish to marry?"

"Oh! As soon as you can arrange matters would suit me."

A small kiss was bestowed to the tip of her nose. "I shall speak with a vicar or as many as I require, I shall pen a letter to your father, inviting your family, and make the arrangements. You are to shop with my aunt, Anne, and Georgiana on Monday?"

"I am, but I am certain they would not mind—"

"No, I think Tuesday or Wednesday would be better days. I would also have time to obtain a common license should my uncle fail."

A weight suddenly exerted itself upon her chest as she took a straggling breath. "You want me to have no regrets, but will you regret me?"

His head jolted back. "Whatever do you mean?"

"I have a pittance of a dowry, few connections—"

"I do not care."

"Regardless, they are a problem, and my mother has always bemoaned that my father educated me. I also have seen the ladies in London. They are a far cry more handsome than me."

"I am enamoured of your wit and intelligence." He brushed a curl back from her face. "And I do not know why you think yourself less than the most handsome woman of my acquaintance. I see naught of any other lady in your presence, and when I am not with you, I still pay them no heed. In my eyes, you have no equal."

Her vision blurred and she sniffed. "My mother has said—"

"Your mother is blind and fit for Bedlam if she does not see your beauty." Fitzwilliam pressed his cheek to hers. "I want no more of this nonsense. I love you, and I shall wed no one but you. Do you understand?"

A soft laugh overrode the sob leaving her throat. "I do understand. I feel the same, but I had to ask."

"Do not doubt me, Elizabeth. I shall never have cause to repine."

"I love you."

Her voice was a croaky whisper, but Fitzwilliam paid no mind as he said, "I love you, too." His lips descended upon hers as he kissed her as though he were starved for her, pressing her against the icy window to the outside. They remained thus entwined until the irritated and loud voice of Lady Fitzwilliam intruded.

"Fitzwilliam, remove yourself from her at once!"

[1]Standing Budge – a thief's scout or spy

Chapter 24

A brisk knock roused Darcy from his ledgers. "Enter!"

Without introduction, Richard in gentleman's dress strode in and closed the door behind him. "Why is it I always find you in this room? You have this grand home, here and at Pemberley, but you spend the entirety of your time in the study."

"One could comment that you have an uncanny ability to appear only at those times as well."

"Touché." Richard glanced at the clock on the mantel. "I understand from Mother that the ladies are to arrive in an hour?"

"Yes, which is why I was attempting to complete these figures. I wanted to have my day free to accompany them to Bond Street." He looked to Richard's cravat as he dipped his pen in ink. "Do you have plans for today?"

"I intend to accompany the group as well."

Darcy's shoulders tightened and he placed his pen on its stand. "You? Shopping with ladies on Bond Street? What do you know that you are not telling me?"

Examining his cuff as though it was the most important piece of his wardrobe, Richard shifted and gave a one-shouldered shrug. "I have naught to report."

"How do you keep secrets for the military when you are a terrible liar?"

"I am merely incapable of telling falsehoods to family. You have witnessed me lie enough at social functions to know the truth of the matter."

He had a point. Richard could deceive the matchmaking mamas at his mother's balls, but he became awkward when making the attempt with those for whom he was closest. As a child, they never escaped punishment since Richard could not spin a convincing tale to his parents.

"Mr. Gardiner has men accompanying us as well as the three men I brought from Pemberley. Why do you feel the measures we have will not be adequate?"

"I have told you how we lost the man from the pub a few nights ago." Darcy nodded and gestured with his hand for Richard to continue. "I mean, Gardiner's men are good, but mistakes and barking dogs happen. I do not blame them." He ran his palms down the legs of his trousers with an awkward stretch. "I have had this feeling in my gut since that night. This man might become desperate. We do not know who is behind this nor why, and I shall not see you, Miss Bennet, or Georgiana harmed when I could prevent it."

As Darcy leaned back from his desk, he caught Richard's eye. "Regardless of what occurs, I appreciate all you have done, cousin."

"You sound as though you expect the worst."

"No, I worry that if one of us is harmed, you will blame yourself."

"You fret like a woman," Richard groused. "I shall not permit any of you to come to harm—not while I am present."

The sound of a door opening caused the study door to shift in its frame as the sound of ladies voices, muffled by the heavy oak panel, brought Darcy to stand and make his way to the hall where Elizabeth and Georgiana were removing their pelisses and gloves.

"You were not expected for almost another hour."

A radiant smile lit Elizabeth's face when she turned, and his breathing hitched. Her eyes sparkled and her skin glowed with health and happiness. She was going to be his! Maybe not today, but in a mere few days!

Georgiana rushed forward and kissed his cheek. "I wished for a gown I had here, so Lizzy accompanied me." She stepped past him and hugged Richard. "I shall be swift." With a glance at both Darcy and Elizabeth, she pressed her hand to Richard's arm. "I am under strict orders to ensure they are not left on their own."

"Georgiana!" he and Elizabeth cried at the same moment.

Richard chuckled. "Do not fret. I shall ensure they behave in my presence."

Georgiana hastened up the stairs as Richard started. "I almost forgot. Father's call on Doctor's Common met with success." A paper was pulled from Richard's inside coat pocket. "He returned with this yesterday and requested I deliver it to you."

Darcy's heart gave a jolt. Could it be the license? He took the document, unfolded it, and perused it to ensure there were no mistakes. "Thank you and thank your father. I shall have to find a suitable gift to repay him for his help in this matter."

Elizabeth's small hand tilted the paper. "Does this mean we can wed when we wish?"

"That is precisely what it means."

Her arm wrapped around his and hugged him a bit closer. "When my uncle discovers you have received this, he might insist on an immediate wedding."

Despite the company of his cousin, he pressed his lips to her hair. "I would welcome his demand and request the vicar myself."

Her uncle had been little pleased by events a few days ago. Darcy's aunt refused to conceal their misbehaviour in the conservatory, revealing all to Mrs. Gardiner, who in turn, divulged their lapse of propriety to her husband. If not for the lack of license, Mr. Gardiner, without delay, would have marched Elizabeth to Darcy House with her trunk on the back of the carriage for the ceremony.

"I did tell Georgiana I would ensure you behaved in my presence, so at least give me a moment to depart the room before you become too lost in one another." He began to walk in the direction of the library. "You wed in two days' time. You would think you could behave with decorum. Darcy is a besotted fool as it is. What happens once you are wed and he..."

Richard's voice faded as he closed the door, and Elizabeth arched an eyebrow at her betrothed. "And you what?"

"I am afraid to venture a guess." His eyes darted from where Richard departed and back to her. He knew, but did not want to say! Before she could question him further, he grabbed her hand and pulled her inside his study. "I have a present for you."

"You do?" His dimple shown in his cheek as his entire being radiated joy. She was so fortunate to be betrothed to Fitzwilliam. He was an honourable man—a good man and he loved her. Who knew what she had done to deserve him, but why question good luck?

He left her by the fireplace where she was warm from more than just the fire. The familiar click of a key in a lock could be heard as he fiddled with a side drawer on his desk where he removed a wooden box. When he stood before her once more, he lifted her hand as he set the case on her palm. "You may wear it every day should you choose."

The polished wood was smooth to her fingers as she traced the length to the clasp, which she lifted. As she cracked the lid, she gasped. "It is lovely!"

"Do you truly like it?"

She studied how each pair of gold flowers resembled a heart shape that joined to another of the same at the top, while a round peridot was between the two dimples and one teardrop shaped peridot sat in the middle of each heart. Pearls accented the arrangement. The floral pattern repeated and was held together by tiny loops of gold between the sections.

He removed it from the velvet and wrapped it around her wrist, joining it together at the clasp. "I have carried it with me the past few days. I wanted to present it to you when you wore your green gown."

She drew his head down and bestowed a simple kiss to his lips. Her uncle had chastised her for almost an hour the last time they were caught flaunting propriety. They would be wed in but two days, so while his embrace beckoned, she pressed her palm to his chest and stepped back.

His forehead crinkled and his eyebrows dipped in the centre. "If you do not care for it, I can—"

"I think it beautiful, and I intend to have it upon my wrist always. You will have all the ladies of the ton whispering of my poor taste behind their fans because I will not only have a pearl ring upon my finger but also pearls upon my wrist at all hours of the day."

With a casual step, she began to walk the perimeter of the room. He was too close! Her heart begged to find solace in his arms and never leave. It was imperative she separate herself from him before she received another chastisement from her uncle.

A particularly thick book drew her eye, and she stopped to ascertain the title. Before she could proceed, a large arm wrapped around her stomach from behind as heated lips seared the flesh where her neck and shoulder met.

"Fitzwilliam!" Her voice sounded strange as it broke and was a bit ragged. "We must not again be caught thus."

His thumb stroked her ribs, grazing the underside of her breast as it followed the same path again and again. As the tip of his nose nuzzled behind her ear, his breath prickled her skin.

"You do not play fair."

"I have no restraint when we are alone, Elizabeth. I know we have but two days, but my fingers itch to touch the velvet of your skin and hold you to me. I can think of nothing else."

Lord help her as it was all she could do to distract herself from the same thoughts! She turned in his arms, but had no opportunity to dissuade him as he claimed her lips and pressed her against the bookcase. His desperate kiss and the feel of his silky tongue against hers rendered her unsteady on her own feet. She clutched the heavy wool of his topcoat at his waist as he returned to her neck; her eyes rolled back and the room disappeared as her eyes closed.

The sensation of his strong body flush to hers, his throaty groan, and the endless massage of his hand across her lower back and side was dizzying. Her breathing was laboured and panting as she shifted to allow him access to her collarbone.

"You left them alone!"

Fitzwilliam hurtled back with such force, he knocked over a side table as she sagged against the metal lattice-work doors that protected the books behind her. Georgiana's censure of the colonel grew louder as she approached the study, and Elizabeth's hand flew to her chest. She must look affright!

"Do not doubt that I shall tell Aunt Charlotte who left them without a chaperon!"

"Georgiana, they will be wed on Wednesday and no longer require this constant supervision. Besides, your brother would never do more than steal a kiss in one of the more public rooms—especially when he expects your return."

Elizabeth's hands began running over her chest and neck while Fitzwilliam hastened to put the table back as it was. Was part of her gown out of place? Would Georgiana and Colonel Fitzwilliam know when they entered?

"Nothing is amiss in your appearance, Elizabeth."

Her eyes darted to his. "You are certain?"

"As long as you relax, she will have no reason to be suspicious."

With a hurried pivot, she opened the bookcase and began to run her finger along the spines of the books. Wordsworth? Well, at least she had a fair knowledge of his poetry in the event Georgiana asked.

Colonel Fitzwilliam burst in first as though he expected to catch them as they were a mere few minutes before while Georgiana pushed him aside and entered. Her eyes narrowed as she glanced between them.

"The pair of you know you are not supposed to be alone. How could you? Aunt Charlotte trusted me to ensure you did not breach propriety." Her shrill voice prompted a wince from all present as she pointed her finger in their general direction. "If she discovers, she will hold me responsible."

"You left them to me, so Mother would not direct her ire towards you, Georgiana. You know well she would not find fault with your actions." With a tilt of his head, the colonel appraised his young cousin. "Are you at sixes and sevens because of the planned trip to Bond Street? I know you were not completely comfortable when we attended services, so your unease would be understandable."

Her hands clenched before her as her entire body sagged. "I so want to go, but I cannot prevent myself from trembling at the thought. My mind has insisted upon turning the same thoughts over and over."

Elizabeth abandoned her ruse and wrapped her arms around the poor dear. "Forgive me. Over the last few days, you have become increasingly ill tempered, but I had not considered this trip to be the cause. You could have unburdened yourself to your aunt or me instead of concealing your anxiety."

"You have been occupied with other matters." Georgiana sniffled as she returned Elizabeth's embrace. "Do not think I did not trust you or feel you could not be of aid. I wanted to conquer this on my own."

She pulled back and cradled Georgiana's face in her hands. "While your resolve is admirable, you have not had much time to heal since August. Give yourself more time."

Fitzwilliam's embrace engulfed them both. "Our first appointment is with the modiste, which is, I believe, what you do not want to miss?"

A dip of Georgiana's chin provided his response as Elizabeth dabbed the girl's cheeks with a handkerchief.

"Then accompany us to the modiste, and when the appointment is complete, you may return here directly. Elizabeth's aunt has purchased the fabric, so a trip to the drapers is not necessary, and we can walk to the milliners and Gunther's from Madame Guiard's shop."

"You would still take part in choosing my trousseau. You would also have gone beyond your previous limitations by leaving the comfort and security of Clarell House for a destination you have not visited since before Ramsgate."

Fitzwilliam kissed her temple. "I am proud of the strides you have made. Even had you opted to remain behind today, my feelings would not have changed."

As Fitzwilliam hugged his sister, cleared his throat, and stepped away, the colonel took his young cousin's hand and tugged her to face him. "They are correct. Do not force yourself to do more than you ought."

Voices from the hall drew their attention just before Lady Fitzwilliam entered, her appraising eye flitting to each of them. "Has something happened?"

Georgiana sniffed and drew back from Elizabeth's embrace. "No, Aunt, but I shall depart Madame Guiard's when Lizzy has completed her shopping and return here to await our party's return for dinner."

Lady Fitzwilliam's eyebrows gave a small lift, but instead of responding, her eyes landed upon Elizabeth's wrist. "Really, Fitzwilliam," she chided, lifting Elizabeth's arm. "First her ring, and now a bracelet? You will have the entire ton gossiping that your new wife does not know the absurd rules of London fashion."

"Perhaps I possess more of a conceited independence?" Her eyes met the great lady's and they stared for a moment before both dissolving into laughter.

"I like you more by the day, Elizabeth Bennet. I shall enjoy promoting you within the ton. We need a spirited lady such as yourself to make things interesting." She wrapped her arm around Georgiana's elbow. "We must depart. The carriage is waiting and Madame Guiard does not hold appointments when her clients are late."

Lady Fitzwilliam wrapped her other arm through Elizabeth's. "Your aunt does have an eye for exquisite fabrics. I am quite envious of the selections she has made for you. I will have to persuade her to accompany me on my next trip to the drapers."

The heavy, steady footfalls of the men followed them to the hall where they donned their coats and joined Aunt Gardiner and Anne in the carriage. Once the colonel joined the driver atop the equipage, the carriage shifted as it began to move through the streets of Mayfair towards Bond Street.

The trip to Madame Guiard's establishment was swift as were her employees when they arrived, who ushered the ladies of their party to a room in the back, while the men awaited them in the front.

As Lady Fitzwilliam had indicated, the fabrics Aunt Gardiner selected were the finest she had ever seen, and when combined with the fashion plates they chose, would make the most splendid, well-made gowns.

Georgiana calmed a great deal once in the privacy of the modiste's, but her relief was evident when Elizabeth kissed her on the cheek before her return to Darcy House. Once the carriage departed, Fitzwilliam offered Elizabeth his arm, and they began their walk to the milliner's a few shops down, surrounded by their party and several men dressed as lesser gentlemen who led or followed, giving the appearance they were not part of the group. When had they arrived?

As they approached the shop front, a selection of bonnets and gloves in the window caught her eye. They were not just the simple straw front hats to which she was accustomed, but also had selections in velvet, silk, and other expensive materials. Once inside, she continued to peruse the items on display until she almost ran into Fitzwilliam when he made an abrupt stop.

"Mr. Darcy!"

That voice! She knew that voice. With a turn of her head, she spotted Miss Bingley at the opposite side of the shop, her sister standing nearby.

"Why, it has been too long!"

Her betrothed stood unyielding as he gave a curt bow. "Mrs. Hurst, Miss Bingley, I do hope you are well."

The presumption of this woman to address them as though she were an old friend after her actions at Netherfield! Was she sane?

Mrs. Hurst curtsied. "Mr. Darcy, Miss Bennet, Miss de Bourgh, I am pleased to see you again."

Without a formal greeting, Miss Bingley rushed forward and grasped Anne's hands. "I am so pleased your betrothal to my brother is official at last! I cannot anticipate more the day I shall be able to call you sister."

Anne leaned back from Miss Bingley with wide eyes as the latter spoke. Caroline Bingley's name was mentioned often while Elizabeth resided at Clarell House and never on good terms. Anne's feelings were quite the opposite of Miss Bingley's to be sure.

"We shall be such a merry party this summer at Rosings, will we not?"

Miss Bingley regarded Anne with the most unaffected smile Elizabeth had ever witnessed. She was ecstatic to be gaining Anne as a sister whether Anne reciprocated those feelings or not. One thing was certain. Anne would never allow Miss Bingley to set one toe into Rosings.

"Miss Bingley," began Anne in a controlled voice.

"Oh! Please call me Caroline!"

"Miss Bingley, while your brother and I have not discussed our plans for the summer months, I have no intention of entertaining guests so soon after our marriage."

"Oh tosh! You will grow bored with only Charles for company."

Anne gave a strange almost high-pitched chirp. Was she stifling an incredulous laugh?

"Mr. Bingley and I have waited nearly two years to begin our lives together. I shall not require more than his companionship; I assure you."

With a wave of her hand, Miss Bingley scoffed. "You will change your mind; mark my words. Besides, if I am living with you and Charles, I cannot remain behind in London."

"Caroline?" called Mrs. Hurst. We should return to have luncheon with Mr. Hurst. You know how he complains when the meal is late."

Miss Bingley did not appear to have heard Mrs. Hurst. "I shall send a note to Charles this afternoon. We should have tea. I would *adore* becoming better acquainted."

Mrs. Hurst came from behind her sister and looped her arm through Miss Bingley's. "We do truly need to depart."

One of Miss Bingley's nostrils lifted, distorting her face in an unattractive fashion. "Of course, Louisa. We would not want to keep your husband from the trough."

Oblivious to Mrs. Hurst's sudden crimson complexion, Miss Bingley's expression then altered to her usual false smile. "You should join us for tea when a date can be arranged, Mr. Darcy. We shall soon be related, you know." Fitzwilliam did not respond, but remained stock-still as Miss Bingley's attention returned to Anne.

"I predict we shall be the best of friends. I anticipate Charles' invitation for tea." After a curtsey, Miss Bingley allowed Mrs. Hurst to guide her from the shop.

"I would burn Rosings to the ground before I allow her within its walls." Anne muttered the statement, yet all within their group heard since they either chuckled or smirked. "Charles was meeting with the solicitor today about her establishment. She will not be pleased with the results."

Lady Fitzwilliam leaned into her niece's shoulder. "Do tell."

Anne smirked. "Are you familiar with the small cottage in Doddington that is part of the Rosings estate?"

Fitzwilliam's shoulders began to shake before his laughter was heard. "I am. It is eight miles west from Rosings and small, as is the village. Is Bingley to move her household there?"

A mischievous glint lit Anne's eyes. "She has made a constant practice of overspending her allowance since she came out. He warned her she could not be so frivolous, yet she has not heeded his words. Due to her habits, Charles is concerned that if she remains in London, she will not have enough of her fortune left to sustain her for her lifetime." She picked up a nearby bonnet and turned it in her hands. "The cottage would require some upkeep, but the estate provides for such necessities as it is. Her abigail and companion would move with her, however, maids and a cook can be hired in the country."

Aunt Gardiner, who Miss Bingley had ignored, smiled. "They will not require as high a wage as those in London."

Elizabeth stared at Lady Fitzwilliam. Miss Bingley had stolen glances at the lady but had not attempted a conversation. How peculiar!

"Lady Fitzwilliam, I understand why Miss Bingley would snub my aunt, but why did she not attempt to engage you in conversation?"

Lady Fitzwilliam took the bonnet from her niece's grasp and threaded the ribbon through her fingers with a grin. "I have made it quite clear I have no wish to make her acquaintance, so while I am sure she knows who I am, she does not speak to me as we have not been introduced." She handed the bonnet back to Anne. "She once made an effort to force an introduction by speaking of me in my presence. I admit I walked away."

"You cut her?" Elizabeth bit back a wince at the high pitch of her own voice.

"In a manner of speaking, yes. She and her sister hope to ascend into the ton by sharpening their claws on those they feel beneath them. Their poor manners have admitted them into the company of those who thrive on gossip and that sort of behaviour, though Miss Bingley's acceptance has waned since her brother formed her establishment."

Anne replaced the hat and picked up a different one. "They assume she has either lost favour by behaving in a scandalous manner, or Charles has decided she is on the shelf. From what Charles related in his letters, her friends dwindled when she moved to her own apartments."

After brushing her palms together, Lady Fitzwilliam took Elizabeth's elbow and steered her further into the shop. "Enough about Caroline Bingley. We need to sort out your purchases, so we can go to the shoemakers and have tea."

The next hour was dizzying as Elizabeth and Anne selected their hats, gloves, and a few silk and cashmere shawls of Indian origin that the proprietor stocked as well. Once the lot was tallied and arrangements made for delivery and payment, they were again walking down Bond Street.

The day was not terribly cold for January, but tolerable with her pelisse and gloves. The sun had emerged from the clouds while they were at the milliner's, which also helped warm those who were shopping for the upcoming season.

Elizabeth gave a gentle squeeze to Fitzwilliam's arm as his thumb traced along the top of her knuckles. His presence beside her for an excursion that must have been a tedious bore to him made her heart swell. He would never fail to see to her safety or abandon her for the whims which many high society gentlemen indulged. She was stuck with him—not that the notion bothered her. On the contrary, every part of her hummed in satisfaction at the thought.

She leaned forward to glance at her aunt who was on Fitzwilliam's other arm, but she was taking in the sites around her as well. Colonel Fitzwilliam strode ahead of them with Anne and his mother as they pointed at different shop fronts and laughed.

A moment later, Lady Fitzwilliam pulled her son to the window of a jeweller's and exclaimed over the few pieces he displayed for the public to see. "His work is lovely. Richard, do not be missish in mentioning this shop to your father. Our anniversary is next month, you know."

The colonel gave a bark of a laugh. "You have enough jewellery, Mother. Surely, Father can think of a more useful gift."

Lady Fitzwilliam slapped his arm. "I shall put you over my knee if you say such nonsense to him, Richard George William Fitzwilliam!"

Elizabeth watched their exchange, smiling at their light-hearted banter and teasing. A glance at Aunt Gardiner revealed her hand to her mouth and her head down as she listened and found amusement at their antics as well.

As her head turned back to the pavement in front of the shop, a man emerged from those walking with a glare fixed on Fitzwilliam; her eyes riveted to him as he continued to stride forward. Without stopping, his hand reached into his coat pocket to remove what appeared to be a piece of wood; however, when sunlight reflected from the object, it created a glare. She shook her head and focussed again—to see a blade now extended from one end! Her heart began to pound as if it would burst from her chest.

"Fitzwilliam?" Her voice emerged as no more than a croaky whisper. Why would her legs not move? She opened her mouth to call Fitzwilliam's name again, but nothing happened. Why could she not make another sound?

"Yes, my love."

She could not breathe! Her hand flew to her chest just at the base of her neck while she attempted to suck in air as though someone held a pillow to her face, her surroundings appearing as though they were a dream unfolding before her.

Fitzwilliam turned and followed her line of sight as the man quickened his pace and advanced. His arm bearing the blade swung back as a scream rent the air or was it several piercing shrieks? Chaos ensued as her back scraped painfully against the stone of the building she was propelled against and the side of her head smarted where it struck the wall. Her vision blurred as Fitzwilliam's body pressed flush to hers. She put a hand to her head, but her knees collapsed as everything went dark.

"Elizabeth!"

Chapter 25

"Fitzwilliam?"

By the croaky sound of her voice, Elizabeth needed to clear her throat. London air was notoriously foul, and she had been exposed for too long today.

He watched his aunt and Richard's amusing interaction. "Yes, my love?" As soon as a pause in the conversation gave him an opportunity, he would propose they return to Darcy House.

When she did not respond, he turned. Elizabeth's wide eyes, panting breaths, and ever increasing grip upon his arm made him follow her line of sight to a blade held back, ready to swing.

"Richard!"

His cousin whirled around as Aunt Charlotte and Anne screamed, followed a second later by Mrs. Gardiner. Elizabeth's hand was at the base of her neck, but she was frozen in place. Darcy grabbed her and propelled them both against the wall of the nearby building. Elizabeth gave a short, high-pitched gasp when she hit the stone. Had the wind been knocked out of her when she hit the wall? Was she hurt?

A searing pain tore through his shoulder. Grunting and scuffling came from behind him. The men began to yell. Feminine screeches came from too far away to be from one of their party but pierced his eardrums.

Spots appeared before his eyes, and he blinked hard. He had to remain alert and rational! Regardless of what happened behind him, Elizabeth must remain safe!

"Get the carriage!"

"Follow them! Ensure the colonel catches him!"

"Stay with Mr. Darcy!"

Without warning, Elizabeth sagged and relinquished her grip on his arm. "Elizabeth!" He wrapped her in a tight embrace, his heart pounding. Had she fainted? As he prevented her from crumpling to the pavement, he pressed a kiss to her temple. The faint sound of her even breaths reached his ears, and he leaned his forehead against the cold stone. Thank God!

"Sir!"

Oliver Morely, who had been one of several men Darcy had transported to London when the threat was first perceived, stood just over his shoulder.

"Sir, the carriage should be here soon. One of the men went to fetch it and alert the house servants to send for the doctor. Colonel Fitzwilliam took off after the hector. Ran like the coward he is, that one."

Mrs. Gardiner's harried and tear-streaked face appeared beside Morely. "Mr. Darcy? Is Lizzy well?" Her voice was frantic; she had been crying.

With the danger presumably gone, Darcy bent and lifted Elizabeth into his arms, turning so Mrs. Gardiner could see her niece with her own eyes. She ran her hands over Elizabeth's face, down her arms and skirt, and along the portions of her back that could be reached.

"She does not appear to have suffered an injury."

Aunt Charlotte approached and brushed the curls from Elizabeth's face. "Could be she fainted from the shock?"

"I thought she struck her head against the wall," offered Anne. "We may find a bump when we return to Darcy House and let down her hair."

Morely held out his arm as the carriage approached, ensuring they were all inside before he strode around to the back of the equipage and climbed aboard. The last of the men clambered atop with the driver.

Darcy sat with Elizabeth clutched to his chest and gazed down at her beloved face. He had acted with such haste to press her against the wall and protect her with his own body, but had he pushed her with too much force? How could he forgive himself if he caused her any harm?

His heart ached as he stroked the soft skin of her cheek with his knuckles. "Elizabeth, please open your eyes."

As his aunt entered, Mrs. Gardiner pulled the shades on their side of the carriage. "We do not need all and sundry to witness Lizzy in your lap."

He stiffened. "We have no room to lay her upon the seat, and she would fall on her face should we attempt to have her sit. What else would you have me do?"

"Fitzwilliam Darcy, do not speak to Marianne in such a manner! Our predicament has attracted a crowd, if you had not noticed. Regardless of whether Lizzy can walk or sit on her own at the moment, you must admit that gossip is best avoided. We shall have enough talk from the attack without giving people more to spread. Do you not agree?"

"Yes, of course."

A groan came from Elizabeth's lips.

"Elizabeth?"

Her eyes fluttered open, she winced, and brought her hand to the back of her head. "What happened? I remember my head striking the wall and not much else." She attempted to rise, but paused as her eyes met his. "Fitzwilliam, am I in your lap?"

Anne grinned. "Yes, and in front of witnesses no less. My cousin has no shame, behaving so before your family and his own."

With a slap to her niece's arm, Aunt Charlotte rolled her eyes. "Ignore her. You could not sit on your own when we entered, and we are now approaching Darcy House. You may as well stay where you are."

"He was heading in our direction... with that knife. I have never seen one unfold as it did. How did he not harm one of us?"

"My son managed to hit the vile beast, who ran when he noticed Richard and the other men surrounding him. Richard pursued him along with the men." Lady Fitzwilliam looked down to a handkerchief clutched in her trembling hands. "I saw him before we turned to look in the window. He had just crossed the street and appeared to be watching the carriages and horses rather than us. How did everything go so wrong in such a short amount of time?"

"He fooled us all, Aunt. My attention was drawn to your conversation with Richard. I did not know what was afoot until Elizabeth said my name—even then, I had to look at her to see there was trouble."

Mrs. Gardiner took his aunt's hand. "We should be grateful his attack did not injure any of our party."

Elizabeth's arm wrapped around his shoulders, her brows drew down, and she looked at his back.

He gave an ever so slight shake of his head. "'Tis a scratch," he whispered near her ear. Truth be told, it smarted terribly now they were safe, yet how could he have her fret when she had just had such a fright?

"We shall call for a doctor when we return." Her voice was soft, but he still glanced to their aunts and Anne, who were still discussing the attack. Could they hear what they were saying?

"We shall, but to ensure you are well. I do not want to take any chances since you struck your head."

With her other hand, she took his face and turned it to her. "The wound could become infected. You must allow a doctor to see it, or I will postpone the wedding until you do."

He grinned. "People on the street witnessed me press my body against yours as well as my removal of you to the carriage where I placed you in my lap. Your uncle and father would never allow you to carry out your threat."

An amusing growl came from her throat. "You are insufferable!" She narrowed her eyes. "Very well!" She leaned up to his ear. "Then perhaps I shall be too exhausted for a proper wedding night. I would not want you to overexert yourself if your injury is too severe."

He gave a loud bark of a laugh, but composed himself when the aunts and his cousin sent curious stares in their direction. How he itched to squirm in his seat! "You would not dare."

She held his steady gaze as they stopped before Darcy House. "Of course I would, or I would not have threatened such a thing." She cocked that infernal eyebrow and shifted to the seat beside him. "I am capable of walking. After all, my head was knocked against a wall. I have not lost the use of my legs."

Her aunt watched their interaction and laid her hand upon Elizabeth's arm. "Do not allow your stubbornness override your sense. I am certain Mr. Darcy is very worried."

"I am, Mrs. Gardiner, thank you."

His heart had dropped to his stomach when Elizabeth removed herself from his embrace. Could she be serious? The wound stung, but why could she not understand that he needed to ensure her safety first? She was more important than a mere flesh wound!

He helped their aunts and Anne alight, and held out both hands in the event Elizabeth became light headed. She rose with care from the seat and held the frame of the door as she peered down upon him.

"Please allow me to be of use."

Tears welled in her eyes as she nodded and accepted his aid. She fumbled a bit as she stepped to the pavement and walked into the house, yet it would not have been noticeable to passers-by.

When they entered, Elizabeth swayed, and he steered her to a chair along the wall. "You should have allowed me to carry you."

"I am certain it is merely the stress of the day."

"Mr. Darcy, one of the men alerted us to your imminent arrival and departed again with haste to summon Mr. Baines in the event someone was injured. Rooms are being prepared for each member of your party to refresh themselves or to consult with the doctor when he arrives."

As Jobbins finished his speech, Aunt Charlotte strode around Darcy and pulled at the fabric of his great coat. "Take this off at once."

"Aunt!"

"Do as I say, Fitzwilliam. If this is what caused the childish standoff between you and Elizabeth in the carriage, I stand with her on the matter."

"You do not know all."

"I can see your shirt and some blood through this rip. I do not require the entirety of your argument as I believe Elizabeth was insisting upon Mr. Baines treating your wound."

He groaned. "'Tis but a scratch."

Aunt Charlotte took the collar of his coat and began to pull it down his arms, forcing him to stand. Once she had removed the heavy wool piece, she began to shift the layers of fabric remaining as the flesh of his shoulder began to throb and sting.

She gave a huff. "I need you to remove your topcoat and waistcoat if I am going to see the severity of the cut."

With an abrupt pivot, Darcy faced his aunt. "I will not disrobe in company, madam. When the doctor arrives, I shall allow him to treat my shoulder as he sees fit."

A giggle drew them all to look at Elizabeth, who had her hand over her mouth. As Darcy glanced around, Mrs. Gardiner and Anne were both suppressing their mirth as well.

"May I ask what is so amusing?"

Elizabeth's eyes twinkled. "You sound like a boy refusing his porridge."

"Mutton," interjected Anne. "Fitzwilliam has always detested mutton." The ladies all burst into laughter.

"Thank you for clarifying, Anne." He spoke through his clenched teeth. Why did they insist on teasing him now? This was not the time for silliness!

Anne smirked. "I am pleased I could be of help."

Darcy scooped Elizabeth into his arms and searched until he found Jobbins near the servant's corridor. "Miss Bennet requires a bedchamber." The butler proceeded up the stairs and down a corridor as they followed with their aunts and Anne close behind.

"Fitzwilliam!"

He ignored Aunt Charlotte's call as Jobbins opened a set of double doors to reveal the mistress' suite. A comforting fire was lit in the grate, though the room was not yet warm.

"These chambers have already been prepared, sir. Phoebe will return with hot water as soon as it is available. Miss Bennet, please ring should you require a comfort we have failed to provide."

"Thank you, Jobbins." Darcy set Elizabeth upon the bed and began to brush the curls from her face, but she stayed his hands.

"Please do not be cross with Anne, your aunt, or even me. I daresay we need to laugh lest we all be nonsensical, which would do good for no one."

"Forgive me for making sport of you, cousin, but Elizabeth is correct. If I dwell on what occurred on Bond Street, I would sit before the fire, inconsolable." Anne held out a quivering hand. "We may be safe within these walls, but I am still quite distressed."

He closed his eyes and took a few slow even breaths. Where was Richard? Why had neither he nor any of the men returned from their chase?

"Until I know how or why, I cannot rest easy."

Aunt Charlotte walked around to the opposite side of the bed. "I would take Richard's continued absence as a good sign that we shall know all soon enough. Had he lost the rogue, he would have returned directly, and if my son has caught him, he has three men to assist him."

"In the meantime," said Aunt Gardiner, as she stepped forward, "we should take down Lizzy's hair, so the doctor can look at her head. You should have your valet prepare you as well."

He stared at his hand joined with hers. How could he allow her to leave his sight? The near constant contact they had shared since the attack was what kept him grounded. How would he cope without her?

"You will manage for an hour or so." His head darted to his aunt who folded her arms in front of her and tilted her head. "Oh, do not look so shocked. Your forlorn countenance speaks volumes as to what is in your mind."

Ignoring the three amused women watching, he bestowed a kiss to Elizabeth's temple and whispered, "I love you."

She squeezed his hand and pulled him a bit closer. "I shall miss you as well."

He cleared his throat, rose from where he knelt by the bed, and departed through the door to his chambers. He did not look back; he could not or he would return to Elizabeth's side.

When he entered, Clarke awaited him, holding his dressing gown. "Sir, water will arrive in a moment. Would you care to prepare for the arrival of the doctor?"

He looked behind him to the door. Elizabeth would be furious if he did not allow Mr. Baines to examine his shoulder, so he dipped his chin in agreement. "Yes, and you will need to dispose of the ripped pieces since they are no longer of use."

"Cook's young nephew is in need of some clothes as he has grown several inches and his father is again searching for work. Would you mind if I laundered the torn garments and gave them to her? Even with the damage, enough wool remains to make him some fine trousers."

"Yes, of course. I would prefer her make use of them than to sell them to the ragman. You may as well include the greatcoat I wore today as well."

Clarke was not rough, by any means, but Darcy hissed as the topcoat was removed. Why was his shoulder so painful all of a sudden? He handed the piece to Clarke and unbuttoned his waistcoat, again gritting his teeth as the valet pulled it from his shoulders. When he turned his back to the mirror, he gaped at the flush of red that soaked through the white lawn of his shirt.

"You may be unable to salvage much from this."

Clarke pulled the tail from his trousers. "A good soak in cold water should remove it. If it is too stubborn a little lye should do the trick."

Darcy began to unbutton the fall of his trousers, which were damp along the back with what was certain to be blood. How had he not noticed the moisture before now?

He followed Clarke into the room beside his dressing room where his bathtub was kept. No carpets adorned these floors; so any dripping of blood would be easily cleaned.

The heated water stung when it made contact with the ripped flesh, but the pain was nothing to when, after a pop behind him, the pungent smell of brandy flooded the air. His teeth clamped shut as he squeezed his eyes tight. Blast! Even as a boy, he had never liked when Clarke tended his wounds, though the diligence was to be lauded since it had prevented his past injuries from festering.

"They said in the kitchen that Mr. Baines has been fetched?"

"Yes, why?"

The valet began towelling his back. "Forgive me for speaking freely, sir, but Mr. Baines does not think so high of himself that he will not do stitches. He is a good choice."

"You believe I require them?"

"The wound will never close on its own."

He wiped a few beads of sweat that had collected along his hairline. "Where did you put the brandy?"

Clarke pressed the towel to Darcy's back. "If you will allow me a few minutes, I shall fetch you a glass of good brandy. This is the cheap bottle we use for medicinal purposes. You do not want to drink it as it might rip a hole in your gut."

Once he donned an old pair of breeches, he sat before the fire in his bedchamber with a glass of his preferred brandy in hand while Clarke tended to the wound. Darcy sipped small amounts, until after a knock, Mr. Baines was escorted into the room. Upon seeing the old doctor's face, he downed the remaining and held the glass aloft for his valet to refill.

Once Darcy's back was stitched, Mr. Baines departed to examine Elizabeth while Clarke helped Darcy to dress. A tedious task— especially after one drinks three glasses of brandy. Not that it dulled the pain. Well, maybe it did... no, it did not.

As his valet left to retrieve a fresh waistcoat, the door leading to the corridor burst open and Richard rushed inside. "We have him! He is in the custody of the magistrate. I have questioned him, but he would not admit to much before he pretended to be mute. Two of Gardiner's men remain at the gaol, keeping watch while I retrieve you. I think the one person he may confess all to is you."

"Me?" He steadied himself with the back of the nearest chair to stop from swaying. He was swaying, was he not?

"Darce, are you pissed?"

With the heel of his hand pressed to his forehead, he attempted to focus. "Mr. Baines just stitched my shoulder. I drank to dull the pain."

Richard jumped forward and pulled the back of Darcy's shirt over his shoulder. "How deep?"

"Deep enough that it would not have closed on its own," stated Clarke when he returned. "I apologise, Mr. Darcy, but since you could not see the cut, I took the liberty of answering."

The room still had a slight movement to it. "I am not upset, Clarke."

With an appraising eye, Richard took the clothes his valet held in his hands. "Bring us some strong coffee and bread. I shall help him dress until you return." A laugh escaped at the doubtful look Clarke levelled at Richard but he did as he was bid without argument.

"How did you catch him?"

"He took a wrong turn, which had no exit, and we cornered him. He was rather well dressed for a man who does such work, and he is not familiar with Wickham. I am certain of that." Darcy attempted to button his waistcoat, but Richard batted his hands away. "How much brandy did you take?"

"I sipped the first glass, but once Mr. Baines arrived, I am afraid I hastened to drink the last two—all three were filled to the top."

"I cannot blame you as I would do the same, but it is at a damned inconvenient time."

Clarke returned as his last boot was pulled on and set a tray of cold meat, cheese, and bread upon the table. "Cook insisted the master required more than just bread."

Richard laughed. "Of course she did." He pushed Darcy to the table. "Eat!"

Once some food hit his stomach, the room and his mind ceased some of the infernal whirling. He took a sip of the coffee, wincing at the bitter flavour. "Clarke brought cream, so why do you insist on torturing me by making me drink it black?"

"I need you sober, not sick. How do you feel?"

"My shoulder is beginning to smart."

"Capital! We need to return to the gaol."

The room remained still when he stood, which was a good sign, though Richard did not wait to see if he was sure-footed. Instead, he hastened down the stairs where they happened upon Aunt Charlotte, who was giving instructions to the housekeeper.

"How is Elizabeth?"

"Mr. Baines sees no cause for alarm since the dizziness has subsided, and Mrs. Rowley prepared her some willow bark tea for a mild headache. When I left her, she was fatigued and desired to sleep for a time. Georgiana has been with her since she discovered our return. She now reads while she sits at Lizzy's bedside."

"What of Anne and Mrs. Gardiner?"

"Anne wished to return home as Bingley was to call this afternoon. Mrs. Gardiner received a letter at half two. The Bennets arrived a day early." She giggled. "As Marianne boarded the carriage her husband sent, she groused how she was certain it was Mrs. Bennet's doing since Mr. Bennet would not have listened to his wife's incessant pleading for any length of time." She looked to Richard. "Did you catch him?"

"We did, but I require Darce present. I am certain he has no affiliation with Wickham, but I need Darcy to shake the truth from him."

"If Elizabeth awakens while I am away, please inform her of my whereabouts, and how anxious I am to see her upon my return."

Aunt Charlotte's lips curved in a soft smile as she patted his cheek. "I shall, and I shall remain through dinner this evening. I know Georgiana is with her, but I do not want to leave her alone."

He grasped her hand and squeezed. "Thank you."

Richard started and glanced between them. "Are you quite finished? We do need to depart."

They donned their hats and greatcoats and mounted the horses they had requested while Darcy ate. When Richard turned towards

Westminster, Darcy called after him. "Would he not be in Newgate?"

Richard turned his mount in Darcy's direction. "He was taken to Tothill Fields, but will be moved when they next transport prisoners to Newgate. Unless he goes to trial before then, that is. In that case, he would likely go to the hulks while he awaits transportation instead. He will wish he had remained at Tothill Fields once he is moved."

Tothill Fields replaced Gatehouse almost five and thirty years before, so it was newer, as well as smaller, than Newgate and the hulks. The living conditions were certain to be vastly superior to the latter two gaols—as long as you had money to pay for them, of course.

Once they handed their horses and a sovereign to the bedraggled boy who offered to guard their horses, Richard led Darcy inside where his cousin spoke with a man for a few moments. When they appeared to come to some sort of an agreement, Richard gestured for Darcy to follow him further inside, stopping when they met the men he and Mr. Gardiner had hired outside a cell door.

Stale air, excrement, urine, and sweat singed his nostrils. If this prison was preferable to Newgate, he never wanted to set foot inside Newgate!

"He's been whining since ya left," the tallest of them chuckled. "He believes he doesn't belong in here with tha riff raff. He thinks he's gonna go off with the fall of the leaf."

Richard gave a humourless laugh. "He should be so fortunate. He may wish for death once he is aboard a boat."

"Oh! The jailer went inside while ya were gone and managed to get a name from 'im."

"Really?"

Richard peered to Darcy and back to Gardiner's man. "Did he share this information?"

A gap-toothed grin appeared. "Sure did! He claims to be Erasmus Cade."

A wailing came from inside the room beside them, and the men shook their heads or rolled their eyes to the ceiling. One of the other men handed Richard a key, and the group of them entered, the men standing to either side of the criminal, who was shackled to a chain that attached to one corner of the floor.

No greeting was given, no handshake, or bow. Richard merely leaned closer to the man's face. "Tell me of Wickham."

The prisoner yanked at his restraints. "I told you I do not know a Wickham! Now, release me from these before my employer knows what you have done!"

"Your employer?" With a step to the side of his cousin, Darcy appraised the man before him. His suit was not of top quality, but tailored well. He received ample pay for his work, whatever it might be. "Who is your employer? Why would he want you to attack me? I have done nothing to provoke or warrant such an action."

"My lord has naught to do with this." He clutched his hands into fists at his side. "Mr. Darcy is a rogue and a knave! He will pay for what he has done!"

Darcy made to lunge forward to strike the man, but Richard held him back. "I deny any such accusations!"

When Cade looked closer at him, recognition flashed across the man's features. "You... on Bond Street."

"Yes, before you charged at my betrothed with a blade."

Cade lunged at Darcy, but the men grabbed his arms and pinned him to the wall. "I never meant to harm her! It was you! I meant to kill you!"

Without looking away, Richard stepped close to the prisoner and crossed his arms upon his chest. "Why would your employer pay you for such an act? Why would he wish to harm my cousin?"

"My employer has naught to do with this!"

"Then why would he hire a man such as yourself?"

After a sucking breath, the man sputtered. "I am the steward of an estate just outside of London! He will come for me! He will not allow me to rot in this place!" Spit flew from Cade's mouth as he screamed and struggled with the men holding him in place.

"Then who hired you to harm Darcy?"

"Because of his caprice, she has lost everything! He was to marry her, but changed his mind when he met that strumpet! She is broken-hearted. I did this for her!"

"Who?"

Cade turned his head as though he could ignore Richard's booming voice in his ear, but before Richard could repeat himself, Darcy put a hand to his shoulder.

"I have never been betrothed to any lady or courted any lady until Miss Bennet. I am afraid you have been deceived, but we cannot know why until you tell us who persuaded you to do this."

Cade's eyes met his. "You lie!"

"I do not. Disguise of every sort is my abhorrence. I swear to you I have never misled or jilted any lady!"

"She would not deceive me!"

"Who?" Despite his attempts to calm Richard, Darcy's voice now boomed through the prison.

Cade shook his head in a violent fashion. Why would he not simply confess?

"Who?"

He whipped his head back and forth as spittle flew in all directions.

Richard grabbed Cade by the lapels and shook him. "Who?"

"Lady Althea Carlisle!"

Chapter 26

Fury threatened to burst through his flesh as Darcy rapped the knocker upon the door and shifted from foot to foot, waiting for the butler to open the blasted door. He reached for the knob, but a hand set upon his chest.

"Calm yourself." His uncle moved in front of him. "Good Lord, Richard. He might run Carlisle through if we cannot restrain him."

"Would that be such a bad consequence?"

"Carlisle is not responsible. I would wager all I own he has had nothing to do with this. His wife and daughter, however, are not cut of the same cloth, so I would not put the deception of that man past one or the both of them."

Once they had questioned Cade until they were satisfied, Richard insisted they not confront Lord Carlisle without the aid of his father. If nothing else, Lord Fitzwilliam's political consequence, title, and long standing friendship with the man would place them on more even ground. They were fortunate the earl was not only at home, but also incensed by what happened.

An aged butler opened the door and eyed Darcy and Richard before he bowed to the earl. "Lord Fitzwilliam, I do not believe Lord Carlisle expects you today."

"I hope he is not busy or from the house. It is imperative I speak with him." His uncle's tone was direct but did not reflect the anger they had witnessed earlier.

"He indicated he had no wish to be disturbed while he was addressing estate matters."

His Uncle stepped towards the servant and looked him in the eye. "Estate matters are easier solved with one's steward. Is he missing one this morning, perchance?"

The man's eyes flared for a second before he schooled his expression. "I shall inform Lord Carlisle of your desire to meet with him. Would you gentlemen care to step inside?"

Darcy jumped ahead of Richard. He would not be shut out and would have an audience with Lord Carlisle. This entire situation would be solved that very day if he had anything at all to say about it! He would not walk away without the answers he needed.

The butler did not take long to return. He held out his arm. "If you will accompany me."

They were led up a flight of stairs, past some garishly decorated rooms, and into a small library where Lord Carlisle sat at a desk littered with ledgers and papers.

"Fitzwilliam!" he boomed as he rose and came around the desk to shake the earl's hand. "I had not expected you to call today, but Simons indicated you had news of some importance for me."

Darcy scanned the room, until his eyes lit upon a familiar face in the corner. "You!"

His uncle and Lord Carlisle halted their greeting as Richard stepped forward and grabbed the man by the arm, thrusting him forward.

Carlisle looked between Uncle William and Richard. "What is the meaning of this?"

"Excuse your butler and close the door." His uncle's voice was lowered as he leaned closer to Carlisle. "I assure you that you do not want this to be made public."

"Simons, we do not require anything further at the moment. Thank you." The butler bowed but stared at Darcy and Richard as he closed the dark panelled oak door.

"Now, I insist you unhand my understeward!"

"Release an accomplice to a murder attempt? I think not."

As Richard pushed the man into a chair, the understeward began to splutter. "I have done no such thing! I would never—"

"Yet, you followed my cousin," Richard pointed to Darcy, "on the orders of Erasmus Cade, did you not?"

The man's head whipped back and forth between Richard and Darcy. "Mr. Cade said he owed Lord Carlisle money. All I did was watch him, and tell Cade what he did and anything I overheard."

Carlisle stepped forward. "Have I ever asked this of you in the past?"

"Only when your eldest daughter was courted by Lord Sexton. You requested we watch him and tell you of his habits. I have heard rumours of your daughter and Mr. Darcy. I assumed you were ensuring your daughter's welfare as you did before."

"Yet my cousin has never indicated an interest in Lady Althea Carlisle and is betrothed to another."

Lord Carlisle put his hands, palm out, before him. "Before we proceed further, are you saying Erasmus Cade attempted to kill someone?"

"Not just anyone, but my nephew, Darcy." His uncle placed a hand upon his shoulder—his good shoulder, thankfully, as he was already gritting his teeth to bear the pain of the other. "If it had not been for the quick mind of my son, he might have escaped after the attempt."

"I do not understand why." Carlisle shook his head. "He has a good position. I pay him well. What could drive him to harm another?" He looked at Darcy. "Though he does not appear to have done you any damage."

"That is due to the swift action of my servants, sir, who acted with haste to notify my physician. The wound is stitched, though painful. When Richard had news of the culprit, a resolution to this nightmare became my priority. This man put my betrothed, my cousin Miss de Bourgh, as well as my aunt Lady Fitzwilliam, in danger with his foolhardy attempt on my life. I must see this resolved before I lick my wounds." Darcy's voice was hard. Could Carlisle be innocent? Cade declared him to be so, as did his uncle, but how to trust the man who raised such a daughter? "I can summon my physician should you wish for his testimony."

Richard's hand motioned towards the injured shoulder. "Or he could show you the wound for that matter."

"Richard!" his father cried.

Lord Carlisle's Adam's apple bobbed as he waved his hand. "Of course, not. I do not require proof of that nature."

His uncle turned to face his long-time friend. "Cade has claimed Darcy abandoned your daughter, Lady Althea, for Miss Elizabeth Bennet, and broke Lady Althea's heart."

Carlisle's brow furrowed as he turned his attention to Darcy. "No understanding ever existed between the two of you. You were introduced just recently, after your courtship began with Miss Bennet."

"That is correct, sir. I have spoken with your daughter on a few separate occasions: at church, Clarell House, the ball. I never gave her any indication to hope. In fact, Miss Bennet was present during several of those meetings, yet one of my uncle's footmen informed us he had overheard a mother and daughter speaking after the ball of Miss Bennet and myself. They indicated they would end my understanding with Miss Bennet in order to ensnare me to the daughter. Based on the description and what I now know, I believe the mother and daughter to be your wife and Lady Althea."

"Cade has confessed Lady Althea claimed she had an understanding with my cousin, he reneged, and engaged himself to Miss Bennet. Based on what Cade has said, we believe your daughter feigned a broken heart and persuaded him to take revenge on Darcy."

"The entire situation is preposterous!"

Richard sat in the closest chair to the understeward. "Why would Cade lie?"

"He would not, but I..." Lord Carlisle speared his man with a heated glare. "Fletcher, what did Cade ask of you? I want to know it all."

His man looked to each of them in turn and jerked his head back and forth. "I swear I thought he was operating under orders from you. When you arrived in town and requested a meeting to go over the books for Edgemoor, we came as you ordered. On our return to the estate that evening, Mr. Cade said he had a task for me. I was to take the two Jenkins boys and follow a Mr. Darcy."

"He claimed Mr. Darcy owed me money?"

"Yes, sir. Two days later, he took us to Mr. Darcy's house in Grosvenor Square and explained where we would meet to inform him of Mr. Darcy's comings and goings, whom Mr. Darcy met, and other details we might find important." Fletcher licked his lips and pointed towards Richard. "Cade became angry when this man followed us to St. Giles. He said he no longer required our help. I heard no more of the matter until today."

"You indicated you knew of my betrothal to Miss Bennet." Darcy did his best to maintain a steady voice. While Carlisle appeared bewildered, this man in a matter of moments had been reduced to a panicked, panting mess.

"I read of it in the paper, sir, but Mr. Cade had first asked us because of a supposed debt. I assumed I had been incorrect and did not question Cade's orders. I have never had reason to do so in the past."

"What of Cade's relationship with Lady Althea?"

"I have had reason to believe Mr. Cade fancied her." His eyes darted to Lord Carlisle as a bead of sweat trickled down his nose. "I thought I once saw a drawing of her, but Cade shoved it into his desk before I could be certain."

After clenching his jaw several times, Carlisle dipped his pen in ink and began to write on a piece of paper, which he sanded and folded. "I need you to return to Edgemoor. You are to crate the contents of Mr. Cade's desk and have them delivered to me here."

Fletcher glanced around with wary eyes and stood. "Sir, I cannot be without work."

Carlisle pulled a book from his desk, placed the missive he just penned on top, and handed it to Fletcher. "Do as I ask. Cooperate with any information I, Lord Fitzwilliam, or Mr. Darcy request of you, and you will not require a new position."

He bobbed his head and gave a short bow. "Thank you, sir. I shall, of course, give you any information I can, though I am afraid I do not know much."

"Just pack his belongings and have them sent to me. I also expect you to keep today's conversation as well as any knowledge of what comes about to yourself."

"Yes, sir. I hope you know I would never share your private business. I never have." He looked to each of the men before he departed through the servant's exit.

Once they were alone, Lord Carlisle turned from them and leaned upon his hands at his desk. "I have known Cade since he was a babe. I cannot fathom his attempting to harm another."

His uncle placed a hand upon Carlisle's shoulder. "He has claimed Lady Althea told him she was betrothed to Darcy. She convinced Cade that Darcy abandoned her. If what Cade has confessed is true, your daughter deceived him cruelly." Carlisle's head whipped to the side and his mouth opened. "I know you wish to deny she could do such a thing, but you must consider the possibility. What if it is true?"

Carlisle crumpled into the nearest chair. "When my son Lawrence died from an outbreak of influenza in ninety-four, we were so thankful Thea was spared that we indulged her. She was a temperamental child, unlike Lawrence, who was good-natured and always wore a smile.

"Her elder sister was in school, so Thea was our last child at home. We took great joy in lavishing her with any trinket or gift that would make her smile. Philippa and I tried for more children, as I required an heir, but we were never blessed. Thea never wanted for anything as a result."

"I knew she had set her cap on you last season," confessed Carlisle, as he tilted his head to look at Darcy. "But we refused to allow any gentleman to court her during her debut season. We were not ready to let her go, and we felt a year might help her gain perspective and maturity on the situation as her sister had."

His uncle sat in the chair beside Lord Carlisle. "The practice has become rather common these days, I believe."

Carlisle nodded. "I know she is spoiled and selfish, and I confess I am terrified Cade is being truthful. She has decided she desires nothing more than to be Mrs. Darcy. I promised to make the introduction at the ball, but you had already entered a courtship with Miss Bennet. She begged, pleaded, and demanded I make you court her in Miss Bennet's stead. I attempted to reason with her, yet she would not have it." He cleared his throat and sniffled. "I hoped she would learn from the experience. She cannot bend others to her will to have all she desires."

"What of your wife?" asked Richard. "Would she attempt to indulge your daughter in this?"

His eyes glistened as he swallowed. "Philippa cannot abide when Thea becomes upset or angry and attempts to placate her. I honestly do not know." With weary movements, he rose and rang for a servant. When a maid responded to the summons, he requested his daughter be brought to him as well as his wife.

Lady Althea swept into her father's study as though she owned it all. A wide grin erupted upon her face when she found Darcy standing near the fireplace. "Mr. Darcy! I did not know you had a meeting with my father. I do hope you are well."

With a huff, Lord Carlisle grasped his daughter by the elbow and thrust her into a chair. Where he was stoop-shouldered and appeared weary before her entrance, his expression was now implacable and stern.

"What do you think you are doing, Papa? How dare you!"

Lady Carlisle's high-pitched gasping shriek rent the air. "What are you about?"

He pointed to a chair across from their daughter. "You will take a seat. I have questions for both of you, and neither of you will leave this room until I have the answers I seek!"

"But to treat Thea in such a way!"

"Philippa, that is enough!" His wife's jaw clamped shut. Had he ever spoken to his wife in such a manner or had he allowed her and their daughter to simply run amok?

Carlisle gazed down upon his daughter, whose lips were drawn into a fine line. "I want to know of your relationship with Erasmus Cade."

"We played together when we were young, but you are well aware of that." She waved a dismissive hand in front of her. "He is now one of your stewards as his father was before him."

"You have continued a friendship with him?" Lord Carlisle's eyes narrowed.

"We are now more acquaintances than friends. Why would *I* be friends with your steward?"

A smirk and a glance in his direction made Darcy stiffen. She had no care for Cade. Her father would never obtain the answers they required to prove her guilt. Lady Althea had too many years bending him to her will. His affection for her was also his greatest impediment.

Richard's quiet but firm words indicated his agitation had been noticed. "Calm yourself." Despite speaking to him, Richard still stared at Lord Carlisle questioning Lady Althea.

How could he tell him to be calm? The lady was misleading her father with great success. "He is angry, but she is playing him false."

Richard made no response except to step in front of Darcy to stand before Lady Althea. "Cade claims you have exchanged correspondence." Lord Carlisle's jaw dropped and his wife's exclamation was unintelligible.

"I would never exchange letters with a man who is not family or my betrothed. What is this about?" Her eyes darted to Darcy, and he stepped back.

A harsh laugh escaped Richard's throat. "You can wish for my cousin to your heart's content, but he will never have you." Her nostrils flared for but a moment, and Richard stepped closer. "Your contrived manner and fawning disposition repulse him, did you not know?"

"Colonel!" cried Lord Carlisle, though Lord Fitzwilliam restrained him with a hand to his arm.

Her chest rose higher with her unsteady breath. Could this truly work? Would she become angry enough to reveal her part?

Richard lifted one nostril in a disgusted sneer. "You are not good enough for my cousin. He would not so much as ask you to dance, yet you presume you are the best candidate for his wife?"

"He would be fortunate to have a wife such as me." Her eyes bore into Richards as she spoke through clenched teeth.

"He would not deign you worthy to bed in a brothel, much less offer you his hand."

"Fitzwilliam! Control your son! He goes too far!" screamed Carlisle as his wife screeched.

Lord Fitzwilliam threw himself bodily in front of Carlisle, and Lady Althea shot from her chair as though catapulted. "I will not be treated thus! I demand you remove yourself from my path, so I can leave at once!" She was furious, but would Richard's cajoling be enough? Perhaps because she was enamoured with Darcy, he would be more apt to obtain a severe reaction than his cousin.

He strode forward, grabbed her arm, and thrust her back into her seat. "He is correct, though you have never cared to notice." He placed his hands upon the arms of the chair and leaned into her face, ignoring the cacophony around them. "I may not have been introduced, but I remember you from last season. Many a gentleman commented on your coy manner and how freely you flirted with them. I also witnessed your haughty disposition and the selfish pleasure you took in the gossip you spread. I have more respect for my heritage than to make a lady with such loose morals the mother of my children."

Her breath came in pants and her hands clenched in her lap until her knuckles drained of colour.

"Miss Bennet does not find enjoyment in belittling others. I shall never have any cause to question her devotion or loyalty to me. She will make an ideal wife." She was close to buckling. "I remember the speculation last season amongst the men. I believe there is a bet on the books at Whites and Boodles as to whether you have been plucked. Still, a few men would have you for your dowry if you were willing."

He straightened and backed from her, not removing his eyes from hers. "I shall never regret taking Miss Bennet as my wife as I would you."

Lady Althea launched herself from the chair and slapped him. "When she is gone, you will come for me! I never fail to get what I want, and this time will be no different!"

Richard darted between them and restrained her before she could pummel Darcy as she appeared she might. She kicked and fought, but Richard held tight.

Did she mean to harm Elizabeth? Had that been her plan, but instead, Cade attempted to harm him, despite Lady Althea's wishes?

He tilted closer. "Erasmus Cade has been jailed for stabbing me this morning on Bond Street."

His suspicion proved true when her jerking and flailing halted. "You? He stabbed you?"

Her shrieking tone pained his ears, but he did not move. "Yes, me. Elizabeth received no more than a bump on her head."

"Simpleton!"

While Richard attempted to hold fast to her struggling body, Lady Althea screamed and ranted as her mother ran from the room. Lord Carlisle called after his wife, but she returned in a matter of minutes with a vial and a glass of wine in her trembling hand.

"Thea, drink this."

"No! Unhand me at once!"

Tears dropped from the countess's eyes as she grasped her daughter's chin and tipped the goblet back as far as it would go. Lady Althea spluttered, but as she had no choice, swallowed the wine. She continued to fight until, after a time, she calmed in Richard's arms.

Lady Althea's wide pupils stared at Darcy. "I should have known Cade would make a bungle of this." She mumbled some words they could not understand.

"What could you mean, Thea?" asked Lady Carlisle.

"I told him Miss Bennet was at fault, but he insisted on blaming Mr. Darcy." She giggled as Richard eased her back into the chair. "He was always sweet on me. Did anything I asked." She bit her bottom lip with a wicked grin. "I once told him the butcher's son made an improper overture to me. Cade beat him for it. He had not even so much as glanced at me. I lied—"

"Dear Lord!" Carlisle gripped the arm of the chair. "What else have you done?"

A weak murmur followed, but her eyes closed as she leaned her head to one side and fell asleep.

"Philippa?" Lord Carlisle looked between his wife and daughter.

"Laudanum to calm her."

He placed a hand to his forehead and held it there. "Did you know?"

"I knew she wanted Mr. Darcy, and I attempted to introduce them at the ball. When his courtship with Miss Bennet became public later that night, she began to speak of forcing his hand. I told her we would find another way. I said you had men in your employ. My intent was to prevent her from making a fool of herself."

Her attention moved to Darcy. "Any person could see you are besotted by your betrothed, sir. I did pay my brother, who is a bishop at Doctor's Common to destroy your petition for a special license. I knew you would wed regardless, but Thea was pacified in knowing that I was attempting to help her. I assumed that when you wed, she would decide you were not worth her time, and find a new gentleman to pursue."

"You did not stop her from her blatant flirtations in the company of Miss Bennet."

"No, betrothals have ended for one reason or another. I decided to leave her be as she was doing no one harm. I never knew." She gulped. "I knew she could be ruthless but no more so than the usual ladies of society." As she sank to her knees, she caressed her daughter's porcelain coloured cheek. "Over the last year, I have come to realize that we were mistaken. We allowed her every indulgence and never taught her to temper her behaviour. Even so, I had no idea she had become this."

His uncle stood behind Lady Althea's chair. "What will you do?" He held Darcy's eye. "My nephew would like to ensure he and his betrothed are safe from your daughter. As long as you see to it she cannot harm him or his family further, I believe he will be satisfied."

"I have no wish to ruin your family. If you can assure me you will curb her threats, I shall trust you in the matter."

Lord Carlisle leaned against his desk, once again weary. "My nephew inherits my title and my estate when I die. The scandal would mean little to him, but *I* do appreciate your discretion and willingness to allow me to deal with this matter. I have no wish for people to remember me by the horrible actions of my daughter.

"I must conclude my business here, but I have an estate in the northern part of Ireland. It is rather remote, which will serve our purposes well. We shall remove from London and journey there as soon I can settle matters.

"Regardless of her behaviour, Thea will not return to London. She has proven I cannot trust her, and as much as it pains me, we must arrange her future elsewhere. A meeting between the two of you or Miss Bennet might stir old feelings and ill will." His voice was soft as he stared at his daughter. If one did not know better, one might believe he was talking aloud to himself.

He cleared his throat and looked to Darcy. "Does that suit?"

"I believe your plan a sound one. I appreciate your consideration towards Miss Bennet and myself."

The man before him was not the proud, confident gentleman Darcy had met at the ball. He no longer held himself straight and tall, but sagged and was downtrodden. His suit was crumpled, his forehead creased, and dark circles framed the undersides of his eyes. Despite their triumph in forcing a confession from Lady Althea, this was no victory. A family was in ruins, and though through no fault of his own, their situation was pitiable.

Darcy stepped forward and offered his hand. "Lord Carlisle, I believe you have been long desiring our absence. Should you require any help to conclude your business endeavours prior to your journey, I would be pleased to be of aid."

As Carlisle's hand wrapped around Darcy's, he cleared his throat. "You are too charitable. Had I acted as a more responsible parent, we would not be in this situation."

"It is possible, but we cannot know if the outcome would be different. Since you are willing to rectify the situation, I bear no grudge against you or your family."

His uncle moved to his left side. "I can help conclude your argument in the House of Lords should you require it of me."

"I shall, no doubt, be in contact, Fitzwilliam."

Carlisle had a difficult time holding their eye as they said their farewells, but Richard offered no more than a nod before the butler was called to show them to the door. Once they were standing upon the pavement, Darcy scanned the façade of the noble exterior.

"I do not envy him."

"Nor do I," agreed his uncle.

"Do not become complacent yet, Darcy."

He turned to his cousin. What could he mean?

"We still need to locate Wickham."

"You will forgive me if I wish to do no more than return home and spend time with Elizabeth."

"Do not forget to take a bit of laudanum for your pain." His uncle peered at him over his spectacles. "Carlisle may not have noticed, but I can tell by your posture that you are in a great deal of discomfort."

"Nothing until I retire." He grasped Richard by the sleeve. "Do you think you can bring a vicar to Darcy House this evening?"

"What are you thinking?"

"Elizabeth's family arrived this afternoon amongst the chaos of what happened on Bond Street, and I intend to wed her this evening—even if I must tell her father that she has been residing in the mistress' chambers since the attack."

His uncle grinned. "Given your lack of propriety, I do not think such a disclosure necessary."

"I am taking no chances. Wickham's target will remain on her back whether she is my wife or betrothed. At least if she is under the same roof, I can be assured of her safety."

Richard guffawed. "She is perfectly safe at Clarell House. You just want your wife."

"That I do, Richard. That I do."

Chapter 27

"Look at this house!"

Elizabeth closed her eyes as her teeth screeched across each other. Her mother was not even within the walls of Darcy House and her voice could not be missed!

Lady Fitzwilliam placed a hand upon her arm. "Whether you choose to believe this or not, I shall not hold your mother against you. She will not be the first or the last exuberant lady I meet in this life."

"Yes, but she is not your relation. I love my mother, though at times, I do wish she could behave with decorum." She wrung her hands before her. "I fear what she will say. I do not want to lose the servants' respect due to her behaviour."

"The servants have seen enough of you in the last fortnight to know you do not resemble your mother. If they were so mistaken, Mrs. Rowley would never tolerate any disrespect towards you or my nephew. Do not let such a trifling matter disturb your equanimity. This is to be your home. No one should make you feel out of place. Do you understand?"

"Yes, ma'am."

As her family's voices carried down the hall, Elizabeth stood with Lady Fitzwilliam backing her while waiting for them to be announced. As footsteps drew nearer the door, she drew a long breath and released it in a heavy stream of air.

"All will be well. You will see."

After one last glance at her future aunt, she drew herself up as tall as she could. She was to be mistress of this house and was not responsible for her mother's actions or the thoughtless behaviour of Lydia or Kitty. At least Jane and the Gardiners were relations for whom there was no reason to blush.

Jane rushed forward and embraced Elizabeth when she entered. "Aunt has told us what happened on Bond Street. You cannot truly be as calm as you seem."

"I was terrified in the moment, but I cannot dwell on what could have happened. He has been captured, and for that, I can be nothing but grateful."

"Elizabeth, may I have the pleasure of an introduction?"

She linked arms with Jane. "Lady Fitzwilliam, this lady is my beloved elder sister Jane. Jane, Lady Fitzwilliam is Mr. Darcy's aunt and the mother of Colonel Fitzwilliam."

Her sister curtsied. "I am honoured to make your acquaintance, my lady."

"Lizzy! You never mentioned in your letters how grand Mr. Darcy's home is! 'Tis larger than Longbourn!" Her mother looked between her daughters and Lady Fitzwilliam as her elbow dug into Elizabeth's side. "Are you not going to introduce us?"

After a slight nod, Elizabeth stepped around and one by one introduced the remaining members of her family. Once they curtsied and bowed as propriety dictated, a loud, mocking sound erupted from Lydia.

"Lawd, Lizzy, it is no wonder you accepted Mr. Darcy. I could even put up with a tedious man like him to live in a house such as this." Despite her sister's remarks, Lady Fitzwilliam gave no more reaction than a twitch of her lips while her Aunt and Uncle Gardiner, Jane, and Mary turned to the youngest Bennet sister agape.

"Forgive my daughter, Lady Fitzwilliam," came her father's voice from behind the ladies. "I have made an attempt to teach her proper deportment and discourse these past weeks, but find it has come to naught." He took Lydia by the elbow. "Come, Mrs. Bennet. Your daughter must be returned to your brother's home, and she requires a chaperon."

"Oh, let Mary accompany her. As Lizzy's mother, it is my right to be here."

Lady Fitzwilliam brushed by Elizabeth. "Have a servant come for me once this has been settled. I fear your father requires my absence."

When her future aunt departed and they were in private, her mother puffed herself up. "See what you have done, Mr. Bennet! You have offended a countess!" She crossed her arms over her chest. "I do not give a care for your reasoning, I shan't leave."

Her father stepped toe to toe with his wife. "Since you have exited the carriage, you have loudly exclaimed over the house, insisted on an introduction to Lady Fitzwilliam, and made a spectacle of yourself."

While he spoke, her mother's jaw dropped lower and lower; however, when she began to speak, he raised his hand. "I have allowed you to continue unchecked and to teach Kitty and Lydia the most dreadful manners. You think them accomplished and able to attract a husband, but I beg to differ—no gentleman will consider them as long as they are so unabashed and free with their words. I do believe Kitty has improved since I have taken more of an interest in their lives, yet Lydia has not. We have both created what she is, me by my lack of attention and you with your example. I have spent miserable evenings at social functions keeping her in check, and now, 'tis only fair you have your share."

"I have done naught to deserve such punishment!"

"I shall not return to my uncle's! Mama claimed we would go to the theatre and balls while in London. We shall order new gowns—"

He gave an incredulous laugh. "Until you learn to behave, you are no longer out, young lady. Your place is in the nursery, not a ballroom."

"Mr. Bennet!" exclaimed her mother as she fluttered her handkerchief.

He peered at Elizabeth and then, to his wife. "My Lizzy has endured enough today without your embarrassing antics. Come, it is time to depart."

Her mother whipped around to face Elizabeth. "Lizzy does not object to my behaviour."

Her chest burned, she swallowed the lump in her throat, and bit her lip. Her mother would be hurt if she responded with the truth. How could her father say such a thing!

When she could not make a sound emerge from her throat, her mother covered her mouth with her handkerchief as Elizabeth took a sudden interest in the rug beneath her feet, staring at the floral design.

"Come, Mrs. Bennet."

A sniffle came from in front of her before it was concealed by the shrill objections of Lydia as she was led back to the hall.

"Oh, Lizzy! I am so sorry Papa scolded Mama and Lydia as he did."

Aunt Marianne wrapped an arm around her shoulders. "You were present as was I, Jane, when your father detailed his expectations for this visit. Your mother and Lydia chose to ignore him, Lady Fitzwilliam was kind to give us privacy, and no servants were present since she ensured they left with her. No harm was done."

"I could not lie to Mama."

"Nor should you." Her aunt lifted her chin. "Your mother has wilfully ignored the effects of her behaviour on you girls for years. Now that Kitty and Lydia have emulated her to such an extent, it is imperative she learn."

Elizabeth started and moved to ring the bell. "Lady Fitzwilliam indicated she would return once matters were settled."

Kitty approached as she pulled the cord. "I hope you know I do not share Lydia's sentiments."

"You did not giggle or state any agreement to her words. I have no reason to hold them against you."

"Thank you," she breathed.

"I am happy to see you, Kitty." Elizabeth embraced her younger sister before Mary approached to hug Elizabeth in greeting. "I am also pleased Papa's rules have made an impression."

"Oh, Lizzy! The ball at Netherfield was dreadfully dull! I want Papa to trust me if for no other reason than to keep company with my friends when I am not dancing."

"I still cannot believe Papa danced with you." Mary grimaced. "He gave me charge of Lydia for the half hour. I thought she would never cease her whining and complaining."

"Lizzy?" Kitty grabbed her arm, but was staring at the entry. "Who is he?" Elizabeth followed her eyes to where Lady Fitzwilliam and Viscount Milton led her father into the room and made their way in her direction.

"The gentleman is Mr. Darcy's cousin, Viscount Milton." Elizabeth suppressed a laugh at the dramatic sigh that came from Kitty.

"He is quite handsome."

Elizabeth tilted her head as she appraised the man in question. She supposed he was attractive. He was not as dark as Fitzwilliam, and Fitzwilliam's blue eyes were more to her liking than Milton's green.

"He is coming towards us. How should I behave?"

With a smile, Elizabeth bumped Kitty's shoulder. "Should you question whether you are proper, think of Jane's comportment in public, but be no one other than yourself. Be amiable, but guard your heart. I imagine he will seek a wife amongst his father's political allies. Despite my betrothal to Mr. Darcy, we are still the daughters of a country gentleman. Not many men of society would consider us."

They each took seats and a conversation began as though the events of the Bennets' arrival had never happened. Lady Fitzwilliam took an instant liking to Jane, who was invited to spend the season with the Fitzwilliams. By the familiar twinkle in the older woman's eye, she had a gentleman in mind for Jane.

Her father accepted the glass of port Milton offered as he watched more than he spoke. If one did not know better, they might believe him at a play rather than a family gathering.

Mary clasped her hands in her lap as she sat without speaking. She responded with politeness to any questions posed to her, but did not venture into the discussion further, while Kitty made more of an attempt to join the group, particularly when Georgiana entered and introductions were made.

After an hour, Elizabeth checked the clock. Half-seven? She took a sip of her sherry as her father took the seat beside her. "I am certain he will return soon."

With her thumb, she turned her ring so the setting was once again on top of her finger. "I just wish Colonel Fitzwilliam could have dealt with the matter. Fitzwilliam was injured. He should be home, resting."

"He would not be the honourable gentleman you love had he done so. I admire his dedication to ensuring your safety."

"Am I being unreasonable?"

He smiled. "Perhaps a mite. I am unaware of how serious an injury he sustained, so I cannot judge the situation fairly."

A giggle came from Kitty, drawing their attention. "I do believe you are correct about Kitty's improvement. Regardless of her reasons, she has made an effort to change."

"She has given a reason for her alteration?"

"Kitty does not wish for your constant companionship at the next assembly."

His eyes twinkled with the upturn of one side of his lips. "I should have suspected as much, yet I agree with you. If I have no cause to worry for her behaviour, I shall allow her some freedom. Can you imagine what Lydia's response will be?"

"Kitty is older, and if she has proven herself, she deserves her reward."

"I agree. Perhaps the perceived insult might prompt Lydia to correct herself." He rubbed a hand to the back of his neck. "Then again, I doubt it will do a thing. Her recalcitrance is remarkable."

Voices resonated through the hall, and her head turned to the door. "You must not give up on her, Papa."

"A part of me wishes I could, but I shall not."

The door opened and Fitzwilliam's eyes scanned the room until they rested upon her. He did not tarry or pause, but strode directly to her side, kneeling by the chair. "Are you well?"

"I shall have a sore spot upon my head for a week or so, but Mr. Baines gave me leave to resume my usual activities." She covered his hand that rested on the arm. "What of your injury?"

"'Tis but a scratch."

Why did he look to her father before he answered? She lifted her brows. "You are attempting to prevent my worrying. It will not work."

Her father laughed behind her. "I would never hide a thing from my daughter, son. She will learn the secret whether you want her to or not."

"Fortunately, Mr. Baines has trained as a surgeon. He sewed the wound, which now smarts and throbs, closed."

"Why could you not tell me that in the first place?"

"I sent Richard for a vicar, and I thought you might not marry me tonight if you believed my injury too grave." His eyes remained upon her cheek as he spoke in low tones.

"You are a ridiculous man, Fitzwilliam Darcy." He gave a jump and looked her in the eye. "Perhaps I would marry you tonight in order to persuade you to rest." Her heart quickened as he studied her.

"So you will? Tonight?"

"We had planned for two days hence. What difference does a few hours make?"

Her grin matched his as he stood. "I should refresh myself before Richard returns."

She rose and grabbed his sleeve. "What of the man who attacked us?"

"I shall tell you later. We still have Wickham, who might cause mischief, but I should not be followed any further. All threats from that quarter are at an end."

"You are certain?"

"The man from the street is in prison. He will be moved to Newgate in the next few days. While questioning him, he divulged who was behind the entire incident. The story is a long and confusing one, and though it is done, I am certain there is information missing from what we do know."

"But you will tell me all later?"

He reached out and brushed a curl back from her cheek. "I promise."

"I beg your pardon," her father's voice interrupted from behind. "But did I hear you say you intend to wed tonight?"

The room, which had maintained a low hum with the entire group's conversation, was overcome with a sudden quiet. "You intended to wed on Wednesday as it is, Brother." Georgiana's tone was incredulous.

Lady Fitzwilliam's lips twisted into a wicked grin. "Lizzy was seen by all and sundry on Bond Street carried into a carriage by your brother and placed in his lap."

Her father's one eyebrow rose. "You were?"

Her entire body burned as Georgiana and Kitty covered their mouths to restrain their amusement. Aunt Marianne grasped Mary's arm before she could spout some proverb or religious quote.

Georgiana gave a sharp inhale. "She was placed in the mistress' suite when they returned from Bond Street."

"Yes, she was," agreed Lady Fitzwilliam.

Fitzwilliam stared at the floor as his shoulders shook. He was laughing! Her respectability was in question, and he found it humorous?

Uncle Gardiner came to stand by her father. "We have had a deuce of a time keeping them within the bounds of propriety."

She began to shake as she opened her mouth. How could he? Her father's hands to her shoulders halted her tirade before she could begin.

"Your uncle and I discussed the possibility upon learning of today's events. I am afraid we are all having some fun at your expense, though you might keep in mind that the levity is also beneficial after such an ordeal. Forgive us."

Aunt Marianne stood and put an arm around her shoulders. "I packed the remainder of your belongings today—including the rose gown you had saved for a special occasion. I believe your wedding fits such a description."

Her eyes stung and blurred. Of course, Aunt Marianne would remember. "It does indeed." She peered at all assembled. "But what of Mama and Lord Fitzwilliam?"

"My uncle stopped at Clarell House to dress for dinner."

"We can send for your mother, as well, Lizzy. She will need to return to mind Lydia when the ceremony is completed as I do not want Marianne's servants to quit on account of your youngest sister's ire."

"Lydia will remain at Uncle's, will she not?"

He glanced around at everyone. All were laughing and once again enjoying each other's company. "Yes, I know if I had exerted myself sooner, I would not have to work so hard to control her, yet it must be done. I may have begun this to prevent her from being ensnared by Wickham, but if she does not learn, she alone could be our ruin. After witnessing her behaviour with the officers, I am convinced she would not think twice about eloping with one of them. Her mind would pretend the repercussions did not exist and she would declare it all a romantic adventure.

"Lydia embarrassed you earlier, as did your mother. I have ignored or found amusement in those antics in the past. I shall not do so in the future."

She embraced her father and sniffed. "Thank you, Papa."

As he withdrew, he patted her arm. "Well, I thought of marrying her to Mr. Collins and saving myself the bother, but after your abrupt departure for London, he decided Charlotte Lucas suited him better."

"What?"

"Oh!" He reached into his pocket and removed a letter. "She asked me to pass this along to you. No doubt, it contains the announcement."

"Charlotte and Mr. Collins?"

"Not everyone has your good fortune, my dear." His lip curved to one side as she took the missive. "She is reaching seven and twenty and no one in our neighbourhood has taken an interest in her. He is likely the sole proposal of marriage she can expect."

A warm hand rested upon the small of her back. "Your father is correct. Mr. Collins may not be an ideal husband to your way of thinking, but he is a prudent choice for Miss Lucas. She will have her own home. With Bingley and Anne taking charge of Rosings, she should be content in her situation."

Her heart hurt. Charlotte could not love such an idiot. Her dear friend would never know the contentment of coming home to someone who holds a part of her soul. Her first kiss would be one of obligation without the all-encompassing thrill that curls your toes and makes you dream of more. The notion was heart breaking.

"She is not you, Elizabeth. Her concerns are different."

Her father clapped his hands together. "I must arrange for a carriage lest your mother remain with Lydia. She would never forgive me the impolitic cruelty of not witnessing her daughter married to a wealthy man." After he stepped to the door, he spoke a few words to Jobbins and departed as her aunt pulled at her shoulders.

"We should get you changed. When the vicar arrives, we do not want to keep him waiting."

She caught Fitzwilliam's eye and curved her lips upward. "No, Aunt. I have no intention of being late to my own wedding."

Nothing but a warm contentment settled in his chest as his arm rested upon the back of the sofa, his thumb tracing light circles on the back of his bride's neck. How he wanted to whisk her up to their suite! Yet, while her father departed with her mother after the ceremony, the remainder of their family had not followed their good example and remained chatting in the drawing room after dinner. This was his wedding night. Would they never leave?

He leaned close to her ear. "You are tired."

"My head aches."

His hand cradled her head as his thumb stroked across her cheek. She bore dark circles under her eyes, visible indications of the long, strenuous day they just put behind them. With their marriage, they had, at least, made the day a happy one, as that event would take precedence in their minds. "Then we should get you upstairs."

"Fitzwilliam..."

Before she could protest, he rose and pulled her to stand with his good arm. "If you will excuse us, Elizabeth is feeling unwell as am I."

"You are throwing us from the house, then." A glint in Richard's eye indicated they would be teased mercilessly for this.

"Hush, son," chided his aunt, "they were both injured today unless you have forgotten."

After a barrage of well wishes and hugs, the remaining members of their families departed, a collective exhale escaping from the servants as well as the bride and groom when the door closed behind them.

"Jobbins, please have some willow bark tea brewed and delivered—"

He smiled and laced his fingers with hers. "Have the tea brought to our sitting room." With a tug of her hand, he started towards the stairs, but made an abrupt stop on the first step. "And remove the knocker. We are not at home to callers, though we shall see family if they have news of great importance."

Jobbins bowed. "Yes, sir."

After a glance down to his wife's pink cheeks, he led her into their sitting room where he wrapped her in an embrace. "In case you have forgotten, this door leads to your bedchamber." One arm held her secure to his chest while he pointed with the other. He swapped arms, pointing left this time. "That door leads to mine." His lips tasted a velvet soft bit of flesh behind her ear. "What will we do while we await our tea?"

Her lips brushed his. "I thought we would change into our nightclothes. I have a hairpin digging into the bump on the back of my head that I am desperate to remove."

One by one, he found each offending pin and collected the lot in his palm as she giggled. "I must comb my hair, Fitzwilliam, or it will become a mess of tangles."

His fingers raked through her loose auburn curls. How he adored her hair! Her long tresses sprang from his grasp as he pressed a kiss to her forehead. "Then you should ring for your maid. While you prepare, I shall have my valet help me change for the night. When I am ready, I shall return and await you here."

With lowered lashes, she withdrew and made for her chambers, looking back with a small smile before she closed the door. She was his!

His triumph was short lived as the throbbing of his shoulder intensified. He tilted his head to the left. Perhaps the pain would ease a bit... nope, bad idea! Hopefully, the willow bark tea would bring some relief. He had no desire to be rendered unconscious by laudanum on his wedding night!

Clarke had his nightshirt and a dressing gown laid upon the bed when he entered his chamber. His valet said little, as was his wont, but took Darcy's clothing as he shed each piece until the time came to remove his shirt. Putting the garment on had not been a comfortable endeavour. Was it necessary to remove it?

Clarke returned from the dressing room. "Sir, if you will bend some at the waist, letting your arms hang, I can gently pull it over your head and perhaps we can slide it down your arms without moving your shoulder more than necessary."

"How did you know?"

He lifted his chin so Clarke could untie the top. "I have never seen you appear wary at my entrance, but you did so when I returned just now. I assisted Mr. Baines as he treated the wound. I am certain it is painful." Darcy straightened and clamped down on his jaw. "Would you care for a brandy before we make an attempt?"

His hand rubbed the back of his neck. "No, I do not wish to be in my cups when I return to my wife."

His hands tightened to fists and released as he took in a bracing breath and blew it hard out of his mouth. After one more, he leaned forward. Clarke drew the shirt up under his arms, shifted to grasp the hem, and began to manoeuver it over Darcy's head. Aside from the lancing pain that shot through his shoulder when he let his arms hang forward and the increase in the throbbing while they remained in such a position, the procedure was effective.

"Sir?"

"It was not as bad as I expected." The nightshirt caught his eye. "But, I shall not put myself through the torture of donning more than my dressing gown."

"Mr. Baines left laudanum should you—"

"No, thank you. Should sleep not come, I might welcome a few drops, but you know I have no preference for that particular remedy."

Clarke slipped the sleeve of the dressing gown up his sore arm. "I thought I would mention it."

Once the robe was over his shoulders, he tied the belt. "I appreciate the offer, but my wife has requested willow bark tea to be delivered to our sitting room. I shall ring when I require you in the morning."

"Very good, sir."

Darcy closed the door behind him and took a seat before the fire. The tea service was placed on the table, but he stretched his legs in front of him, staring into the flames. A click stirred him from his occupation, and he gawked as a vision made her way beside him.

"You should have poured your cup. It is much better when it is hot." She took a seat beside him, but his eye was drawn to where her dressing gown gaped open as she leaned to pour them each a serving. Her trousseau was still being made, so what was beneath her robe?

He took a sip of the cup she handed him and struggled to swallow. Gah! It was vile!

"Sugar might help the bitterness." She giggled as he poured some cream into the cup to cool it and then gulped it down.

Elizabeth took a bit longer, but when she finished, he took the cup and placed it on the tray. Her head rested upon his chest as he kept her wrapped in his good arm. He had no wish to disturb her before they retired, but because the disclosure was necessary, he told her about Lady Althea.

Unable to resist, he ran his fingers in the barest of touches down her arm as he spoke. She asked questions here and there, but at some point, her body grew heavier against his side.

He nuzzled the top of her head with his lips. "Elizabeth?"

After no response, he placed a finger under her chin to lift her face, but before he could see her eyes, she murmured and shifted, curling into his side and her face tilting back against his shoulder.

Her eyes were closed and her breaths deep and even. She had fallen asleep. Now, how was he going to get her to bed?

Chapter 28

Elizabeth woke with a start. What was that noise? Despite the current silence, her heart thrummed against her sternum—no doubt due to the combination of her abrupt awakening and the nightmare she had been having. A moment later the sound resumed from the direction of the fireplace, and she settled back into the mattress. The scullery maid had entered to replenish the fire. One day she would again sleep without waking in such an abrupt fashion at every noise. That dream where she relived the events of Bond Street would hopefully fade as well.

While her eyes became accustomed to the minimal amount of light within the bed curtains, she ran her hand along her husband's arm, which was draped over her stomach, then rolled with care in his embrace. After a se'nnight, his shoulder, while improved, was still painful, and she had no wish to jar his wound.

A gentle finger brushed a curl from his temple as she kissed his forehead. He was cool to the touch, thank goodness. With a rough breath, he shifted as she drew back and relaxed.

Since the injury, he had remained warm for several days, though never enough to concern Mr. Baines, who after checking his wound saw no signs of infection. She and Georgiana, on the other hand, were in a near constant state of nerves. Georgiana even returned to Darcy House on a permanent basis to keep abreast of her brother's condition and to be nearby in the event he worsened. They were thankful he never did.

The fever, of sorts, may not have been present for the last two days, but Elizabeth reassured herself often of his continued recovery. He knew what she was about, but since she used her lips to confirm his health, he tolerated her kisses and cosseting without complaint.

He even requested she be certain he was in good health more and more as the days passed.

His hand tightened upon her back, and he groaned. Blue eyes appeared between lazy eyelids, which opened just enough to see her before him, and closed once more. "Are you certain I have no fever, my love?"

She lightly slapped his forearm at her waist. "If you must know, I kissed your forehead but a few minutes ago. You are not the slightest bit warm."

His lips curved into a wicked smile. "You can never be too careful. I think several touches of your lips are required to be absolutely positive of your initial determination."

"You are incorrigible."

He pulled her closer, pressing her hips to his. "We have done naught but sleep in this bed since we were married. I have submitted to each examination by Mr. Baines as you insisted, and still we have not—"

"Fitzwilliam Darcy!" She gave an incredulous exclamation at his pouting bottom lip. "As you are well aware, I had no intention of falling asleep on our wedding night! Let us also not forget that you did take a touch of laudanum the next few evenings while the pain in your shoulder was at its worst."

At his low rumble of a laugh, she sat and propped herself over him with one arm. How dare he laugh! "You—"

Before another word could be hurled in his direction, his hand cupped the back of her head to pull her down for a demanding kiss, but she pushed herself away with a palm to his chest. "You were trying to make me angry."

"I confess I was. Now, save your breath and put those lips to better use. Kiss me."

He claimed her lips again, his tongue sneaking in as she gasped against his mouth. He was insufferable. He was hers, however, and she would have it no other way. His good arm dragged her atop him, his touch branding her thigh where her shift had risen to her hips.

His deep moan vibrated against her chest and her heartbeat quickened. Nimble fingers threaded into her hair and a moment later, her plait was no more as her curls cascaded down around their faces.

He opened his eyes and stared while he brushed the tendrils from her face with one hand. "You are so lovely. You have the most expressive eyes I have ever seen. Did you know?"

She shook her head. "They are a simple hazel."

He bestowed a gentle kiss to each of her eyelids. "There is nothing simple about your eyes. They show every emotion in your heart, and when you are frustrated or angry, they become more vibrant." His hands cradled her face. "I love you, Elizabeth."

"I love you, too." Her voice came as a hoarse whisper. When he wished, he could express himself well—better than well. His words touched her.

She leaned down and caressed his lips with hers. He pulled her shift to her waist. "May I?"

Her body froze. "You want to remove it?"

"I would, but only if you are comfortable."

She was not at ease, by any means, yet her trust in him was absolute. How could she not comply with his request? With uncooperative fingers, she untied the ribbon at her chest and rose to pull it over her head. How could she watch when he saw her unclothed? Butterflies frolicked in her chest and stomach, yet she managed to hold his steady gaze as he stroked up her leg and around her hip, his eyes never leaving hers. His touch left a burning sensation in its wake and she exhaled a shaky breath.

"You are beautiful."

Her laugh was husky and odd to her own ears. "You have not looked beyond my face."

He rose to a seated position and took her in his embrace. "All of you is beautiful, Elizabeth, but what is in here," he placed his palm over her heart, "is what draws me to you most. It is why I love you and want to be near you." His eyes grazed down her front before returning to her face. "Your body and looks are all that is pleasing, but what makes you stunning is the woman inside."

Her vision blurred. She had loved him at the Netherfield ball, yet her feelings had increased since then. How did he always find the words to further bind her heart to his? With more confidence than before, she brushed his top lip and then the bottom with hers.

He returned the gesture, but did not move otherwise. She opened her eyes and gazed at his face. His eyes remained closed, his long, dark eyelashes lining the lower edge. Could he be waiting for her?

Before his eyes could open, she kissed him without restraint, dipping her tongue inside his mouth to touch his. With her bold move, he was no longer the passive lover. His hands stroked over her back, buttocks, and thighs without ceasing as she pressed herself flush to his chest.

She gripped the soft silk of his dressing gown. Would he care if she touched him as he did her? Without warning, he sank back and rolled atop her, hissing in the process.

"Your shoulder?"

His coarse chin scraped against her cheek as he nodded. "I forgot for a moment." He shifted above her, using his good arm for leverage until his set jaw relaxed.

After brushing his nose against hers and trailing it down her cheek, Fitzwilliam nuzzled her ear and ran his lips down her neck, the heat from his breath radiating throughout her body.

"Remove my dressing gown."

Her hands, which were clenching the fabric in her fists, were supposed to untie the belt? She could scarcely think, much less make her fingers cooperate! Her incessant trembling slowed the process as she shifted and worked the knot until it loosened and came free.

"Elizabeth."

Her gaze moved from where she held the silk sash to his beloved face. His eyes conveyed such warmth and affection. How could she be so anxious when he loved her as he did? He would suffer injury or death rather than allow her to be harmed; he had done so that day on Bond Street, had he not?

She shifted the front panels to bare him, treading slowly when his injury could be jostled. Once the garment was removed, she flung it away. Broad shoulders and a muscled chest were the first of his attributes to come into view as her fingertips traced from his neck to the dark patch of hair upon his chest.

He pressed her palm flush to his skin and shifted her hand around his side to his back. "I am yours Elizabeth, as much as you are mine."

He kissed her as he ground his pelvis into hers. She whimpered and her breath began to come in short pants. Why did she feel as though she had been running, and when had her legs lifted to cradle him? His hips shifted down as he lifted hers to press firm against him. She could not think. She could barely breathe! He was so close, yet he was not close enough!

Rap, rap, rap! What was that?

His lips trailed down the centre of her chest, kissing the side of each breast until he reached her belly where he nuzzled and licked her flesh as her fingers clenched the soft hair upon his head. His tongue dipped into her navel while his eyes remained fixed upon hers.

Rap, rap, rap!

With a growl, he lifted his head. "I said we were not to be disturbed! We will call when you are required!"

His lips skimmed her skin, working his way back towards her head.

"Sir, I would not have awakened you, except Colonel Fitzwilliam is awaiting you in the drawing room! He indicated it is important!"

Fitzwilliam glanced outside the bed curtains and moaned. "What business requires him to appear on our doorstep at such an indecent hour? The sun is not even in the sky. He has lived in society long enough to know London hours and what the absence of a knocker indicates."

"Yet, you are the one who gave him permission to call if he had news of some import."

His forehead dropped to her stomach with a great exhale of air. She threaded his curls through her fingers as he shifted to rest his chin upon her chest. His eyes met hers and held her gaze. "He can have nothing which needs to be resolved at this time of morning." He lifted himself onto his good arm. "Please show my cousin to the dining room and serve him whatever he wishes! I shall attend him when I can."

"Fitzwilliam!" A giggle erupted from her lips. "You cannot make him wait!"

"Why not? He is the one who chose to call at this ungodly hour." Before she could retort, he ensured her silence with a passionate kiss. "I have waited this long to love you, and I intend to finish what we have started."

"You cannot mean..."

Her husband's lips to her mouth again prevented her argument and were quite convincing with their persuasion. Soon, Elizabeth could not have cared less whether the colonel waited for days or weeks! Her husband shifted to kiss her collarbone. When he glanced up, a wicked grin adorned his face as he disappeared under the coverlet. As her eyes rolled back and her eyelids pressed closed, her mind became a muddle. Who was waiting in the drawing room?

Elizabeth hummed while Lucy placed the last few pins upon her head.

"Will that suit, ma'am?"

She turned her head a bit to each side. "'Tis lovely, Lucy."

With a satisfied smile, her maid lifted Elizabeth's breakfast tray from a nearby table. "Will you be needing anything else, Mrs. Darcy?"

Elizabeth stood while she studied herself in the mirror. "No, thank you."

She toyed with the pleats upon the waist of her gown and trailed her fingers along the edge of her bodice. Fitzwilliam left no marks this time—at least not where anyone could see them; her gown hid any evidence of their morning's activities.

> He threw off the coverlet. "'Tis too warm!" He resumed his place on his stomach and reached to lace his fingers with hers.

> Lord, how she ached for him to touch her again! Her other hand still clenched the bedclothes with white knuckles as her pulse echoed in her ears. He was going to continue, was he not?

> His teeth scraped the inside of her thigh and her body clenched. Oh, please!

> She lifted her head as he shifted. At the first touch of his tongue, her head dropped back to the pillow, her back arched off the mattress, and her toes curled.

She bit her lip as her cheeks burned. A book! A book was just what she required to distract her.

A volume of poetry her husband recommended soon was held in her grasp as she moved to their sitting room. She opened the cover, flipped a few pages to the beginning, and stared into the fire until a knock distracted her.

"Come in!" She glanced at the clock. An hour? She had been wool gathering for an hour?

The door opened a fraction and Georgiana's face peeked inside. "Do you mind company?"

Blinking rapidly in an attempt to focus, she waved her new sister into the room. "Not at all." Elizabeth closed the book. She had no need for a ribbon since she had not read more than the first few words.

"I do not mean to disturb you."

"Georgiana, I decided to read until I knew you were awake. Please ring the bell so we can order tea and sit down."

Once she tugged at the cord, Georgiana sat upon the sofa and tucked her feet under her. "I have been in the music room for a while now. I had not realized how much I missed home until I returned. I cannot wait to depart for Pemberley. I have missed it the most!"

A maid entered, and once tea was requested, she departed swiftly.

"Your brother and I spoke of Pemberley last night. We made the decision to forego this season and spend the time in Derbyshire in its stead. Gossip abounds from the incident on Bond Street, and we have no desire for spectators when we attend the theatre or a ball. Your brother wishes to return home, and so do I for that matter. Another scandal will have interested the ton by the time we are next in London. We may get some stares, but not like the present interest should we remain."

Georgiana clasped her hands together. "I cannot wait for you to see Pemberley. My brother speaks with fondness of our home, but it is so much more than can be described."

"It does sound a magical place."

"I have anticipated returning for so long." Georgiana gazed at the window. "Since Ramsgate, I have wanted nothing more than to be home."

"Your brother requires until the end of the week to settle his affairs and for us to attend Anne's wedding. Saturday morning, we shall travel to Hertfordshire; Mr. Bingley has loaned us the use of Netherfield where we will remain until Monday morning when we continue on to Derbyshire."

"Will we be in company with your family?"

"We will visit a short time on Saturday, attend church with them on Sunday, and my mother will insist upon us dining at Longbourn after services. Longbourn chapel is small by comparison to the church here, and you are familiar with my family—"

"Oh! Do not mistake me! I enjoy your sister Kitty's company. I look forward to speaking with her again."

"Kitty would do well to adopt some of your poise and manners now that she's decided not to follow Lydia's lead."

Georgiana's nose crinkled. "Why would she want to emulate Miss Lydia?"

"My mother has always doted on Jane for her looks and Lydia for her temperament; she tells all and sundry how Lydia is as she was when she was young. Perhaps Kitty thought she would gain more of Mama's favour if she behaved as Lydia does. To be honest, I am not certain why. She might not even know herself."

"Did you ever wish to resemble Miss Bennet?"

Elizabeth's chest was tight as she paused, cleared her throat, and straightened her skirt. She had wanted to look like Jane many times in the past, but always for different reasons: her mother's notice, to have gentlemen find her pretty. Jane never expected such attention or became conceited, but yes, at times she had coveted Jane's beauty. The admission was not an easy one to make.

"I did."

"But you are handsome in your own way. I think Miss Bennet is lovely, but so are you."

Her face warmed as she shifted in her seat. "I have never thought myself unattractive, by any means, but I have never thought myself Jane's equal. As much as I wish my mother's words had no effect, they have had more than I would care to admit."

"So, it is not far-fetched that Kitty would emulate Miss Lydia to gain your mother's attention?"

"No, I suppose not."

Georgiana perched on the edge of her seat with her hands folded in her lap. "When we are done with our tea, would you care to practice the pianoforte with me? We could perhaps prepare a duet for after dinner this—"

Both of them started when Morely burst through the door. "Mrs. Darcy, Miss Georgiana, you must come with me!"

Elizabeth sat straight, while Georgiana jumped from her seat. "What is it?" She grabbed Elizabeth's arm and heaved her to her feet. "Mr. Morely would not make such a demand without good reason. We must go!"

"I—"

With Elizabeth's hand in hers, Georgiana followed Morely through the door to her chambers. She stared at her bed's rumpled state as they passed and cringed. Why had Lucy not tended to the sheets as she was told?

She was jolted back to the situation at hand as they passed through another doorway where they made an abrupt halt. Morely began shifting her gowns. "Here! You need to hide here."

"Why?"

Georgiana tugged, but Elizabeth refused to budge.

"What has happened?"

"Mrs. Darcy, we believe there is someone in the house. Until we have caught him, I am asking you and Miss Darcy to hide. Please."

She gave way to Georgiana's pulls and followed where they would be partially concealed by a trunk and her gowns hanging overhead.

"Do you truly believe this will protect us?" The room had a slight spin, and though she was not shaking, her limbs felt weak.

Without a word, Morely darted to a table near the door, opened a top drawer, and removed a small pistol.

Elizabeth's eyes hurt as they bulged. "Why is that in my dressing room?"

"In the event it is needed, ma'am, 'tis a pocket pistol. If someone other than myself enters, pull this piece back and then squeeze the trigger. Have you ever fired one?"

Georgiana's earlier courage dissolved as she shook her head in a frantic back and forth motion. Her eyes were wide and her breathing erratic. She was going to faint if she continued as she was.

Elizabeth drew herself straight and grasped the gun. "My father has taken me shooting a time or two."

"I shall return as soon as I can. I will call before I enter, just so you know it is me." He bobbed his head, turned, locked the door to the servant's hallway, and then exited out to the main corridor.

She stared at the pistol in her hand. Regardless of how inelegant it was, her father had taught her to shoot. With no son, he instructed her on a few less than lady-like practices, but she never thought those skills would be put to practical use. What lady needs to know shooting or Latin?

After joining Georgiana behind the trunk, she put her arm around the girl and rubbed her arm. "I am certain your brother will be home soon. Besides, no one will find us hidden in here."

A steady trail of tears flowed down Georgiana's cheeks despite Elizabeth's whispered reassurances. "Do you truly believe that?"

Elizabeth swallowed down her doubt. "I do. You will see."

Georgiana's eyes darted to the pistol, which was resting in Elizabeth's hand on the trunk. "Were you telling the truth earlier? Did your father teach you to shoot?"

"He did. My mother never knew or she would have succumbed to one of her legendary fits of nerves." One side of Georgiana's lips tipped upwards. Good, perhaps she would relax. She could not remain as anxious as she was.

"Are you a good shot?"

"My father claimed I was. He took me to this one glen where a few of the trees had fallen limbs or holes in the trunks. Those were my targets. Once he explained how to aim, he would tell me what to shoot."

Georgiana studied the wood and iron weapon. Mr. Bennet's pistols were rather plain, but this one was engraved with a floral detailing that was inlaid with silver on the dark stained handle.

"Do you think my brother would teach me?" Poor Georgiana trembled as she huddled to Elizabeth's side.

"You will not conquer your fears by learning to shoot." The mood needed to be lightened regardless of their present situation. "After all, ladies do not carry pistols in their reticules."

Georgiana lifted her chin. "I could create a new fashion." Despite her current state of anxiety, Georgiana's lips curved once more.

"You have been in my company too much if you are teasing at a time such as this."

Footsteps plodded outside the door, and they both froze in place, waiting. Who was it? Her heart hammered her sternum with an unsteady cadence. Would whomever it was enter? Elizabeth aimed for the door, but soon, the plodding footfalls passed as a shadow travelled across the crack under the door, then continued down the corridor.

Elizabeth sank back onto her heels as she again rested the gun upon the trunk. She blinked at her eyes burning. She would not cry!

Georgiana would never remain composed if she began to weep! "What do you wish to do first when we reach Pemberley?"

"Play my pianoforte. Once I have spent several days occupied by my music, I intend to ride my horse."

"Are you an accomplished rider?"

"Fitzwilliam and I often ride together and at times we race. I have bested him on several occasions."

"I know little of horses, but Fitzwilliam is an impressive rider. If you have won a race against him, you must be quite skilled."

Georgiana settled as they spoke, though she never relaxed, which was understandable. She told Elizabeth at length of her horse, as well as the different footpaths around Pemberley. Elizabeth's love of walking was certain to be the motivation behind her detailed descriptions of the scenery, but no complaints would escape Elizabeth's lips. If it kept Georgiana from thinking of the matter before them, she would allow her to talk until she was hoarse.

At the sound of footsteps thudding once again down the corridor, they both froze in place, their conversation forgotten. The pistol, which had been set on the flat top of the trunk while they whispered, was once again aimed at the door with both of Elizabeth's hands clenched upon the handle. The joints of her fingers ached she gripped the metal and wooden handle so tightly. She could not allow her fear to get the better of her; she could not tremble!

Pleas and prayers to God echoed through her head. Please pass the door! Please pass the door! Elizabeth bit her lip as her pulse thundered against her eardrum. Her fingers stretched and clenched the handle anew in an attempt to dry her palms; however, the footfalls grew louder as they drew closer to the door. *Thump... thump... thump.*

The doorknob creaked as it began to turn. That was a figment of her imagination, was it not? She blinked hard and squinted, her hand gripping the pistol with as much strength as she possessed. No, the knob was indeed moving.

A whimper came from Georgiana, who huddled behind her. The latch clicked when the handle could be turned no longer, and the hinges squeaked as the large dark stained panel began to inch open.

How could she shoot someone? How could she watch a bullet tear into a person's body with a design to harm? She clenched the weapon and shifted the barrel upwards. Such an aim would hit most men in the chest, would it not?

Oh God!

Her eyelids pressed together, she took in one long gulp of air, steeled herself, and pulled back on the trigger as a scream from behind pierced her ears. Her arms were shoved to the side as a deafening blast rent the air and jarred Elizabeth's shoulders. She landed upon the floor with someone atop her and groaned.

Chapter 29

"What the..."

Wait! That voice! Sick rose in her throat, causing her to gulp in order to prevent its escape. "Oh no!"

With a hand to the floor beside them, Georgiana pushed herself off Elizabeth as her head whipped towards the door. Elizabeth swallowed again as she rose. What would greet her when she could see the entrance?

As the trunk cleared from her line of vision, Colonel Fitzwilliam's fearsome glare came into view followed by her husband's dropped jaw and bulging eyes. "Elizabeth?"

A sob tore from her throat as she dropped the pistol as though it burned her palm. She almost shot her husband? Lord help her! She almost shot her husband!

"What in blue blazes!" He shoved Richard to the side, strode forward, and pulled her from behind the trunk into his arms. "Why do you have a pistol?"

She shook her head, hiccoughed, and gasped; however, she could not force even one word from her throat as a spasm prevented any sound from being formed. Georgiana sniffled by her ear, but was soon drawn into Richard's consoling embrace while Fitzwilliam cradled her face in his palms.

"Elizabeth, breathe."

That first inhale was a struggle, but his steady gaze and calm voice soon helped the choking sobs to subside. Her arms shifted under his great coat to cling to the back of his topcoat as Morely burst into the room.

"Sir! I did not know you had returned!"

"We arrived close to a quarter hour ago. Jobbins was not at his post, but as usual, I carried a key, which the colonel and I used to enter. I then went to the cellar to access the strongbox for some of my mother's jewels. I intended to put them in my wife's dressing room."

"Sir, Jobbins locked the front door while he went below stairs. When he returned, the door was unlocked and not pulled shut, leading us to believe we had an intruder. I notified Mrs. and Miss Darcy, hid them there," he pointed behind the trunk, "and gave Mrs. Darcy the pistol to protect herself in the event they were discovered."

He tugged at his collar. "My sole thought was their ability to keep themselves safe. We had not expected you back until later this afternoon and it never occurred to us to search the cellar." His eyes shifted to the hole made in the wall by the bullet and his jaw opened and shut several times before another sound was uttered. "Thank the Lord she missed."

The colonel stepped around Fitzwilliam. "We have Miss Darcy's quick action to credit for Mrs. Darcy's bad aim. She pushed Mrs. Darcy's arm to the side when we entered." His voice was firm and held a note of derision. To anyone who knew the colonel, he was not pleased with Morely's handling of the situation.

A noise from the doorway drew their attention to the flood of servants who had come to defend their mistress. Several footmen, Jobbins, the scullery maid with her pail and shovel, and cook, brandishing her largest knife, all stood poised and ready.

"Sir!" Jobbins scanned each person within the small dressing room. "Please forgive the intrusion. We did not know you had returned."

"Well, I have." His hand rubbed steady circles upon her back. "I entered almost a quarter hour ago and from what Morely tells me, must have left the front door slightly ajar. Please inform the servants there is no intruder." Jobbins turned to depart. "Oh! And please arrange for someone to repair the hole in this wall."

The aged butler ushered the staff away from the dressing room and back to their posts as Elizabeth's nails continued to clench his topcoat.

"Elizabeth?"

She shook her head, keeping her face buried in his chest. "I am so, so sorry. The idea of shooting someone terrified me, so I shut my eyes. I could have killed you with my silliness."

"Dearest, look at me." His bent finger tipped her chin until her hazy gaze met his. "I cannot imagine how frightened you must have been. Morely hid you, gave you a pistol, and left you alone. Most ladies would not have had the mettle to touch the weapon much less fire it. I am not angry with you. None of what occurred was your fault. Do you understand?"

A reflexive hiccough caused an odd sound from her throat. She pressed a hand to her mouth as he grinned. "Richard insisted we depart directly, so I had no opportunity to speak to you before we left."

"I was with my maid when I received your message. I am not upset you accompanied your cousin."

"Elizabeth, I did not mean what you think. I need to tell you why Richard called so early this morning."

"Oh?" She did not remove her eyes from his beloved face.

"Late last night Richard received word of Wickham's capture." A gasp came from Georgiana.

"But how?" Elizabeth straightened and glanced between the colonel and her husband. "What could he have done to reveal his whereabouts?"

Richard gave a derisive laugh. "The imbecile squandered the money he stole and has been attempting to raise his passage to Ireland by playing cards in a pub down by the docks. Two nights ago, he made the mistake of cheating a few navy officers. A brawl ensued in which a man was killed and Wickham was sent to the closest gaol."

He smirked. "Wickham attempted to hide his identity, but one of the other patrons who he had cheated was a blab. He revealed Wickham's name, which I had bandied about the docks with rumour of a reward for information."

"I paid the man well for his notifying the army." Fitzwilliam cuddled her closer. "Wickham has a trial set for next week, but if it were not for Anne and Bingley's wedding Saturday, we would depart for Pemberley on the morrow. I have had enough of London for this year."

The colonel clapped her husband upon the shoulder. "You have me here to ensure Wickham's punishment is met. After the incident at the pub, I do not think he will escape the noose. He has too many crimes to his name. Wickham will dance upon nothing before the cheering and jeering crowd before the month is out."

She shuddered and looked to Georgiana, whose eyes were closed. "Georgiana, are you well?"

Georgiana's head jerked to attend her. "Oh, yes. I cannot pretend that I shall not feel safer with him unable to cause me further harm, yet he wasted his life so."

"Which was his own fault." Fitzwilliam held out his hand to his sister, who set hers within his palm. "He was given every opportunity to establish himself in a respectable position and was never satisfied. I am thankful my father did not live to discover what his godson became."

"What he always was," clarified the colonel. "He was never good or true. His grasping ways were present when he was young. You should never forget that."

"I wish I could."

The colonel cleared his throat and offered his arm to Georgiana. "Would you walk me to the door? I am certain your brother would like some time alone with his new wife, and you would enjoy some time with your harp or pianoforte."

Elizabeth's hand shot forward and grasped the top of her husband and Georgiana's joined ones. "We have both had quite a fright. You do not need to be alone."

She kissed Elizabeth's cheek. "I believe music will help settle me. I should like to spend a few hours in the music room, but I shall not be alone as Mrs. Annesley will accompany me."

"I do not doubt your fondness for Mrs. Annesley, but you are certain?"

Georgiana kissed her brother's cheek and took the colonel's arm. "I am determined. You are just wed and deserve time together, though I shall expect both your company after dinner."

"Not for dinner?"

Elizabeth's head whipped to her husband whose lips were lifted to one side, and she struck him upon the chest. "Fitzwilliam!"

"I am merely teasing."

"Careful brother, lest we think you have become Richard."

With a smirk, Richard tugged her arm. "Come, I need to return to Horse Guards before I am reprimanded for my tardiness."

Once they were alone, Fitzwilliam held her in a firm embrace against his chest. "You have not ceased shaking since we entered."

"I nearly took your life."

He planted a firm kiss to her forehead. "But you did not. I am still here." His lips clasped hers and reaffirmed his life and warmth. Despite her attempt at defending herself and Georgiana, she had failed. Thank goodness!

Fingers, aching to steady themselves, threaded through his curls to prevent his withdrawal. She needed to touch him! She needed to verify with her own eyes and hands that he was one and whole.

She pushed under his greatcoat and topcoat, shoving them from his shoulders to the floor. A button of his waistcoat might have fallen to the carpet in her haste to remove it as well. When her fingers found their way beneath his lawn shirt, he groaned at the contact.

"Elizabeth?"

With a palm to the back of his head, she brought his lips back to hers. He slowed their exchange and lifted her into his arms, her legs wrapping about his waist while she suckled a particular spot just beneath his earlobe.

"Elizabeth, I cannot think when you do that!"

Her back met the plush mattress and counterpane. "I do not want to think. I just want to feel you against me. I need you." Her voice was breathless. Why did it always sound strange when they became amorous?

Nimble fingers reached around her back and began to unfasten the hooks one at a time while his lips bestowed feather-light kisses upon the swell of her breasts. He lifted to claim her lips, drew back, and ran his knuckles down her heated cheek. "I can deny you nothing."

Clarell House was decked in flowers and finery for the wedding of Charles Bingley to Anne de Bourgh. Though not as ostentatious as the ball he had attended a short month or so ago, the house was an elegant reminder of his uncle's status and wealth.

"I can guess the subject of your reverie." A feminine hand wrapped around his arm as he turned and raised an eyebrow. "You are thankful our wedding was as simple as it was. We had no need to attend a wedding breakfast or entertain a large number of overtaxing guests."

Elizabeth knew him too well. His mind had indeed taken that turn not a few minutes prior to her approach.

"Perhaps," he responded, covering her hand with his own. "Do you find you regret the method of our marriage?"

Her musical laugh prompted a few heads to turn in their direction. "Not at all. Your aunt has introduced me to a gaggle of ladies this morning, who were more interested in my status as Mrs. Darcy than myself. We had those we love around us, which is what matters most to me."

His heart calmed within his chest. He had needed to hear those words, to know she had no regrets. "Come with me."

He laced his fingers with hers and led her to the library where he slipped through the doors and pulled her into his embrace. He grazed a nip where her neck and shoulder met and kissed below her ear.

"My uncle had news for me upon my arrival."

"Did he now?" How he adored that breathy voice she had when they were intimate! He loathed mentioning the topic that he had ensured their solitude to discuss.

"Rumours have been rampant with Lord Carlisle's swift departure from town."

"I heard he left within a few days rather than the week you mentioned after the incident on Bond Street. I admit to wondering why."

"He read Cade's journal." An adorable little crease appeared between her eyebrows. "She was intimate with Cade but managed to keep the affair a secret."

Elizabeth's eyes appeared as though they would burst from the sockets.

"When she was sixteen, the family stayed at the estate Cade managed. They had a short affair during that time, but while Cade thought she would one day run away with him..."

Her eyelids pressed tight. "Instead she rebuffed him for a gentleman in possession of a fortune."

"Precisely. His ire towards me was from the beginning it seems. He ranted and raved about my supposed engagement to Lady Althea, yet was incensed when I broke her heart." He pulled her closer as she had shifted away just a little while they spoke. "Lord Carlisle wished to distance himself immediately from town. Lady Althea had become more troublesome since our encounter with her, and he worried of society linking her to Cade."

"They still might."

"Cade was hanged three days ago. If any gossip were to come from that quarter, I think it would have made the rounds of society. My uncle agrees."

"I still find it difficult to believe he was hanged."

He nuzzled her temple and brushed a kiss to her hairline. "He attempted to harm a prominent member of society who is related to a wealthy and powerful political figure in the House of Lords. My aunt's presence at the incident also sealed his fate. My uncle did not speak against him, but our connection to the Fitzwilliams was Cade's downfall. I also wonder if Carlisle influenced the decision in some manner."

They jumped when Richard opened the door and sauntered inside. Without looking in their direction, he strode to the liquor decanters and poured himself a generous glass. "I thought you two might be hiding in an empty room. Can you not remove your hands from one another long enough to appear in company?"

"Richard!"

Elizabeth giggled and leaned against Darcy's arm. "He is just making sport. We shall have a turn at him when he, one day, is in a similar situation."

The colonel bared his teeth as he swallowed and tipped his glass at them. "I appreciate your confidence in my finding a wealthy heiress to support my dissolute lifestyle, but since I have entered society, the ladies have flocked to my brother or Darcy here. I am under no delusions that I am a good catch in the ton. I am a mere second son."

"Perhaps when Milton weds?" Her head was tilted as she appraised his cousin.

"I find it doubtful, but I shall allow you to plan the event for me. I expect I shall be married to the army for as long as she will have me. Besides, I am poor husband material. I am moody and set in my ways. Can you imagine my disposition in another ten years?" He shuddered. "Do not wish that upon any woman."

His wife walked forward, and with a hand to Richard's shoulder, gave him a sisterly kiss on the cheek. "You are loyal, protect those you love with your life, witty, and caring. I believe she would be a fortunate lady."

Various shades from pink to beetroot emerged upon Richard's face, which brought a hearty laugh from Darcy's lips. "Richard does not accept praise well. You best return to me, my love, before you embarrass him further."

Before she could step back, Richard took her hand and pressed his lips to her knuckles. "I thank you for your compliment. Please forgive me if I choose to believe your kind words are the biased attempts of a family member to lift my spirits." He straightened and cleared his throat. "While we are assembled thus, I have been remiss in correcting your address of me, Mrs. Darcy. We are family, so I would have you call me Fitzwilliam or Richard rather than colonel."

A tinkling laugh was music to Darcy's ears.

"I cannot call you Fitzwilliam, but if I am to address you as Richard, you must call me Elizabeth or Lizzy."

With a hand to her waist, Darcy drew her back to his side and bent to her ear. "Elizabeth is for me alone."

His wife rolled her eyes. "Forgive me, but it seems you are relegated to calling me Lizzy, though Georgiana calls me Elizabeth."

"Quite a different situation." A fire lit in her eyes as she turned and lifted a finger to his chest.

"Do not quarrel on my account," smiled Richard. "I do not require the use of your given name. Lizzy is sufficient."

A noise from the entry revealed Bingley peeking his head into the library. "I have wondered where you disappeared to. You will miss the entirety of my wedding breakfast should you hide yourselves away in here." His line of sight rested on the glass in Richard's hand, and he hastened to remove it. "You can become well into your cups after Anne and I depart."

"I am no drunkard!" Richard trailed after Bingley as the latter exited in the direction of the party. "I have yet to ruin a social occasion by being in my altitudes. My brother, on the other hand..."

His cousin turned one last time before he disappeared through the doorway. "By the by, my mother is searching for the two of you. She has learned of your intended departure for Pemberley and disapproves."

With a growl, Darcy dropped his head upon her shoulder. "How much longer must we remain? Aunt Charlotte will not take no for an answer. She will lecture and preach until we concede."

Elizabeth's dainty hand reached into his pocket, retrieved his watch, and flipped open the lid. "Another hour, at least, lest we be considered rude. Do you believe your aunt will be so stubborn? She should understand our reluctance to remain in London."

"I am sure she does. Her concern is likely due to rumours and establishing you in society."

"I do not give a whit about the season." She wrapped her hand around his elbow and tugged him towards the corridor. "Perhaps if we are seen enough today, your aunt will not press."

He pulled her back into his arms before she reached the doorway. "If only we could be so fortunate!" His teeth grazed her ear, and his pulse began to accelerate at the sound of her sharp inhale. "We could remain here rather than retuning to the festivities."

Her small palm pressed to his chest and his shoulders dropped. "Fitzwilliam, we must return." She bit her lip and backed towards the door. "If you are polite and friendly for the remainder of the wedding breakfast, I promise I shall reward you well when we return to Darcy House."

Her teasing manner made him sensitive to every brush of his shirt against his chest and every rub of his wool trousers against his legs. "What is my reward?"

With a provocative lift of her eyebrow, she watched him from the corner of her eye as she proceeded without him. She had always been skilled at teasing, but when did she learn to become so flirtatious?

He awoke from his trance when her head peeked around the corner. "Are you going to join me?"

His feet hastened to follow her. After all, how could he refuse?

Chapter 30

At last! The end of the interminable season was upon them! Once he and Elizabeth departed this infernal ball, they would be free. Free to pack their belongings, free to return to Pemberley, and well, free to do anything but remain in London!

Darcy's eyes followed his wife as she moved through the current set with Richard, who was sure to be speaking of the ridiculous; Elizabeth's diverted expression was proof enough that his cousin was speaking nonsense. Well, that and his mouth had not stopped moving since he had retrieved Elizabeth for their set.

His gaze remained on his wife as she passed nearby and bestowed a brilliant smile in his direction. Despite his naturally poor mood in company, at least his wife was enjoying herself.

"I know you detested remaining in town, but you must admit it was for the best." His aunt took his arm as she watched the dancers turn with the music. "I know the callers and the gossip were a trial, yet you and Elizabeth did well—very well."

Aunt Charlotte had indeed caught them before they could leave Anne and Bingley's wedding breakfast, sequestering them inside his uncle's library for close to an hour as the two convinced them of the ills of forgoing the season.

> "The entire town is gossiping of what occurred on Bond Street as well as the incident at Darcy House. Should you journey to Pemberley, you will appear as though you are hiding—that you did wrong. You must remain and face those who would spread their lies."

> Darcy clutched Elizabeth's hand. "I care not for the talk of idle minds! We have endured enough since our arrival and want nothing more than to go home. You must understand."

His uncle clutched Darcy's shoulder. "We do understand, but you must accept that your aunt is merely considering what is best for you. We are thinking of your reputation, the honour of the Darcy name, and when the time comes, the standing of your children."

Lord Fitzwilliam removed his glasses and wiped the lenses with his handkerchief. "Because she is the daughter of a country squire, many in society are prepared to treat her as an interloper. They cannot comprehend that she has the grace or intelligence to make it in our sphere."

"I care not for such small-minded people."

"Whether you care or not is irrelevant. Lizzy must be allowed to prove them wrong, or your task will be even greater next year.

"We have seen and heard the rumours surrounding such marriages in the past. Please, trust us to lead you in this. We can ensure the Darcy name remains respected by those who matter, but they must see Lizzy—they must speak with her.

"The matter of what occurred on Bond Street has been bandied about with no regard for the truth. We also cannot forget the gunshot that is known to have taken place at Darcy House." Aunt Charlotte looked between the two of them. "You must remain in town."

Elizabeth placed her other hand upon his chest as his careful travel plans eroded before him. "I have no wish to remain, but what if your aunt is correct?"

"I know I am correct, dear."

As soon as he had heard talk of Elizabeth's gunshot, Darcy, with the help of his aunt, traced the rumour back to a neighbour's servant. It had been his own footman who had spoken of the possible intruder with one of the maids; however, the rumour spread like a plague infiltrates the poorest parts of London—the dissemination was rampant.

The worst was the conjecture that he had shot at Elizabeth's lover as well as speculation that he had not only killed the man but also hidden the body—not that anyone had a name or location for the man in question or the corpse.

In the end, the best they could do was ignore the whispers behind the fans of the matrons and maidens and hold their heads high. After all, they had committed no wrong.

His aunt was correct, Elizabeth had done well—no, more than well. She had been outstanding. "I am exceedingly proud of Elizabeth." He smiled as his wife's eyes met his. She curtsied to his cousin as they began the second dance.

"As you should be." She motioned with her hand towards Miss Bennet, who stood up with Sir James Audley. "What does Elizabeth think of the match? I must admit to being surprised. I had no notion of his interest when they were first introduced. I admit that I expected her to attract a husband but not a baronet."

He watched a few ringlets of Elizabeth's hair bounce as she turned her back to him. "She is pleased. Sir James estate is too distant from Pemberley for her to be overjoyed."

"Sir James is a good man."

"He is, which is why she is happy for her sister's good fortune, though I understand Mrs. Bennet was quite put out with a meagre baronet for her eldest and most handsome daughter."

Aunt Charlotte rolled her eyes. "Should Mr. Bennet pass before his wife, perhaps you should have that woman sent to Bedlam. From my observations and Elizabeth and Marianne's comments, I question the woman's sanity. Not every man can afford to wed a lady of little fortune."

"Sir James was prudent not to waste his wife's dowry after her passing. Not many men would have appreciated the freedom that could be attained with the excess funds. It has allowed him to wed a lady more of his choosing this time."

His aunt leaned closer. "I have heard Sir James' mother is not pleased with the match. She hoped for the daughter of an earl."

His hands clenched at his sides. "She might wish for her son's happiness rather than more money for their coffers. Sir James has done well with his estate. I understand he recently purchased a small parcel of land adjacent to the west of his park. Amongst its attributes are a wood suitable for hunting and a fair-sized cottage."

His aunt bit her lip, as she turned to him, her eyebrows lifted in question.

"He has already had any necessary repairs done to the house and had it furnished. It will make an excellent dower house."

A laugh came from beside him. "And when did he implement these plans?"

"They were in place prior to his betrothal to Miss Bennet. The owner of the land approached Sir James almost six months after the death of his late wife. As his mother and Lady Audley often disagreed, he wasted no time in negotiating a price and beginning the repair of the cottage.

"Once he decided upon Miss Bennet as his bride, completing the project became a necessity. Her placid nature was all the more reason for his mother to remove to a dower house. He will not abide any abuse of his wife."

"Good man!"

"Indeed."

The music stopped and Darcy searched through the people milling about until he spotted Richard moving in their direction with

Elizabeth on his arm. When Elizabeth reached Darcy's side, she took his other arm, caressing the underside with her thumb. His heart thrummed with contentment at her touch.

"If you will excuse us." With a glance back at his wife, he led her past the refreshment table to the hall and through a set of French doors. The night air was cool and did not yet have that musty odour he detested about London in the summer. A few people milled about the garden, but a place of quiet and solitude was to be found in the back corner.

He removed his topcoat and placed it upon her shoulders as he pulled her into his embrace. "We depart directly after supper."

Her shoulders shook as a soft laugh came from the direction of his chest. "I have promised a set to Milton as well as Sir James, and I am afraid your aunt will prevent us from sneaking away."

"We depart London in two days. She cannot force us to remain."

"'Tis but a few hours."

"An eternity." His voice was petulant, even to his own ears. The season had dragged by so, but why did the moments he wanted to hold close to his heart escape his grasp with such an unexpected swiftness?

"Come, the season was not as dreadful as you predicted."

No, the entirety of the season was not cringe worthy. He and Elizabeth had taken great pleasure in many of the plays they had attended as well as several art exhibits. The queen's suspension of drawing rooms for the year had done a great deal to lift his spirits. Elizabeth had not been forced to endure that ridiculous tomfoolery, though Aunt Charlotte had dragged them to Almack's. Lord, but he despised that pompous, preening event!

He brushed a tendril of hair from her eyes. "Some events were tolerable."

"Tolerable?" she laughed. "Such high praise."

"I am pleased by your success. I am proud of you."

Her brow arched as she tilted her head. "I cannot say I have worked for the success you and Aunt Charlotte perceive. I was merely myself when your aunt made the introductions." Elizabeth's connection to the owner of two reasonably sized estates (despite his roots in trade), her status as Mrs. Darcy, as well as her friendship with Lady Fitzwilliam, helped her forge alliances that would see her through future events with the ton.

The gossip of Bond Street and what occurred in their home was eclipsed by Gwyllym Wardle's humiliation in Parliament in late February and the recent re-instatement of the Duke of York to Commander in Chief of the Army. Thankfully, such salacious tittle-tattle of more prominent men than him and their public scandals directed the gossip elsewhere.

With a quick lift to the tips of her toes, she planted a kiss to his nose. "We should return before we are missed." Taking his hands in hers, she stepped back and tugged him in the direction of the house. "I promise to make the remainder of the night worth your while."

"Little can make a crowded ballroom worth my while."

A glint appeared in her eye as she crushed her soft breasts to his chest; her cheek pressed to his. "Can you think of nothing?" Her breath against the sensitive flesh of his ear caused a tingling sensation that prickled down the back of his neck. As though he required further torture, she grazed her teeth against his earlobe before she backed away, turned, and peered over her shoulder while she sauntered in the direction of the doors.

He hated to admit he was wrong. Well, why did he have to admit such a thing?

With a tug to straighten his waistcoat, he took one dignified step forward before lunging. Elizabeth gave a shrill giggle as she dodged his extended arm and threw his topcoat at his chest.

He was so close!

His appearance was back in order when they emerged from their hiding place. One or two couples stared in their direction, but he held himself tall and ignored the attention as Elizabeth took his arm and squeezed. Talk was sure to be rife in tomorrow's drawing rooms of an assignation between them in the garden. Oh well! If he was to be scorned for loving his wife, so be it!

As they entered the hall, a hard clap on the shoulder jerked his attention to Bingley at his side. "Should Aunt Charlotte or Lady Catherine inquire, I have escorted Anne to take the air."

Anne's peaked eyes and green countenance prompted Darcy to step to the side with haste. "Are you well?"

Anne gave an exasperated huff. "I wish everyone would stop asking if I am well."

"Perhaps it is the heat of the ballroom?" offered Elizabeth.

With a hand to his wife's back and a brilliant toothy grin, Bingley pressed her through the exit. "I am certain you are correct."

Once the door was closed behind the Bingleys, Darcy leaned towards his wife. "I cannot understand why he smiles so when his wife is suffering."

She peered around at the few people milling in the room as though searching for someone before she looked him in the eye. "Anne suspects she is with child but does not want Lady Catherine to know as of yet."

He looked through the nearby window where Anne and Bingley appeared to be having a discussion. "I would want to delay that conversation as well. Her mother will be insufferable."

"At least she has come to terms with their marriage." Elizabeth lifted her free hand and began to nibble upon her thumbnail.

He lowered the offending thumb with his hand. "Stop and tell me what is bothering you all of a sudden."

"Are you disappointed I am not yet with child?"

He ran his knuckles down her cheek. A sharp inhale came from behind his shoulder, but he disregarded it. If some interloper had issue with his touching his wife, then they could look elsewhere. "I must admit that I am not ready to share you yet. A baby will come soon enough. I intend to enjoy every moment we have without that responsibility."

A small line was between her eyebrows. "You are certain?"

He squinted a bit as he studied her eyes, which bore into his. "You opened your mother's letter." Why would she not wait as he had requested? Mrs. Bennet's correspondence never failed to put a damper on her spirits, and he had not wanted her downtrodden tonight. If he could but throttle that woman!

"The parcel was not thick. I hoped it was nothing more than a quick note."

"She chastised you again for not being with child?" He and Mr. Bennet had interrupted Mrs. Bennet's less than tactful questions and advice when they journeyed Longbourn at Easter, which had curtailed any further discussion of babies for their visit, especially since they stayed at Netherfield. In return for Bingley's allowing them to use the estate, Darcy gave Bingley an expensive case of brandy for the service since he would not have survived the week at Longbourn and remained in his right mind.

Elizabeth shifted her head a bit from side to side. "Amongst other matters."

He turned her to face him. "What other matters?"

"Where do I begin? Lydia's new governess is mean-spirited and too strict for a girl as lively as her youngest daughter. She believes Milton is better suited for Jane than Sir James and expects me to convince Jane to end the betrothal. Oh! Since Jane has stayed at Clarell House, we have the room to invite Lydia—never mind that we leave a mere few days after her letter arrived."

"Her words should be relegated to the grate." His hand clenched and released. "Mrs. Simms is just who Miss Lydia requires. She is strict, educated, and will brook no silliness from your youngest sister. Your father was wise to offer her the position as your sister requires near constant supervision." He ran his fingers through his hair. "And to think just a few weeks ago, your mother bragged to the neighbours of what a governess meant in terms of status."

"Mary has indicated Mrs. Simms does not allow Lydia any sort of freedoms. She accompanies her to exercise every morning, yet maintains they are not to walk to Meryton, which vexes Lydia. Lydia has lessons she must complete, and Mrs. Simms has told Lydia to retire without dinner for her lack of respect and manners." An adorable noise of contempt escaped his wife's control. "Mama claims Mrs. Simms is stifling Lydia's lively personality."

"What of your father?"

"He remains in his book room and ignores it all. Once he hired Mrs. Simms, he seemed to wash his hands of it."

She grinned towards the entrance of the ballroom. When he turned, Jane was speaking to his Aunt Charlotte as she held Sir James' arm with a beatific smile. "As for Jane, my sister loves Sir James. I am convinced she and Milton, regardless of his current courtship of Lady Amelia, would never suit.

"Besides, the license has been purchased. Mama, whether she likes it or not, must accept Jane's marriage to a mere baronet." She took his hand and gave it a squeeze. "Forgive me, but for the moment, I wish to forget about Mama. Do you think we could just enjoy the remainder of the ball?"

"If we departed straight away, then yes." He jumped at the sharp pinch she gave his ribs.

"I see your aunt and uncle there. We should join them."

Despite his wish to return home, they did not enter their carriage until nearly dawn when he escorted a yawning and groggy Elizabeth to their equipage. The next few days were occupied with packing, taking their leave of their friends and acquaintances, and preparing for the journey to Derbyshire. As each chore was accomplished, another weight was lifted from Darcy's shoulders. They were going home!

A putrid odour enveloped London the morning they boarded their carriage and set off for the north. It was unfortunate that the morning was humid and warm; the sticky air did not help the smell.

Georgiana and Elizabeth held handkerchiefs scented with perfume to their noses until they were out of the city. During their first stop to change horses, they opted to take the fresh air than enter the confines of the busy inn.

While Georgiana was accustomed to such travel, he ensured Elizabeth suffered no signs of undue fatigue or sickness caused by the motion of the carriage. On the contrary, she bore the strain of a three-day journey with aplomb, almost bouncing in her seat as they entered the boundaries of his estate.

"When do you think we will reach the house?" Her eyes glowed as he tucked a curl away from her cheek.

"Patience, my love. We must still pass through a fair amount of pastureland first."

She turned to watch the passing hills and valleys dotted with sheep. "I am overwhelmed to finally see a place of which I have heard so much, but I am also nervous. What if your housekeeper does not like me?"

"Mrs. Reynolds will adore you!" protested Georgiana. "She will be so relieved Fitzwilliam did not wed Miss Bingley. From what my maid has said, the servants have spoken of that fear often below stairs."

A shudder rippled down his spine. "As if I would marry such a woman!" Elizabeth's merry laughter made him smile as he kissed her hand. "My sister is correct, though. Mrs. Reynolds will appreciate you and respect you due to your position, but you will earn her approval due to your kindness and intelligence on your own. Mrs. Reynolds is a fair woman. You have nothing about which to fret."

His stomach fluttered when they took the last rise. His home could be seen from the ridge, where the wood ceased. As they cleared the last of the trees and curved around to begin their descent, Elizabeth's sharp inhale could not be missed within the confines of the carriage.

"Is that...?"

Where it had remained for the last few centuries, the large, handsome stone building sat on the opposite side of the valley. The imposing structure stood well on rising ground and was backed by a ridge of high woody hills. In front a stream of some natural importance swelled into a lake, but without any artificial appearance. Its banks were neither formal nor falsely adorned, which suited him well.

His home inspired great pride and love, and now he could share it with Elizabeth. His heart expanded as though it would burst from his chest. His arm wound around her stomach from behind as he pressed his cheek to her hair, his lips near her ear.

"Welcome to Pemberley, my love."

About the Author

L.L. Diamond is more commonly known as Leslie to her friends and Mom to her three kids. A native of Louisiana, she has spent the majority of her life living within an hour of New Orleans until she vowed to follow her husband to the ends of the earth as a military wife. Louisiana, Mississippi, California, Texas, New Mexico, Nebraska, and now England have all been called home along the way.

After watching *Sense and Sensibility* with her mother, Leslie became a fan of Jane Austen, reading her collected works over the next few years. *Pride and Prejudice* stood out as a favourite and has dominated her writing since finding Jane Austen Fan Fiction.

Aside from mother and writer, Leslie considers herself a perpetual student. She has degrees in biology and studio art, but will devour any subject of interest simply for the knowledge. As an artist, her concentration is in graphic design, but watercolour is her medium of choice with one of her watercolours featured on the cover of her second book, *A Matter of Chance*. She is a member of the Jane Austen Society of North America. Leslie also plays flute and piano, but much like Elizabeth Bennet, she is always in need of practice!

Leslie's books include: *Rain and Retribution, A Matter of Chance, An Unwavering Trust, The Earl's Conquest*, and *Particular Intentions*.

Acknowledgements

As always, I have to thank Jane Austen, whose timeless works have inspired me and others to re-imagine her unique and beloved characters into countless scenarios as well as time periods. She had a talent few possess for words and though she meant them to be more satires than romance, I appreciate both aspects when I read one of her wonderful works.

Huge hugs and thanks to my betas, Lisa Toth and Suzan Lauder, who have spent their free time pouring over, critiquing, and correcting these chapters. Big thanks to those who helped me with proofreading! The hard work of my betas, my editor and my proof readers (Brandon, Brenna, and Tresha) help make this suitable for reading! As we say on the boards, all mistakes are mine!

Speaking of editors, big thanks to my new editor Brynn Shimel. I know JAFF was probably not what you had in mind when you decided on your degree, but thanks for giving it a go!

I would like to thank those who run and frequent the JAFF forums, especially A Happy Assembly and Darcy and Lizzy. You have provided me a launching pad for my work and helped me become a writer. I appreciate every comment! The community has been great in terms of support and friendship. I wouldn't be where I am today without it.

The amazing authors at Austen Variations have also been great with their encouragement and sharing their knowledge. I can't wait for our next get-together!

My mother always encouraged my creativity. She purchased just about any art supplies I required as a child. She was my first piano teacher (I will forever associate Claire de Lune with her. She played it often). She bought me my flute, and fussed when I didn't practice, which was often. (I'm afraid I'm a bit like Elizabeth Bennet in that I don't practice like I should.) My mother was also a reading teacher and never denied me a book, and when I was twenty-two, she introduced me to Jane Austen. I miss her every day. I love you, Mom!

I have a husband and three children who have to endure my crazy Jane Austen addiction. They have suffered through National Trust homes, as well as trips to Ramsgate, Bath, and Lyme Regis. Despite my torture of them, my children still brag that I am a writer and my husband has taken to chatting up my books in airports when he travels. One of my daughters begged to attend Jane Austen Regency Week this year, and my other is now pushing for me to take her next year. Perhaps there's hope I can turn them to the dark side!

Thank you to everyone who has bought a copy of one of my books. You make it possible for me to write! My muse thanks you as well!

59992260R00204

Made in the USA
Charleston, SC
18 August 2016